THE YEAR OF MY HUMILIATION

*To Dominic —
with warm regards,
CJ Sursum*

THE YEAR OF MY HUMILIATION

C.J. SURSUM

LILYFIELD
PRESS

THE YEAR OF MY HUMILIATION

Published in the United States by Lilyfield Press

Copyright 2025 © C.J. Sursum

All rights reserved in all media. No part of this book may be reproduced, transmitted, or stored in any form by any means—electronic, mechanical, recorded, photocopy, or otherwise—without prior permission in writing from the author, except for brief excerpts in critical articles or reviews.

This book is a work of fiction. Names, characters, places, and incidents either are the product of the author's imagination or are used fictitiously, and any resemblance to actual persons, living or dead, events, or locales, is entirely coincidental.

Book and cover design by Magdalene Kennedy

ISBN 978-0-9671492-6-4

Yet I know that good is coming to me—that good is always coming; though few have at all times the simplicity and the courage to believe it. What we call evil, is the only and best shape, which, for the person and his condition at the time, could be assumed by the best good.

— GEORGE MACDONALD, *PHANTASTES*

Day 1

I expected today would be the hardest.

Around 7:00 am, I stood at the bottom of the stairs, waiting for my wife to wake up. I waited until I heard the familiar sounds from above—the bed creaking as she rolled herself to a sitting position and again as she hoisted herself to her feet. I waited for her footsteps shuffling down the hallway to the bath, and the toilet flushing as it always did—twice.

That was my signal to withdraw to the kitchen, where I filled the kettle and placed it gently on the burner. I labored over the choice of tea—various canisters of loose leaves confronted me. How to decide? Twenty-four years of marriage, and I'd never before made my wife tea. Why couldn't she drink coffee like a normal person?

After several minutes, the kettle began to rumble and hiss. I lifted it from the heat just before it shrieked. Herbal lemon, I decided, was a safe bet. The strainer, however, was nowhere to be found. Nothing was organized; it was hardly my fault that I never attempted to cook in there.

Patton must've sensed my frustration. He tapped his moist snout on my bare thigh, just below my running shorts. I reached for the underside of his jaw and massaged the loose skin while looking into his eyes. "Hang in there, fella," I said, although I was the one wanting reassurance.

After much discreet opening of drawers, I located the strainer, then searched for a mug. My wife's favorite, the one with the imprint of Michaelina's drawing, sat at the front of the cabinet. I looked past it. Not because of its chipped handle, though that was irritating enough. Why then? Because I couldn't go that far, not so soon.

Nor did I want a mug with an aphorism or ad. No *Carpe Diem* or *Tea Solves Everything* or *World's Best Bank*. Meaning could be construed from even the most innocuous phrase. Why didn't we have any solid-colored mugs? Because she did the shopping, and apparently, she couldn't drink a mug of tea without it telling her what to think.

I settled on one with a romanticized winter scene—a sleigh whooshing down a snow-covered slope towards a snug little house with a lamp in the window.

Rosie likes milk and two heaping teaspoons of sugar in her tea, that much I know. By heaping, I mean she re-dips the spoon several times in the sugar bowl to get every possible granule she's capable of perching on it. The crystals cascade down the sides as she absentmindedly scoops and re-scoops. I've asked her why she doesn't just admit she likes three normal teaspoons of sugar. She looks at me as if she has no idea what I'm talking about.

God, how I hate that look. Why doesn't she just tell me to shut the hell up? At least I could respect that.

But no, no, no—I need to wrench myself away from hypercritical thoughts. It's that very lack of respect for my wife that's caused my current plight.

I'll admit here that the disrespect is decades long. I suppose infidelity was the initial manifestation. Less than two years into our marriage, the first occasions for temptation emerged. Medical school was grueling and intense. I needed fun, some release, during the brief windows between study sessions and stress-filled training. Only other students could empathize. When they went drinking, I joined them. Brief hook-ups followed with an easy inevitability, requiring little effort on my part—I was attractive (still am) and in fighting shape. The women were openhanded in their offerings, but cautious in their expectations—they didn't want a commitment either, to have their bright medical careers so soon encumbered with husbands or babies.

The first, a one-nighter, sported long dark hair like my wife, but a more athletic build. I can't recall her shadowy face, only her muscular body—a contrast to Rosie's soft, lax limbs. The woman had a birthmark beneath her left ear—a dark, convoluted port wine stain. I whispered in her ear that when I got my license, I'd remove it for her. She tensed at first, but relaxed after I began kissing the area amorously. Another tryst was with an egg-headed sort of girl, whose clinical performance in bed gave me the distinct impression that she'd read up on the subject at length.

Mostly, though, these memories blur into a disjointed amalgam of body parts and fragmented guilt. I took no true delight in scratching that sexual itch—what kind of husband would? Deep down, I wanted Rosie to recognize that her lack of honest enthusiasm and inability to apprehend and allay my fears were driving me away. Yet she was resolute in her ignorance, and her apathy only grew.

Later, during my residency, the flings subsided as my free time dwindled further. The absence of affairs, though, did nothing to improve our relationship. Oh, we had sporadic moments of bliss—I want to be clear about that. But those times served too as a painful reminder of what we'd lost.

When the odd chance came for us to get away, it helped. We couldn't afford a sitter, but my mother-in-law would sometimes take the boy, enabling Rosie to break out of the cocoon she'd constructed around herself and him. We'd go hiking or on a picnic or a drive around the lake. Occasionally the freedom would spark in her that whimsical sort of behavior I could never decide if I hated or missed. On the hiking trail, she'd sometimes announce herself to be a wood nymph and appoint me as hunter. Before I could react, she'd take off out of my reach. Usually I'd ignore her silliness and make her come back to the path.

Once, though, in a remote state park, she ignored my command to return. She bounded into the woods, across the pine needle blanket, her behind bouncing like a deer flicking its tail. I was forced to follow but refused to run. When I glimpsed her slipping behind a large oak, I crept up silently, then leapt out at her with a roar. She startled, even though she'd been expecting me, wanting me.

That scenario, gratifying in its way, didn't bear repetition. Moreover, my mood had swung to irritation on the drive home. I'd served as prey, not the other way around—she'd plundered my self-control and hoodwinked me into foregoing protection. In the end, nothing came of it.

By the time I finished my residency and was situated in my practice, the boy was in school. Rosie approached me then, supposing that since my paycheck had become substantial, I might reconsider enlarging our family. I resisted—we were deeply in debt, and frankly, the way she was raising our son hardly inspired me to further reproduction.

And then there was that other, more formidable reason.

Back to the tea. I took a few sips to pretend I was making the tea for myself, but the addition of all that sugar nearly made me gag.

I was stalling but couldn't make myself move faster. Rosie had to be back in the bedroom by then, probably sitting in the chair near the window where she said her morning prayers. I'd spent days mentally preparing for this moment. I had to act—once she came downstairs it'd be too late.

The real difficulty wasn't in making the tea. It was taking it to her—wrapping my fingers around the mug, climbing the stairs, walking into the bedroom, and handing it to her.

I feared what would happen then. She'd look at me with damp eyes and ask me why I was doing this. There was no answer to that question, or none that I could give her.

I gulped down the rest of the tea and took Patton out for a run.

Day 2

Years later, one woman nearly supplanted my wife: Heather, a pharmaceutical rep with a slightly exaggerated jaw and sharp gonial angle, like Audrey Hepburn or Angelina Jolie. The jaw gave Heather just that aura of authority that made her more tantalizing. Her flawless features afforded me a measure of relief—I could set aside my otherwise obsessive need to analyze a face for potential surgical improvements (a hazard of my trade). Intellectually, she was sharper than the nurses I'd been liaising with since my residency, and I could converse with her on topics that would completely flummox Rosie.

Heather traveled often and maintained a tight schedule. When she was in town, though, we connected frequently.

Sex with Heather was a step up from the nurse variety. She was more exacting, and demanded more give and take, in a way that felt respectful and mature. The predictable nature of the act—almost formulaic—redounded to our pleasure, and strengthened the emotional bond between us. We'd chat in bed amiably before and afterward—the process in-between lubricating the rails of our conversation. That sums it up: mutual comfort, respect, and physical satisfaction. Wasn't that the very definition of good sex, if not of love itself?

Most critically, nothing lurked beneath the surface of our sex, as it did with Rosie. No brutish craving, no terrifying abandonment, no awful dependency. No confusion about the meaning of our coming together, or opposition over our intentions.

But that was then. Circumstances have changed. Sure, I'm still a surgeon, a man who helps mitigate facial deformities, who repairs the results of ghastly accidents, who's witnessed the deaths of children. Yet now I'm a man who dreads taking his wife a cup of tea.

But yesterday I did it—I made the damn tea. Yesterday counted.

This morning I got up earlier. I stepped out onto the back deck. The sun wasn't yet above the tree line, and the early March air was frosty and painful to breathe. But I'm not the shivering type. Standing in the bracing air reminds me of my courage and fortitude. So why do I so abhor taking my wife tea?

I need a new approach. I need to force my efforts into a ritual as mundane and mechanical as nurse-sex used to be.

Imagining Rosie's reaction is getting in the way—I fear she'll misinterpret the whole endeavor. She'll think I'm feeling guilty or something, when nothing could be further from the truth. In fact, this enterprise has little to do with her at all—I'm not doing it for her benefit. She's merely the recipient, a conduit, because she happens to live in this house. It's my decision and my plan, which is why I haven't told her and never will. She can come to her own conclusions.

That, unfortunately, is the rub.

In the kitchen, the granite counters sparkled, the cherry cabinets gleamed, and no crumb could be found on the Tuscan tile floor—the cleaning lady must've been in yesterday. However, a dirty pot from last night's dinner, filled with greasy water, was settled in the sink.

I ignored it, opened the cabinet, and reached for Rosie's 'special' mug. Surely today I could handle it. I examined Michaelina's drawing, simplistic as any four-year old might make—a lopsided black oval for the head, long brown stick hair, and blue dots for the eyes. A thin red line stretched across for the mouth, culminating in a smile at one end. A dysmorphic face if ever there was one.

I set it on the counter, my fingers hovering over the rim. After a moment's discomfort, I turned the picture on it away from me. The symbolism of that act shattered my composure.

Even so, I left it that way. The painful feeling it engendered worked as a salve of sorts. Again I made the tea—that part at least was easier. I concocted it just as Rosie would, going so far as to re-scoop the sugar several times.

The toilet flushed above as I stirred the mug. Time to quit procrastinating. A voice in my head screamed out against this violation to the moral order. I couldn't ignore it, only beat it back as I headed upstairs. I placed the mug on the windowsill in her room, then crept out. The second flush sounded as I neared the bottom of the stairs.

Patton leapt for joy as I leashed him.

During my run, I thought again of Heather. When she and I had begun making plans, I believed I was leaving my dependency on Rosie behind.

That is, until that night five years ago.

Day 3

It happened when I was in Connecticut for my father's funeral. My father's life, not a long one, ended with a massive myocardial infarction at age 72.

My feelings for him were complicated, although he wasn't a complicated man. He avoided affection. While my mother accepted his aloofness in stride, I, as an only child, found the lack of warmth distressing. In my adult years, I rarely spoke with him, although I believe he cared about me in his own abstract fashion.

After the funeral, I was faced with the disposal of his remaining possessions, of which I discovered remarkably few. He'd been a plumber his entire working life, and was of the penny-pincher type common in that generation. Combing through my modest boyhood home again, I realized anew what he'd given up for me, and how little I'd returned. I never loved him, or I thought I didn't, yet once he was gone I regretted not having seen more of him. His sudden death caught me off-guard.

Rosie and I stayed in a hotel for two nights—same room, separate beds.

On the second night, after the funeral, I was out of sorts. I don't know why—my life would carry on in the same way without my father. Certainly any inheritance I'd receive would be negligible compared to my own assets.

What undid me was the flooding back of painful childhood memories. Maybe it was seeing my father's face manifested in his sister, my Aunt Shirley, at the funeral. As a child, I'd been her favorite. Now, she was a stranger to me, one with a strangely familiar face. Or maybe it was realizing that my father might've enjoyed seeing more of his grandson, and how little effort I'd made in that direction. That made me think of my son and his leaving us, and that I had no idea where he was living.

Whatever the reason, or combination of reasons, I ended up having a lot to drink. I don't recall going to bed, but I do remember waking up in the night sobbing. Not just for the loss of my father, but for my mother as well. She'd died years earlier, also unexpectedly, while I was away at college, immersed in my studies. I'd never fully grieved for her.

I tried to stop—or at least silence—my outpouring, yet I soon felt Rosie's soft arms around me, her hair brushing against my skin, her soothing voice in my ear. I don't recall what she said—words didn't matter.

Swallowed up in the confusing nature of my loss, I was helpless. I allowed Rosie to minister to me. I sank my face into her hair, drawing in the familiar vanilla-shampoo scent of it. Her arms circumscribed me, held me captive. I gave in to my distress, to my grief, without restraint. I emptied myself of the bitterness flowing through my veins. And she absorbed it all. Every resentment against my father, every childhood hurt, every regret about my mother, were forgotten in those blessed moments of release.

Afterward, I fell into a deep slumber until she woke me in the morning to leave for the airport. I said nothing to her on the trip home except the commonplace, and even that was subdued. She was likewise quiet, not wanting to break what must've seemed a spell, probably wondering whether this event marked an alteration in our daily existence.

The change, however, didn't last. How could it, when nothing else in our lives had? Once we were home, the barriers that demarcated our lives re-emerged and overshadowed us once again. The first night, Rosie lingered downstairs at her usual bedtime. I sensed her hope that I'd invite her to my bed. But I couldn't, I couldn't. And when that first night passed, there was no hope for another rapprochement.

The barrier was Heather. By the time of the funeral, I'd made an implicit commitment to her. My one-night stand with Rosie felt like infidelity to Heather. Although I revealed nothing to Heather of my indiscretion, I spent the next several weeks trying to make it up to her. I presented her with an expensive ring, which she rightly took as a pledge of my intentions.

However, six weeks after the funeral and barely back on track emotionally, the announcement came from Rosie about her pregnancy. I didn't speak to her for three days. In the end, though, nothing could be done. It was one thing to divorce Rosie when I had a grown son I never saw anyway. To abandon a 39-year-old pregnant wife, however, was another thing altogether.

So that was it for Heather.

There was a scene at work. I was unprepared for the ferocity of her opposition. I waffled, trying to keep open future possibilities. But Heather, realizing she wanted nothing to do with a man tied to an ex-wife by means of a new baby, cut things off herself in the end.

I resigned myself to the situation, and Rosie tempered her displays of enthusiasm. As the pregnancy wore on, though, and the image of Heather receded from my horizon, a change came over me. I began to look forward to the second chance. The raising of our son had been a disaster, though I wasn't to blame. By the time I'd completed my residency, he was already spoiled.

But this time it could—it would—be different. I was settled and successful in my practice. I could take as many or as few surgeries as I wanted. I could make time for this child—this daughter—from the start, and prevent Rosie from ruining her.

That was my plan.

Day 4

Today, tea again. This time when I brought it upstairs Rosie was sitting in the alcove with her prayer book. I concentrated on the tea to avoid spills, though I felt her eyes on me. If she'd said, "Thank you for the tea," it would've ruined the entire undertaking. Those words would be tantamount to saying, "So— you voluntarily performed a service for me today. You thus admit that I'm a person of value, someone who has a claim on you. I'd just like to acknowledge that and rub it in your face." Yes, that's what *thank you* means implicitly.

Patton awaited me at the bottom of the staircase. I sat down and buffed the top of his head until the sheen of his brown-gray coat glistened. He tilted his head and looked at me approvingly, as dogs will do.

Day 5

What a relief to settle into my office chair today. Even Rosie couldn't bother me there, not without facing the nurses' gauntlet. And they can be formidable, even where my wife's concerned. I think they take perverse delight in keeping her on hold while they 'search' for me. I must've telegraphed the notion to them that I was ambivalent about speaking with her.

I generally spend mornings in rounds and afternoons in clinic, unless I have surgery scheduled. It's a full day, intense and rewarding. When a child needs reconstructive surgery of the middle or upper face—from a congenital defect, rare disease, car accident, burn, animal attack—I'm the man to see, the best pediatric craniofacial surgeon in the state.

Before catching up on some documents, I picked up the framed photograph of Michaelina from my desk. It's an official preschool picture, the kind with harsh lighting and a background of soft blue swirls. In it, she sits up straight, chin lifted, wearing the slightly goofy but exuberant smile that any four-year-old might produce on demand.

In my profession, I need to apprehend what is considered beautiful. I do that by analyzing faces. Not only my patients' faces with their deformities and disfigurements, but every face I encounter—normal, ugly, lovely. It's a game to me—scrutinizing a face's imperfections and deciding which ones, if I could alter them, would render the face more attractive.

It's also a burden. Others seem able to accept a person's face, including its irregularities, and even consider it beautiful if they love the person behind it. It's not so simple for me. With my extensive knowledge of craniofacial anthropometry, I'm acutely aware of the infinite ways in which a human face can deviate from scientifically documented reference points.

However, I didn't look at Michaelina's facial landmarks today, nor did I analyze her features. I looked only at the shiny brown hair behind her shoulders, at the way the light struck it and made some strands appear luminescent. One tress was separated from the others and lay in front on her chest, satisfied and defiant. I've grown to love that misplaced lock, the way its thickness tapers off to a point and curls slightly at the end.

That's what I focused on today. Just her hair.

Day 7

Dr. Ji-young Kim, the hospital's Chief Medical Officer, called me in first thing. Ji-young is a short, well-built woman with arms that hang slightly away from her body, trailing off into small curled-up fists.

I've never had a satisfying conversation with Ji-young. It's the job of a CMO to make the medical center run efficiently, a goal in direct contradiction to the best medical care, and sometimes even to common sense.

Today was typical. Ji-young said I needed to chat with a staff psychiatrist.

I asked why.

Her little fists tightened and she attempted to swallow a rough noise in her throat. "To make sure everything's okay."

Ji-young had a habit of nodding her head when wanting affirmation to a statement, and shaking it for something you likely didn't want to hear. The nods and shakes were minute movements on the axis of her neck, as if subliminal messages to prompt the desired response.

When I assured her I was perfectly fine, she bobble-nodded, saying, "I appreciate your self-confidence," with no appreciation whatsoever in her tone. "Nevertheless," she said, "it would behoove you to go."

Now, when someone throws out a "behoove," there's trouble in the air. Or at least major inconvenience. Her head bobbled to the negative. "I wouldn't want to have to suspend your surgical privileges."

Ahh, so that was it.

Evidently, the legal department had requested a sign-off on my mental fitness to satisfy liability concerns. Ji-young had already checked my calendar with the division admin and scheduled a slot for tomorrow, as I had a canceled operation and was 'free.' I'd be one of the first patients of Dr. Matilda Thurman, who was new to the medical center.

A dozen protests formed in my throat but died on my lips. Must I be the guinea pig for a new doctor? And why a woman? How would she be able to determine my mental state as it relates to how well I fulfill my duties as a surgeon?

However, in hospital bureaucracies, it's axiomatic that what legal wants, legal gets.

Day 8

I made my way across campus this afternoon for my appointment and was ushered in without a wait. The fast-tracking struck me as a good sign—this issue could be dealt with expeditiously. I'd just need to project a cheerful attitude and choose my words with care. Also, if this psychiatrist was newly minted, I could over-awe her with my gravitas.

Those were my thoughts, anyway, as I entered the office. Dr. Thurman was standing behind her desk. My first surprise was that she wasn't a new doctor at all, but a woman of roughly my age. I'd describe her expression as quizzical—so I wiped the sunny smile from my own face. If I hoped to engender empathy, I'd need to mirror her attitude.

A handshake seemed appropriate. When I offered, she extended a meaty hand that registered no warmth. She motioned me to the brown leather sofa opposite her desk. I attempted to sit but the cushion sagged so much that the motion was more like falling, with my ass landing lower than expected. I wondered who she'd inherited this lousy sofa from and made a mental note to suggest she replace it.

Dr. Thurman, instead of sitting on the other side of the sofa or in the upholstered chair next to it, retreated to the chair behind her desk. She turned to her laptop, I presume to bring up my electronic health record.

That gave me a chance to examine her for clues. Not much there. Hers was a peasant's face, with largish nose and close-set eyes, suggesting an Eastern European background. Her hair was brown-black, or had been in better days, merging with dark gray at the temples. The entire nest-like mass fell just below her shoulders. Her bare calves, visible under the desk, were smooth, interrupted only by the long ridge of the tibia's anterior margin. One foot was poised on tiptoe in front of the chair, and the other behind it to the side, as if positioned to lift a load to her shoulders. I could picture her in a dirndl with a yoke across her muscular shoulders, a pail of milk hanging at each side.

She began typing. Without looking away from her screen, she shook her head and clucked twice. "Such a business," she said, and turned to me. "What can I do for you?"

That opening afforded me some cautious optimism. I explained that the legal department needed an all-clear on my psychiatric status. A completed form for their records. It'd probably take only a sentence or two from her to set things to rights.

In response, she looked at me and tilted her head slightly while narrowing one eye, as if looking through a telescope. Or maybe a microscope. It struck me that I'd seen this woman somewhere before. I couldn't place her, though, and didn't want to get sidetracked by bringing it up.

I told her this visit was a formality, that Ji-young Kim had said as much. I repeated that we just needed to satisfy those darn actuarial types in the legal office. "Clearly they anticipate no problem," I added, "as I've been operating with no problems since the incident."

"*Hoo*," she said.

I decided to interpret that vague ethnic articulation as agreement. Leaning forward on the sofa—not an easy feat—I said, "Great, we're on the same page then. If you could just type that into my record…"

Her fingers froze on the keyboard. She turned and gawked at me.

I stared right back. Wasn't that the way to win—to state your request, then steel yourself and wait for the other person to break the awkward silence?

Several seconds later, she did break it, but her scope-eye didn't leave me. Spreading her hands flat on the desk, she asked, "Have you ever hurt yourself?" *No,* I said. "Any plans to hurt yourself?" *No.* "Thoughts of suicide?" *No.* "Ever seriously hurt someone else?" *No,* I said quickly, not allowing the nuances of that question to interfere with the robustness of my response.

"Any *plans* to hurt someone?"

At that question, I threw my hands in the air, accidentally bumping the arm of the sofa, which was elevated in relation to my low-slung position. "No. I'm a surgeon. I'm a pediatric craniofacial surgeon."

The psychiatrist's face betrayed no reaction to my declaration. I noticed, though, that she seemed to be grinding her toes into the carpet. She was readying herself, but for what? I only hoped she wasn't about to leap out at me. I was unsure I could triumph in a tussle.

But no—all she did was pick up a pen, grip it near the tip, and tap it on the desk. Her left eye opened wide and narrowed again, as if readjusting the focus of her microscope, centering me more precisely on the stage. "Tell me what happened," she said.

I leaned against the sofa back and adjusted my position. The creaking support structure beneath the cushion shifted with me, as if I were a child squirming on its grandmother's flabby lap.

With a faint chuckle to soften the mood and prepare her for disappointment, I said, "What happened is well known."

"I want to hear you tell it," she said.

I took a long, steadying breath. "A recitation of the lurid facts seems gratuitous."

"Skip the lurid part then."

"What exactly do you want?"

"To know why you're here."

"I told you, to get a statement—"

"No, not the statement, the reason for the statement."

"The hospital needs to cover itself."

"Why does it feel the need to cover itself?"

"Lawyers always feel the need for coverage."

"Why do they feel the need in this particular case?"

"How should I know?"

"If you don't know, there's the problem right there."

I gripped one arm of that spongy grandmother of a sofa, strained forward, and enunciated my answer. "In a case like this, the legal department needs to document that I can still operate without complications. They need a professional opinion by the likes of you to state that I've been unaffected by the incident."

"*Hoo*. And that's what you're saying? That you've been unaffected by this so-called incident?"

"My *competence*," I said. "They want to know whether my *competence* has been affected."

"Has it?"

"No. I've operated since then, perfectly successfully."

This sort of exchange went on for another ten minutes or so. Finally, I told her she had no reason not to clear me.

"I'm the judge of that," she said. Then, after rapidly typing a few words on her keyboard, she said we'd meet again next week.

I opened my mouth to protest, but before I could formulate a response she stood and walked to the door, using the time-honored physician's technique to move patients on their way.

She made me feel like a dog being banished to the backyard after pissing on the carpet.

Day 10

I needed to get the bad taste of Matilda Thurman out of my mouth. Being Saturday, I spent a good hour pruning my roses. The forsythia are in bloom, signaling the time is right. I've cultivated a fair number of rose varieties, including antiques, climbers, and even some shrubs.

My gardening tools are essentially coarser versions of the precision tools I use in my surgery. Wielding them is a respite, a sort of rustic retreat. If I shear too much off a rose cane, or if the hoe carves a divot from the root, no big deal. The stakes are infinitely higher when shearing through a child's delicate skin and tissue with what is essentially a sharper version of a razor blade. Any error or imprecision will worsen the scar, haunting the child's face forever.

Today I tackled the Madame Isaac Pereire out back. With my loppers, I removed the dead wood and suckers. Next I worked my pruning shears, opening up the center of the bush to maximize air circulation. No blood, no sutures needed. Only a drop of Elmer's on each exposed cut to discourage cane borers.

I won't let Rosie touch my roses (not that she's ever shown interest). Sometimes, though, I'll cut an armful of blooms and put them in a vase on the dining room table. She knows (on some level) that they're for her. It would seem crass, though, to give them to her directly.

Rosie has her own pursuits. One of them is crossword puzzles. I helped her develop that interest early in our marriage. We used to work on them together in the evenings for cheap entertainment. I use the phrase 'work on' loosely—we had a sort of game going. We'd answer clues for a while in all seriousness. Then, one of us would respond to a clue with some word that had a sexual connotation. And at that stage of life, it was amazing how many words could remind one of sex. *Slapstick, durable, nosegay, flare, exculpate.* We'd catch each other's eye, grin like the adolescents we were, and make love, whispering the word between us, each repetition heightening the mystery and intensifying the focus of our desire. We rarely finished a puzzle.

Rosie still does a crossword every day, claiming it's her way of improving her mind, without having to leave the house. I suppose it's more edifying than watching TV. I don't have the time or desire to do them with her anymore—they long ago lost their erotic magic.

Day 11

Thankfully there's no proscription against my surgical work while seeing Dr. Thurman. This morning I operated on a 4-month-old infant whose two front plates had fused prematurely, a condition known as trigonocephaly. The skull bones are supposed to be separated on top of a newborn's head, with the soft spot allowing room for continued brain growth. This infant was already displaying the beginnings of the classic triangular-shaped forehead from the compression of her brain as it expanded and found no outlet. A case like this can cause neurological deficits as well as physical deformities if not corrected early.

Operating on the skull of an infant is exhilarating, giving me a rush of adrenaline that comes with the initial cut of the scalpel. Carving through that fresh newborn skin is like an act of vandalism. I can sense the skin's shock and surprise at being desecrated this way—the integrity and cohesion it has worked so hard to achieve in its young life obliterated in an instant. I slice, but it takes a moment for the despoiling to register. Then the flesh around the incision blushes and a crisp red line forms—the tiny drops of blood emerging one after the other, in angry succession.

I wrest open the flaps of skin, and the messiness of suction begins. My exhilaration takes a different turn as I begin sawing through the skull. The craniotomy removes enough bone to relieve the cerebral compression. Typically, a number of transosseous veins are encased where the bone plate suture has closed. Dissecting those veins from the bone is a delicate business. A tiny tear can cause massive, even life-threatening bleeding.

The spiral blade of my electric craniotome whirs, its guide angled against the inside of the skull to prevent penetration of the dura surrounding the soft matter of the brain. I cut through the portion of skull needing removal, while preserving in place the small triangular bone on which the originating veins are attached. This method allows me a better sight line to detach the veins from the surrounding bone structures and control the bleeding prior to removing that final small piece of frontal bone.

The surgery was successful. Because of the precision required, the technique I used was especially time-consuming. The neurosurgeon working with me had advocated beforehand for what he termed a "more efficient approach." I'd ignored him but sensed his disapproval.

When we finished, he met my eyes and snapped off his gloves.

He doesn't see what I do. He doesn't see death loitering around the operating table, nonchalantly, as if a disinterested observer, trying not to appear greedy. But I know death's pretenses.

Day 12

Making and delivering Rosie's tea is finally becoming routine. Today, while passing her the mug, I even managed to grumble "G'morning," but in such a way as to make it clear that no response was desired or welcome. For once, my signals worked.

Every day, Patton waits at the bottom of the stairs to get his rubdown. It soothes my nerves, that skin-on-fur contact. And dogs know how to receive affection without humiliating the giver. He looks at me as if to say, "Why are you going to all this trouble? I don't deserve this. You're the most awesome being in the universe!"

But, routine inevitably becomes rut. I've only just begun to fulfill this damn bargain. Time to move onward. Next mission: no eye rolling, no matter what senseless words usher forth from Rosie's mouth.

I was tried severely today in this endeavor. After Rosie's early morning doctor's appointment, I agreed to meet her to drop off her Lexus at the mechanic. As I drove her home, she made one of her typical pointless comments: "If you get in the left lane here, it'll be easier to make the turn up ahead."

"Right-o," I replied, in pun-ish contradiction. I didn't roll my eyes though—I only squinted them a little harshly. It's true she would've been unlikely to notice my restraint, since we were both facing the same direction, but still.

However, she then insisted we stop at the pharmacy to pick up her medication, which her doctor had called in for her. I knew perfectly well it wouldn't be ready that quickly. She maintained otherwise.

Sure enough, the pharmacy assistant said we'd have to wait 20 minutes. Rosie glanced at me apologetically, and my eyeballs started their customary ascent. But by a series of facial contortions, I managed to push them back into place before they'd made a full rotation. She looked at me as if I were having a seizure or something.

I walked away to prevent saying something I'd have to chastise myself for later. While waiting for the pills, fuming internally, I browsed the magazine covers of attractive women, which spun my thoughts to nurse-sex. For years that had been my go-to cocktail when frustrations mounted. Even now, all it would take was a phone call—two names popped into my head. Then a quick ride to an hourly-rate hotel for a socks-wearing rendezvous that would slake that particular thirst.

But no—I've sworn off nurse-sex for good.

Day 13

Okay, so maybe I didn't put the time into my relationship with Rosie that I should have, back when it might've altered our trajectory. I was busy professionally. The early years in my practice would determine the course of my career. I had to make time to stroke other physicians for referrals.

Dealing with Rosie was fraught; sex with her exacted an emotional toll I couldn't always handle. Nurse-sex was so much simpler—any emotional component could be safely avoided. Nurses were plentiful—beautiful young women, excited to be away from home, grasping for control of their own destinies, eager to sleep with a surgeon. Perhaps deep inside their lovely young psyches was an unacknowledged financial goal. But their immediate aim was to throw off the incomprehensible strictures of their parents' morality and eat the thrilling, forbidden fruit for the gaining of knowledge.

It didn't matter to them that I was married. They seemed to know instinctively, as if sniffing it in the air, that my marriage was problematic. Once I got involved with the first one, word got out and a succession followed over the years. They're a gossipy lot, milling about the nurses' station when they should be caring for patients. I became a source of competition among them. Not just concerning who could bed me—I was accommodating enough—but who'd be the one to push my wife out for good.

Nurse-sex was delectable in its way. Like a fast-food combo, I could order my preference, wolf down the cheap meal, and toss the wrappings in the trash. I'd come away sated, if not entirely satisfied.

For a while, that's what I thought I wanted from Rosie—more detachment and predictability, less emotional entanglement. But I'll admit this now, although it pains me: there were times I was in bed with a nurse that I'd fantasize about Rosie, that we were making love the way we did in the early days of our infatuation. I'd imagine myself possessing her with that old clownish joy, so overcome with its glory that there was no brain space left to face its meaning.

Day 14

More work, and progress, on the eye rolling today. Three times I held myself in check by squeezing my frontalis and orbicularis oculi together.

Why is eye rolling even a problem? I'll admit, on the rare occasions when someone rolls their eyes at me, such as a poorly trained cashier who can't comprehend a simple request, I find it maddening. Rolling your eyes is saying, in effect, *you are an idiot*, and it's only due to the unfortunate situation in which I currently find myself that I'm forced to deal with you.

This morning, Rosie mentioned that her sister Maude was coming over for dinner.

"Again?" I said.

"She always comes over on Thursdays."

This would typically be occasion for an eyeroll, accompanied by a semi-suppressed sigh for good measure. Today, though, I just stared and swallowed hard.

The fact is, I didn't think Rosie would press company on me, not so soon. But she took my silence for assent.

Little was said during the meal. Afterward, I heard the two of them on the deck, laughing. Or maybe it was crying—you often can't tell with women, especially when the reverberations have that slightly insane tinge.

Day 15

Here's how Rosie and I met.

One summer evening, prior to my starting medical school at Duke, I was walking through the historic district on West Main, heading home. Up ahead a young woman in a short denim skirt was traveling in the same direction. My pace was faster; I gained on her. The closer I got, the more her figure demanded my attention. I enjoyed the way her hips moved. Not swaying in the loose way some women have, but in a tighter, more controlled fashion, revealed primarily in the counter-sway of her long and lustrous black hair.

When I'd nearly overtaken her, and while in the midst of a fantasy regarding those hips and that hair, something hard and sharp hit me on the head. I yelped, as you might imagine, and twisted around in alarm to look for an attacker. None was in sight. Turning back, my eyes locked with those of the woman, just a few yards away, who had turned around to face me. She was startled, even a little fearful, a response that only heightened my interest.

I reached for the top of my stinging head, and brought down fingers streaked with blood. My injury evidently allayed her fear. Becoming solicitous, she stepped towards me, fishing in her purse and producing a helpful wad of tissue, while asking what'd happened and whether I was okay.

I speculated that a bit of debris—a chip of brick or stone from one of the timeworn buildings lining the street—must've become dislodged. The woman searched the sidewalk, picked up a fragment that looked plausible, declared success, and offered it to me on her open palm. I laughed and declined. She curled her sweet fingers around it and I didn't give it another thought.

She insisted on escorting me home. We walked in the direction of my apartment for a couple of blocks, chatting about the various freak accidents we'd heard of in our lives. I could be quite entertaining in my descriptions, and her laughter was unrestrained.

At some point it occurred to me to ask about her own destination. It turned out she was headed to work at a nearby movie theater. We altered course, and when we arrived at the theater, I decided to take a rest. I stayed through two shows, until her shift was over, then walked her home.

I saw a lot of movies after that.

After we were married, I noticed that distinctive rock fragment on top of our dresser. When I asked why she'd kept it, she said she'd never throw away a piece of angel dust.

I smiled. "Isn't dust soft?"

She replied, "You're thinking of the kind that's made of flakes of skin or specks of dirt. I'm thinking of the dust that might fall off a piece of flint when you strike it to get a spark."

I added that it also seemed a bit large for dust, and she replied, "You have no idea how big angels are."

Day 16

Today I performed a distraction osteogenesis procedure, installing a mid-face titanium device in a nine-year old to promote bone growth. The operation went fine, fine. The results will be good. As I was about to cut through the hypoplastic maxilla bone, however, it suddenly appeared as if the bone were actually a tubercle of rib. Confused by the visual disturbance, I asked the nurse to remove my goggles, which must have clouded. That wasn't the problem though. It was a trick of perception, an optical illusion. When I looked away for several seconds and blinked hard a few times, I was able to correct my misperception and make the cut properly.

Life is rife with illusions. Here's one that's always stumped me. Why is it that the traits you find most appealing in a potential mate are the very ones that drive you out of your mind once you're married? The rule of opposites attracting must be an evolutionary ploy to amplify genetic variation. You fall in love with a person, for example, who doesn't obsess about cleanliness. It's somehow endearing the way they'll pick up an apple off the ground and eat it without washing it. You only discover later this means you've married someone who leaves smelly bras hanging in the dressing room or dirty cutlery on the countertop.

Or you're charmed by someone who's playful and spontaneous. A person who pulls you out of the drudgery of your studies and delights you with their sunny outlook and resourceful imagination. Later, you realize what you initially perceived as spontaneity is actually capriciousness, and what you experienced as liveliness is really imprudence.

At the time, though, those personality characteristics are beguiling, entrancing. Rosie's playfulness pervaded our early conjugal life. For starters, she wouldn't call me Michael. Too formal, she said. Over my objections, she began calling me *Mac*. I explained to her that 'Mac' was a lower-class substitute for 'Sir,' when addressing a man you didn't know. As in, *Hey Mac, need a cab?* That information only encouraged her. It annoyed me at first, but I tired of correcting her. And when she addressed me that way in bed, whispered it in that suggestive way she had, it made my hair stand on end.

Bed, though, was different from real life. There, I wasn't myself—I was a foreigner, dispossessed, someone whose spirited actions I couldn't fathom in the cold clarity of day. In which case, why not assume the persona of this animated fellow named Mac? It felt good. In bed, our very names held the secret of the ages, a secret I was certain only we possessed. Why couldn't we name ourselves whatever we wanted? We were Adam and Eve, the archetypal man and woman. We ourselves were the originators of sex, of true fulfilling sex, because surely this was something new under the sun. Else, why weren't its glories being shouted from every rooftop? Instead, people around us went about their daily business, while we, meeting each other's eyes, relished the conspiracy behind our god-like exertions.

So I became Mac to her, though never completely to myself.

Looking back now, I'm a bit ashamed at the extent of my play-acting. I should've known I couldn't keep up the impersonation indefinitely.

No, I couldn't pretend forever.

Day 17

I spoke with Ji-young this morning to ask if I could see some psychiatrist other than Dr. Thurman.

"She doesn't suit me," I said. "A man would be better."

She bristled. "How should gender matter here?"

"I don't click with her." People are very into 'clicking,' as if our species were some kind of beetle.

She gave a few minuscule shakes of her head. "No need to click. She just needs to attest to your mental fitness." Her head bobbled to the positive. "Surely a woman doctor is capable of that?"

"Yes, but—"

"And why didn't she sign off already when you saw her?"

I wanted to say because she's a pain-in-the-ass, but instead, I stayed silent.

Ji-young's small fists tightened. "The legal department is anxious to resolve this."

Victory. Ji-young had given me permission—a mandate really—to push ole Matilda Thurman to sign off on my clearance.

So at my afternoon appointment, even before sitting down, I relayed Ji-young's expectation that we wrap things up today.

"That's up to you," said Thurman, in that way people have of manipulating you into believing you have some control over a situation. The way a parent might trick a child into sitting quietly in the car in hopes of stopping for ice cream.

"Great! If it's up to me," I said, "let's get that clearance signed off and be done with it."

She trained her scope-vision on me. "Have a seat. Thirty minutes is good for something."

I sighed and descended into the abyss of the sofa.

"How are your surgeries going?"

"Hunky-dory." I recalled the rib-bone hallucination I'd experienced the other day, but that surgery had turned out fine. Not worth mentioning to Thurman.

"And how are you getting along with patients?"

"Good, good." That was true, for all I knew.

"And the other doctors and the nurses?"

"Fabulous," seemed the proper response.

"How about your wife?"

She placed a slight emphasis on the word 'wife' that I didn't like. Here she'd gone too far. My relationship with Rosie was none of her business and I told her so.

"*Hoo*," she said, with a flat wave of her hand, as if petting a dog. "So touchy there."

"Not touchy, just being clear," I said.

"I understand," she said, though obviously she didn't. "It's just that your wife—"

I stopped her right there. "Your job," I said, "is to examine my mental state as it relates to my ability to serve my patients. That's it." I crossed my arms.

She clamped her mouth shut and pulled her lips inside, as if restraining herself from saying something ill-advised. As an alternative outlet, she picked up a pen and tapped it lightly on the desk, then unsealed her lips with a tiny pop. "My job is mine to decide. I'm deciding right now. I won't be signing off on anything. Not until you prove you're okay."

"Prove it? I prove it every day by doing my work and doing it well. You don't need more than that."

"I do need more. You've been through mental trauma. I need to know how you're coping mentally."

I began a litany of my successful surgeries, but she stopped me, saying, "There's no checklist, no precision process. I use my professional judgment."

"Exactly my point," I said. "Psychiatrists don't need to care about precision. You're holding me hostage without a clear path out."

"You like to attack," she said without emotion. "And you're so uptight. So much resistance. Why so intent on burying your feelings?"

"Feelings are immaterial here. It's my work performance that's under review."

I expected a retort from her. Maybe I even wanted one. But all she did was sniff once and turn to her computer.

"I'm giving you a prescription for Xanax."

"That's your answer? That I need sedation?"

"Your anxiety is over the roof."

"The phrase is, 'through the roof,' not over it. And I'm *supposed* to feel anxiety—that's built into a surgeon's training."

"It's not anxiety about surgery that concerns me."

"But that's all you're supposed to be concerned with—my competence in surgery."

"The human brain can't just put itself into compartments like that."

"You know nothing of my brain."

"That's what I'm trying to learn about."

We talked in circles like this for the full half hour, with no resolution. As she walked me to the door, she said, "You may be Mr. Expert on human faces, but I'm the expert on human shame."

I didn't ask her to explain that remark, yet I couldn't help wondering how much she knew.

Day 18

Today started badly. I was anxious to get out with Patton, but Rosie was late getting up. The morning tea, in the prescribed mug, stood on the counter, its steam coiling upward and filling the kitchen with a treacly raspberry odor. Here I was, doing this service for her, and she didn't even have the consideration to get out of bed at the expected time. I paced around the kitchen, my goodwill draining out of me with each step.

Patton was aware of my annoyance. He stood in my way as I paced, flapping his big ears. When I ignored him, he lay down on the rug in front of the sink, obstructing my access.

After nine minutes, I finally heard Rosie rise and go into the bathroom. I took the now lukewarm tea upstairs and left it for her. I could have re-heated it in the microwave, but I needed to teach her a lesson. If she was going to sleep in, she'd just have to drink it cold. I got out of the house with Patton as quickly as I could, not waiting for the double-flush. Didn't she even know how to flush a toilet properly?

Then at dinner, she made this ambitious sort of stew, beef bourguignon I think it was, which she'd grossly over-salted. I chastised her casually, almost jokingly. In retrospect, perhaps I shouldn't have noted the countless times she'd made this same mistake, but I wanted her to understand that I wasn't rebuking her for an isolated mistake.

She took it harder than she should have and started tearing up. I stood slowly and left the room, my uneaten stew in my bowl. In keeping with my bargain, I should've eaten my portion and said nothing, or even better, complimented the chef. But that would do us both a disservice.

I suppose that's not the point, though. No matter how ludicrous and ill-advised, no matter how unfortunate the consequences, I ought to have held my tongue. When I couldn't manage that, I should've apologized. But I didn't. I couldn't.

I had no more ability to do that than to raise someone from the dead.

Day 19

I'm a sound sleeper. About an hour ago, though, a loud noise—some kind of crash or bang—woke me. It was the kind of abrupt noise that startles you, but because you were sleeping so deeply you can't determine exactly what it was or where it came from.

I turned my head and cupped my ear. It must be Rosie, I thought, groping around for something in the hallway. Hauling myself from my warm bed, I flicked on the light to investigate. I opened the door to Rosie's bedroom. The outline of her figure under the blankets expanded and contracted with each breath. The noise hadn't woken her—maybe I'd only been dreaming.

I turned on the light in Michaelina's room and peered in. All was undisturbed: the small vanity with her comb and brush arranged neatly on top and the satin chair underneath; the posters of Disney princesses lining the walls; the stuffed animals sitting expectantly against pink velvet cushions on the child-sized sofa; the bed with its gauzy canopy, and the pristine white coverlet stretched smoothly beneath.

I switched the light off and paused. If there were an intruder downstairs Patton would bark. I listened intently, straining not to miss the lowest growl or whimper. Some dogs are fickle in their barking, but I could trust Patton.

I wanted him to bark. Not because I wanted an intruder, but because I was spring-loaded now, ready to respond. I wanted him to call me to action. I stood there 15 minutes, wishing for it, pleading for another chance.

But there are no more chances, or none that matter. I gave up on sleep for the night.

Day 20

I'm embarrassed by my ramblings in yesterday's entry. It's unsettling, the ideas your mind can drum up when you're half asleep.

Next up is avoiding criticism. No, I haven't perfected either the tea ritual or the avoidance of eye-rolling, but I can't spend the entire year working on those two behaviors. I need to attack from every possible angle to hold up my side of the bargain. I'm not a person who goes back on his word, ever.

Sure, I'll admit there was a time I seriously considered divorce, and some people might consider that going back on your word. There's a way around that, however—annulment. It's a clever invention by Catholics by which some canon lawyer can decree your marriage was never valid in the first place. Thus, an annulment would mean I wasn't rescinding a promise, only recognizing that the vow I thought I'd made didn't really count. My wife is Catholic and we married in her church, so I have this process available as an out. I've looked into the rubrics. An annulment isn't just for cases of non-consummation. It can also be pursued when one or both parties are forced or pressured into a marriage, in which case I'd have valid grounds.

Why? Because we were essentially forced to marry when Eurosia got herself pregnant. Yes, that's her real name—Eurosia. I think it's some obscure saint's name. What her parents could've been thinking I have no idea. Anyway, when I was 22 the name Eurosia struck me as alluring—redolent of ambrosia and erotica and Eurasian. She's not Eurasian, but when she was 18, she was plenty alluring.

When we first began sleeping together, she told me to call her Rosie. That wasn't much better than the name Eurosia, in my opinion. I've always thought of *Rosie* as a cow's name, like Bessie or Buttercup. But at the time I was so smitten that I would've called her Star-catcher if she'd asked me to.

Day 21

Well before I met Rosie, I possessed a fascination with the details and proportions of the human face. I noticed Rosie had an incomplete lip seal, meaning that her lips don't close completely when at rest. The gap is only a few millimeters—not enough to register as a deformity, although still noticeable. When she was young, it gave her an adorable look of innocence, of surprise at my advances, of awe that I found her enchanting and wanted her.

And she resisted nothing. I should've taken precautions, but it all came up so unexpectedly and deliciously that I couldn't forgo the moment to go in search of a drugstore. Although I told myself I'd plan more carefully the next time, it was already too late. She always contended she hadn't understood what was going on, that she trusted from the start that I knew what I was doing. I'm still convinced she had at least a subconscious plot to reel me in. That must've been why her parents had sent her off at such an early age to live in the city, unchaperoned.

We were married the day after her 19th birthday—three months into the pregnancy. Being the eldest of seven children, her parents were only too glad to unload her, especially onto a young man just starting medical school and full of promise. It wouldn't surprise me if they'd purposely held off teaching her the facts of life in hopes of just such a bonanza.

Rosie was bright, in her benighted way. Her light, like a firefly's, ignited frequently yet unexpectedly—you never knew where the spark would show up next, just that it would. Her glow attracted me, but wasn't radiant enough to illuminate much. Later, her intermittent nature exasperated me. She lacked focus and ambition.

I take that back. She did have focus. Her focus was on our son. He's 24 years old now, and a more inveterate skirt-chaser than I ever was. I managed medical school while supporting a wife and baby, while I doubt he's done anything with his life—certainly nothing to earn respect from me. Anyway, I don't know why I'm talking about him. I hope never to see his jack-ass face again.

I've gotten completely off track. But I do have cause for resentfulness, and reasons that make it difficult to restrain my frustration.

And I haven't revealed the worst of it.

Day 22

I filled the damn Xanax prescription to have it on the record, in case it matters for obtaining my clearance. I have no intention of taking it, so no need to concern myself with Thurman's direction to take it only in the early evening to avoid any impact on my operating ability.

The best anxiety buster for me has always been sex. At times I do find myself wishing Rosie had held onto her inventive nature with respect to our intimacy—I could use the kind of thought-obliterating relief it afforded.

Back when we were newlyweds and Rosie was already pregnant, sex flowed freely. I'd established my virility, and she, her fecundity. There was nothing left to prove, nothing left to fear. Her expanding belly only enhanced the excitement. And the baby inside her needed no tending—its occasional jostling signaled to us that it was both accomplice to and product of our dizzy joy.

Rosie demonstrated her gratitude bountifully to the man who'd given her the gift of this baby. Sometimes she'd surreptitiously light scented candles to prepare the bedroom for us. I'd be studying, unaware, until the smell of vanilla (her favorite) drifted into the living room where I sat at my desk. I became Pavlov's dog, my body responding vigorously without my volition. Not that I objected to being used in that way. And while Rosie wasn't always an initiator, she was an eager enough responder. I'd approach her, she'd blush and grin, then chuck her clothing and pretend to hide coyly behind that lustrous mane of hers. I can still recall the sensation of that hair floating over me and her hands gliding across my skin, the anticipatory tension building in my flesh like a tightly strung bow.

If only, if only...

Day 23

It was Rosie who insisted on naming the baby *Michaelina*. I was concerned it might be too unusual, like Eurosia, causing her not to be taken seriously later in life. Rosie feared, on the other hand, that I wouldn't put up with another child, not after the disappointment of the Jackass. So she insisted the baby be named after me: Michael, Michaelina. In a rare moment of superstition I agreed, hoping against hope the child would take after me.

And she does. Did. She learned to read early, and although she wasn't particularly precocious in her speech, she was observant and displayed a remarkably keen understanding of relationships. She recognized when her chatter was endearing and welcome, and when she ought to stay silent.

She had a fascination with princesses, natural enough for a four-year old girl. She liked the very construct of princesses, the idea that one could be selected by fate to rise above other mortals and rule them. Despite her tiny frame, she was far from a delicate damsel. A fearless explorer, that's what she was, who wanted to do everything herself. I started calling her 'Princess' at some point, and she understood the irony, even at that age. Stoic in the face of pain, she'd bounce right up if she fell or hurt herself. She never complained, and never blamed other people for anything.

Day 24

Why does sex become more serious as life goes on? Why, at some point, is it no longer possible to play at it in the same happy-go-lucky way? For Rosie and me, that transition into seriousness came suddenly, out of nowhere. And when it did, it stripped sex down to its bones—and those bones were rigid, brittle, and unforgiving.

I'll explain.

This evening, when I arrived home, Rosie was nowhere to be seen. Her car was there, but she wasn't. There was no written note, no message on my phone. I called her cell, but the ring went to voice mail.

In the kitchen, no dinner preparations were underway. I checked her bedroom and closet, looking for clues. No suitcases were missing that I could tell. Her clothes were in a jumble—hangers askew and coats on the floor, evidently where they'd fallen from overloaded hooks. I hadn't entered this closet for so long, though, that I had no baseline—it was plausible this was the normal state of affairs.

What to do next? I sat on her bed. It was unmade, but that I recognized as the status quo. I tried to collect my thoughts. Rather than collecting them, however, they dispersed further, flying in random directions until one alighted—a memory from many years ago when something similar had happened:

Our son was just a baby then. I'd arrived home from med school late. Rosie wasn't there. Neither was the car. This was before the ubiquity of cellphones.

We'd had an argument that morning—I wanted her to avoid driving the car whenever possible to save on gas. She had a stroller for the baby and could easily walk to the grocery store, library, or park. But that day she wanted to drive somewhere. I can't remember where—it's immaterial now. But I said no.

I'd looked in the closet that time too. Surely she wouldn't leave me over an inconsequential argument? My mind began entertaining all sorts of possibilities. Could there be another man? If there were, maybe they'd gotten so involved that she hadn't noticed the time. Maybe she was using the car for regular trysts with him.

That idea was preposterous—even then I recognized it was my lizard brain acting up. Nevertheless, I went to the dresser and was relieved to see her 'angel dust' stone sitting in the same place as always. Surely that was a good sign. But then I thought, no—if she were leaving me, there'd be every reason to leave it behind.

Yes, I'd been angry with her that morning, but in reality it wasn't so much about the car. I'd been anxious about an exam that day and was sleep-deprived from late-night studying. As things turned out, I'd done well enough on the test, but the stress had left a dent in my psyche that hadn't yet popped back into place. When Rosie wasn't home upon my arrival, that dent filled with apprehension and soon flooded to overflowing.

Maybe I needed to eat something, I remember thinking. I hadn't had anything since an early lunch. I went to the kitchen, but didn't have the motivation to make even a snack for myself. I sat at my desk to study, but my uneasy thoughts returned to Rosie at the end of every sentence.

I gave up studying and stared at the wall. My irritation, my needs, and my fears were bundled into a tight ball, one I mentally turned over and over. After my long day, I'd forgotten about the car issue, but suddenly it made me angry all over again. In essence, she'd stolen it, taken it somewhere against my explicit wishes. Okay, maybe not to see a lover—I couldn't countenance that thought—but for something petty and stupid. When she finally returned, I'd give her a tongue lashing, then not speak to her for a week. I'd make her understand I wouldn't allow this behavior—not only taking the car, but not being home and not leaving a note of explanation.

I undressed and ran the water for a shower. Rosie would surely arrive before I finished. She'd apprehend I couldn't care less whether she was late or not—I had my own agenda and didn't need her. Her realization of that fact would serve as a chastisement in itself. I stood for a long time under the showerhead. The hot water shooting down the back of my neck soothed me, made me recognize how silly I'd been to worry. I heard a muffled sound—a baby crying. Rosie was home, then, and would be starting dinner. I wouldn't rush out to welcome her. She'd be anxious to explain herself, but I'd take my time toweling off.

When I exited the bathroom in my robe, however, I found the apartment undisturbed. The crying sound had come from my over-active imagination.

My anxiety returned in a whirlwind. I wondered whether I should phone the police or call around to the hospitals. When someone was brought to the ED from a bad accident, the focus was on saving them before searching their belongings to find contact information for relatives.

I stood and paced. By then, I'd been home alone for hours. The dime-store clock hanging on our kitchen wall ticked out its jarring strokes. My pacing followed in rhythm. Time itself mocked me with the way it strode forward, relentlessly, the clock-ticks like the throbs of a bad headache, drumming into me the fact that I was still there and Rosie still wasn't.

I was half crazed by then with not knowing where she was. Even so, I wouldn't attempt to discover her whereabouts. Contacting the police or hospital would make it too real, escalating the worst possibilities into probabilities. I didn't have phone numbers for any of her friends. Nor would I stoop to calling them—I'd appear needy and foolish, unable to control my own wife.

Those thoughts brought my fury again to the fore. I was in the midst of refining my plan for Rosie's punishment when the sound of footsteps on the exterior stairs reached my hyper-alert ears. Then came a fumbling at the door latch. I took my stance several yards away. I wouldn't open the door for her—I needed distance for the confrontation. Once assured of her wellbeing, there'd be time enough to release my anger.

In stepped Rosie with the car seat. The baby was strapped into it, snuggled under a blanket, fast asleep. She set him down carefully and closed the door behind her. When she turned and met my eyes, I read fear there. Was it fear that our morning argument was about to recommence? Or was it the knowledge that she was about to be castigated for her transgression? The gap from her incomplete lip seal widened just a bit as she drew a breath to speak.

But she didn't need to say a thing. Transparent tears were issuing from her eyes. Those, coupled with the expression on her face, convinced me she had an excuse for being late, and a good one too. She'd been tormented by her inability to get home or to reach me.

My weighty plan for her punishment dropped from my grasp like a greased bowling ball.

"Rosie," I said. My fear and longing were encapsulated in that one word, that one name. She froze for a second, then flew into my arms with a sob. Her head found its harbor against my neck. I held and rocked her for a minute or two, my hands stroking her hair. My hands were restive—I felt an overwhelming need to touch every part of her, to assure myself that all her flesh was still there, every bit I'd grown accustomed to, every piece I loved and craved. I lifted her shuddering frame, held her against me, and bore her to the bedroom, where I laid her crosswise on the bed. This was no time for candlelight or crosswords. None were needed or wanted. This was different; this was serious.

I dropped my robe to the floor, not taking my eyes off her. I had to have her all at once then, every morsel of her—the soft arms, the lustrous hair, the narrow hips, and everything in between. I kissed her, yes, but in a frenzied way, not savoring, not even enjoying. Not the way I had before.

I met no resistance, but half out of my mind as I was, I'm not sure I'd have noticed any. She knew my need, she was ready. The narrow hips tilted upward in that way she had, hips nudged open like a gate, then growing wide in welcome. I held on to her for dear life, because that's what she was—my dear, my life. Still, there was a grimness, a desperation about it. I gripped those narrow hips like a drowning man with a life preserver, flailing, fighting not to be pulled under. It was now or never, drown or survive. I had to have her all at once, like gulping a stiff drink. All at once, like tearing off a band-aid.

All at once, like swallowing the bitter pill it was.

Day 25

I couldn't finish writing last night. I don't know what I was thinking. That memory...was it pleasure or pain?

Regardless, I couldn't help recalling it when I noticed Rosie's absence last night. And then, still engrossed in that unsettling recollection, I encountered Rosie herself at the top of the stairs. I stopped short in surprise and our eyes met. She wore an expression of fear that again took me back to that night in our apartment 20-plus years ago. The gap between her lips again widened as she prepared to speak. Again, I spoke first, before I could even think.

"Rosie," I said, with that same longing, that same anguish.

But Rosie failed to recognize my agony. She didn't cry. She didn't fly into my arms. I didn't carry her to the bedroom. We didn't make desperate love.

The fear on her face signaled something else entirely. It wasn't fear of being separated from me, or despair that she'd kept me waiting in anxiety. No—she was hiding something. And she was afraid of my questioning her.

"I didn't expect you home this early," she said.

"Nevertheless, here I am."

She mumbled a few words about the traffic and forgetting her cell phone at home.

But something else clearly lurked behind her excuses. I didn't press her. I didn't care she was late, or that she'd forgotten her phone. What I hated was that she didn't come to me when I said her name.

I suppose she never will again.

Day 26

I've endured my final session with Dr. Thurman. Thank God.

It didn't start well. First, she asked if the medication was helping. I told her yes, which was true in the sense that by agreeing to fill the prescription, I was bringing myself one step closer to getting her sign-off on my healthy mental state.

"Let's talk about the day of the incident," she began.

"Let's not," I said.

"Not talking about this event, repressing it, is a problem," she said.

What she didn't know was that revealing the details of it would be worse. So I said, "Can't you accept that some people are simply more mentally stable? That some of us are more resilient, more able to move on with our lives, to discharge our duties even in the midst of grief?"

"Okay, at least you're admitting to grief now."

I didn't respond. The more I spoke, the more she seized on my words and twisted them to her own purpose.

My silence bothered her. She fixed her scope-eye on me and said, "If I don't sign off, Ji-young will suspend you. I'm leaning that way unless you can give me more."

I ran my hand along the sofa arm, caressing its pitted surface, exploring with my fingertips the rough cracks and crinkles of the aging leather. What was I supposed to say to this woman? Letting her into the recesses of my psyche wasn't just repugnant, it was an impossibility, no matter the consequences.

She didn't see that. She somehow believed that if she kept pushing, kept probing, I'd eventually see the sunbeam and open up my soul to her like a morning glory blooming at dawn. Then we'd rejoice together in its beauty.

Beauty, though, was the last thing she'd find there.

As if she sensed the source of my defensiveness, she said, "Tell me how you see yourself."

That was easy. "As a highly competent pediatric craniofacial surgeon."

She shook her head. "Tell me about your childhood, about your parents."

I provided a brief summation to demonstrate my cooperativeness, but included nothing titillating for her to latch onto.

All the same, she said, "I'm thinking maybe you're a classic case. Not a narcissist really—no, I sense anxious-avoidant attachment syndrome. What was done to you as a—"

I cut her off. "Nothing was done to me."

She turned to her computer and began typing. "It must be trauma-informed—"

I stood. "No, no, no. No trauma, informed or otherwise. I have nothing to tell you there."

"You mean, nothing you *want* to tell." She was typing furiously, not even looking at me.

"Stop recording that bullshit. I don't agree to any of that."

"You don't agree right now. Fine." Squinting at her watch, then staring me down, she said, "Let's go back. Tell me what happened that day. Your last chance." She leaned forward, clamping her mouth shut.

I sat back down but said nothing. She tilted her head sideways and fixed me in her eye scope.

That mannerism struck me as familiar. It set off an internal alarm. I scrutinized her features from my redoubt deep in the sofa.

I knew this woman from somewhere.

I glanced about the room but the walls were bare. A translucent plastic bin, overflowing with files and other office detritus, sat on a chair in the corner. Why hadn't she finished moving in?

I turned back and looked her in the eye, her scoping eye. It wasn't the scope of a microscope, but more like the scope of a gun.

I said, "I know you."

She blinked a couple times. "You think so? From where?"

"I don't know, but I'm sure of it."

"Well, I don't know you."

"I don't forget faces."

"You're off the point."

I couldn't place her but I found I could read her. That was all that mattered. I could read her—she was bluffing.

"Go ahead," I said. "Tell Ji-young I'm unfit. But you have no grounds for it."

She picked up her pen and rat-a-tatted on the desk, a virtual unloading of her gun into the dirt. Once the barrel was emptied, she sighed and said, "With what little bits you've given me, I can't stop you."

I smiled.

She took on a strange coaxing tone then, one I hadn't witnessed before, and said, "You know, even if I sign off, you're welcome to keep seeing me. In fact, I want you to come back. I can help you."

The hubris of this woman!

"No, thank you." This was a correct usage of *thank-you*, to end a conversation and be rid of someone.

"We can work through the problems. No need to tell Ji-young about them."

"Not on your life."

Our time was up, but she seemed reluctant to end the session.

I stood to leave.

She remained seated and leaned forward, eyes full-bore. "Good job," she said. "You make yourself into someone not even touched by this crazy tragedy. I have plenty of notes to protect me, and that's good, because I've seen lots of patients, Michael—"

"I'm not lots of patients. I'm not a patient at all. I'm a surgeon."

I didn't like her calling me Michael either, instead of doctor. Beyond that, though, was the way she said *Michael*. The 'k' sound had a softness to it, a tiny breeze that sounded like the 'ch' in *chutzpah*. I'd heard that somewhere before.

But I didn't stay to figure out her identity. What did it matter? She'd agreed to sign off and I was home free.

As I headed out the door, she said, "Watch out. Deniers like you can come to ruinous ends."

Day 27

Humility is what I'm seeking, and that means I must be patient. An impatient person is essentially claiming his time is more valuable than yours, that he's a person of greater worth and higher status than you. If impatience denotes pride, then ipso facto, patience implies humility.

I needed a reminder to exhibit greater patience with Rosie this evening. In her presence, I'd surreptitiously move my wedding band up over my knuckle. The irritation of it being placed incorrectly on my finger would prompt me to reflect more consciously on my response to whatever she said or did.

This tactic worked on a few simple matters. I was able to ignore her speaking too loudly to Maude on the phone, forgetting to put the condiments on the table prior to sitting down to dinner, and even her making two inane remarks as we ate.

I was tried more thoroughly, however, in a larger affair. After dinner, I reclined on my easy chair in the den, perusing the opinion section of the paper. Rosie, instead of relaxing on the sofa with her feet up as she typically did, sat forward, forearms on her knees. She asked if we might visit her family over Easter.

Spending time with Rosie's family was not my version of enjoying a holiday. I asked whether she couldn't go alone. She said no, "Because we're married."

I suggested we celebrate at home, but the mention of the word 'celebrate' turns out to have been a trigger. Her eyes filled. She said she didn't want to spend the day here.

My thoughts turned to Easter of last year. I recalled Michaelina dashing about the yard, searching for plastic eggs, running haphazardly from the shrubbery to the swing-set and back again. The neighbor boy, Trevor, peeking over the high fence between our yards (as he did frequently), watching the hunt with such interest that before I could say something to prevent it, Rosie invited him to join in. I don't like interlopers as a rule, but Trevor wasn't so bad. I appreciated how the boy deferred to Michaelina. He carried her basket and helped her obtain a few hard-to-reach eggs, like the one wedged in the notch of the willow tree. Although older than Michaelina, he's tangibly younger in terms of social skills. His face is quite appealing with his wide blue eyes, perfectly formed nose, and mop of thick brown hair. His facial expressions, however, are lacking in what you'd expect of a seven-year-old. He never furrows his brow, for instance, and I never once saw him smile in response to the jolly chatter Michaelina directed his way. No—his smile emerges only when he finds something internally satisfying or amusing.

His speech is odd too. He seldom talks, and when he does, his enunciation is exaggerated, as if he's concerned about making himself clear. Anyway, the friendship was one of pure convenience. If Trevor peered over the fence and saw Michaelina playing outside, he'd invite himself over. Michaelina could prattle on endlessly and he never interrupted her or seemed to mind in the least. I rather doubt he was paying much attention. He was mainly interested in Michaelina's toys, as far as I could tell. He liked to upend her bicycle and spin the tire while Michaelina talked.

Even so, on Easter, I ensured he scrammed before dinner. Rosie had made roasted lamb with garlic and rosemary. I can smell it even now. And there were herbed new potatoes, lemon asparagus, fresh baked rolls, and some sort of pastry that Rosie made every year, from a recipe of her mother's. She'd even made homemade buttercream eggs. I don't know about Lenten fasting, but the papists sure know how to put on a feast.

There'd be none of that feast this year, though, unless we ate at her parents' house. That fact was written all over her countenance.

I twisted my wedding band and jammed it back down my finger. Maybe the trip wouldn't be such a terrible idea. Rosie's brothers were competent fishermen, and one of them was sure to take me out on the lake. They were fun to needle, too, about their ill-considered political leanings. So I agreed to go.

Then the irritations began.

Rosie started by asking whether we should fly or drive, a not inconsequential question. To get to Fayetteville was too long for a drive but too short for a flight. If we drove, it would mean more time away from the hospital. With security at the airport, however, and then getting a rental car and driving to Fayetteville, a flight would be nearly as time-consuming. And then we'd have to adhere to a schedule—we couldn't just pick up and leave her family when I'd had enough. We batted it back and forth, and although both options would be royal nuisances, I chose flying. At least I could have a glass of wine on the flight and lose myself in a book.

Next she wanted to know whether we should stay at her parents' house or at a hotel. I said hotel, but then she started up with her objections: the distance from her parents, the inconvenience of parking, the offense her parents might take.

"Then you stay with them. I'll stay at the hotel."

"That would defeat the point of our going together."

We wouldn't get separate beds (my preference) at her parents' house. I was uncomfortable pointing that out to her, so I suggested we decide later.

Then she wanted to know about what kind of car we should rent. And whether she should make the buttercream eggs and bring them. Would she be allowed to bring them on the plane, or should she get some dry ice and pack them in her checked luggage? She wondered (aloud) what the weather would be, what coat she should bring for Easter Mass, if she should check multiple bags.

I fingered my wedding band again as my patience ebbed. There had to be some strategy to refill the tank. I tried answering her incessant questions monosyllabically, but that didn't deter her. Each additional question battered my patience. When she asked if we should buy Easter gifts for her nieces and nephews, I told her I didn't know or care, and that I wasn't going with her after all.

What I want to know is this: do I get some kind of credit for the patience I initially displayed? I answered more than a dozen questions patiently—almost certainly a record for me. But if, after being pressed far beyond what any sane person could possibly bear, I finally boil over, am I to be judged only on the finale?

Day 28

It's ironic, for sure. Rosie's the beneficiary of my efforts when she was the one at fault. Still, I'm the one who made the bargain. I'm the one who has to lower myself, to pursue humility in all its forms, no matter what the cost to my dignity or to her improvement.

So today I bit my tongue until a little white sore developed on the tip.

Thinking about Michaelina reminds me why I'm doing this. Framed photos of her adorn our walls. All were taken by Rosie, who's become a fairly proficient photographer. I was pleased that after Michaelina's birth, she'd at last professed an interest in some kind of hobby. As encouragement, I bought her a decent camera. A few months later, she asked for some special lenses, so I purchased them as well.

On occasion I'd ask her to take a photo of Michaelina and me. She'd fumble around with the equipment as if she had no clue what she was doing. I chalked it up to nervousness, her fear of stumbling in front of me, and didn't make a big deal about the less than stellar results. She must've known how to use the camera correctly, though, as the photos she took of Michaelina when I wasn't around were quite artful.

Several of my favorites are of Michaelina at the local park. In one, she's clutching a fistful of daisies, her favorite flower. In another, she's perched atop the slide, grinning with triumph at having climbed up herself. Her skinny little arms barely reach to the sides and her grip is tight, poised to launch herself into the depths. Rosie told me that she'd scraped her leg at the bottom on that very trip, but nevertheless continued climbing up the steps and hurtling down with abandon.

While I wasn't with her on that particular occasion, I did spend as much time as I could with my little girl. When I pulled into the driveway after work, Patton would bark furiously until the front door was opened. Then he'd race out to me without a hint of decorum, claiming his bit of attention first. I'd crouch down and buff his gray-brown noggin with my fist.

My eyes, though, were on Michaelina. She'd stand in the open doorway, her snub nose in the air and a suppressed smile on her lips—a Disney princess amused at my boorish dog-handling behavior, yet deigning to receive me, a commoner returning from his labor.

I'd walk with feigned obeisance to the porch, ascend the steps, and bow deeply in her presence, at which point she'd lose all control and jump up into my arms. She was an ethereal thing, a mere wisp, weighing less than my doctor's bag, or so it seemed. I'd carry her back to the car and set her in the front seat next to me. Riding like a grown-up, even for the very brief trip from the driveway into the garage, was a treat for her.

Then, I'd hoist her onto my shoulders and pony-trot into the house, tossing her like a sack of potatoes onto the sofa, and tickling her until she screeched so loud with delight that Rosie would yell from the kitchen, "Can't you leave the poor thing alone?" Then I'd stop and we'd whisper together until we were called in to dinner, or if it was late, until her bedtime.

If I tickled her for too long or dumped her too roughly on the sofa, she'd cross her arms and frown, bottom lip out. We had a little signal we used in those cases. I'm not the apologizing type, but when I offended her, I'd rest the tip of my index finger lightly on my bottom lip and lift my eyebrows just slightly. Her response was a tiny, quick dip of her head. I didn't teach her to do that—she understood instinctively that I was making myself vulnerable, that this apologizing and forgiving was a delicate thing, not to be treated as a broad gesture or carried to the point of embarrassment. To be sorry was to humble oneself, and to forgive was to exercise an awful power. And once done, it was done for good—the incident was behind us.

Day 29

In contrast, when I was a young child, my father and I were not close. He had no gift for play. From him, it was always, *You idiot* this, and *You moron* that. For years I accepted the belittling as the norm between fathers and sons. If it hurt, at least I could comfort myself that hurting was normal. That is, until I witnessed other fathers treating their own sons differently, respectfully.

That respect was a revelation to me. I must be doing something wrong in relating to my own father, I concluded, but couldn't figure out what. I was smart and worked hard in school, yet I never could count on his approval. When I produced a straight-A report card, the most he'd do was grunt, and possibly refrain from calling me names for a week or so. I tried to think of some way to change the dynamic, but I didn't have enough life experience to formulate a strategy.

My father did possess one favorable attribute. While he didn't have a lot of money, what he did have he used for my education. He made plenty of sacrifices to contribute to my college and med school tuition—I recognize that in retrospect.

The largess was halted, however, the moment he learned of Rosie's pregnancy. If I was to be a husband and father, he said, my finances were henceforward my own responsibility.

I'd feared that exact outcome, so before presenting this unwelcome news to my father, I tried to salvage the situation. Rosie wouldn't think of a termination. I'll admit, though, that I'd suggested that option only half-heartedly. Not only was I besotted with Rosie, but a juvenile pride rose up in me that I'd generated this new life in her. Pure evolutionary hogwash, I see now. Still, I was young and there it was.

Even with my intelligence and academic preparation, medical school was no sleepover. My father's continuing assistance would've helped enormously. Without it, Rosie and I experienced some very trying years, both financially and emotionally. We eked by with careful budgeting. One time, in my early residency, I arrived home exhausted from 36 straight hours on call. I found Rosie sitting on the floor with the boy, counting a pile of loose change. She apologized that dinner wasn't ready but said there was enough money for her to run out to the grocery store, if I'd watch the boy for a few minutes.

I vowed then to work even harder, to prioritize my profession, to provide well for my family. As a result, I was home little during the boy's infancy. When I was present, I mainly studied and slept. Rosie was responsible for all the feeding, diapering, soothing, and playing. She had a talent for it.

Her life, if not yet financially comfortable, was a relatively easy one. She cared for the baby and our small apartment while I slaved over my books. I didn't begrudge her that ease per se. It would've been one thing if she did her share by keeping the place clean and well organized, the laundry done, the groceries purchased. But she often failed in those domains. I'd come home late at night to toys littering the living room floor, clothes scattered on the sofa—whether clean or dirty I had no clue—and dinner either half-cooked or cold.

Oh, she managed the boy's needs all right, in her unsophisticated way. I never worried for his safety, or that he was fed. They'd go for walks, to the park, story hour at the library—any place that was free. She'd sit cross-legged on the floor with him for hours, narrating elaborate stories and acting them out with little figures she'd collected from rare Happy Meals or that she'd purchased for a few dimes at Goodwill. Cardboard boxes and pots and pans were turned into forts and castles. She'd sit at the table with him and create all kinds of crafts.

The two of them were inseparable; Rosie took attachment parenting to the extreme. When the boy was nearly two and he requested the 'other side,' I knew he had to be weaned, but even then Rosie was reluctant.

The main problem, though, was that she wouldn't discipline him. When I returned home, drained from my studies or work, the boy was still up. Like a wild creature, he jumped on the furniture, threw his toys about, and began back-sassing as soon as he'd learned enough words. I tried to avoid calling my own son the names my father had called me, at least in his early years. But my restraint got us nowhere.

As time went on I recognized my father's wisdom. The world is harsh and a boy needed to be prepared for that. Rosie babied him, so to compensate, I had to be tough. That strategy had worked for my father—so what if I'd hated him when I was a boy? I see now that he did the right thing by me. If my son hated me, I believed it to be a passing emotion. He'd thank me when he grew into a mature, successful adult.

That firmness took a lot of effort. Even so, my chastisements were no match for Rosie's leniency. Her indulgence ruined him. He's been gone five years now, and never even met his sister.

Day 30

In his later adolescence, the Jackass became a master of concealment. Every direct question from me was answered with a monosyllable devoid of expression—positive or negative—and with a face as frozen as Mount Rushmore. He wouldn't let me into his life one iota. Not after the incident with the car, anyway.

It was Rosie's car, not mine. He asked her if he could borrow it to attend a party. In the other room, I overheard the request, and came in to intervene. As far as I was concerned, his grades didn't merit any form of partying. I insisted he stay home and study. Surprisingly, he didn't argue. I was so pleased by his acquiescence that later I went up to his room to offer some words of encouragement.

He wasn't there.

I questioned Rosie, whose expression of panic at the news of his absence instantly relieved my fear that she'd crossed me. A quick look in the garage confirmed my suspicions.

Despite Rosie's pleas, I called the police to report a stolen vehicle. They found it—and the Jackass—in less than an hour. He spent the night in youth detention. When I picked him up, I expected a chastened child and an apology, but none was forthcoming.

After that event, even his monosyllabic answers were gone. He devoured his meals with us in hurried silence, then excused himself. If I insisted he stay, the increased tension in the air would only cause me indigestion. As time went on, I lost any desire to speak to him either. He managed to graduate from high school, but I didn't attend the ceremony. What would've been the point?

A few weeks later, on his 18th birthday, he took the possessions he could rightfully claim as his own—and a few questionable ones—and left us without a word. No, I take that back—he no doubt gave his mother a heartfelt adieu. I wasn't home at the time.

I told Rosie that if he didn't want to be part of our lives, then we'd have no part in his. I was owed an apology, and until he produced one, there was to be no communication with him from our end, and no money. "But not to worry," I reassured her. "He'll be back at the trough in no time."

That's where I was wrong.

Day 32

Sunday mornings I don't bother with Rosie's tea because she sleeps in and fasts before Mass. I relish her absence during the hour and a half she's gone. Beforehand, I take an extra-long run, timing it so I arrive home just as she's leaving. Even if it means foraging for my own breakfast, it's a relief to have the house to myself and not be concerned with what she might say to me or how I might respond. A break from humility.

The break was particularly needed this morning, after she left a wet towel draped over the sink, made a trivial comment on the neighbor's new siding, and stood with her arms crossed near the bathroom door, nearly blocking me, with a daft expression on her face.

Even her question about whether I slept well was annoying, because it was a thinly-veiled attempt to take my emotional temperature, and thereby to control me, or at least to manage me. Only by colossal effort did I manage to forgo a snide comment in response. Couldn't she tell just by looking at me that her every word, her every action irritated me? And once she'd pushed me so near the edge, even her hustling off to church afforded no respite. It was as if she'd set the pot on the highest setting before leaving. By the time she returned, it was boiling over.

The moment she walked in the door, I informed her I was leaving for the hospital to catch up on some paperwork. Her face fell. She shouldn't have been disappointed. I was no company for her, not in my present state.

I very nearly took a Xanax.

Day 33

I'm relieved to be done with Thurman. One more step in getting past this.

Certain questions she raised, though, continue to circulate through my mind.

Identity, for one. She believes personal identity develops in childhood. Agreed. Surely some of that identity arises from our appearance. We see ourselves in the mirror and compare ourselves to others. We notice how people react to us.

My patients are often teased or bullied because of their disfigurement— or 'facial differences,' as the new lingo would have it. That affects their identity more than anything else in their lives.

I can empathize with that. My own identity was affected in middle school when—

No, scratch that.

Day 34

Just as irritating as *thank you* is the word *please*, which typically comes in the guise of a request, such as *Please turn that off.* Even if you try to make it more polite, as in *Would you mind please turning that off,* it still constitutes a command.

I concluded years ago that it's inappropriate to use the word *please* when addressing one's superiors because of its imperative nature. I generally view it as disrespectful when my admin or my wife uses it. The admin, if she has a legitimate request, has learned to phrase it thusly: "I will forward the letter for your review." She would never say, "Will you *please* review the letter."

Likewise, Rosie might say, "We could use some bread, if it's convenient for you to stop on the way home." She knows better than to say, "Will you *please* stop and get bread?"

So today, when she slipped up and said, "Will you please call the credit card company about that mistake on the bill?" I didn't take it well. I suppose a humble person would have accepted the command in quiet submission. So that will be my aim.

My future aim, that is. Not today. Today I stared at her without expression, which is an expression in itself. It was intended to convey, "How dare you? You, who have caused this cataclysm in my life. How dare you command me to do anything?"

Day 35

Speaking of please and thank-you, a few weeks ago I was searching for Rosie, and when I looked in her room, my eye was drawn to her dresser. The usual jumble of lotions, stockings, and jewelry so covered the surface that I couldn't spot Rosie's piece of angel dust. I wondered whether it was still there. I wasn't ready to dig for it, though.

Then I noticed her desk. The mess there had been pushed aside, evidently to make room for a large stack of blank cards along with sheets of return address labels and stamps. Nearby lay a hand-written draft of a thank-you message, partially completed but marred with crossed-out words and phrases. The verbiage was clearly meant to be heartfelt, yet there was no mistaking its triteness. Triteness—yes—that's exactly what's called for in these communications.

After noticing the cards, I started monitoring Rosie's progress—or lack thereof—in completing them. The envelopes had been addressed, and the labels and stamps applied. But no thank-yous had actually been written. It's been well over a month since the funeral—what was she waiting for?

So last night, when I woke up at 3:00 am—as I often do these days—I got up and slipped into her room, took the materials, and brought them downstairs to my office. Over the next two hours, I wrote them all out, using some semblance of Rosie's verbiage. I signed her name and mine, sealed, and stacked them.

Then, on my way out for my run, I deposited the whole batch of cards in the mailbox with the flag up.

Day 36

While out running this morning, I approached a woman a dozen yards ahead who was bent over, scooping up her dog's business. The woman's hair, which had fallen over her face, reminded me of Matilda Thurman's. I picked up my pace and raced past her, an imagined conversation flitting through my mind.

She says, *Tell me how things are going.*

I reply, *Fine, just fine.*

How's the grief coming along?

Great. I'm better each day.

No problems with surgery?

None whatsoever.

Hoo. Maybe not yet. It's not the end of your story though. Deniers like you come to ruinous ends.

You're wrong. I'm proving you wrong.

As I write this now, I don't think it was Thurman. The hair wasn't the same.

Day 37

I'm ready to explain what I started to write about the other day. In middle school I had a classmate named Trey, who envied my intellect and grades. He was forever following me around to copy completed homework assignments from me. In class, he'd speak up too often, attempting to sound intelligent, but his answers were off base. When focusing on his work, he'd close his mouth and puff out his cheeks, as if that would help.

One day, I caught him copying my answers on a test. Out of pity I didn't report him, but the next time that I caught him concentrating with those puffed-up cheeks, I called him *Butt-cheeks*. I said it to his face, with the sort of smirk that emphasized how fitting and witty the moniker was. I didn't specifically intend to hurt him; if the name upset him I didn't notice or care. I said it to please myself.

At some point a teacher heard about it and pulled me aside. She informed me that the boy had some sort of learning disability. I wasn't used to being chastised by a teacher—she managed to make me feel guilty and embarrassed. After that I avoided Trey as much as possible.

But I've never forgotten the name I called him—*Butt-cheeks*.

Day 40

Today's case was a 6-year-old girl with CHARGE syndrome involving hearing loss, poor balance, and bilateral facial paralysis. I'd operated on her since she was a newborn, mainly to correct issues affecting breathing and swallowing. She and her parents had learned sign language, but the girl's inability to use her facial musculature to form a smile was a particularly devastating aspect of her genetic condition.

I'd discussed with the parents the possibility of performing a procedure to excise two small pieces of muscle tissue from her chest and implant them in her cheeks. One end of each piece would be attached to the corners of her mouth, and the other to her cheekbones. This procedure was far from routine, and I'd spent months of meetings with our team to work out specifics. The end result, we hoped, would be to enable this child to engage those new muscles in her face to produce a smile.

I rarely make an incision in a child below the jaw line, but the removal of the muscle tissue in the girl's chest should've been the easy part. I had, in fact, no trouble slicing into her, but as soon as I retracted the layers of skin my heart began racing. The blood was suctioned away effectively, but I found myself staring at the tissue beneath, struggling to go forward with the excision of the necessary muscle. My vision blurred, I became lightheaded, and my stomach seemed to float up into my ribs. I thought back to what I'd eaten the night before and whether I'd been exposed to anyone sick. In the hospital, bacteria are everywhere.

I left the OR briefly—an almost unheard-of breach—but no team members commented. I beelined to the nearest single-occupancy restroom, where I promptly vomited up my breakfast. Forcing myself to breathe deeply didn't help my pumping heart, but I was able to return to surgery after re-prepping.

There, my vision normalized and I completed the procedure. Still, I couldn't stop myself from repeatedly checking the vital signs display. Monitoring patient status is the anesthesiologist's role, not mine. This compulsion interrupted my focus and slowed my work. I avoided eye contact with the rest of the surgical team, but my peripheral vision caught them exchanging glances.

Day 41

I had trouble sleeping last night. Results from the surgery won't be determined for some time, and I have no reason to believe the operation wasn't successful. My momentary lapse still concerns me though. I can't fail now. In the future, I'll eat a lighter breakfast prior to surgery.

As I lay awake, the image of Dr. Thurman, that damn psychiatrist, plagued me. I'm still bothered by my inability to identify where I know her from.

Today, though, I was fine. A doubling down on my efforts at humility will give my mind something else with which to occupy itself. Lately, I've been focusing on not having to be right. I've made several attempts in conversation with Rosie to keep myself in check.

Success, however, has eluded me. The problem is this: what if I am, in fact, right? The truth is that I know far more than Rosie does on virtually every subject.

Today, for example, I tried to hold my tongue, despite her erroneous views regarding the proper length of time to simmer a poached egg, what type of weather cumulonimbus clouds portend, and the origin of the saying 'the die is cast.' These topics arose spontaneously in conversation, and when they did, Rosie made several statements that were verifiably wrong. In each case, I hesitated and reminded myself that I didn't need to demonstrate my greater knowledge at every opportunity. Acting the know-it-all is the antithesis of humility.

But I couldn't do it. Ignoring ignorance is morally absurd. I have a duty to the truth. Being right isn't the same as being overbearing or forcing an ill-considered opinion on a weaker person. No—being right is merely a matter of superior knowledge of facts.

So in the end, I was compelled to correct her every time.

Day 42

This morning I was in a hurry. I had an early vascular malformation repair, but still wanted to squeeze in a brief run. I brought Rosie her tea, piping hot. She was still in the bathroom, although I expected her out any moment.

In my rush, I accidentally bumped my elbow into her prayer book, sending it flying and scattering the bits of paper she had tucked inside. I reached down to gather them up. On top of the pile was a dog-eared photo of her and our son when he was maybe in middle school. I successfully resisted an urge to toss it in the trashcan.

The other items were some chicken-scratched notes to herself and a couple of holy cards. One caught my eye: *Litany of Humility*. I scanned the first few lines, then deposited the card in my pocket.

This evening I read through the entire prayer. I'm copying it here so I can slip the original back into her prayer book:

> O Jesus! meek and humble of heart, Hear me.
> From the desire of being esteemed, *Deliver me, Jesus.*
> From the desire of being loved, *Deliver me, Jesus.*
> From the desire of being extolled, *Deliver me, Jesus.*
> From the desire of being honored, *Deliver me, Jesus.*
> From the desire of being praised, *Deliver me, Jesus.*
> From the desire of being preferred to others, *Deliver me, Jesus.*
> From the desire of being consulted, *Deliver me, Jesus.*
> From the desire of being approved, *Deliver me, Jesus.*
> From the fear of being humiliated, *Deliver me, Jesus.*

From the fear of being despised, *Deliver me, Jesus.*
From the fear of suffering rebukes, *Deliver me, Jesus.*
From the fear of being calumniated, *Deliver me, Jesus.*
From the fear of being forgotten, *Deliver me, Jesus.*
From the fear of being ridiculed, *Deliver me, Jesus.*
From the fear of being wronged, *Deliver me, Jesus.*
From the fear of being suspected, *Deliver me, Jesus.*

That others may be loved more than I,
Jesus, grant me the grace to desire it.
That others may be esteemed more than I,
Jesus, grant me the grace to desire it.
That, in the opinion of the world, others may increase and I may decrease,
Jesus, grant me the grace to desire it.
That others may be chosen and I set aside,
Jesus, grant me the grace to desire it.
That others may be praised and I unnoticed,
Jesus, grant me the grace to desire it.
That others may be preferred to me in everything,
Jesus, grant me the grace to desire it.
That others may become holier than I, provided that I may become as holy as I should,
Jesus, grant me the grace to desire it.

If that's what humility looks like, it's unattainable for any mortal. I can't even believe anyone would want to attain it. There must be some reasonable level of humility, a healthy level, that doesn't go so far as that.

Day 44

My own mother, unlike Rosie, was of a practical nature. Treated by my father with utmost respect, she was joined to him in a way I couldn't comprehend—almost as an extension of him. Together, they formed a monolithic bloc. Affection between them seemed superfluous, too much like hugging yourself. My mother wasn't hard like my father—she never called me names or responded harshly to me, but neither would she gainsay any pronouncement that issued from his lips. Not once do I recall her defending me against his severity, or sensing reluctance from her in acceding to his mandates. From all appearances, she completely agreed with him. If I approached her first for permission to go somewhere or do something, she'd always insist I ask my father.

If he hadn't been present in our lives, she may have been softer. But would that have helped me? Maybe I wouldn't be where I am today. Maybe I owe her gratitude for that. Still, my father, acting as a wedge between my mother and me, hindered my developing a truly personal relationship with her.

Being an only child, and a late one at that, I spent my teen years conjecturing internally as to whether my coming into being had been an unanticipated and perhaps not wholly desirable event in my parents' estimation. Perhaps that was why my father seemed to dislike me so much. Mainly, though, my speculations have been blind. Neither of my parents were the type with whom such issues could be examined or discussed. If I'd had siblings, we could've dissected our parents' personalities and motivations. Maybe then I could've achieved some understanding. But as it is, both my mother and father are gone. Tracking down my Aunt Shirley and asking her such questions is unthinkable. And really, what would be the value now?

I have no immediate family left besides Rosie. And, I suppose, the Jackass. That's why he troubles my thoughts so much lately.

Day 46

Becoming an adult means no longer needing your parents' discipline, because you're mature enough to discipline yourself. That's what I'm doing now, disciplining myself. An added benefit is that I can demonstrate to Rosie how it's done. For example, how to keep silent when appropriate.

It's true she's been more reticent lately, clearly trying not to aggravate me. However, I expect her efforts to subside any time now, once she's gotten over the worst of her grief. She wants me to forgive her—I see that readily enough. The nicer dinners she's been making, always on time or kept warm for me if I'm late, ensuring my shirts get to the cleaners, holding back the clutter in the house more than usual. Sure, it's easier now that she doesn't have a four-year-old in the house.

Even so, all her efforts, weighed against the enormity of her offense, are useless, weighing an ant against an elephant. Her meager attempts to make up for her sin, to make up for the tragedy she caused, are futile.

I'm well aware these thoughts don't square with my efforts at humility. But if I were in complete possession of my thoughts there'd be no need for this year of penance.

Day 49

Rosie always wanted more children—I think she'd have been happy with a dozen. But early on, we didn't have the money, and I didn't have the time and energy to be involved in their upbringing. As it was, I witnessed daily the way she and the boy clung to each other, such that I felt like an intruder. He came first. He was always there, in our bed, between us. No longer the silent partaker of our joy, but an interloper interfering with it. When he was old enough that his thrashing disturbed my sleep, I told Rosie he needed to sleep in his own room. He did, and half the time Rosie went with him.

It wasn't a suitable time for more kids, a fact so obvious I shouldn't have needed to justify it. Rosie said she didn't mind if we all had to squeeze into a tiny place. Little ones only wanted love, she said, no need for "fancy living." And weren't my prospects good?

I disliked her banking on me that way. Even though I was her husband, it came off as grasping to talk about money in those terms. Furthermore, I was never one to borrow on the future, not even my own. I'd inherited that sensibility from my father.

Rosie opposed contraception on religious principle, so I had to take matters into my own hands to guard against an adverse outcome. That unsettled her. In her mind, it was as if the flimsy rubber barrier between us acted on some metaphysical level. While for the most part she kept her objections to herself, she said one time that it felt like I was cheating, that I wasn't having sex with her, but with the sheathe itself.

Part of the problem too was this: although my desire, my need for her was greater than ever, my discovery of the seriousness of sex preyed upon my outlook. That time when Rosie was late and I'd recognized with horror my dependence on her was never far from my mind. Rosie hadn't been privy to my epiphany. It was too demeaning to discuss, a secret I couldn't share.

These conflicting subtexts encumbered our sex life. Rosie still worked to make it fun, but that was the problem. Intercourse became a form of work for her, even a form of lying. She wanted sex to be carefree in the deepest sense of the word—that we should be free from caring about its outcome. Like a tight-rope walker performing without a safety net, the potential for an outcome of pregnancy was what thrilled her; it constituted the very basis of her enjoyment in it. Absent the risk of conception, she had to pretend a level of interest and engagement she didn't feel. It irked me. I had my needs, but also my pride. If she wasn't going to respond to my overtures with genuine enthusiasm, or at least some level of sincerity, I'd stop asking.

Okay, I didn't stop asking, not completely. Even if we couldn't enjoy each other the way we had at first, we were still young. All the same, I couldn't escape the feeling that sex had been ruined for us, like eating a dinner of spoiled meat when on the brink of starvation—despite your fears and even disgust, your body needs whatever nourishment it can still provide. Your senses, and the very construct of dinner, require you to make an effort to enjoy it. But it makes you sick. I believe that's the reason I'd often snap at Rosie after sex. Instead of it drawing us closer, my qualms and her reservations forced us further apart.

I had to consider these facts before approaching her. Most times, my calculations told me that sex with Rosie wasn't worth the cost. If she was bothered by the decline in our sex life, she didn't let on. We probably had it often enough to convince her that everything between us was fine. She merely diverted her playfulness to her interactions with the boy. Gone were the candles and the crosswords—I was left with the remnants of her energy and creativity. I resented that.

From then on, I often refused to show her any joy, no matter how I felt. To show happiness or contentment to a spouse is to admit they're doing something right. It's acceding to their wishes, and acceding is ceding control.

Day 50

Despite all that, Rosie eventually got her wish for another child, after my father's funeral five years ago.

Once Heather was fully out of the picture, the remaining months of Rosie's pregnancy rated among the best of our marriage. We experienced a welcome increase in physical intimacy, for one thing. Not that it was the same as when we were newly married, but Rosie's excitement and gratitude over the new state of affairs spilled over into our sex life. The conflicting subtexts were temporarily whisked away—I had no need for a prophylactic, and Rosie, no need to be troubled by one.

Also, I withheld criticisms more than usual for the sake of Rosie's emotional state and the health of the gestating baby. Rosie responded in her own way, turning to me more. It was a subtle difference, but not lost on me. Occasionally I caught her looking at me in that enamored manner I recalled from our early years. She quickly hid it, fearing my contempt.

Why was it so hard to endure her open adulation? In my professional life I seek and receive it. I doubt many people at the hospital care for me personally. I imagine they find me remote and condescending, which, given my status, is as it should be. They respect my talents and achievements and give me my just due.

But with Rosie it was different. In our early days she'd insisted on revering me. The more she did so, the more I took charge. The more she appeased me, the more I expected appeasement. It had to be part of human nature, or just nature generally. Apes exhibit the same behavior—submission by one calls forth increased domination by the other.

That analysis, however, makes it seem as if we humans have no control over ourselves. I reject that notion. I can control myself. I'm proving it even now.

Proving it by completing my side of this bargain.

Day 51

Yes, I made a bargain. That's what this year of humility is about.

I made the bargain with God. Or with whatever it is that people refer to as God. Rosie's a believer, and always has been. She believes in a transcendent God, one who wills only good for his creatures and is beyond reproach. Rosie attends church weekly without fail. She used to take our son with her. I kept out of it. For one thing, I wasn't brought up with a strong religious faith. My parents were descended from a motley assortment of Protestant denominations with beliefs so diluted that by the time they reached me they were virtually homeopathic.

Nonetheless, I somehow deduced that my parents believed in God. Their belief wasn't like Rosie's. For them, believing in God was like believing in drapery. It existed in the background and was often useful for avoiding exposure, but wasn't something you took any regular notice of. Their beliefs held little relevance to their daily lives. Or, by extension, to mine.

Another hindrance to my churchgoing in the early years of our marriage was that I often studied or worked Sunday mornings. Patients might be taking a day of rest, but that didn't mean I got one. I never formed the church-going habit. These days, Sunday mornings are an opportunity for an especially long run, an excellent way to clear my mind, and a chance to read in the den or on the deck, uninterrupted by Rosie, undisturbed by her very presence in the house. Running and reading bring me far more peace than church ever could.

Rosie and I were married in the Catholic Church. It was important to her and a point of indifference to me.

No—that's not completely true. At the time of our marriage I intended to convert. I took the required classes, learned the beliefs and rules of Catholicism and thought I'd accepted them. By the time I finished, I knew considerably more about the faith than most cradle Catholics.

But I continued to have a problem with the concept of God. I couldn't pin that concept down into anything concrete, anything that could exist within a building or a service. The concept of God was instead tangled up in my mind with the reality of Rosie. She was my church, my temple. It was her body that enabled me to experience splendor and awe. If God existed for me, it was within the ineffable bestowing and receiving that graced my physical intimacy with Rosie.

The plan was for me to be received into the Church on the Easter vigil just after we were married. On Holy Saturday, I was to make my confession. I'd put it off as long as possible and had asked Rosie not to come with me—I wanted to carry out this highly personal ritual alone. Maybe, though, I had a foreboding.

I went to the church and entered the pew. A few other penitents were scattered about, sitting or kneeling. I'd learned in the class that the time to express my contrition to God was not during the sacrament but beforehand, when I was unhurried and not focused on performing the rite according to norms.

But I couldn't work up any contrition. For weeks I'd labored over the inventory of sins I planned to catalog for the priest. Reviewing them yet again, I discovered the problem—I just wasn't sorry for any of them. Not for the various times I'd dissembled, not for taking the Lord's name in vain, and certainly not for sins of a sexual nature, especially for sex with Rosie before marriage. I'd married her, hadn't I? Would that have happened without sex beforehand? I doubt it.

I pondered the large crucifix above the altar. Christ died for my sins, they'd said in class. For *my* sins? For my piddly, silly sins? For my sins of passion with Rosie? The idea was absurd. I'd never asked for this Christ to die for me, especially not for the sins I'd commit again in a heartbeat if placed in identical circumstances. I wanted nothing to do with this man's long-past death. His choice to die an ignominious, excruciating death wasn't blotting out my sins. No—that would take from me my own free will, the consequences of my own actions, including the value of my good choices. I disavowed that. I didn't believe it. I *couldn't* believe it.

When I returned home, I lied to Rosie, although not by telling her I'd made my confession. I admitted I didn't go, but I told her it was because I wasn't ready, not that I'd rejected its purported meaning and value. She was disappointed but understanding, saying she didn't want me to go forward if I hadn't yet overcome my reservations.

I continued to attend Mass with her, but found nothing in it to convict me. I was at an impasse with faith.

Day 52

As time went on, I began frequently glancing at my watch during Mass, worried about the study time I was missing. Rosie didn't like that I insisted on leaving as soon as the service was over—or sometimes even before—wanting to avoid the worst of the parking lot exodus. Eventually, I deemed the entire exercise impractical, if not pointless.

That ambivalence became the state of my religious life for more than two decades. But when Michaelina lay dying, I was desperate. I witnessed her grip on life slacken over the course of several days. Her internal injuries were so severe that the doctors no longer offered any hope. In that moment, I stopped thinking rationally. I would've done anything—cut off my arm, swallowed poison, committed any atrocity known to man, if only my daughter would live. I was ready to grasp at any religious or paranormal scheme, no matter how far-fetched.

Rosie prayed. Did she believe God would swoop in and save Michaelina? My mind latched onto that idea. If an all-powerful God did exist, he'd have the power to save Michaelina. And 'miracles' did occasionally happen. I'm a man of science, a believer in the world we perceive through our senses. At the same time, it's impossible to have worked in a hospital all these years without getting wind of a random, unexplained cure. A patient who couldn't be resuscitated despite intensive effort by an entire team of medical professionals, yet who, hours after the sheet is drawn over her head, suddenly begins breathing again. A tumor that's on the MRI one day and gone the next. A doctor I know personally had a case in which a child's hearing was lost in an accident—his cochlear nerve was damaged beyond repair, yet he regained his hearing after his family prayed for a saint's intercession.

Such medically mysterious cures are exceedingly rare, and someday we'll be able to explain them. But at the time they happened, they were inexplicable. That's what tugged at me. If miracles existed, then couldn't Michaelina qualify for one? Death was wiggling the latch at her door. If there were only the most miniscule of chances that God might perform such a feat, I had to snatch at it.

Day 53

So that was the genesis of my bargain. Life was seeping out of my daughter. Her situation had gone beyond the bounds of what medicine could do. So I reached out to Rosie's putative God. Being experienced in the transactional nature of relationships, I knew that if I asked something of him, he'd want something from me in return. What, though, could I offer in exchange for Michaelina's life? It's not as if I could become a monk. Moreover, my vocation as a pediatric craniofacial surgeon was surely acceptable to God already—I'd been instrumental in giving countless children back their lives. In that way, I was god-like myself, so this exchange shouldn't be all that difficult.

Rosie's feverish prayers for Michaelina were evident in the unremitting jangling of her rosary beads. God, however, wasn't responding. And why should he? He already had Rosie in the bag.

I knew instinctively that I was the one he wanted. The standard bargain—a promise to attend church every Sunday for the rest of my life—was a weak proposition. If God was indeed all-knowing, he'd look down from his grand perch and see me sitting in the pew, bodily present, but my mind elsewhere. It'd be a hollow offering, a waste of time for both God and me.

No, I had to propose something more tantalizing, a deal so enticing he couldn't refuse the exchange. I needed something that would make his mouth water.

Then it came to me: God was jealous. Jealous of *me*, in some petulant way. I was an achiever, and justly proud of my accomplishments. God wanted me to defer honor to him, even for those things I'd worked my ass off for. He didn't like people showing him up. He was a manipulator at heart, getting back at those who were a little too full of themselves. I'd experienced his maneuvering before—he'd tricked me into marrying Rosie, then gave me a reprobate for a son. He'd sent me those family travails to bring me down a notch, make me come crawling to him for consolation and assistance. But his strategy hadn't worked, so now he was poised to take away Michaelina, the only person I've ever loved purely—a love unadulterated by my own needs or desires. If I wanted to keep her, I'd have to give God what he wanted. So I offered him all I had:

God, give me Michaelina, and you can have my pride. All of it.

Day 57

I had a cleft palate case today. The operation should've been routine.

The trouble was that in the midst of it my vision clouded. I tried blinking it away, but the problem wasn't tears or discharge. The blurring originated in the back of my eyes—somewhere near the retina.

I turned the procedure over to a resident. That hadn't been the plan going in, so I had to make it appear as though I'd decided—mid-operation—that she was ready to perform it. The rest of the surgical team seemed to be studying me across the operating table—I avoided looking at them.

It turned out all right in the end, more or less. Certainly it was better for an inexperienced surgeon to complete the operation than one who was having difficulty seeing.

Day 60

God, it turns out, declined to accept the offer of my pride in exchange for Michaelina's life.

Her funeral was huge, a real crowd-pleaser. That's what happens when a child dies—gossip, rubbernecking, pity.

Rosie had chosen St. Bartholomew's downtown because of its ability to accommodate the swarms of people. The church was an old one, with vaulted ceilings, imposing columns, and orderly rows of age-blackened wooden pews. The stained-glass windows needed cleaning, as did the kitschy statues and morose paintings. Faint odors of candle wax and incense wafted about me.

The cavernous nature of the space enveloped me and provided a sort of shield. Rosie was calm—the Valium was doing its job. Yet her face had a frozen, brittle look to it, as if one tap would shatter it.

Before the service began, we stood next to the casket, greeting people as they entered. It was mostly a mechanical affair. I quickly discovered that people expected hugs in this situation, as if such a hyperbolic display of emotion would comfort me. I began reaching out my hand before people approached, in hopes of a simple handshake. That staved off most of the hugs, but some folks couldn't take the hint.

The line seemed endless. The out-of-town relatives, predominantly from Rosie's side, all showed up. Aunt Shirley—my dad's sister—attended. I hadn't seen her since my father's funeral. She was more wrinkled and portly, yet unbent. She looked at me with my father's hooded eyes, then wrapped her arms around me in a bosomy squeeze, the first and only embrace I'd received that conveyed true sympathy. She greeted Rosie with less enthusiasm, and in fact, nearly snubbed her. She'd heard the rumors I'm sure.

Many from the hospital attended, along with their spouses. And plenty of neighbors too, including the woman from down the block with the overabundance of cats, and even that annoying Herman and his wife from next door, probably there to gloat over our misfortune. I noticed they didn't bring their boy Trevor with them, which was just as well. Poor little fellow would've been traumatized. With the exception of Rosie and me, Trevor must've felt Michaelina's loss more than anyone.

The parents of several of my longer-term patients also attended, although most stayed in their pews, as if frightened by encountering me in such a profoundly personal situation. The number of complete strangers astonished me. Was it possible Rosie knew all those people?

The proximity of Michaelina's casket to the ornate baptismal font struck me as ironic. Just after Michaelina was born, Rosie wanted to arrange a baptism. I pointed out that baptism hadn't done the Jackass any good. She was undeterred, so I gave in. I've come to terms with her stubbornness about religious matters. And what harm could the ritual do, really? I told her she was free to do as she wished, but I wasn't interested in attending, or hosting any sort of reception. To this day I don't know when she had it done.

I didn't want a funeral Mass for Michaelina either. Once again Rosie was insistent. The type they have for little children, *Mass of the Angels*, is presumably a nod to their innocence. The choir's plaintive chant and polyphony echoed through the rafters with a searing sort of resonance that I would've called beautiful if my mood had allowed it. Who were these people, giving up their Saturday morning for this? Probably being paid—by me. But even so.

I glanced around the church. The old-fashioned confession box stood over to the side, its heavy curtains obscuring the dark guts of the enclosure. It reminded me of the confession I never got around to making decades ago. Confession, or 'reconciliation,' as they fashion it now, presented itself for the first time to me as holding some concrete appeal.

The main crucifix, high above the altar, sported a corpus that looked down at the congregation in resignation. I wished for a moment I'd been there. If the Son of God could allow my little girl to be maimed and killed, he deserved all that suffering, and more. If I'd been there, I'd have searched him out myself in the Garden of Gethsemane. I'd have spotted him—yes!—surrounded by his coterie of sycophants. I knew who he was—who wouldn't? He was the center of attention—no humility there.

In my imagination, I dashed up to him and he looked at me, trying to convey something. What—disappointment? Good! I wanted him to be disappointed in me. His disappointment in me would never match my disappointment in him. I kissed his sallow cheek. A nurse-sex sort of kiss. I stepped back and smiled. Let the strongmen do their thing.

I followed the rabble to the high priest's courtyard, then cozied myself by the fire with Peter as he denied his best buddy three times. When that cock crowed, I myself crowed in laughter.

I stuck close by as Jesus was transferred from one authority to another, hands bound, then back to Pilate. At the pillar I took up the whip and got in my lashes too. Anyone claiming to be God, claiming to be the Almighty, yet who would sanction the mangling of a child deserved to be mangled himself. I swung the whip, landing it plumb on his back and watching with delight the involuntary whipsaw from the jolt of pain.

Pilate suggested releasing Jesus, but he must've known that'd never fly. The crowd preferred Barabbas—an ordinary thug. If Barabbas were killed, what would that satisfy? Jesus was the necessary one. I knew it and so did the crowd. I was the first to shout it out. "Crucify him! Crucify him!" The crowd took up the chant.

When Pilate washed his hands of Jesus, I thrust my hands in the water too. I could wash away my part in this punishment as easily as Pilate, because I saw that Christ had chosen it. By choosing to be God, by choosing to permit evil in the world, he'd chosen to suffer for it. I was only a cog in the machinery of fate.

I played my role with gusto, jamming the circlet of thorns onto his head, dressing him in purple, taunting him for his supposed kingship. I followed him every step on his way to Calvary, jeering him, blaming him, rejoicing at his suffering. There'd be no retribution from him—he'd made himself powerless to stop me from getting my fill of bloodlust.

I watched with increasing glee as the soldiers nailed his hands to the cross. Noticing my presence, they laughed and handed me one of the nails. It was a spike, really, long enough go through both feet. It took me a dozen blows to pound it through to the wood, securing the feet at the bottom of the vertical just above the footrest. It was this footrest that would enable the true torture of the cross. To breathe, to live, he would have had to push up on this footrest to expand his lungs. That action would be painful in the extreme. In between breaths, he'd rest himself by allowing his body to hang. But he couldn't breathe while he did so, adding to the psychological torture. After hours of this, when he no longer had the strength to hold himself up, he died from exhaustion asphyxia and hypovolemic shock.

Even when he was dead, surely dead, I wanted one last chance to vent. A lance appeared, ready to hand. With my knowledge of physiology, I chose the spot under the lowest rib on his right side. Angling the weapon upward to the left, I thrust it in with full force, penetrating the heart. I withdrew it in one smooth motion.

Bizarrely, blood and water spouted outward in distinct fountains. Both streams landed on me, drenching my hair and running down my face. I leapt backward and watched as the surge lessened and petered out. Only then did a shadow of doubt pass over me.

I shook it away. Michaelina, unlike Christ, couldn't avoid her death. God had allowed it. Christ had condoned it. I would avenge it.

Day 61

Oh, I should mention that after I offered my bargain to God, Michaelina did open her eyes one last time—we had a final communication—but I can't talk about that right now.

Then she died.

I couldn't comprehend this God at all. I thought he was hungry for souls. Here I was, in essence offering mine, and he shoved it away. Perhaps he wasn't all-powerful after all. I wondered if I should've made the deal with Satan instead—maybe my soul was more appealing to him—but it was too late for that.

So the bargain was null and void. God didn't bite. I had offered to lower myself, going against my own principles, to no avail. My first thought was that if he didn't want what I'd offered him, offered in sincerity, then to hell with him. To counter him, I could throw it all back in his face. Thoughts of revenge circulated through my consciousness. What if I left a subtle glitch in each face I worked on? What if I refused the hardest cases? If God wouldn't grant me the one favor I'd ever asked, what was the point in continuing to do good work?

In response to God's non-response, I should've rejected the whole notion of his existence. My proposing the bargain, however, was a tacit admission that I believed—on some level—that he was there. Yes, he existed all right. The decision to let Michaelina die was a cosmic one. Someone powerful was behind it.

So far he'd outsmarted me. He'd injured me, treated me unjustly. I was determined, though, to get the better of him. I owed it to Michaelina.

Day 62

I wanted to get back at God in some tangible way.

To devise an effective scheme, I'd need to think like God. I considered his essence. Was he a vain, frivolous fellow with arbitrary whims? A grandfather-like figure, who in his dotage preferred taking a nap while the grandchildren had their way of the house? Or an active miscreant, leveraging his infinite resources to bring down those who refused to pay him homage?

During the funeral, the priest had delivered an unremarkable homily, observing that those experiencing grief needed to lean on someone greater than themselves. That someone was God, of course. I had pulled out a missalette from the pew and began flipping through, in a somewhat futile effort to disengage.

I happened upon a passage about the mother who demanded that Jesus let her sons James and John sit at his right and left when he came into his kingdom. I almost burst out laughing. Mothers are forever the same—interfering harridans who want a cushy path for their sons, who won't let them take the hard road needed to become real men. In response, Jesus put the woman in her place, saying no, her sons couldn't have those places of honor. Then came the kicker: her sons would have to endure the same ignominious treatment as he would, anyway. I'll bet that mother never lobbied Jesus again.

What really struck me, though, was the statement Jesus made afterward, that whoever wished to become great had to be a servant. It was a turnaround of expectations, a reversal of normal relationships. That's what I wanted—a reversal. God was high and mighty, and I was the lowly one, the powerless one. He'd demonstrated that dynamic by taking Michaelina away from me.

Day 63

How could I accomplish such a reversal? I reviewed my life experience, the times when people sought revenge against me for some hurt. Those incidents, I figured, might provide a clue.

What about the nurses with whom I'd had affairs? They could be a spiteful lot. I recall one in particular—Lupe, a Latina nurse with a pristine olive complexion, aquiline nose, and well-defined nostrils. Unfortunately, her personality was like that of a horse, forever standing in my way or nudging me in some direction I didn't want to go. When I ended it, she sought retribution by ignoring me, berating me to the other nurses when I was in earshot, and calling my home number just so she could hang up when Rosie answered. Her pathetic attempts to wreak revenge amused me. Even her threat to tell Rosie was ineffectual. I was beyond caring.

And then there was Herman, the lantern-jawed jerk who lives next door. We've never been friendly, despite his son Trevor playing frequently with Michaelina. At some point early on, Rosie and Herman's wife, whose name I forget, had a fender-bender on our street. Herman claimed Rosie had caused the accident. The insurance companies, however, faulted neither of these hapless women. That didn't satisfy Herman. He acted as if I'd personally contrived to turn the insurance judgment in my favor. As punishment, he began avoiding me, not even looking in my direction if we both retrieved our mail at the same time. He let his dog bark at me without calling him in. He failed to return a ladder he'd borrowed, whereas before the accident he was always quick to do so. All the while, I pictured him sitting in his armchair, hunched over and stewing, ranting to his wife, while his vindictive actions affected my existence not one iota.

Herman and the nurses, I decided, were examples *not* to imitate.

My colleague Owen is a different case entirely. Owen is a tall, youngish doctor at the hospital, a maxillofacial surgeon who often works on my surgical team. Sadly for him, he's got a classic case of neoteny—round, baby blue eyes, undeveloped nasal bone with rounded apex, and a restricted labial commissure that makes his lips appear to be pouting when at rest—all set in a smallish head on a stalk of a neck.

Once, some years back, Owen second-guessed me in a team consultation. The patient was a five-year-old boy needing a septoplasty. I recommended that the surgery be delayed a couple of years due to the potential for later problems with development. Owen, however, cited new research suggesting it could be performed safely in children as young as two, and that delaying it could actually increase deformity and asymmetry while negatively affecting nasal and facial growth. He couched his comments as a question, making it appear he was actually deferring to me. But everyone in that consultation knew he was challenging my decision.

I was taken aback. An ancillary doctor on my surgical team should not openly question my judgment, especially in front of others. I stuck with my original decision and was proved right in the end. I operated a year later, and the boy's nose is now as perfect as could be hoped for.

Soon after the incident, a prestigious pediatrics chair opened up. I was a senior member of the selection panel. I scuttled Owen's nomination by throwing my weight behind an alternative candidate, one who was less deserving but who had demonstrated appropriate deference. That was the right way to exact revenge.

Or so I thought.

Owen knew I'd been behind his failure to get the position—word gets around. I expected some backlash, to be undercut, challenged again. I was prepared to shoot down his efforts to retaliate.

But that's not what happened. To my surprise, he acted as if nothing untoward had happened at all. He deferred to my judgments as he usually did. He said hello in his same pleasant way when we passed each other in the hall, and he gave me as many referrals as he always had. These new patients said that Owen gave me his strongest recommendation.

After my initial bemusement, I laughed at him behind his back, thinking him weak and clueless. He didn't realize everyone pitied him. Then it occurred to me that he was trying to get back into my good graces. I could make or break his career, he must've thought, and he needed to please me. Pathetic. I soon began watching for the expected obsequious behavior. But it failed to materialize.

Months later, in a group consultation, he again questioned a procedure I planned to use. He explained his reasons in a measured and dispassionate tone. All eyes in the room settled on me. It was painfully evident to everyone, myself included, that I'd missed a critical detail about the patient's condition. Owen, recognizing my awkward position, chose his next words to make it appear that it was all merely a discussion, and that he and I, rather than having opposing viewpoints, were both of the same opinion.

All the same, everyone knew he'd bested me. I thought to strike back. Somehow, though, I didn't want to. I found myself respecting him, almost against my will. Ever since then, I've felt increasingly friendly towards him. He alone, among all those I'd injured, was able to turn around my judgment and regain my esteem. In the end, he'd won. How? By not seeking revenge. He'd accepted what befell him by my hand, and returned not anger, not servility, but only a pleasant, respectful meekness.

I applied the same logic to my plan to retaliate against God. If I tried to rebuff him, insult him, swing my fists at him, he'd only stand back and laugh, like I did with Lupe or my neighbor Herman. *I wouldn't give God that satisfaction.* I would instead act like Owen. No matter how painful, I'd accept what befell me by God's hand with meekness.

God hadn't kept his part of the bargain, but I would keep mine. I'd act with humility, like Owen. I'd abjure my pride, root it out, eliminate it from my thoughts and actions. By humbling myself, I would chasten God.

Day 64

My idea needed a method of execution.

If the rule was that the greatest person had to become the servant to demonstrate his superiority, then I'd become a servant. But whose? God himself didn't need one, not if he already had everything he wanted and did as he pleased. I concluded that it must be in serving a mere human being that the precept would be satisfied.

So I needed a proxy, someone robed in mortal flesh to be treated as if God. Someone who'd be in my presence day in and day out. Someone it would humble me to serve. Although I fought with the answer, it was obvious from the start.

I'd need to serve Rosie.

What would that accomplish in the end? I wasn't sure. The concept was a mind-bending paradox. But at the time, I was overwrought with the fact of Michaelina's death, a raw reality I couldn't confront or ignore. I knew only this much—her death couldn't be the final say. I wouldn't accept that. By adhering to this bargain, I was sticking a finger in God's eye. I was sliding a wedge into Michaelina's coffin as God tried to slam it shut.

Day 65

No bargain, of course, could bring Michaelina back, but at least this bargain gives me something to grasp at, something to prove. I'm doing it for Michaelina's sake. In some way it gives new meaning to her brief existence and avenges her untimely death.

Using my history with Owen as a reference, I decided it would take a year to achieve my goal. Thus, I am humbling myself with a methodical, systematic plan for a full twelve months.

I started with the tea-making and other menial tasks, performing them unasked. Then I worked on the eye-rolling and snide remarks, as well as holding my tongue when irritated. Next I'll offer to help Rosie, a step that's far more difficult than bringing her tea, because it's less under my control— who knows what she might ask for? My humble response to her requests must be cheerful and prompt. I will also listen attentively to her without interruptions. After conquering the externals I'll work on the inside, trying to avoid even internal criticisms.

Yes, Rosie's the primary beneficiary of my plan. Objectively, she's not deserving of my efforts—not after her betrayal.

But there are complicating circumstances.

Day 67

There's no way to direct my humility towards the Jackass, not with our being out of communication. He had a hand in Michaelina's death, too, even from a distance. I've tried to excise him from my life, to bar him from the sphere of my existence, but still he's managed to secrete his toxins from afar.

I have money, and I sometimes wonder if he's out there just waiting to lay his hands on it. Maybe he's hoping I'll die from an early heart attack, like my father. My death would be his jackpot. Even though everything would go to Rosie, she'd be overly generous with him.

From an early age, as soon as my son could understand money, he wanted it from me. He didn't want to earn it—he expected it to be dropped in his lap. Would I buy him that new toy, that bike, that computer, that cellphone, that car? Why not, if I had the cash just sitting there in the bank? He didn't see the purpose and value of work, of achievement, of saving for something. It would've been one thing if he were a scholar. I'd gladly have financed his education, as my father had done for me. His grades, though, were lackluster. He dabbled in sports but was unremarkable, weaseling out of practices whenever possible.

Rosie did nothing to get him headed in the right direction. On the contrary, she made an art of concocting excuses for him. "He shouldn't practice if his leg's still hurting." "He can't write notes well because he's not an auditory learner." "The teacher is expecting the impossible." The more she justified his behavior, the more I needed to counterbalance the effects, or there'd be no hope for him.

Rosie triumphed in the end, if you can call it a triumph. The boy grew accustomed to her coddling, so that when he reached physical maturity, he was emotionally and intellectually a baby-man. With his man's body he chased girls. He netted plenty of them too, was my impression. I tried to nip those relationships in the bud, but I couldn't watch him nonstop—he found ways to tomcat around at night. I counseled him at length, trying to impress upon him the folly of this approach to life, how he needed to be serious or he'd get into trouble, how his reckless actions could rob him of a promising future, or at the very least, bind him in an unequal relationship.

I was never sure how intelligent he was. He did possess a kind of cunning and doggedness that might've served him well enough in adulthood. Once, when he was around nine years old, I gave him a mechanical toy for

Christmas—a metal tower that could be built in various configurations and had several attachments, including a crane and pulley. He'd played with it intently for not more than an hour when the pulley broke. He brought it to me. I had neither the time, nor, frankly, the inclination to repair it, and told him so. After his continued nagging, however, I examined it closely and discovered that a small plastic plate in the mechanism had broken. I explained to him that there was no way to fix it. His eyes welled up, and I noticed Rosie looking distraught. In a moment of holiday-induced magnanimity, I told him I'd buy him a new one come Saturday. He took the toy back to his room without a word. The next day, though, I found him playing with it again. He hadn't fixed the plastic plate, but he'd built some sort of workaround with a bit of wood, a couple of screws, and a rubber band, such that the toy was functional again.

I figured that inventiveness and tenacity might one day serve him in good stead. Instead, they only seemed to provide him with more clever ways to get around me. Probably he's shacking up with some girl right now, doing who knows what to support his lifestyle. I wonder if Rosie's found a way to secretly subsidize him. I've had to keep the purse-strings tight all these years to avoid just that.

During the Jackass's teen years, he fashioned himself an artist. Sure, he could draw well, at least to my fatherly eye. What kind of a living, though, could be made from that? I strongly encouraged him to take as much science as he could in high school. Becoming a doctor was the way to make a good living, to leave your mark, to make a difference in the world. He was resolute, though, in his resistance to common-sense advice. Maybe he wasn't capable of competing in medicine, but couldn't he at least try? That's how you got started, and the rest would follow. Try it, and work hard until you're good at it.

When I was that age, I respected my father. I tried to please him, only to be berated anyway. That was unjust. I'd sworn to myself that when I had a son of my own I wouldn't repeat the pattern. I suppose in some ways I have, but only because my son's personality and approach to life were so different than mine were. Whereas I'd been motivated to prove myself, my son seemed to have nothing to prove. Or maybe he did. Maybe he wanted to prove that he wouldn't give anything a chance if I were the one to suggest it.

In his early adolescence, I could force him to listen to me. With each passing year, though, he pushed me further away. The failure to obey was bad enough. But at some point late in his teen years, he began to laugh at my advice. *Laugh.* Not out loud—I could see it there in the curl of his lip. He wasn't able to suppress that, or perhaps he stopped trying to. It implied that what I was saying was so absurd that it didn't even merit the trouble of laughing out loud.

And when he left us, it was his choice, not mine. I want to be clear on that. I never asked him to leave. But once he moved out, I gave up hope of his making anything of himself. I disavowed all responsibility for him.

His existence has been a forbidden subject between Rosie and me ever since. I prohibited her from communicating with him. I'll say one thing for my wife, she's always been compliant. Sure, she has her faults—flightiness, disorganization, inefficiency—but willful disobedience wasn't one of them.

So Rosie deferred to me about not communicating with the Jackass. That's what I believed.

Until the day our world came to a halt.

Day 74

I had an epiphany this morning about being right. I need to come up with a topic that Rosie knows more about than I do. For example, she knows more esoteric crossword puzzle words, especially those two- and three-letter ones that aren't true words in any functional sense, but are just a way for puzzle aficionados to pretend they have sophisticated vocabularies. The usage of such words, in my view, constitutes a form of cheating. However, I couldn't come up with any way to initiate a conversation about such trivia. I suppose an added fear was that she might think I was trying to dredge up memories of how she and I had used such crosswords in the distant past. That would never do.

My next idea was photography. That seemed a sure winner, as my knowledge of it is fairly minimal. So I asked Rosie for a lesson on how to work the camera. The final photos she'd taken of Michaelina were particularly good, and I told her so.

Her face paled. Her reply was flustered. She begged off, claiming she was poor at explaining things and wasn't a very good photographer anyway.

What am I supposed to do when out-humbled by my own wife?

Day 79

I was feeling the need to produce just a little success in one area before moving to the next. So today I again searched for a topic Rosie is knowledgeable about, so she could appear the superior one.

Unexpectedly, an opportunity presented itself in the evening as we were sitting in the den. Rosie was lying on the couch with her crossword puzzle in hand. She stopped working on it momentarily to inform me that her sister Maude, a nurse, had just been offered a new position.

Now Maude, while distinctly less physically attractive than her sister, is admittedly on the sharper edge of the mental knife. That doesn't make me like her any better. In fact, less so, because she uses that intelligence in a smart-alecky way that's supremely off-putting. Even though she's younger than Rosie, she lords her education and career over her sister, bossing her around, trying to bully her into being a different person than she is. She's a negative influence on Rosie, who is all too vulnerable to being influenced by anyone she loves and looks up to.

Anyway, Rosie insisted that the new job would be much better suited to her sister because it was in the cardiology department. Maude would purportedly have more responsibility and more say in how things were done.

Reflexively, I readied myself to burst the bubble of these thoroughly baseless assertions. The pin was poised. Then, realizing my chance, I stopped myself. I refrained from pointing out to her that even the nurse managers (which Maude wasn't one of) had minimal say in hospital procedures. I didn't remark that if Maude was dissatisfied in her previous department because no one listened to her ideas there, I could guarantee there'd be no improvement in a new department. Nor did I explain that coworkers are the same all over, and if you're a complainer in one position, you'll be a complainer in the next one too. And where did she get the idea that cardiology was superior to endocrinology? I suppose she decided that the heart was more important than glands and hormones.

I wanted to say all these things. Instead, I swallowed them, took a mammoth breath, and said, "How nice for Maude."

Rosie jerked her face in my direction and let her pencil drop to the floor, where it rolled under the sofa. Then she frowned and said, "You weren't even listening to me, were you?"

Day 80

After yesterday's semi-success, I was motivated to push things further. That's the way to develop a habit—repetition.

I had another good idea this morning, or so I thought—we could talk about Michaelina.

Although I have the greater insight into our daughter's personality, Rosie has more surface knowledge. I understood the topic was a sensitive one, so I bided my time, waiting for a circumstance in which inserting a comment about her into the conversation would sound natural. Saying her name would confer the additional benefit of moving towards a normalization of the situation—a situation that was anything but normal.

My chance arose at the dinner table. As Rosie was passing me the meatloaf, I said something like, "Ah, one of Michaelina's favorites, wasn't it?" I had no recollection if meatloaf was one of her favorites or not. My plan was to initiate a conversation and bow to whatever Rosie's opinion was.

However, the moment the words left my mouth, Rosie paused, the plate of meatloaf gripped between her thumb and fingers, frozen in mid-air. I had been reaching for it, but then had to withdraw my hand awkwardly.

Rosie slowly lowered the plate to the table. But she couldn't prevent it from clattering as her fingers released it onto the table.

Day 85

Early this morning I made a trip to the cemetery.

Spring was in full throttle there, the trees sporting their newly minted leaves and the flowers flaunting their colorful bonnets. The soft wind was warm, the sun dazzling, the entire atmosphere charged with the brilliance of nascent life in all its delicate beauty and tender expectations.

This tangible glory maddened me. Deflated as I was with the solemnity of the day, I didn't want earthly beauty; I wanted to be with Michaelina in her underground desolation. The forlorn among the dead.

This would've been her fifth birthday. Not having visited many cemeteries before, I was unsure of protocol. Random vehicles were pulled up to the side of the paths—following their example, I parked and searched on foot. This was my first time here since the burial, and I couldn't recall the exact location of Michaelina's site, just that it was near a clump of beech trees—ones that were climbable.

The atrociousness, the indignity of death confronted me here in a way that it never had at the hospital. For Michaelina to be deposited here in a cleft in the soil, with no choice in the matter, seemed inhuman. Why had I consented to this? She should've been cremated, her remains flung out from a spaceship soaring through the Milky Way, not sealed up in a coffin where no ray of light could penetrate.

I identified the correct cluster of trees and walked in that direction. A few other visitors ambled about or bent over graves. Up ahead a young couple, their backs to me, were just making their way from the area.

I found Michaelina's marble marker. Someone had planted daisies around it; the soil was newly turned. Rosie hadn't yet left the house, so who could it have been?

I contemplated for a moment the bleak specifics on the gravestone, but the thoughts that came to me were those of the ghastliest sort. Why had I come? Unable to make sense of my presence, I didn't stay long.

Getting back to work was a relief. I remained at the hospital as late as I could. When I arrived home this evening, the smell of rosemary chicken wafted through the doorway.

So it would be dinner as usual.

Without greeting Rosie, I went upstairs to change, then headed directly to the dining room. Dinner was on the table, but something else lay there as well—a beautifully wrapped birthday gift in Michaelina's spot.

I turned to Rosie, who stood looking at me with eyes strangely bright.

"What is it?" I said.

"Open it," she said. "Michaelina can't."

Rosie wasn't one to issue orders, especially emotionally laden ones. By the edge in her voice, I knew this was one time I should obey.

I untied the ribbon and tore the paper off the box. It's been nearly three months since the funeral. Did she really go to a store and buy a gift for a dead girl? Or had she already purchased it before the accident? I pulled open the top flaps and peered inside.

A new bike helmet—a pink one. Circling it was the image of a purple, gem-laden crown.

I mumbled something to the effect of, "Michaelina would've loved this." I put it back in the box and left it right there on the table in Michaelina's place.

Day 90

Today I received a voicemail from Heather. It's been over five years since we communicated. Her voice was smooth and controlled, with what sounded like a practiced, upbeat lilt to it. Even with its note of falseness, it was balm to my ear, reminding me of happier times past, before the heavy encumbrance of grief. She offered her condolences—briefly and belatedly—and asked whether I'd meet her for lunch. As simple as that. The child that had come between us was dead, suggesting there was nothing left to prevent a rapprochement.

I considered the offer. If I accepted, it'd be a way to leave this sorry mess behind. A clean break, a fresh start, a cliched new beginning. It would mean abandoning my plan to 'one up' God, but what of it? I'm tired of it. It'd be a fitting revenge, too, for Rosie's betrayal.

Could it hurt just to have lunch, to see if Heather was as attractive as before, as easy to take? My current existence consisted of a stressful work life and an emotionally fraught home life. The temptation to see Heather again—no, not a temptation, merely a decision—beckoned me.

My reverie lasted no more than five seconds. I deleted the voicemail and blocked her number.

Day 92

That call from Heather motivated me to redouble my efforts at humility. I was rewarded with success today. When I took Rosie her tea, not only did I say, "Good morning," I asked her how she'd slept. Pathetic, I know—this is my wife, for God's sake. That's what makes it so difficult. Saying these things to a stranger would be nothing. Saying them to your wife, when you haven't said them in so long, is like wearing those shoes from the back of your closet, the ones that didn't fit right when you bought them. Never having been properly broken in, they're as painful as ever.

The compulsion to adhere to a pattern, no matter how useless or destructive, gums up my ability to change. Getting in a rut is how it's always put. Or a groove if it's good.

Rosie's in a rut, too, playing her own role. Maybe if she broke out of it herself and did something surprising it'd help me. No—that's not true. Three months ago, she did do something surprising, something that shocked the living daylights out of me and ultimately forced me into the confounded situation I'm in now. However, that's not the point I'm trying to make.

When I asked how she'd slept, she said fine, except for Mrs. Croney's cat howling on the fence around midnight. I was about to remark that I'd slept right through it—even with an undertaking one has so little control over as sleep, I maintained my competitive edge. Instead, after clearing my throat, I managed to cough out, "I hope you got back to sleep without too much trouble," to which she replied in the affirmative. This was roughly fifty more words exchanged than on a typical morning.

Then, after my morning run, I was reading the paper, with Patton napping at my feet. Rosie asked if I could help her lift a heavy box off the closet shelf, "If you have a moment to spare before work," she added. After a brief internal struggle, I folded my paper and completed the task. I then asked if she needed help with anything else while I was up. (Unfortunately, the addition of "while I was up" implied I wouldn't be willing to help any more once I sat back down. Something more to work on.)

Complying with her modest request may seem unremarkable. Before my pact, however, here's how the situation would've unfolded: Rosie would ask me for a favor. First, I'd glare at her for five seconds or so, to be sure she was aware she was interrupting my reading. Then, depending on my view as to whether the requested favor had any real importance, I'd either harrumph and say I didn't have time before work, make her wait until I finished reading the paper or at least the article I was on, or else I'd throw the paper down noisily and heave myself to my feet with an exaggerated sigh. There are numerous ways to express displeasure and irritation and to make someone understand just how much they're inconveniencing you.

But I didn't do any of those things. I just got up and helped her. It was a victory. I'm still rather amazing, only in a different way.

Day 94

I've reread Rosie's absurd litany of humility a hundred times. Never have I encountered something so utterly in opposition to human nature. And yet it's stuck in Rosie's prayer book. Either it's just a convenient bookmark, or else Rosie prays it herself. If she prays it, does that mean she practices it?

To experiment (I was going to say for the fun of it, but I doubted it would be fun), I decided to attempt one of the traits cited in the prayer. Many of them mean the same thing: letting go of the desire to be esteemed or respected.

I had to come up with a circumstance, in advance, in which I anticipated desiring exactly that. Preferably a scenario I could test out on others before working my way up to Rosie. The idea I arrived at was to let go of the need to assert my superiority at work. During rounds, instead of berating the residents for their stupidity, I'd praise one of them for an astute observation. This plan was predicated, of course, on one of them saying something remotely astute. Once in a great while that happened. On those occasions I generally downplayed it to protect them from getting puffed up into overconfidence.

So today I queried the residents about a ten-year-old female patient presenting localized vitiligo, which had been unresponsive to conventional therapies. What surgical treatments, I asked, might be indicated to replenish the patient's melanocytes? I expected to be met with blank stares, but one resident, a rather stout young woman with no shortage of skin anomalies herself, immediately suggested minipunch grafts and suction blister epidermal grafts. My typical response in such a situation would've been, "What about thin Thiersch grafts, cultured melanocyte suspension, or transplantation of epidermal cell suspension? Did you forget those?"

Instead, I bit my tongue and said, "Excellent answer, Dr. Prezic. Can anyone add to that?"

The residents offered nothing more. I believe they went away wondering if I was being sarcastic. It was actually rather fun.

The ironic thing was, I don't think they esteemed me any the less for it.

Day 96

The parents of my patients insist they're not asking for beauty, just for their child to appear normal like everyone else. They don't realize that to the extent I capture 'normal,' I *am* capturing beauty. That's what beauty is—conforming to the norm, not deviating from it. Beauty is generally out of reach for them, because normalcy is.

Michaelina was beautiful. What typical child isn't? I gazed at her face as she lay dying in that hospital bed, struck anew by her beauty. Although her innards were mutilated, the bike helmet had protected her lovely face.

The ventilator masked her upturned nose and rosebud lips, and her eyes were closed. I wanted to see those eyes again, the cerulean blue irises with the midnight blue rims. I wanted to see life in them. I wanted her to look at me.

I had something of extreme importance to communicate.

Day 97

Back to that litany of humility. I can't see how it's possible not to desire being esteemed. Isn't that desire, and its fulfillment, what has made life bearable throughout the ages? If I can't be superior to my neighbors, what's the point in putting up with them?

Yet here it is before me, this quest for humility. I'm sensing the need for a role model to improve my execution. I don't hang around in circles of humble people. Rosie might be humble, but that hardly counts—she doesn't have any real achievements to fuel her pride.

Dr. Babyface—Owen—is probably the closest to a humble man I've ever encountered. He's an accomplished, well-respected surgeon, but whenever someone compliments him, he makes a self-deprecating joke or returns an even larger accolade. Deep down, though, he must enjoy praise as much as anyone. Maybe more, because he knows perfectly well that his attempts to deflect it only produce for him greater esteem from others. There's the irony—that he's celebrated for being humble. I've never heard anyone bad-mouth him, and I'm sure that's why. That's his strategy.

I may not be humble, but at least I'm not a phony.

Day 99

Another incident with Owen occurred today, one which made me think his humility might be genuine. We were discussing a patient with congenital velocardiofacial syndrome in a team consult. The medical case was standard, or so it seemed to me. The discussion turned on the issue of whether, beyond correcting the submucous cleft palate, facial reconstruction of the over-prominent upper jaw should be attempted at the same time.

Owen is the team leader for this case. His knowledge of how I'd previously undermined him would've justified his ignoring me or brushing off my opinion. Instead, he actively solicited it, saying, "I'd like to hear Michael on this." His statement wasn't uttered as a challenge; rather, it was stated as a sincere desire on his part to invite my counsel, as if I were the hermit on the hill. Such a simple gesture, but the weight of it dumbfounded me. I wouldn't have done the same had our roles been reversed.

I can't deny the goodness of his behavior, although I've tried for a long time to deny that his way was better. If there is such a thing as a saint, Owen comes closer to fulfilling the requirements than anyone I know.

Day 101

The past several days have gone exceptionally well from a humility standpoint. Each day has ended with a gratifying feeling of progression, of building momentum. I've not only come to terms with the difficulties of the past several months, but I'm getting beyond them.

Take that, Dr. Matilda Thurman.

Today, though, a blip occurred. The morning's tea ritual went well enough. However, things fell apart after dinner. Rosie was working on a crossword puzzle. She usually starts them in the morning, and any words she can't figure out she waits and asks me about in the evening. What's a five-letter word for *can't bake*? What's a twenty-letter phrase meaning *far gone*? I answer enough of the tough ones that she can usually complete the puzzle, gaining for herself some measure of satisfaction.

Sometimes the process aggravates me though. I have my own interests to pursue during the little free time I have in the evening, and there's nothing more exasperating than her interrupting my reading with a clue that she ought to know the answer to.

Tonight something unusual happened. Rosie first asked me about a seven-letter word meaning *fumble*. I tried several possible answers, including *blunder* and *misstep*, but none would fit. Then she said, "I know, it's *mistake*." That answer wasn't nearly as appropriate as my guesses, which is another reason I dislike crosswords. And if Rosie could figure it out herself, she shouldn't have disturbed me with it.

She didn't stop there. Next she asked me a nine-letter word for *disgust*. I had no immediate idea on this one, and after a pause, she said, "Actually, I think it's *antipathy*." I could see she was quite pleased with herself for coming up with two difficult words before I could, and I began to feel irritated. She asked if I could help her once more with one she was really stuck on. Desiring to regain the upper hand, I agreed.

"The theme is *Actors and Actions*," she said. "The clue is *projectile thrower*, and there are 17 spaces. In the first space is *H*, then in the fourth space is another *H*." I told her to show me and we looked at it together. I racked my brain. Nothing occurred to me.

Then she blurted out, "He who is without sin!"

She must have seen my annoyance because she immediately said something like, "You would've gotten it in a minute."

Patronized by my own wife. It was too much. I smacked the paper and told her never to bother me with her damn crosswords again.

Day 102

I narrowly avoided Matilda Thurman today. I was just exiting the main hospital when I spied her from a distance walking in my direction.

Ducking into the nearby campus Starbucks, I positioned myself at the end of the long line at the counter. A group of students arrived and queued up immediately behind me. I kept an eye on the window, waiting for Thurman to pass by so I could continue on my way.

To my chagrin, however, Starbucks was her intended destination. As she opened the door, I turned my back to her. Trapped, I felt her eyes boring into me from behind. I judged it unlikely she'd bypass the line to approach me, but once I had my coffee I wouldn't put it past her to accost me. Even if she's powerless now, I have a queasy sense that it's in my best interests to steer clear of her.

When it was almost my turn to be served, I realized my wallet was in my desk, not my pocket. Moreover, if I didn't hustle I'd be late for my cross-campus meeting. I solved the problem by making a show of looking at my watch, harrumphing loudly, and exiting out the side door. Thankfully she didn't follow.

Although I feel a fool, I'll admit it disturbed my equilibrium, just the glimpse of Thurman.

Day 105

Today being Saturday, I didn't need to go in to the hospital. Sitting on the back deck, I imbibed my post-run coffee in a leisurely fashion while scanning the morning headlines. Though the temperature was about right for mid-June, I was sodden in sweat from my run. The air was absolutely still, a hint of the stultifying summer to come.

Encountering no news article worth reading in its entirety, I folded the paper and attempted to enjoy the scenery. I shifted my chair so it would face the rose bushes instead of the driveway. Many buds were preparing to open, while others were in full bloom or even starting to fade. Roses need care, discipline even, to promote proper growth—pruning is key to producing voluptuous blooms.

Michaelina hated my roses, calling them "Daddy's stinky woses" after she pricked her finger on a thorn when she was three. I was at work at the time. Rosie told me that Michaelina had squeezed the pricked finger until it bled, then ran to her with wide eyes, "I amn't going to die, am I?" Rosie put a band-aid on the wound and assured Michaelina all would be fine, and sent her off to play.

An hour later, Rosie couldn't find her. After a thorough search downstairs and outside, Michaelina was finally discovered in her bedroom, dressed as a princess and lying in bed, pretending to sleep. She whispered, with eyes closed, that Prince Charming was on his way to wake her. Sure enough, Trevor from next door soon showed up at the door. He put on a green cape and cardboard crown that had been laid out for him. But when he looked at himself in the mirror and said, "Mirror, mirror, on the wall, who's the fairest of them all?" Michaelina hushed him, saying that wasn't Prince Charming's part. She wouldn't endure an actual kiss, so she whispered to Prince Charming to tap her on the lips with one of her magic wands.

I'm not sure a typical seven-year old boy would agree to participate in such a ritual, but this boy, as I've said before, was odd. A professional evaluation would likely yield an interesting diagnosis. The boy seemed innocent enough, and the neighborhood was short on little girls. I could never be sure of his intelligence, as he rarely spoke, but when he did, much of his language contained large swaths of dialog lifted straight from Disney movies. No wonder he and Michaelina got along so well. Too bad his father, Herman, was such an asshole.

The very thought of the man caused me to glance over at the high fence I'd built between our yards. I couldn't be sure, but it seemed that just as my peripheral vision reached the top of the fence, the brown mop of Trevor's hair disappeared beneath it.

Day 106

Rosie can still look damn good when she makes an effort.

Tonight was the hospital's annual Physician's Dinner. We've always gone in the past, but this time I gave her a chance to back out. When I asked if she wanted to attend, she searched my eyes, then said yes. It wasn't a particularly enthusiastic response. On the other hand, she's barely left home since the funeral.

Her makeup had been applied with her usual practiced skill, and she wore a black cocktail dress with a lacy black shawl. While it was appropriate for the occasion, I wondered if she was making a statement with the color. I let it slide and instead complimented her. I expected a smile in return, but none was forthcoming.

At the dinner she seemed low-spirited, with nothing to say. Perhaps that wasn't surprising, seated as she was between me and a cardio-thoracic surgeon who was a known bore. I caught occasional snippets of a long-winded story he was relating to her. I used his engagement with Rosie to my advantage, chatting with the pretty young wife of a podiatrist seated to my right.

But when someone asked Rosie to pass the salt, I turned in her direction and noticed the carefully-applied mascara was smudged. After that I paid closer attention to the surgeon's ramblings, and realized to my horror he was relating an incident about a child he'd operated on with a punctured lung.

I excused myself to the podiatrist's wife, stood, and guided Rosie by the elbow to the ladies room so she could fix her face. When she came out, her makeup was corrected, but not the expression beneath it.

I took her home.

Day 107

I made Rosie her tea this morning and handed it to her with a pleasant greeting. My plan in that sense is working. A problem I've encountered, though, is that even in my acts of humility, I still desire control and expect the appreciation of others in response. And then there's the impossible paradox that if I achieve a measure of humility, I become inordinately pleased with myself. But self-satisfaction is the antithesis of humility, isn't it?

I considered it on my run with Patton. To win this thing, I had to get it right. An idea came to me. What if I executed some act, even a small one, that neither Rosie nor anyone else witnessed? It'd be like the proverbial tree falling in the forest with no one to hear it. She couldn't increase her respect for me if she didn't realize I'd done anything.

For starters, I decided to give Rosie a little more spending money. I located her purse. What an ungodly mess inside—everything from used tissues and crumpled receipts to melted cough drops and gooey lipstick tubes. I put it all out of my mind, though, and found her wallet. There was $13 inside. I threw in another ten. I'd have added more, but then it'd be too noticeable.

I felt sneaky and clever. Rosie's response, though, wasn't quite what I'd anticipated. She discovered the additional money, figured out I was the one behind it, and thanked me in confusion.

That defeated the purpose. I needed another idea, one unrelated to money. Performing a service would be more humbling. I came up with a plan to shine her leather boots, a task she rarely undertook on her own initiative. Typically, she'd wait until the boots were so scuffed that I shamed her into doing it.

So this afternoon, when she was out on some errands with her sister Maude, I polished every pair. I had to restrain my irritation that she'd allowed them to deteriorate to such a dreadful condition. Then, I laid them gently back onto the heap in her closet.

Day 108

Though the weather was on the warm side today, Rosie wore her brown dress boots to church. She said nothing about them being newly polished. Either she didn't notice (entirely possible) or else chose to stay silent.

I couldn't decide whether I was pleased or annoyed.

Day 109

I must listen attentively to Rosie, even if she blabs on and on. I must not interrupt her. I must not demonstrate my impatience for her to get to the point. I must not crave that she leave me in peace.

Those were my resolutions today.

I worried I'd have no chance to carry them out, with Rosie's mood so subdued lately. But an opportunity did arise. Maybe my shining her boots prompted it. She came to me with a pair of shoes, a favorite of hers, but one I never particularly liked. With their black patent leather and big buckles on the vamp, they looked like something a Pilgrim man might wear. What little there was of a heel was worn down and partially broken off.

Rosie wanted my opinion on whether to have them repaired or buy a new pair. It may have appeared to her that I was merely relaxing in the den, and thus open to her stray musings. In actuality, I was thinking about tomorrow's surgery. I'm concerned because the surgical simulation computer shut down unexpectedly today. Even though the IT folks got it working again, the source of the problem eluded them. If it acts up tomorrow, the operation will be in trouble.

True to my resolution, however, I wrenched those weighty thoughts aside to consider the shoe issue. Rosie rattled on about the benefits and disadvantages of repairing the shoes (over $80) versus buying a replacement pair (in the $200 range), assuming she could even find a pair she liked as well.

I looked at her and nodded in what I felt was an encouraging manner.

Evidently, that wasn't enough. She needed me to make the decision for her. I said either choice seemed reasonable to me. Okay, I didn't exactly phrase it that way. I said something like, "I'm not sure what difference it makes. Are you sure you don't have enough shoes already?" Not a perfect response, I recognize in retrospect, but at least I was listening, and keeping the conversation going.

She brought up the fact that these shoes matched several outfits in a particularly harmonious way.

"Can't you ask Maude?"

"No, she's out of town at the nurse's conference," said Rosie. "And I'd like to do something about this now."

Normally, I would've shut down such a conversation well before reaching this juncture. But I had to tackle this fault. Surely the humble response was to exhibit patience while trying not to think about how I could be occupying my thoughts far more productively elsewhere.

Again she ran through her litany of pros and cons as a prelude to requesting my opinion on whether to get the shoes fixed.

I suggested she toss a coin.

She tightened her lips, then said I wasn't being helpful. She needed my honest opinion.

When someone says they want your honest opinion, the one thing you can be sure of is that they don't. In my experience, the person requesting advice wants an affirmation of what they've already decided. I tried to divine what answer she wanted. In this case, though, I couldn't tell. I only knew I was becoming irritated, resolution or no resolution. I'd made it clear I wouldn't fault her for either choice. Why couldn't we leave it at that?

Finally, in a tone that probably sounded less benevolent than I intended, I said, "Why don't you get a new pair, maybe something a little more feminine?"

Her face fell. She tucked the shoes under her arm and left the room.

I can't figure out how to win this game.

Day 110

Today's surgery could've gone more smoothly. Yes, the computer worked as needed. The problem was of a different stripe altogether—nausea again. Just as I opened the patient up, my mouth filled with saliva as it prepared to facilitate the emptying of my stomach. I swallowed repeatedly and was at last able to fight it back. My vision blurred again, but just briefly.

Why is this happening? It's Thurman's fault. I was fine before seeing her—totally fine. But she implanted a subliminal suggestion that's wormed its way deep into my brain—that my surgery should be problematic because of unexplored grief. I need to force that idea out, to squeeze my brain until the seed of that notion pops out or gets sufficiently buried that it won't be able to grow. In the meantime, I'll take an anti-emetic before operating. I don't know what to do about my eyesight. Seeing an ophthalmologist for a problem that occurs intermittently would be a waste of time.

Back to Rosie. After being less than successful yesterday in how I responded to her shoe dilemma, I made another attempt today. This time, though, I was the one to start the conversation. That way I could tolerate it better, or at least exercise a little control. By practicing in a limited context I could work my way up to a solid habit.

The plan came to me while out on my run. Rosie's always wanted to travel. I, on the other hand, have had more than enough travel by attending various professional conferences every year. Rosie sometimes accompanies me, and she's afforded ample time to sightsee and shop. Even so, over the years she's occasionally expressed a desire for a non-work-related vacation.

Eventually she gave up asking. Surely it would be a welcome surprise if I brought it up now of my own accord. Such a trip would serve as a wellspring of conversation over the weeks of planning and allow me to practice patience in answering the many queries and concerns she'd come up with.

I sauntered into the kitchen as she was sautéing some vegetables and casually mentioned the idea of our going on a trip together.

She dropped the spatula in the pan.

No, she didn't drop it, she sort of threw it down in a jerk of her wrist.

She turned to me, eyes blazing. I attempted to decipher her expression. How is it possible to convey disbelief, dismay, outrage, and concern all in one look? I don't know, but that's what I saw.

I said, "You don't look too happy about the idea. I thought that's what you wanted all these years."

"Maybe I did."

"Not anymore?"

She turned back to the stove, picked up the spatula, and began stirring the contents of the pan with determination.

"No," she said. "Not anymore."

Day 114

I don't mention Michaelina much, even though her death is still so recent, so fresh. In other ways it seems long ago. Unlike Rosie, there are limits to my anguish. Maybe it's that I'm better at facing facts. Michaelina is dead, and we're stuck with life.

Rosie mostly hides her grief—Michaelina's birthday was an exception. Maybe she fears any outward signs of sorrow will cause me more grief, as if what holds me together is her avoidance of the topic.

But she said something today. I was out front tending to my rose bushes, when Rosie, after returning from an errand, removed Michaelina's booster seat from her car. (Why it was still in there I have no idea.) She came over to me, carrying the seat as if it were some sacrificial offering or the child's fatally injured body itself, and said, "Michaelina always buckled herself in, ever since she was two years old. I always wanted to check, to be sure the belt was tight, but she'd say, 'Got it, Mom.'"

I watched as the tears layered up in Rosie's eyes until ready to tumble over her lids.

Nasolacrimal ducts, or tear ducts, constitute one of the more difficult elements of facial reconstruction. We take them for granted, but their function is critical to eye health. Without those ducts we can't cry. Even more important are the thousands of times we blink our eyes each day, washing away the particulate matter that continually lands on our eyeballs. That debris would scratch the surface without lubricant from the tear duct.

My own eyes narrowed as I observed Rosie. She could see I wasn't buying into this circus.

The waterworks from her ducts never made it down her cheeks—she was able to blink the whole mess back under the tent of her lids.

I told her to take the damn car seat to Goodwill. Why had she even shown it to me? A car seat can only keep a child safe within a car. I needed no reminding of that fact, least of all from her.

I've never shed a tear over Michaelina. That would do nothing to bring her back.

Day 120

Rosie has always looked up to me. On nearly every subject she bows to my judgment. What TV shows to watch, podcasts to listen to, candidates to vote for. She asks me what websites to follow, my thoughts on the city's proposed light rail project, whether it's worth spending extra to buy organic produce, etc.

The only arenas where my opinions never held sway were her mothering of the boy and her faith. Whenever I voiced arguments on the unlikelihood of her religion having any particular claim to the truth, she just nodded and continued practicing it in the same way—Sunday Mass week after week, year in and year out, and sometimes even on weekdays. I mostly refrained from commenting, although I could hardly remain silent when a priest was caught in a scandal, or some high-flown Catholic was exposed as a hypocrite.

I couldn't understand why she persisted in the belief and ritual, absent any compelling evidence of God's existence. I allowed her to live in that world, as it seemed to mean so much to her. At times I wondered if it was all a show for my benefit—her reading that well-worn prayer book every morning (didn't she ever tire of it?) and the surreptitious blessing she said to herself before meals. Once, though, I came upon her unexpectedly as she was kneeling by the bed. She jumped up, embarrassed. I felt as if I'd walked in on her in the bathroom. I retreated without a word.

I didn't bother to state the obvious—that her prayers were never answered. I was well aware of the content of those prayers. She wanted me to love the boy more—to spend 'quality' time with him, to encourage him, to be more sensitive to his nature.

I knew better. I executed the formula that countless fathers before me have used instinctively with their sons to straighten them out, toughen them up, and teach them not to make excuses or blame others. It's the formula that helps a boy become a man.

Rosie was incapable of comprehending that. She couldn't see what to me was self-evident—that even if it were temporarily painful, the boy would thank me in the end for cultivating resiliency in him. The world is harsh. Rosie could see only the present; I could envision the future. She saw the boy's hurt and pitied him. I saw the boy's potential—what there was of it—and disciplined him.

At least I tried to. She ran interference on every occasion, making him believe he was soft and needed care. I tried to make him see he was strong and could withstand the buffeting of life's headwinds.

To be clear, we didn't argue overtly over the boy, or should I say, not vociferously. Rosie always deferred to me in his presence, but she had her way of showing her displeasure—pursed lips, downcast look, furrowed brow, watery eyes. The boy saw these things too, and blamed me for what he perceived as severity towards her.

In the end, he chose his own path. He rejected me, so I rejected him.

Day 121

My relationship with Michaelina was different. That's why her death was particularly tragic for me. From her infancy, she reached for me to hold her, read to her, play with her. When she was big enough, I'd lie on my back on the floor, the top of my head against the sofa. She'd stand on my palms, facing me, and I'd raise her up, benchpress-like. At first, she'd hold her arms out to the sides for balance, then, reaching the pinnacle, lift them above her head in triumph. When she finally lost her balance, or got tired of the trick, she'd fall forward onto the sofa in tinkling laughter.

Early on, she mimicked me by rolling her eyes at many of her mother's requests or silly statements, knowing I'd give her a smile of approval. In her eyes, I was magnificent, and she'd do anything I asked. She had a stubborn streak, though, that she saved for Rosie. If her mother told her to pick up her room, she'd be discovered drawing at the kitchen table. If she was asked to go out back and play, she'd sneak to her room and look at books. If instructed to sit and look at books, she'd go out back and ride her two-wheeler with the training wheels.

Rosie believed I encouraged Michaelina to be disobedient, but I was only supporting her independent thinking. In retrospect, though, maybe I did embolden her too much, before she was fully aware of life's dangers.

Day 122

I've been good to Rosie in a multitude of ways. People don't always see that. I provide well for her, I have a generous life insurance policy, and I've never pushed her to get a job. I've encouraged her to improve herself, and have suggested umpteen classes she could take—everything from aerobics and painting to public speaking and philosophy. She always demurs, insisting it would be a waste of time and money. Maybe it would. I thought that after I bought her the camera, she'd at least take a photography class, but even that idea met resistance.

She's always claimed to be content cooking and managing the house. Her life's purpose was to be fully available to her children—first to the Jackass, then later Michaelina. As part of that commitment, she frequently volunteered at their schools. The recollection of her involvement gave me an idea. Today I suggested she get a part-time job at a preschool or daycare center.

When I floated the idea, she paled and gave her head a little shake. Not a shake as in 'no,' but a shake as if ridding herself of a bothersome mosquito. I explained that even though I haven't encouraged her to work in the past, I believed now it could do her some good, providing focus and an opportunity to spend time with children. That's what she loved, wasn't it? She avoided my gaze and said something about it being too painful. I backed off.

I perceive now what the problem is. There's a larger difficulty here that I haven't mentioned before. It's not just that Rosie's dealing with grief. That's understandable, though wearing thin. The problem is that she's also contending with guilt. Maybe that guilt makes her not trust herself around children.

Yes, guilt is far worse than grief. Or I imagine it is.

I can't do anything to relieve her on that score. Absolutely, she's guilty. Her actions were deliberate. They resulted in the death of Michaelina as surely as if she'd taken a knife and stabbed her.

Day 123

A setback today on the tea ritual. It's been going so smoothly—my one area of repeated success. Today, after I handed Rosie the mug, however, she ruined the gesture completely. She asked me for a different kind of tea.

A different kind of tea.

Sure, she softened her request by first saying how much she appreciated my bringing her tea every morning. But then she added, "I wonder if in the future you could make it Earl Grey or something else with caffeine in it?"

I stared at her, open-mouthed.

Then, in an apologetic tone, she said she could use a little "jump-start" in the mornings.

The implication was that I've been giving her the wrong tea for months, and that she'd only been humoring me. Was she attempting to humble me further, or was this some sort of test? She obviously had no conception of what I've been going through, how difficult this already was. My sincere gesture wasn't good enough—she was throwing it back in my face.

Catching her blunder, she back-pedaled, stating that herbal tea was lovely too. When I said nothing, she flashed me an exaggerated, *I'm sorry* smile, with stretched out zygomatics and raised frontalis muscles.

I stood, bowed and said, "Whatever your ladyship desires."

Day 124

Today I made her the damn Earl Grey. I put it in a different mug, though, one that said *Dream Big*. The irony was probably lost on her.

So that was a success, more or less.

Have I had enough successes? I'm a third of the way into the year, an appropriate time to assess my progress. I paged through my journal and read over some of my previous entries. Despite the occasional victories, I have to admit my improvement isn't quite what I'd hoped for. In some ways, I seem to be an even less humble person than when I started.

Some entries cast me in a negative light. How hard can it be, you might ask, to refrain from criticism over the saltiness of a dish Rosie's cooked especially for me? Or why must I attribute her minimal achievements to a lack of motivation? Why would I belittle her for living out her beliefs?

I shouldn't be judged for these flaws. The fact is, my honesty with myself works against me. I do seek truth and goodness. Or at least a part of me does. It's the same part of me that apprehends beauty in the faces I study.

Increasingly often, though, I've become cognizant of a split. Not a split personality, because it's all me, all Michael. It's more like me warring against myself. Some part of me clamors for the opposite of what I know is right, in a way that seems perfectly reasonable in the moment. It's the voice of another part, an internal bully.

I extol discipline and the exercise of self-control, yet I've let this bully push the 'higher' me into the background. It's not that the higher Michael never speaks or acts. He emerges when I manage to subdue or ignore the lower part, as you might a spoiled child. I've given him a name, that lower part of me, because it reminds me of this problematic side. I call him *Butt-cheeks*.

Day 125

Despite the recent glitch regarding Earl Grey, the morning tea ritual has become almost pleasant. Rosie expects it now. There's no more fear of witnessing concern in her eyes. My motives are not suspected. Her discreet *thank-you*, said under her breath, is tolerable.

I've taken to leaning against the wall near her for a brief conversation. It never lasts long—as soon as there's a slight break in the flow, we reach what seems an insurmountable barrier, and retreat into silence. What's left unsaid between us slowly rises and hangs in the air like an unmentionable odor. A gentle cross breeze from an open window might be enough to clear it out. But the window remains closed, as if painted shut.

Day 129

As a craniofacial surgeon, I may be overly clinical at times. I do objectify my patients—I need to focus on my role and not let myself be caught up in their (or their parents') emotional drama. My job is not to cater to psychological needs, but to rectify facial structures.

By doing well what I've been paid to do, I've received many effusive thank-you letters over the years, which I preserve in a manila folder. I occasionally break it out and read a few letters when my work is particularly taxing. Here's a typical one:

> Dr. Michael, I thank you with all my heart for your work with Jonathan. The results have been amazing! He just started at a new school and the other kids barely notice his ears anymore. You've given him a new chance in life! God bless you.

Anonymous online reviews, though, are likely to express the negatives that people won't tell me personally. It occurred to me today that it might enhance my humility to read a few of those. I've reproduced a few here (correcting the annoyingly bad spelling):

> He kept staring at my daughter like she was a jigsaw puzzle or something, not a real person.

> He's done a bunch of operations on my little boy who was born with Stickler's. He knows what he's doing, but forget time for questions! We only keep going because he knows us.

> Okay, he fixed my daughter's jaw, but we didn't feel supported. He wouldn't make eye contact with me, only my husband.

> A total jerk! We couldn't wait to get out of there.

Clearly they'd misinterpreted my actions. One reviewer came to my defense, after a fashion:

> What the hell do people want? Dr. Michael is the most awesome plastic surgeon for kids on the planet! He fixed my baby's cleft palate so good you can't even tell he had one. So quit your complaining that he's not all sugary sweet. Five stars!

I tried to shake these comments off, at the same time wondering if Rosie had read them. Rather than enhancing my humility, the lack of gratitude of these parents only infuriated me.

Day 130

I snapped at Rosie today. I didn't raise my voice, but I was curt. She has this habit of facing away when she's speaking to me. She's always busying herself with something—chopping vegetables, loading the dishwasher, pulling lint off her sweater. It's fine for her to be getting her work done. However, when I can't hear her and have to keep asking her to repeat herself—well, it's exasperating.

I tried to be patient, but she'd done it twice today already. Then, during dinner, I asked her something about the landscaper, and she turned almost completely around to look out the window as she replied, as if she were incapable of answering a question about the lawn without actually viewing it. I couldn't hear her answer, so I told her just to forget it and I walked out of the room.

Okay, I stormed out.

By doing so I was making clear my frustration and teaching Rosie a lesson—that her behavior was unacceptable. Butt-cheeks egged me on.

And yet the moment I cleared the door, I felt a jolt inside, as if something hard and blunt had struck my brain, bursting open a delicate membrane. Dammed-up memories of the last time I'd stormed out cascaded into my consciousness, flooding every nerve and synapse.

In former times, when my annoyance with Rosie had reached a level beyond tolerance, I would've left the house, driven somewhere, called my mistress of the moment. But not this time. This was a test. If I left, I'd never return. Oh, I'd return to the house, eventually. But I'd never return to my bargain. If I couldn't manage to defeat Butt-cheeks here and now, in this particular circumstance, I never would.

I had to go back in, but how? Forcing myself to swim upstream against the very flow of my nature, against the surge that wanted to lift me away from my troubles, seemed impossible. I stood outside that door for a full 30 seconds, fighting against myself. Here was an opportunity, thrown out to me like a life preserver. I had only to grab it and pull myself in. And yet that opportunity was in opposition to all that I was, or knew myself to be.

Looking back, I don't know how I did it. Somehow I was able to ask Butt-cheeks to step aside. Somehow I was able to walk back into the room. Somehow I was able to say softly to my wife, "I'm sorry. Please tell me what you were saying."

Rosie wouldn't meet my eyes. She jumped up, and with one choked sob pushed past me out of the room.

Day 131

To make up for yesterday, I offered to grill steaks for dinner. Rosie appeared to take my offer as I intended it. Her smile—I hoped—expressed her forgiveness for what had transpired in the dining room last night.

While she was in the kitchen making potato salad, I loaded the charcoal and some bits of hardwood onto the grill. I like a big fire. When the blaze erupted full force, I stared at it for a long time. I didn't move to avoid the smoke, but instead let the odor fill my nostrils and pour past me in the breeze, until the intensity of the heat forced me to move a little farther back. I watched until the conflagration cleared and only the white-hot coals remained.

I pulled out the manila folder I'd hidden beneath some newspaper on a nearby chair. Without opening it, I tossed it onto the coals. The intense heat curled around the edges of the folder, outlining them in luminous red. Then the flames flared up. In less than a minute, the folder, and all the cards and letters within, was ablaze. Little flakes of ash sailed into the air, carrying the adulation with them.

It was time to get the steaks from the kitchen. I turned towards the screen door just in time to see Rosie scurrying away.

Day 134

I operated today on a girl who was in an accident a couple weeks ago. The ER doctors had saved her life, but she needed additional reconstructive surgery on her face. We'd been waiting for her to stabilize from the trauma before operating again.

The surgery did not go well.

Day 135

Ji-young called me into the executive office this afternoon. When she stood to meet me, her small fists were already clenched.

I was being blamed for yesterday's debacle in the OR.

That's patently unfair. Although I was the lead surgeon, others were there who could've stepped in. If a pilot has a heart attack, the co-pilot takes over and lands the plane, right?

And no, I didn't have a heart attack. Here's what happened. The patient—the girl who'd been severely injured in the accident—had suffered a double orbital blowout fracture on impact. I was attempting a dissection to release a resulting adhesion. I used traction force, which inadvertently caused an intraorbital hemorrhage. Things went south from there—we had difficulty stopping the bleeding.

So yes, there was a problem. Poor outcomes in surgery do happen. That's why patients sign a waiver. Moreover, it was the original accident that was the proximate cause, not the mishap in surgery. Go after the driver at fault, not me. I was just attempting to clean up the mess.

I said this to Ji-young. She only glared at me.

Except she didn't only glare at me, she suspended me from surgery. I'm allowed to still see patients, still make rounds. What good, though, is a surgeon without surgery?

I protested vociferously. There are inherent risks in surgery, and the patient's family understood that. Was this a liability issue? Was the hospital concerned about litigation?

"It's not only that," she said. "And you know it."

I stared at her, open-mouthed.

"Discuss it with Dr. Thurman."

"I'm not seeing her again."

She shook her head. "You will if you want to get back to surgery."

If I had to see a psychiatrist, I wanted a different one, but Ji-young insisted that because Dr. Thurman specialized in "these kinds of issues," and because she already had "copious notes" on me, no switch was possible.

"Besides," she said, head bobbling to a nod, "I have confidence in her judgment."

I raised my brows.

"She didn't want you to continue performing surgery. In her opinion, you were on the brink of a breakdown. But I said if she couldn't pinpoint any diagnosable psychiatric issue, we had to let you continue working."

Wonderful.

Her small fists unclenched just so she could have the emotional pleasure of clenching them again. "This time it's her call if and when you return."

If?

"And what're my patients supposed to do in the meantime?"

"I've found fill-ins for your scheduled surgeries. Please refer all new surgical patients to those same physicians," she said. "You can continue your follow-up visits with on-going patients." She head-bobbled to the negative. "Assuming no more issues arise."

My diaphragm froze. I couldn't breathe, couldn't muster a response to this news. Ji-young must've been expecting a retort from me, as her mouth was cocked half-open as she prepared her rebuttal. When I said nothing, she was left hanging. I detected a note of disappointment on her face.

I turned and left her office, hollow and dry. I was an autumn leaf in the street—exposed, blown in arbitrary directions by fickle winds. Or, ready to be ground into dust by the first foot that trampled me.

Even then, further mortification awaited. The averted gazes of colleagues and staff members as I walked down the hall were worse than jeers. Which of them had known this was coming? There had to have been planning and plotting behind my back—it would've taken some quick legwork to find replacements without my knowledge. Other, future humiliations beckoned with their long derisive fingers—inquiries from patients' families about loss of my surgical privileges, and the look on Rosie's face when she learned of my disgrace.

In the lonely trek back to my office, I happened to run into Owen. I grunted in response to his greeting, hoping he'd get the message and leave me alone. Instead, he insisted on walking me the rest of the way to my office. I wondered if he was one of the surgeons picking up some extra patients in my wake. Maybe now that I'd be out of his surgical orbit, the real Owen would shine forth.

However, I observed no indication that he was glorying in my humiliation. Instead, he started right in on a story clearly intended to cheer me up. Something about a mandibular reconstructive surgery that he told the parents was routine, but during which he severed a boy's inferior alveolar nerve. The outcome wasn't good, and Owen was embarrassed by it. (*'Humiliated'* was the word he used. He has no idea what real humiliation is.) The story was hardly relevant to my situation, nor, if it was meant to lift my spirits, did it accomplish the desired effect. Still, I appreciated his attempt at empathy.

At my office door, I shooed him away and sat behind my desk, trying to breathe. Everything there was in order. All was the same as it'd always been. Everything, that is, except me. I was the strange, unrecognizable object in the room. The one that no longer belonged.

Day 136

I blame Rosie. Her actions are the root cause of all my current miseries.

She knew how I felt about the Jackass, knew I wanted him banned from our life, at least until he apologized for running out on us. That was my well-reasoned and emphatically stated intention. If she'd just done as I asked, none of this would've happened. I'd still be performing surgery. I'd still be seeing Michaelina's little upturned nose in the doorway when I returned from work each day.

Rosie's betrayal was revealed in the most commonplace way, almost five months ago now. My morning's surgery had been canceled, and as I was in no immediate rush to get to the hospital, I'd taken a longer run than usual. When I returned home, Rosie's cell phone was ringing, and she was nowhere to be found.

That was typical—she'd frequently leave it behind or misplace it. Anyway, I picked it up, thinking to answer it for her. The caller had hung up. My eye was caught, though, by a text message lying bare on the screen: *Can't make it by 2. Will 3 work?* The caller ID read *John*.

When I saw that name, my chest seemed to grip my heart as if preventing it from leaping out into the open air. There were plenty of Johns in the world. Only one of them could I imagine being on such familiar terms with my wife.

The Jackass.

It was also typical of Rosie not to lock her screen, so I clicked on the message and scrolled through at least a dozen casual exchanges. I didn't need to go back far—I quickly got the gist of it. Not only were they planning to meet that very day, but they'd also clearly been getting together for some time.

There had to be immediate consequences—Rosie would have to pay.

And she has. She certainly has.

My suspension is ultimately a result of her betrayal. But I won't tell her about it—that's not what my bargain's about. I have to suck up this situation in humility. It's just a temporary setback anyway—I'll get back to operating without her being any the wiser.

Day 142

The rumor mill is grinding out bushels of innuendo about the reasons for my surgical hiatus. I'm continuing to round with residents, but they're only half-listening to me. In their eyes I've become the curiosity, the case, the one who needs diagnosing.

Dr. Prezic was the resident who'd assisted in the surgery. My eyes flitted across her face. Her smug expression told me that she, as first-person beholder of the episode, had capitalized on it. She'd dispensed the gossip broadly and garnered a bump in status in return.

I considered stopping rounds right in the middle and explaining what had happened, from my own perspective. It was too late, though, to control the narrative. Explaining is losing. As our group moved from one patient room to the next, I could swear I heard someone whisper, "He lost his child, now he's losing his mind."

I soldiered on, ignoring the murmurings as best I could. The third case on the docket was one eerily similar to my failed surgery—a boy with a facial fracture from a skateboarding accident. I asked what procedures were indicated and the residents responded correctly.

I should've asked what they'd do if they encountered an adhesion. I should've used my surgical debacle as an example to them, to make it clear that nothing about craniofacial surgery is cut-and-dried, nothing about it is easy.

Day 143

After waiting a week for an appointment to see Dr. Thurman, nothing good came of it.

When I walked into her office she didn't bother with pleasantries. The sofa, that old grandmother of a sofa, received me into her sagging lap. She gathered me in, dolefully welcoming the errant child after his long absence. Her bony skeleton shifted beneath my rear end.

"So what's this all about?" was Dr. Thurman's entree.

"You mean the surgery? A routine error."

"I heard something different."

"Don't give too much credence to rumors."

"I heard from Ji-young, and she heard from the surgical team."

"That's third-hand."

"Then tell me yourself."

I explained the procedure in minute detail, so there'd be no mistaking that everything I did had a medical purpose and precedent. She'd have no way to gainsay it then.

But when I finished, she said, "That doesn't match up."

"No? In what particular?"

"Was this traction force decided on with your team beforehand? Ji-young says it wasn't. And more than that—she says it wasn't called for."

"It *was* called for. I just explained my rationale. You're not a surgeon. A surgeon knows you can't anticipate every problem you'll encounter beforehand. And you can't envision every solution you'll need to attempt."

"There were other solutions, better solutions, I was told."

"You were told wrong. Ji-young's a cardiologist. I made my best judgment based on medical knowledge and surgical experience."

Thurman clamped her mouth shut and tucked her lips inside, like a child thinking she could hide chewing gum from the teacher. Then she opened it with that familiar pop and said, "The bleeding was so heavy."

"Moderately heavy, yes."

"How did you control it?"

I was about to reply, but in the fraction of a second it took to open my mouth, something threw me off.

I couldn't remember. I had no recollection of that part of the surgery. The next thing I could recall was the patient being closed up, which Prezic had taken care of.

Recovering quickly, I was able to give Thurman a reasonable account, filling in the blanks with what I would've done in such a circumstance. It sounded quite realistic, in my humble opinion.

The entire time I talked, she leaned forward with her elbows propped on the desk, making no comment. When I finished, she consulted her laptop notes. "All that bleeding. No good for the eyes. Damaged the optic nerve, yes?"

I told her I was well aware of that—I'd seen the patient post-surgery several times already.

"In both eyes I think," Thurman said.

"That was the unfortunate result."

She looked up from her screen. "So now that little girl is permanently blind. Is that right?"

"Yes, the patient lost her sight due to complications of the surgery resulting from her accident."

Thurman shook her head. "You should've kept seeing me before. Now the bar is so high for you to do surgery again." She trained her scope-eye on me. "And that little girl has a name. It's Zoe."

Day 144

The hell with humility. The hell with holding back for Rosie's sake. This morning I needed someone to discuss these events with, someone other than Dr. Thurman.

Rosie was in the kitchen. I went in with a plan to tell her.

I found her leaning against the rim of the sink, washing dishes. Her hair was pulled up in a messy, girlish knot on top of her head. I saw her for a moment as the vulnerable and trusting young woman I'd married so many years ago. Maybe that's why this wouldn't work. That's why I couldn't confide this predicament to her. Just seeing her like that.

So instead, I asked her where the bleach was.

She turned toward me and dried her hands on a towel. "What do you need bleach for?"

"Is it not sufficient that the master of the house desires it?"

She went on the defensive, claiming she merely wanted to know if it was for that wine stain on my dress shirt, which she could take care of for me. "I just wanted to help," she added, pursing her lips and looking at me in expectation.

In expectation of what—an explanation? An apology?

I suppose that the humble person would've proffered both. I was not that person though. Not today. Not after yesterday's meeting with Dr. Thurman. Today Butt-cheeks was in charge. I glared at Rosie so as to reject any and every expectation.

She glared right back as if to say, "Even now, and even in this small way, still you deny me."

When I said nothing further, she turned on her heel and left the room in a huff.

Well, not in a huff. She is anything but a huffy person. However, she walked out with more purpose, more determination, I might even say more frustration, than she typically evinces in such an exchange.

A minute later she returned, plunked the bleach bottle on the counter, and turned it so the label faced me. Then she left the room without a word.

Day 146

I don't see an avenue to explain to Rosie what's happened. I can't have her questioning me or looking at me with pity. So I'm sticking to my usual schedule, and just holing up in my office.

I'll see my patients and be extra pleasant with them. I can squander plenty of time with them now—they'll appreciate that. Word will get out what a compassionate doctor I am. The online reviews will rave.

So I'll have to manufacture a reason as to why I can't operate right now. My patients and their parents won't have heard about the botched surgery—the hospital keeps such incidents under wraps. I'll say I'm having a problem with my vision. That's at least a partial truth.

I strolled through my rose garden today, although the temperature was well into the nineties and the percent humidity not far behind. I haven't paid much heed to my roses this summer, and now the best of the blooms are spent. Every bush is riddled with brown masses of petals, sagging and shriveling. Even now, with time on my hands, I can't seem to muster the needed energy to deadhead them.

They're oddly comforting, these dead flowers. Their presence tells me everything will be all right. Everything will turn out fine because I too, will die. When I'm dead and decaying, all my problems will be over.

Day 150

I was scheduled to see Dr. Thurman today. I'd waited for this day. I need resolution. She called out sick, though, and now can't see me for another week.

I need an all-day appointment with her. One long session to hash it out and be done with it. Surely she must be cognizant of how this limbo affects me, how the uncertainty and the excess free time that I should be spending in surgery wreak havoc with my thoughts and spirit.

I blame her for my brief memory lapse the other day. I remember it now, every moment of that procedure and why I did what I did. I just need the chance to tell her.

Day 151

I have trouble bringing Michaelina's face to mind without aid of a photograph. Spending so much time in my office, though, means too much time to look at the framed picture of her on my desk. She's frozen there. In the most prosaic sense, she's become a set of facts—when and where she was born, eye color, height attained, etc. To others, she's just a scrap of history like all who've lived and died, a mere sentence in the cosmic Wikipedia. I want her to move, to change, to grow. But there's none of that now. I suppose that's what eternity is.

But I can't accept that. There's got to be something more.

Until now, I believed that with her death the Wikipedia entry was finished and done with, the tab closed. Nothing more would or could be added.

I was mistaken though. Her bodily existence was just part of what I've come to see as her life. I refer not to the cliché that a deceased loved one continues "living on in our hearts." I embrace her remembrance, yes, but no new memories are made, so there's no "living on." Some people claim they feel a strong presence of their loved one, or even receive a nocturnal visit from the person's spirit. Those notions strike me as highly dubious, and are far from my own experience of the complete loss of Michaelina's presence.

Nonetheless, Michaelina's existence, set in grand motion at the moment of her conception, didn't grind to a halt the instant she died. At first I viewed her brief life as a wind-up clock whose ticking slowed and then came to a complete stop. Now, though, it seems more like a snowball that gains both mass and momentum as it rolls down a mountain. Or like a fish that leaps and breaks the surface of a lake. When it drops below, wavelets form and spread; the interconnected ripples reverberate over the entire lake. In time they fade away and the water is calm again. However, even if the surface becomes like glass, the water molecules in the lake have been permanently re-arranged, forever disrupted and influenced by that unique event.

Michaelina is gone, but not the disruption and rearrangement. I'm not a mere observer in this disruption—the undercurrent of her existence continues to affect me. My plan for humility helps keep her present. I lie in the shallow water of her life and feel it wash over me.

Day 152

I was the one who composed Michaelina's obituary. Before writing it I studied examples to see how it was done. Listing surviving relatives was easy, though it pained me to include the Jackass. Even typing out his name—John—almost made me ill. No doubt it pleased Rosie to see it there. And I was already in the business of pleasing her, no matter how conflicted it made me feel.

Some obituaries mention, if vaguely, the cause of death, as in, 'passed away after a brief illness,' or 'passed peacefully at home.' What was I to say? That Michaelina died as a result of penetrating torso trauma? In the end, I put nothing—just the cold hard fact of her decease. Everyone knew the cause anyway.

I couldn't bear to share my favorite photo of her from my office, so I asked Rosie to choose something.

In times past, people would bring flowers. That custom has fallen into some disuse, except for the ones thrown onto the casket in the grave. (Roses are generally chosen; for Michaelina it was daisies.) The delivery of large floral arrangements has been replaced by the pecuniary request to donate to a specific charity.

On this front I was again flummoxed. I wasn't much for giving to charities per se. In my understanding, most are run by shysters with exorbitant salaries who may as well be funneling the money into the sewer, for all the good it does anyone. I figured, and rightly enough, that the time and effort I gave to my patients, despite being compensated for it, was my contribution to humanity.

It would sit well with the public, however, if I established a foundation in Michaelina's name, with contributions going to some destitute waifs in a Third World country who needed cleft-lip operations.

But I couldn't do it. That's not what Michaelina's life was about. I toyed with the idea of starting a Foundation to Support the Study of Princesshood. That would've excited her.

In the end, though, I once again put nothing, and just hoped we wouldn't be inundated with flora.

Day 153

What if, instead of dying, Michaelina had been merely disfigured? What if she'd only lost her eyesight? Blindness is a relative inconvenience in the larger panorama of existence—blind people get used to it and learn not to mind it. Zoe will get used to it. She'll be okay.

Faces are complex. A child's face is expected to be smooth and seamless. Even small scars are noticeable and can be intimidating. Disfigured kids win a sort of reverse lottery. It's difficult for them to comprehend their status, why they've been singled out, why other people can perceive them as aliens in this world. Surely, though, the disfigurement can be gotten used to, the same way deafness or blindness can. Still, it's hard.

That's why my son's behavior rankles me so. If anyone's won the lottery of life, he has. Born into a stable family with excellent financial prospects and two caring parents, he squanders it. How many times did I use the example of these disfigured children to help him recognize his advantages and learn to make good use of them?

Day 155

With Michaelina gone, I'm helpless to stop my careening thoughts from veering in my son's direction. We'd named him John, a strong and sturdy name, but Rosie called him Jack. On occasion, making me cringe, she even called him Jackie. To counter that, in his adolescence I began referring to him as the Jackass.

Sometimes, I'll admit, I even called him Jackass to his face. Rosie blanched at that. She couldn't understand that my addressing him as such was motivated by concern, not dislike. Couldn't she see that I'd never call a stranger *Jackass*, at least not to his face? Only someone I cared about, as a father cared about his son. Only someone who allowed me no other way to express my deep parental desire for him to change his ways, to better himself, to find success and thus happiness.

Anyway, it's been over six years since I've last seen him. It was about a year before my father died. I do regret that I didn't visit my own father in his last years. And now, I'm developing a fear that I'll die without ever seeing my son again.

I'd forgive him if only he asked. Or would I? I picture him requesting an audience with me. When he walks into my office, he's apologetic, remorseful for all he's put me through, for coming between Rosie and me, for being greedy and disrespectful. He tells me he wants nothing more than to be the kind of son I've always wanted.

But that wouldn't be enough. I wouldn't be able to stop myself from ensuring he soaked up his share of blame for the underhanded relationship with his mother that caused his sister's death.

Day 156

I've made good use of my own gifts and talents. That entailed sacrifices in young adulthood—late-night studying, financial struggles. And even in recent years it's meant working outrageous hours, attending conferences to keep up with developments in my field, and of course dealing regularly with the difficulties and decisions facing these children and their parents.

Why does society demand more than this? I've devoted my life to repairing faces. Why isn't the world content with that? The bank teller isn't satisfied to handle my transaction discreetly; she's compelled to engage me in lively conversation, goading me with her loud banter into wishing her a nice day. I don't care whether she has a nice day, and I won't be manipulated into saying so.

I prefer my barber, Harris. For fifteen years he's been trimming my hair. He's earned the right to say good morning to me and ask me about my day. Even so, he doesn't abuse the privilege. He offers an occasional pleasantry, but for the most part we communicate in silence, just as it should be. He knows what I want done and he does it.

His is an old-style shop—no wall-length mirrors to examine yourself while the barber works. When he finishes, he offers me a hand mirror. I wave it away. It's become a kind of ritual, my way of complimenting him—*I trust you've done your usual first-rate job.* I tip him generously too. That's why my chair is always waiting for me when I arrive for my regular appointment.

But the rest of the world hasn't caught on. I glare at the bank tellers and they still think it's in their power to make me smile, if only they're more persistent.

As for the nurses and the rest of the hospital staff, I just want them to do their work. I dislike being pitied or a subject of gossip. They all heard about Michaelina's death—many attended the funeral. I've felt even more removed from them ever since. And now, with surgery on the girl Zoe having gone awry, the whispering and furtive looks have increased. Maybe that's part of what makes my efforts with Rosie a little less cumbersome. She understands me, at least on a rudimentary level, when the rest of the world doesn't.

And she misses Michaelina too. She hides it, knowing I abhor crying and carrying on. But I've sometimes seen the light on in Michaelina's bedroom when I come home in the evening. Patton barks as I pull up, and the light goes off. What she does in that room I have no idea. Maybe she lies in Michaelina's bed and stares up at the canopy. Maybe she hugs Michaelina's stuffed animals. Maybe she smells Michaelina's pillow to see if she can bring back the memories.

I eschew such sentimentality, yet I can't ask her to clean out the room and get rid of Michaelina's things. We'll probably need to move from this house before that'll happen.

I don't enter Michaelina's room at all.

Day 157

Before Dr. Thurman could say a word today, I told her I now recalled with greater clarity my efforts to stop the bleeding in the recent failed operation. The one I performed on Zoe.

She wouldn't allow me to tell her, however. She said those details didn't matter now.

"Why not?"

"Because you didn't tell me the truth in the first place."

I wanted to tell her that it wasn't a matter of honesty, that I'd simply blanked out on the memory. But that would sound far worse.

"To get your problem figured out," she said, "you need to show some honesty. Be honest with me and with yourself."

I leaned back in the soft lap of the sofa, but found no comfort there. I was just so tired. I couldn't imagine where this line of questioning would lead. I only knew it promised to bog me down for weeks to come. I wanted to get back to surgery, to make up for what happened with Zoe. But Thurman was perversely drawing everything out.

"Let's start here," she said. "You act as if your daughter's death didn't mess with your psyche. As if it didn't affect you at all."

I weighed my response and decided I could admit to that if it'd move things along. "Of course it's affected me," I said in my best offhand manner.

"Tell me how."

I considered keeping the mood light by cracking a joke about reduced food and clothing expenditures but decided against it. Instead, I returned to the previous issue and said, "Honesty is overrated."

"*Hoo*." She tapped her pen on the desk and said, "Are you honest with your wife at least?"

"It's easy to be honest with her. She has no power over me."

That's what I said, anyway.

She switched the position of her legs under the desk, moving the left one to the back and grinding her toes into the carpet.

"An assignment for you," she said. "A little work. Before next time, think of sometime you were dishonest and what happened."

"How is that relevant to my competence to operate?"

"I'm just thinking. Maybe if you can see the problem with dishonesty, and learn to tell the truth in small things, we can work up to big things."

Day 160

What the hell am I supposed to tell Thurman? If I truly felt the need to unburden myself, I'd talk to a priest in the confessional.

But I'm not interested in that leap. I've made my choices. What value is there in that sort of forgiveness? And if I went down that road, everything would be on the table. It wouldn't be just about the paltry dishonesties.

I'm not convinced, as I tried to tell Thurman, that prevarication is such a negative thing. My own relationships wouldn't survive without it. A well-told lie avoids a lot of angst, heartache, and inconvenience. Honesty, on the other hand, requires an immense amount of time and self-explanation.

Besides, my larger problem isn't dishonesty—if anything I'm too honest. Too often I make observations that are better left unsaid, or I tell people information they don't want to hear.

Still, I do wish I could be more forthcoming with Rosie, especially about what's been happening at the hospital. If only she could listen a little more dispassionately. She carries her emotions too close to the surface. I need to spare her—and myself.

And I still need to come up with a story to satisfy Thurman.

Day 162

Rosie asked me today why I haven't talked about my surgeries lately.

I told her a partial truth. I said I was experiencing occasional blurred vision and that I needed to take a break from surgery until I saw an eye doctor and got it cleared up.

She voiced concern and asked when my appointment was.

I said I'd be making it soon.

Day 164

Rarely was I ever sharp with Michaelina. One time, though, when sitting down to pay some bills at my desk, I found her name, MICHAELINA, etched into the surface. She'd pressed down hard, with my Camlin pen no less, embossing the letters into the varnish. The M was fairly small, but each successive letter increased in size, until the final *A* more or less screamed at me.

I brought her over to my desk and confronted her.

"Mom said to practice my name," she said matter-of-factly, turning her small face up to mine.

"On paper," I said. "Now I'll have to have the desktop sanded and refinished. You've ruined it."

Her rosebud lips tightened and began working. A shine burnished her eyes.

Irritated though I was—and I was mightily irritated—I managed to hold back further remonstration. I relaxed my frown, and put my finger to my bottom lip in apology for my outburst.

Her expression changed instantly. She nodded her forgiveness and wrapped her arms around my legs, then danced off to her next project.

I never did get around to getting that desktop refinished.

Day 171

Today, during my appointment with Thurman, I tried to get away with a few simple admissions of dishonesty. The white lie type. She'd been the one to suggest that small dishonesties would be a start.

So I mentioned that I didn't tell Rosie when a dress was unflattering, and that I didn't admit to the state cop who pulled me over that I'd had a couple glasses of wine at dinner.

She dismissed these examples with a wave of her hand. "Not helpful."

When I had no others to offer, she asked me why I didn't wear a wedding ring. That was a better example of dishonesty, she said.

"Plenty of men don't wear wedding rings," I said.

"Why not you?" She smoothed her hair down. "In American culture it's normal, yes?"

"It's an annoyance during surgery."

"You're not doing surgeries."

"I still see patients. I still wash my hands. That ring is a haven for bacteria. Besides, I do put it on when I get home. If I think of it."

She didn't seem satisfied, so I added, "I've never lied about being married."

"But you don't offer that information."

That line of questioning seemed downright silly and I told her so. Who goes around announcing marital status?

"Fine," she said. "Then you give me a better example."

All I could think of was the big omission. The one lie I'd never tell her about.

She persisted. "Most people are dishonest quite frequently. I just want one real example."

I came up with something else I thought might satisfy her. I said I hadn't fully admitted to Rosie why I was suspended from surgery.

She leaned forward in her chair and activated her scope-eye. "Why not? It's been weeks now."

"Yes, well, I expected it to be temporary."

"Maybe you're avoiding her anger."

"No. Rosie'd never be angry about something like that."

"Then why?"

Pride was the reason. But I said, "I don't like to concern her."

"That's the job of a spouse, isn't it, to be concerned? If your wife was having, to take a random example, a mental health problem, you'd want to know, wouldn't you?"

"I'm not having mental health problems."

"*Hoo*. So defensive. I never said you were."

She was insinuating it at the least. She and I argued the point until the session was nearly over.

My next assignment, she said, was to tell Rosie the complete truth and come back and report the result.

Day 172

I resented Thurman worming herself into my home life. Still, I convinced myself that humility would be served by acceding to her demand. So, while Rosie was reheating my dinner tonight, I gave her more details about the surgery that didn't turn out well. Not all the details—just enough, I hoped, to satisfy both her and Thurman.

Rosie wanted to know if the problem had been caused by my blurred vision, and I said no—there'd been more bleeding than expected but we'd gotten it under control. The child's life was saved.

Rosie's look of relief was gratifying.

Because it was such a close call, however, and because of procedures I'd unexpectedly needed to employ, the case was being reviewed, I told her. The legal staff needed to ensure the hospital would incur no liability. I'd been asked to allow other surgeons to step in temporarily until the matter was resolved.

She appeared perplexed by this, but I discouraged further questioning. I didn't tell her about Zoe's blindness.

Day 175

Once, around two years ago, I took Rosie with me to a medical conference. At times it could be useful—professionally—to have your spouse seated at your side. And Rosie could look downright marvelous when circumstances called for it. I could usually depend on her to act appropriately—staying close by and regarding me approvingly, or at least complacently. Easy enough, as she was generally too intimidated in the presence of such an assemblage of well-educated minds to venture much conversation anyway.

On this particular occasion, however, one of the other wives latched onto Rosie. They talked and giggled. This woman kept refilling Rosie's glass, encouraging her to drink more than was good for her.

Some background here. There are several kinds of doctors' wives. The first type is an equal—physician married to physician. The two usually meet in med school or residency. If these wives come to a conference like this it's because they want to network or flaunt their equality or because their husbands guilted them into it. The second kind is nurses, who've managed to snag a doctor in his first hospital assignment. The third type is one like Rosie, who captures a husband early, before he even enters med school, before the poor guy even realizes his worth. Most of these wives are dropped once the husband gets established in practice and finds a younger, more glamorous mate, which constitutes the fourth kind—the trophy wife.

Anyway, Rosie is usually too cowed to talk much to wives number one and two, or the trophy wives. When she sniffs out one of her own ilk, however—type number three—watch out. I should've realized what was happening but was caught up in an actual useful conversation, rare at these events, with a craniofacial surgeon from New Guinea, who was describing an experimental method for cleft palate repair. Doctors are freer to experiment in economically underdeveloped countries, as whatever they do for such victims renders them heroes. Here, on the other hand, if you try something new and it's not 100% successful, you go down the litigation tube.

The chuckling on the other side of the table became louder and less controlled. I looked in their direction. The wife that Rosie was conversing with winked and tittered while mumbling something I couldn't quite make out.

Rosie, almost choking with laughter, whispered something back to her—I was sure I heard the name *Mac* in there somewhere—and they both roared. The whole table, and even the nearby ones, turned to look.

I glared at her, but she was too far gone to notice. I addressed her across the table, calling her Eurosia to get her attention, but even that didn't work. I would've grabbed her by the arm and hauled her out of there, if such a move wouldn't have made me appear ridiculous. Instead, I had to wait until the dinner was over. In the parking lot I lashed out at her, then refused normal conversation.

Thereafter, I wouldn't sit with her at the dining room table, instead taking my plate into my study. If I had to communicate something, I'd text it, or use Michaelina as a go-between. "Please ask your mother when dinner will be ready," or "Please inform your mother that the salmon is dry," even when Rosie was in the room.

Michaelina would respond with gusto. It was pretty funny, hearing a three-year old say, "The sammin is dwy."

Later, Rosie confronted me, asking me why I wasn't talking to her.

I said, "What do you mean? I'm talking to you right now."

"That's not what I mean, and you know it."

Her protest only impressed upon me the effectiveness of my strategy. I wouldn't give in to her groveling. Sure, I grew tired of maintaining that stance of silence. Even though she was the one being punished, it wasn't all that pleasant for me.

However, there was no smooth exit strategy, no way to extricate myself without appearing to be caving in. I can't recall even now how we eventually returned to the status quo, but it took more than a month.

While instant forgiveness is an impossibility, I do desire to be free of this method and its consequences.

Do I have free will or don't I? Next time, no matter how rankled I am, I promise myself I'll speak to Rosie—pleasantly—within an hour.

Day 179

I told Thurman today that I'd explained my surgery suspension to Rosie.

"Such a relief, yes? Good for the spirit," Thurman said.

"Sure, sure," I said.

In reality, it wasn't a relief at all. I'd given Rosie just enough details to be concerned, while not enough information to be able to discuss ongoing repercussions with her openly. I was living in a no-man's land of honesty.

So it hadn't been a success. In Thurman's, view, though, she'd achieved something. She pumped her leg under the desk. "We'll work on this problem more. No more lying. No more avoiding. No more telling me, telling yourself, that everything's A-okay. Okay?"

Then she went on a long harangue about repression (only she called it "stuffing down your feelings") and how it can lead to mental illness. How some people don't develop psychological disorders until well into middle age. How it can be set off by a traumatic event.

I listened patiently, as I was indeed her patient and had no other choice. We had a few words back and forth. I explained that my mind was healthy and strong and I wasn't going to let her drag me down into a diagnosis just to satisfy some pet theory of hers.

She didn't appear perturbed by my response in the least. She didn't even engage her scope-eye while I spoke. That annoyed me—it seemed as if she wasn't listening, that she was discounting everything I said out of hand.

We were getting nowhere. But then I came up with an idea to throw her a bone.

I shifted on the sofa, trying to sit up a little higher, a little straighter. I needed to be on eye level with her for the admission I'd prepared myself to make.

"My vision," I said. "Once or twice it's blurred on me."

She planted the palms of her hands on her desk and drew a long breath for her next barrage. "You were crying when it happened?" *No.* "Some discharge maybe?" *No.* "You're seeing an eye doctor?" *No.* "Clear vision is pretty necessary for a surgeon I think."

"I'm not doing any surgeries right now."

"How long is this been bothering you?"

I told her I couldn't recall, but believed the problem had cleared up on its own.

"So. You had it for a while." She leaned forward and almost whispered. "Is that problem what caused you to mess up the surgery on Zoe?"

"No."

"Has it happened any time you were operating?"

"Not that comes to mind."

She crossed her arms. "'Not that comes to mind.' *Hoo.* Mr. Precision Surgeon! Not so precise in our recollections, eh? Not remembering on purpose—that's what I see. The way of the liar." She was quick to add, "Not that I'm saying you're a liar. Only some people that don't remember too easily are."

I ignored that and continued pursuing my plan. "I'm suggesting to you that perhaps these couple of incidents of unsettled vision relate to my psychological upset over my daughter's death. Opening up about it to you will clear it from my psyche."

"Just like that?"

"Just like that. But I could also submit to a thorough eye exam. If an ophthalmologist certifies my vision is healthy, that will indicate the problem has been dealt with. In which case, will you then sign off for me to return to surgery?"

She raised her brows so high at my suggestion I thought they might fly off her forehead.

I reiterated my plan since she didn't seem to fully comprehend it. Following through with the appointment would have the added benefit of getting Rosie off my back. She's brought it up several times now.

"Of course. Good idea," she said. Then she added, "You've told Ji-young about this, right? And the other doctors?"

"I haven't had the opportunity. And now, since I'm not operating, it seems immaterial."

She said, "Blurred vision—a serious thing." She typed in some notes. "And your not telling anyone is worse."

I thought of the nausea I'd had in surgery. I'd successfully hidden that from the team too. In my mind, none of this constituted dishonesty. It was self-preservation. Besides, the surgeries were completed satisfactorily. Regarding the one that wasn't, I hadn't had any vision or nausea problems then. The blanking out—I'm less sure about that. I have to believe, though, that the memory lapse was an isolated incident. This psychiatrist was probably the cause. Clueless as she is, she has a way of preying on my mental state. If I can prove to her I'm mentally fit, and be rid of her, these issues will disappear.

So I said brightly, "Well, I've admitted it now, so that's progress, isn't it?" I lifted my chin to emphasize my optimism. "I'll make that ophthalmologist appointment tomorrow. As soon as I have confirmation that my vision problem is corrected, I'll stop by and drop off a copy with your nurse. We won't even need to meet again."

Her jaw dropped. "What? Not so fast. An eye appointment's good, but how can that doctor know if you'll have the problem again next time you're operating?"

I threw my hands in the air. "What kind of a catch-22 are you pulling on me? You're saying I can't operate because of a vision problem that I can't prove won't affect my surgical judgment because you won't allow me to perform surgery."

"I signed off once already, and see where that brought us." She smoothed her hair. "But go ahead, see the eye doctor. We'll discuss then."

Then she narrowed one eye and observed me. "I'm going out of the country for a few weeks."

Another delay. What was I supposed to feel—anxiety, relief, elation? Whatever my internal response, I wasn't going to let her in on it.

Day 182

The more Thurman harasses me about my mental state, the more I'm determined to prove her wrong. I ought to be able to control myself. That's why it was maddening today when I couldn't follow through. It's as if the very act of making a resolution brings on a cosmic, unpassable test of it.

This evening, Rosie wanted to show me an article about some craniofacial surgery being conducted by Doctors Without Borders. She's hinted over the years that I ought to volunteer time with them, but I see no need to travel to a destitute country when there's plenty of work to do right here. And the fact is, those countries have their own way of dealing with these problems. Children with facial deformities are kept at home, where they can be of service and receive some measure of familial love, avoiding shame and bullying in the outside world. I'm not saying that's ideal, but it's better than institutionalization.

In this country, on the other hand, we no longer have such institutions for children, and keeping them home is considered tantamount to abuse. So there's no choice for parents of severely deformed children. Many of them are forced to run the years-long gauntlet of multiple facial surgeries. And I'm integral to that effort. Or I was.

Back to the point at hand. Consistent with my humility goal, I accompanied Rosie over to my desk to view the news article. I wondered (aloud) why she hadn't pulled up the article in advance.

She didn't answer, instead diving right into her search. Her method of using the mouse makes it swerve all over the place such that the cursor can't be located easily on the screen. I could barely restrain myself from reaching over and grabbing it from her.

There followed several minutes of fruitless searching, during which I was forced to tolerate her innumerable clucking noises of surprise when the article didn't pop up when she expected it to. I asked her where she'd seen it in the first place.

"I think on Facebook."

In a huff, I provided her with more precise search terms that enabled her to find the piece—a story from several years ago about doctors in Bangladesh, information I'd heard long ago at a conference. Outdated, irrelevant information.

She was hinting at something, too, making an underhanded suggestion.

That intimation only added to my fury. All thoughts of my plan for humility flew out the window like so many screeching crows. I reprimanded her and left the room.

Day 188

Today was better.

True, Rosie did nothing to try my patience. When I walked in the door, she greeted me pleasantly, then went to the kitchen to re-warm my dinner. I sat down at the table and poured myself a glass of wine.

I invited Rosie to sit down with me, and told her about my day. I informed her I'd seen the ophthalmologist, who had found no problems.

She wanted to know if I'd be returning to surgery and I said yes, soon.

Day 189

I did in fact see the ophthalmologist. I'll take the documentation to Thurman, although I'm not sure what good it'll do. She's determined to thwart me.

I do want to get back to surgery, and yet it won't be the same as before.

These last few years, I'd carved out time from my busy schedule for Michaelina. She infused my life with a pleasure that was different from the satisfactions arising from my own achievements. In fact, those achievements were muted in comparison to simply being with Michaelina.

When she lay dying in her hospital bed, I contemplated life without her. And the way she died—

But I can't go through this again.

Day 192

Memories churn, replaying incessantly. I can't find solace—not even giving a ritual rubdown to Patton relieves me. I couldn't write more in my journal yesterday, nor did my disturbed thoughts end when my writing did. They plagued me well into the evening, flooding my mind, seeming to soak my pillow at night. My brief interludes of unconsciousness couldn't be labeled sleep, broken up as they were by flashes of panic in which I jerked upright, fighting for breath.

Today, I encountered Michaelina's ghostly image everywhere—on the street, in the hospital elevator, on the news. Every attempt to evade the intrusive recollections only brought them on more strongly, like telling oneself not to think of a purple elephant.

Rosie watched me. She tried to disguise her concern, none too successfully. I'm not sure if that made me feel better or worse.

How has she become the one with the greater emotional authority? It wasn't that way on the day of the accident. That day, when we realized

Michaelina had been hit, Rosie became hysterical, sobbing and wringing her hands. The moment the police got out of the squad car, she said, "I'm sorry, I'm sorry," repeating it while she stood over Michaelina. The police asked her what happened. Her reply was largely unintelligible. The word 'accident' came out several times. They turned to me for confirmation, and I managed to choke out, "Yes, an accident."

"How did it happen?" they asked.

"We didn't know she'd gone outside," I said.

Rosie started to say something more but couldn't put two words together. The ambulance had arrived by then, and the paramedics began firing questions at us—blood type, allergies to medications, that sort of thing. They lifted Michaelina onto a stretcher and loaded her into the ambulance. Rosie and I climbed in behind them.

Ambulances are fast, but they're not teleportation. Every fraction of a second spent inside that vehicle tore further at my insides. Never before had I felt such impatience, such urgency, and such an utter lack of agency. The constraints of time frustrated me in their paradoxical nature. Time had to go faster to speed us to the hospital, while slowing down to prevent Michaelina's bodily processes from shutting down before we arrived.

The paramedic pumped intervals of oxygen into her lungs. Her heart still beat, still carried on its plaintive rhythm within its broken little cage. Every moment, though, I feared her flitting away.

Rosie rocked herself, or maybe she was just swaying with the vehicle. She was probably praying. I didn't look at her.

I didn't believe I could ever look at her again.

Day 193

In the hospital, we were pushed out of the way while the emergency team worked on Michaelina. A nurse asked us how it happened. The question only renewed Rosie's hysterics. Another nurse pulled her aside to administer a shot of sedative.

Meanwhile, I pushed my way into the ER, which, because of my admitting privileges at that hospital, was initially allowed. The medical team monitored Michaelina's heartbeat, performed a scan, and prepped her for surgery.

I insisted on staying. I'd wash, suit up, help in any way I could. Once they realized I was her father, they wouldn't hear of it. There were words, heated ones. I didn't touch anyone though—they needn't have called security.

I hovered outside the door but wasn't permitted to stay there either. I found myself relegated to the waiting room with Rosie. We sat, not together on the sofa, but in two chairs across from each other. Neither of us spoke.

The frenzied rush of the previous 40 minutes came to an abrupt halt, at least for us. We could only sit and wait. Some sort of intake clerk and a social worker came into the waiting room. The clerk was a beanpole man with chiclet teeth, and the social worker an expansive, thin-lipped matron who sighed a lot.

I answered the clerk's administrative questions, mostly about insurance. Then the social worker asked what happened. I recalled what Rosie had told the police. I understood what she'd meant by her words, by her apology. She was admitting that her disobedience, her disloyalty to me, caused this tragedy, and she was sorry. But it was only when faced with the social worker's question that I realized how the police must have interpreted her answer. By dint of her apology, they may have made some incorrect inferences. Her agitation, in contrast with my horrified but silent demeanor, no doubt reinforced their suppositions.

So there we sat, answering the social worker's mundane questions, while down the hall they were slicing through Michaelina's abdominal wall to salvage her internal organs. At that moment, in the midst of my agony, I was being asked to describe the accident. I knew what I needed to say—I just had no idea how to do it.

The brain performs funny tricks at such times. The words hung on my lips like icicles on an eave—heavy, suspended, poised to drop, but frozen in place. I couldn't summon the mindset required to release them. I wasn't used to explaining myself.

Even now, it's difficult for me to recall a specific instance when I've been fully to blame for something serious. The reality is, I'm an exceedingly conscientious person, as is necessary in my line of work. I'm careful, aware, meticulous. Carelessness springs from people who are unthinking, distracted, lazy, or just plain ignorant. In my experience, when mistakes are made it's virtually always someone else's fault. If not the actual deed, then the underlying cause.

For example, there was the time I side-swiped an old clunker downtown and sheared off its door. It was hardly my fault that the street was so narrow, and no way could I have anticipated the driver stupidly opening her door just as I was passing. My insurance company paid out, because of some arcane insurance rule. No reasonable person would've blamed me.

Have I ever made a mistake in surgery, one that was my fault? Of course. All surgeons make errors. But the mistakes I've made have been just that—mistakes. For instance, several years ago I operated on a difficult Apert's case, in which I needed to advance an infant's supraorbital rim. I made a couple of cuts near the part of the bone that would be removed. After sawing through the skull, I performed a strip craniectomy and fastened a plate with resorbable screws. I encountered an unexpected difficulty in anchoring the plate at the temple. An error was made with respect to a nerve. The procedure is incredibly involved, the need for precision absolute. It's like connecting the ends of two blond hairs in a container of lemon Jell-O, without touching the massive tangle of brown hairs surrounding them. It's a miracle I don't make more errors than I do. I don't consider these so much personal mistakes as occupational probabilities, an inevitable result of conducting myriad procedures.

Surgeries aside, for every personal mistake I've made, there's always been a mitigating factor—fatigue after a long day, being pressed for time, not having gotten in my morning run, etc. I don't stand for excuses generally. In my case, though, they're justified. That sounds sanctimonious, but there's truth to it. The common man isn't spending hours in the operating room, or enduring the stress of parents who depend on you for the futures of their children.

In my personal life, Rosie is typically to blame when events don't proceed according to plan. Any sane person with a window into our world would agree. As I've made clear, she was at fault in Michaelina's death too—she admitted as much when she apologized to the police.

In the hospital, though, I was too stunned to explain all this. The social worker stood there sighing and pursing her lips. There was just no way to phrase it, to make it clear that even though I was the one at the wheel, Rosie's actions had been the underlying cause. She'd instigated the tragedy by blatantly flouting my orders about the Jackass. But if I put it that way, it would sound self-serving.

The social worker sighed again, looking at me as a farmer regards a cow that won't move into her stall.

It was time to speak. I was having difficulty, however, formulating the right words.

Then Rosie blurted out, "We were in the house talking. I needed to go to the grocery store. I didn't watch out for Michaelina. My husband's a doctor. He did CPR." Then she looked at me, her face blank and bloodless. In a voice as hollow as a dead volcano, she said, "My husband saved her life."

I stared at Rosie in stupefaction. Just as she'd done with the police, she was implying that she'd been the one to hit Michaelina. It made me wonder for a moment if it were true. In my distress, maybe I was the one who wasn't thinking straight. Was it possible I had the story wrong? If only I did!

Rosie had stopped crying. Her eyes, though, were wide and glassy.

I attribute what happened next to the nightmarish situation. I was muddled and confused. The social worker turned to me and asked for my version of events. This was my opportunity to clarify, to correct the record.

I hesitated.

Day 194

Anyone could appreciate the complexity. Offering a different version would bring up more questions, particularly if I outright contradicted my wife. And Rosie had probably told this version to the ER nurse too. I wanted to interrupt the whole process, to take Rosie aside and ask her what she meant by all this. But I couldn't. Not here. I was a doctor in this very hospital.

And I was so mentally exhausted. My thoughts desperately sought shelter, a place of rest where they could turn away from this thing happening to me. More than anything, I wanted to be left in peace, even though I knew, at a deep level, there was no peace to be had.

I couldn't take being questioned. I couldn't put into words the reality of events. I could focus only on Michaelina, who at that moment was under the surgeon's knife, suspended between life and no life. With no understanding of Rosie's motivation, I couldn't parse or address her response. Surely it'd be better to sort it out later, when I could discuss it with her privately.

So I swallowed and said, "Yes, we didn't realize Michaelina had gone outside. When I came out, I saw she'd been hit. I did CPR. Once her heart was going I called 911."

None of this was a lie, by the way. I didn't explicitly accuse Rosie; I never claimed she was the driver.

Ironically, avoiding an overt accusation made me look magnanimous, as if I were trying to mitigate my wife's guilt and support her by not blaming her outright. I comforted myself that blame wouldn't matter in the end, anyway. The surgeons here were excellent. Michaelina was breathing. She would live.

Day 195

To this day, I don't know why Rosie said what she did. The possible reasons rattle over the tracks of my brain as I lie in bed at night:

- She was trying to save my reputation as a respected physician—a child saver, not a child killer.
- She believed that I had, in fact, saved Michaelina's life by performing CPR, and didn't think it was fair that I be blamed for the accident.
- She was trying to prevent me from blaming her, by admitting it herself.
- She recognized that she was ultimately to blame anyway, by fraternizing with the Jackass.
- She did it as a way to win back my affections.
- She was too traumatized or doped up to realize what she was saying.

But none of these reasons ring true. The fact is, Rosie's a stickler for the truth. She's big on total honesty, even in the most trivial matters, like returning a 50-cent undercharge to the store—the Abe Lincoln sort of thing. Once, she was in search of a pen so I gave her a whole box that I'd gotten from the supply closet at the hospital. She refused to take even one of them.

Then there was the time she fretted over an insignificant lie I needed her to tell to get us out of a wedding she'd agreed to attend without consulting me first. She couldn't or wouldn't do it.

So if she entertains scruples in such trivial matters, why would she lie about something so consequential?

Day 196

That's the thing—Rosie fashions herself a saint. Oh, she never claims it outwardly—that wouldn't be saintly, would it? But she displays all her little righteous scrupulosities for the world to see. In larger matters, the ones that count most, she's a failure. What she did—taking the blame in that dishonest way—disqualifies her for sainthood.

A saint, to my way of thinking, is someone who doesn't shrink from harsh truths. Saints don't hide from the reality of sin, thinking if they just leave things alone, or just model their own goodness, the sinner will magically mend his ways.

No, a saint displays more courage than that. A saint not only embraces the existence of human weakness, but draws the sinner away from his sins, not by chastisement, shame, or humiliation. Instead, a saint gently pulls back the curtain to let you witness the absurdity of your sins, to see how you've been fooled. The saint has a way of revealing that he, too, was once fooled. Now he's bringing you in on the joke, so you can laugh together. He helps you see that leaving your sins behind isn't so difficult, because he's done it himself.

This is best accomplished without saying anything about the sin. Words provoke reaction; silence invites reflection.

Here's an example. Around a year ago I made an offhand comment to Owen about a new nurse on the surgical staff, or rather, about a body part of hers (a positive comment, by the way). I expected one of the typical replies that men make to keep the conversation going—either an affirmation of my observation, perhaps accompanied by a smirk, or a disagreement with it, maybe by making a comparison to another nurse.

But he did neither. In fact, he said nothing at all, not at first. There was a slight pause in the conversation—very slight—which I now believe was caused by his mentally scrambling for an appropriate response. He ended up saying something like, "Did you know she was born in Ireland?"

His reply was an elegant rebuke of my off-color comment. He didn't reproach me outright, nor make a sarcastic or sanctimonious comment such as, "All our nurses are beautiful and deserve our respect."

No, he acted as if I'd audibly passed gas in polite company. Rather than remark on it and embarrass me, he delicately directed the conversation away from it, graciously assuming that my words must have seeped out by accident. He seemed to recognize that some lesser part of me was giving voice, and not the inner, better part of me. It was both the gentlest and most effective rebuke I'd ever received, chastising me in a way a verbal reprimand never could.

A saint is someone like that—someone whose behavior you desire to emulate, even when you suspect you're incapable of doing so. And a saint isn't someone who takes the fall for you. That only exacerbates your shame and entrenches you in your guilt. It does nothing to pull you out of it.

Day 199

Back at Thurman's today. She's becoming impatient. Psychiatrists aren't supposed to be impatient, are they? She wanted more examples of how I haven't been honest with myself or others. I couldn't give her any more. Only one lie mattered, and that was the last one I'd dream of telling her.

Still, we had to fill the session. She asked me again about my emotional response to the circumstances of Michaelina's death. That question skirted too close to the big omission. I felt the need to provide something meaty to move her away from thoughts of Michaelina, so I told her I was angry with my wife and son. I told her I'd discovered they were in communication. I changed only the timeline, marking it as happening well before the accident.

I played up the fact that they'd both been unspeakably dishonest with me. I wasn't the only one guilty of major errors of omission. Thurman needed to know that.

I expected a bit of understanding in response. A bit of "Okay, I see now why you might not always be truthful." Or at least some recognition that I was suffering too.

But there was none of that. She pushed me into explaining why I'd cut off communication with the Jackass. I clarified that it was *his* decision, not mine. I was only acceding to his wishes.

Thurman tried to convince me that even there I was in the wrong, that it was my responsibility as a father to reach out to my son for reconciliation, as many times as necessary to make it happen. As usual, she demonstrated no real comprehension of my situation.

She's exactly the kind of woman I avoided marrying. The kind who doesn't hesitate to demean you by telling you, or at least implying, that you're behaving like a child. If it weren't for needing her sign-off to get back to surgery, I'd have told her off and never returned.

Day 200

I lay no claims to sainthood for myself. When Rosie does something patently wrong, I point it out to her. Many of her behaviors, however, aren't so much wrong as simply annoying. To draw attention to them is petty, and I despise pettiness.

For example, she often makes this sort of grimace when she first walks into a room, for no apparent reason. Or she'll sprawl herself onto the sofa. Sure, that may have been a beguiling ploy at age 18. I remember, in fact, the very first time she did it. I'd invited her in to see my apartment. We'd gone out a few times and had necked in the back of the theater when she was off work. That's as far as things had progressed, and I had no particular plan to take them further.

On this visit, though, she wore tight jeans and a blousy white top that worked on me in a way I hadn't been expecting. As soon as she entered my living room, she stretched out on the sofa like a cat, elongating the curves of her frame and accentuating those narrow hips. Gravity pulled down the lapel of the white blouse, like a bit of wrapping paper torn open, partially revealing the plump mounds beneath. Her sleek hair fell across them like a veil.

I recall my shock that a girl would position herself so provocatively, but the expression on her face told me she didn't fully realize the invitation her body was sending. My roommate, sitting across from her, leered openly. I shooed him out of the apartment—no one else should be allowed to look at this beautifully-wrapped present, the one I was about to open.

And open it I did.

Considering it now, I think I believe her after all. I believe her claim that she hadn't fully grasped what was happening.

For that matter, had I? I'll admit something here—this wasn't just Rosie's first time, it was mine too. I didn't tell her that though. I wanted her to think I was experienced, that I was taking charge of things, that I knew what was called for and that I'd handle it for the both of us. I'd dated a few other women, but with them, the inexorable inching toward sex was awkward and discomfiting, threatening to reveal those parts of my essence I was unprepared to expose.

With Rosie, those reservations were nowhere to be found. With Rosie it was different. It was worship. I wanted to fall down before her body in adoration, submit myself to it as I never had to an earthly or heavenly entity before. My willingness—no, my eagerness to entwine myself with her, to divulge my essence to her, seemed courageous and virtuous. By connecting with Rosie I was creating something stronger and better. I was completing that part of myself that was wanting.

Only later did I realize that when it was over and we untwined ourselves, the twine held its new shape. That shape had unique twists, ones that meant we now were inextricably formed for each other. I'd ingrained my own lack into hers and made it permanent. It felt as if my need for her would never go away, even when I badly wanted it to.

I should've recognized that episode for the omen it was. I should've been forewarned of what was to come, of how that twining, that intimacy, would evolve from something full of delight into something so overpowering, so fraught with existential dread, so relentless in its demand for my unabridged self, that I'd find myself working to tear those strands apart.

That's what drove me to nurse-sex. These other women could give me a new shape, one that no longer depended on Rosie to make me feel whole.

Day 201

Rosie still stretches out on the sofa, but the action is no longer beguiling. I'll be sitting in the chair opposite her, reading the news, and she comes in with her crossword puzzle and sprawls herself out on the sofa. She opens the newspaper like a gift, then folds it into a square, presumably so she won't be distracted by the surrounding ads. Then she licks the tip of the pencil before commencing, as if it won't make a mark until she's anointed it with her spit.

Even if she says absolutely nothing, her mere presence somehow aggravates me. It's one thing to take tea to her—*I'm* the one to enter her room, and *I* can decide when to leave it. But here, I can't just walk out when she sits down. Yet the moment she plops herself down, oppressive waves seem to radiate from her, cross the room, and push against my psyche. I can't relax. I can hardly breathe.

When and how did this situation originate? And how can I begin to tackle it?

I have to try.

So today, when Rosie walked in and sprawled herself on the sofa, I attempted to counter my irritation by forcing myself to really look at her.

The familiar elements of her body were all there—the still long hair that now flashes strands of silver, the soft arms that jiggle slightly now when she writes. The skin on her neck is beginning to sag while the tendons are increasing in prominence. My surreptitious gaze ventured to her face. The formerly rosebud lips—the ones Michaelina inherited—are pulled down at the ends into a wilted look. The skin of her eyelids is starting to stretch back beneath the frontal bone into her eye sockets.

I'd gotten just that far in my observations when she must've read a clue in her puzzle that amused her. Maybe she'd come across a word that made her recall our sexual games of so long past. Her face broke into a smile, a grand one, big as the moon, as if she'd completely forgotten her grieving mother mode for a blissful instant.

With that smile, something pure and holy shone forth from her. Beauty, that's what it was, a beauty that emanates from her still. I'd been trying to find fault with her—but to what end? The way her facial features meld together in that smile of hers still holds the power to delight. Her eyes, with the clear gray irises and darkening shadows, signal a deepening of mystery unexpectedly unfolding before me.

Any aversion is of my own making. Most likely, it's a reaction to what I see as her growing aversion to me.

Day 203

She's reading my mind. Thurman, that is. There's no other explanation.

Today she wanted to explore my feelings of guilt.

"Why should I feel guilty?" I asked.

At first, she wouldn't specify, claiming she didn't want to plant any suggestions in my head. I immediately suspected, though, that she knew something she wasn't telling me.

"Well, is it true or not?" she said.

I wanted to move forward on the sofa before answering, but found myself entrenched in the cushion's depressed center, the one that countless sad souls before me had formed. No matter how I attempted to shift my weight, I slid back into the pit.

"I'm trying not to lead you," she said. "You have guilty feelings, though, I know it."

"What would give you that idea?"

"They're all over your face."

I didn't believe that. Nevertheless, the accusation forced my mind to take a direction I didn't want it to go.

"You haven't forgiven your wife for Michaelina's death," she said.

"Sure I have."

"No. You've made some motions to make it seem that way. The way you talk about her, or I should say the way you dismiss her—it's like you're angry with her. You blame her. You can't let go that she talked to your son against your orders."

She'd latched on to some truth. I thought it would stop there, but she continued.

"Inside you know it was really *you* who killed your daughter."

My heart flipped like a steak on a hot grill.

She noticed my discomfiture and hesitation. "C'mon," she said, like a little girl, like a playmate beckoning me. "C'mon," she said, daring me to move to the edge of the cliff.

The dare tempted me. For a second I thought I could do it.

"Guilt is okay. Maybe even good." She bounced her leg under the desk in anticipation.

I took a breath, but no words came out. That sofa pit suddenly felt like a safe place to burrow myself into.

She said, "I made you uncomfortable."

"It's the damn sofa," I said.

"No," she said, "It's guilt. Tell me what you did that day, or maybe what you didn't do."

She trained her scope-eye on me and waited. I tried avoiding her gaze, but when she said nothing further, I ventured a glance.

When I looked into her eyes, I saw knowledge there. She knew exactly what had happened and what I was trying to conceal. I was sure of it.

But I hadn't said anything to give myself away, had I? I'd remember that. I needed to go back and reread my journal entries. I'd have recorded anything like that. Yes, definitely I would have.

Thurman earlier had implied that I might be unraveling mentally, but I couldn't see it. That would be the problem though, wouldn't it? That something's mentally amiss and I can't see it clearly enough to fix it, that something's worked itself loose and I can't tighten it up again. That something's giving way and I can't hold back the tide much longer.

Day 204

But no, no, no. I haven't said anything. I checked every journal entry.

I now believe Thurman was merely implying I was responsible for Michaelina's death because it wouldn't have happened if I hadn't been trying to prevent Rosie and the Jackass from communicating. I hadn't thought of it that way before. So I'm double guilty of the crime. How much more can I take?

Or maybe Thurman's gaslighting me. She wants me to believe I'm going insane.

That shouldn't be her goal, should it? She's supposed to be helping me. She's the supposed expert. It'd be the easy way out to just make a determination that I'm crazy.

She has the knowledge, the skills to make things right. It's not so simple as asking about my guilt. If it were that easy, she wouldn't have needed med school. Any idiot could ask me. Hell, I could ask myself. If she thinks I have some sort of mental illness, some growing tumor of guilt, she must possess the means of cutting it out of me. Expecting me to excise it of my own accord would be like me asking my patients to operate on themselves.

I wish she'd demonstrate more competence, and not by asking stupid questions. Where are her more sophisticated methods? Her sharper tools?

Day 206

Is giving up on life the logical response to death? Maybe Rosie isn't giving up on life, just giving up on life with me. Sex, that ancient life-giving force, and the fruit of that sex—Michaelina—are receding into the past, becoming distant memories. Maybe the sex that brought our daughter into being was the glue that held our marriage together. Or maybe it was Michaelina herself.

And she's gone, forever gone. No matter how many times I think of her and wish for her, she's still gone.

In the hospital, as long as she lay in that hospital bed, I entertained hope. I could contemplate nothing else beyond my all-consuming desire that she survive. I didn't think about the accident itself, who was responsible, or what anyone thought of it. I thought only about Michaelina's struggling little body. I obsessed over every mark on her charts and the tiniest change in her scans.

I was relentless with the doctors, pushing for precise details about her condition. Initially, because I was a surgeon myself, the team gave me preferential treatment. But after the first day, I was rebuffed. The doctors became difficult to locate, didn't return calls, and cut me off when I asked too many questions. I was all too familiar with the routine—I was acting just like the parents I'd endured, the ones who wouldn't leave me alone so I could do my job. Even though I recognized what a pain-in-the-ass I was being, I couldn't stop myself.

Rosie and I barely spoke during that time in the hospital. Not that there was any overt animosity or anger between us. I was a lunatic half the time, and numb the rest of it. Rosie and I took turns sitting with Michaelina while the other one slept, attempted to eat, or paced the halls. I avoided Rosie's eyes as much as I could, although I was quick to inform her when I learned anything about Michaelina's condition that offered the smallest shred of hope.

But the shreds of hope were just that—torn-up, useless shreds.

Day 207

As Michaelina lay unconscious, I began to contemplate reports of near-death experiences.

I had a patient once, seven or eight years old, whom we almost lost (due to an incompetent anesthesiologist) during a craniectomy to relieve pressure on his brain. His heart stopped for several minutes. When he woke from the operation, he claimed to have been to heaven. I only half-listened to the details, and didn't believe a word of what I heard. I've always scoffed at the concept of such an experience, but I had to admit that the patient's belief in it, and his parents' belief as well, redounded to his benefit.

When the parents first brought their son for an initial consultation, they'd been intensely bitter, an attitude reflected in their child. Moreover, the surgery produced an outcome that was not wholly satisfactory. After their son's purported experience of heaven, however, their outlook transformed. Their acrimony, which ought to have intensified after the poor surgical result, dissipated before my eyes. The effect was long-lasting. Whenever I examined the boy at future appointments, he had a smile on his face, brightening his disfigured appearance considerably.

So while I dismissed the reality of a near-death experience, I couldn't completely dismiss the impact. As I sat by Michaelina's bedside in the hospital, I began hoping that such a phenomenon might truly exist. If it did, perhaps Michaelina was experiencing it. The idea consoled me. While I could do nothing to comfort her beyond holding her hand and whispering in her ear, I could imagine her mind disengaging temporarily from her wracked body. I could picture her chatting blissfully with an angel in comfort rather than suffering in a hospital bed with shattered ribs and mangled organs. If she liked princesses, she'd love angels. Even if it were all an illusion, a trick played on her by her distressed synapses, it was a happy trick, like having a dream in which you can fly.

And here's another reason I wanted this experience for Michaelina: if she were asked if she wanted to come back, she'd say yes. Unquestionably. She'd never leave me if she had a choice.

Day 208

In the end, Michaelina did leave me. She died three days after the accident. I should've corrected the record about my role in her death then, but there was still the funeral to plan and get through. You can imagine how emotionally taxing that was—making calls, composing an obituary, and deciding a thousand unpleasant details—choosing a casket, purchasing a burial plot, and arranging for the viewing, service, and refreshments.

The funeral-goers enjoyed themselves immensely. They reveled in not just the food, but at the prospect of telling their coworkers and neighbors they'd gone to the funeral of a four-year old girl who'd been mowed down by her own mother.

She hadn't been though. I was the one who hit her. Of course that wasn't discussed at the funeral. And how could I have changed the narrative at that point? I couldn't just walk around at the reception, stop at each table, and say, "By the way, I was the one to kill Michaelina."

She was gone, and nothing I said or did could change that. It'd be better, I thought, for me to work it out afterward.

An opportunity came the following day. The police showed up at our door—a uniformed cop and a plainclothes sort who introduced herself as Detective Wolanski. Her face sported a fairly serious mandibular prognathism that should've been corrected as an adolescent. That jutting jaw gave her a tough, I'll-take-no-nonsense-here look. It wouldn't look good on a nurse, but was appropriate enough for a police officer.

The detective said their visit would be brief. They just needed our official statements about the accident for the record.

Here was my chance to correct the mistaken impressions. I breathed deeply as I readied my account. I needed to choose my words with care so as not to appear foolish.

I planned to speak up, I truly did. I'm certain I intended to.

But before I could open my mouth, Rosie jumped in. I figured she'd sensed my embarrassment and decided to spare me by correcting the story herself. But that's not what she did. Instead, she began weaving the most fantastic series of lies. She, who dislikes lies in the extreme, turned out to be amazingly adroit.

In her version, she was in the kitchen making a coffeecake for the next day's brunch. The recipe was a favorite of Michaelina's. Rosie needed ground cardamom, she said—the cake wasn't nearly as good without the cardamom—but she was all out, so she decided to make a quick run to the grocery store. She was in a hurry, because the cake needed an hour to bake, and she had to get it out of the oven before taking Michaelina to her ballet class.

She'd grabbed her purse, without bothering to alert me since she'd be gone only 20 minutes. By her account, I was sitting in the den the entire time, reading the newspaper. She dashed out the kitchen door that led directly into the garage. The garage door was up but she didn't give it any thought. Normally she'd take her Lexus, but she'd accidentally grabbed the wrong set of keys so she decided to take the Porsche. (I should note here that Rosie would *never* have taken the Porsche without my permission.)

She started it up, shifted into reverse, and glanced perfunctorily in the rearview mirror. Seeing nothing, and in fact expecting nothing, she backed out. Instantly she realized she'd hit something.

Wolanski interrupted and asked how fast she was going.

"I don't know," she said. "I don't think the speedometer works in reverse."

She asked if she knew Michaelina was outside playing. Rosie said no. She shifted in her seat.

When the detective asked where she thought Michaelina was, Rosie said, "In her room. She said she was going to her room. She has this one doll, Princess Moana, she said was sick with a 'feeber.' That's what she calls it, a feeber."

Rosie let out a truncated aspiration here, halfway between a laugh and a sigh.

Wolanski thrust her misplaced jaw out further and told her to continue.

"She likes to pretend her dolls are sick, and she's the doctor. Her father's a doctor, you know. Michaelina knows—knew—what kind of doctor he is, I mean, about his fixing faces, children's faces. She sometimes played that she was fixing one of her doll's faces, the one that—"

Wolanski interrupted and asked her to get back to the accident.

She did so, the words tumbling out so fast she didn't take a moment to breathe. I'm only recording a fraction of them here. "I stopped the car and turned off the engine and got out and Michaelina was lying on the ground, over in the grass, and I think I screamed, and Patton was barking, and my husband came outside and restarted her heart and gave her mouth-to-mouth resuscitation—did I tell you he's a doctor?—and he called 911 and the ambulance came and took us all to the hospital." Her account was embellished by graphic descriptions of Michaelina's body, as if she took some sort of macabre pleasure in the recounting of it. The level of detail she provided made the scenario seem entirely plausible.

When her narration was finished, she took a breath, a very drawn-out one. She breathed it out slowly as she concluded, "She died anyway."

Wolanski took it all down.

I wonder now about Rosie's previously unknown ability to lie. Had she invented these same kinds of stories to hide her relationship with the Jackass? I'd never asked her point blank if she was still in communication with him. It's entirely possible that she never lied outright. Surely, though, her withholding information was tantamount to lying. The problem is, even Rosie's dissembling sports a veneer of virtue—she could claim she cares about her son, that she wasn't being deceitful for personal gain. Nor was there any advantage in her lying to the police about the accident, or at least none that I could see.

Wolanski questioned me as well, but I maintained my brevity. With such a detailed exposition from Rosie, the detective wasn't inclined to probe. Since I 'wasn't there' when the car hit my child, my statement wasn't as important.

When Rosie was admitting her guilt, I felt a modicum of gratitude toward her. But then anger took over again. If she hadn't gone expressly against my wishes, we wouldn't have argued, and Michaelina would still be alive.

So why should I contradict her confession? I'd never accused her—she was the one to claim fault to the police, not I. It wasn't my responsibility to set the story straight. I hadn't lied.

Even so, and despite my legitimate justifications, I did resolve to confront Rosie privately about her assertions. It was fitting for her to accept partial responsibility for the accident, just not all of it.

However, no opportunity presented itself. Even when the funeral was over, relatives and neighbors continued to stream in at all hours bringing food and yet more condolences.

With each passing day, the notion of clarifying things became more untenable. The thought of confessing—to the police, to the hospital, and later, to that damn psychiatrist—was impossible. I told myself it didn't matter what people thought. Rosie and I both knew the truth—wasn't that sufficient?

Never owning up to my share of culpability is another reason to keep my bargain with God. The penance of humbling myself will appease him, won't it? Or at least it's a way to make restitution.

Day 211

Rosie didn't go to church today. I thought at first she must be sick. She hasn't missed Sunday Mass in all these years of our marriage. I asked if something was wrong, but she just gave her head a quick shake and compressed her lips, not looking at me.

I wanted to inquire further, but was too confused to formulate a question. Was this some capricious whim? Was she making some sort of statement? Or was something dreadful happening that I was slow to comprehend?

Day 214

Today's session with Dr. Thurman did not go the way I intended. It started off with a long back-and-forth on why I was there and the progress I supposedly still needed to make.

I was battle-weary. Why hadn't she freed me? I needed to get back to surgery or I really was headed for insanity.

Something had to give. Because she demonstrated no evident ability to resolve the matter, I decided to take charge, using a new strategy to wear her down. When she asked me questions about my state of mind, I answered in meandering sentences leading nowhere. Once she realized this was all she was getting, she'd sign off on the damn release.

She's dogged though—I'll give her that. As determined as I was not to reveal anything too personal, she was equally stubborn in her attempts to undermine my efforts. Being forced to parry her incessant questions caused my mind to go in circles until it was tied up and ready to explode.

Is this the typical psychiatrist strategy—to harass you into such a mental state that you can't think clearly, that you end up going mad, and can never free yourself from their machinations? I suppose that's how they hold onto you and earn their big money. Yes, that was it—Thurman could help me, but just didn't want to.

The more she interrogated me, the more that explanation made sense. I became increasingly angry. The turmoil registered as a churning sensation in my gut. I had to work around her. It was critical to stay focused, to remain in control, to keep the curtain closed.

She asked me again to describe the incident.

Whatever was causing the churning in my gut moved up into my throat—a danger sign. I told her I had nothing to say. I said it quickly, because speaking when my throat ached only squeezed the throbbing up into my eyes.

She stopped with her questions and stared at me full-bore.

I attempted to breathe, but something seemed to press against my diaphragm. Or maybe it was just that evil sofa contorting me unnaturally in the middle.

I wouldn't—I couldn't—say anything more. Ending the conversation, though, made things worse. The questions I'd left unanswered echoed back and forth in my mind—bouncing here, then there. The more I tried to catch and immobilize them, the more they dodged and taunted me.

I blinked my eyes with force, but it was useless. I swiped my knuckles across my lower lids.

Thurman continued looking at me. Was there a molecule of pity in her eyes?

That gave me an idea of how to use the tears to my advantage. I said to her, "Happy now? This is what you wanted, isn't it? Here's your maudlin display of grief. Now can you please give me that clearance?" And yes, the *please* was uttered as a command.

Her eyes glittered. The molecule of pity, if it'd been there at all, slid away. She waited a moment, probably for effect, and then said, "Those aren't grief tears. They're just frustration. You're crying like a big baby because you're not getting your toy back, the one you broke."

That beat all. I jumped up, freeing my body from the clutches of that masochistic sofa. "What is it you want?" I said, my voice breaking despite myself. "Am I supposed to make up something I don't feel?"

She stood as well. "No, you're supposed to let yourself feel. You need to show what you're hiding."

She indicated the session was over. That only incensed me further. I complained to her that I hadn't had sufficient chance to prove myself today. To prove my mental competence.

"*Hoo*," she said. "You proved plenty."

Day 218

I kept an eye on Rosie this morning. I wanted to make sure she was preparing for Sunday Mass. She got up at the usual time but sat on the sofa doing her crossword puzzle well past the time she should've been showered and ready to go.

When I inquired whether she'd be going, she just gave her head that little shake and looked away. That's two weeks in a row she hasn't gone. I'm less thrilled about this development than might be expected. I don't like change, even those changes that might ultimately be for the better.

All morning I was on edge. I'm used to having a couple of hours on Sunday morning to myself. Her presence in the house at this unusual time was unsettling. I wanted to encourage her to go but didn't see how it was possible. Not after the many times over the years I'd been less than supportive.

Day 220

Nothing is happening. Nothing at home, nothing at work, and no progress with the damn psychiatrist. I spend my time at work pretending to be busy, barking orders at the nurses, drawing out rounds so long that the residents look at their watches.

I'm beginning to hang on to the prospect of seeing Thurman. I don't know why, since I abhor her. Her very face fills me with resentment and disgust. Nevertheless, I've caught myself counting the days until I see her again.

At least it's something to do. At least it's a recurring event that holds some sort of potential to get me past this limbo.

Day 225

Rosie again didn't go to Mass. What is happening? Something about her refusal to go and her not explaining herself disturbs me. It's causing me almost physical sickness. When I ask if she's going and she shakes her head, I feel a worm in my stomach that squirms around there until I'm ready to vomit.

This can't continue. I can't bear it one more day, yet I can't confront her about it. So today I decided that if she wouldn't go, *I* would—but without telling her. To be sure, I had no grand vision for my impulsive action. I thought only this: that my going in her stead was the only way to prevent one of the last frayed threads in our lives from breaking.

By the time I arrived at the church and parked, the service was well under way. I stood erect, arms crossed, against a back wall near the exit. I was aiming only for a physical presence. I was there only to fulfill the necessity of inserting my body into the breach.

I focused on the congregants directly in front of me: a young woman wearing a t-shirt emblazoned on the back with a Harley-Davidson logo, a tall fellow with a bad comb-over who conveniently blocked my view of the pulpit, and a young family parked in the last pew.

A boy, maybe two years old, popped his head up and stared at me with large brown eyes, like a younger version of Michaelina's friend Trevor. I made a face at him and he turned away. He clutched a small toy car that he began running along the back of the pew with accompanying sound effects. By accident, he ran the car into his older sister's shoulder. She turned and scowled at him, a response that so filled the boy with delight that as soon as she turned back to face the front, he did it again, with malice aforethought.

His sister shrieked, grabbed the car from him, and swatted him smartly on the head with it. They tussled for possession of the toy until the father belatedly intervened and wrestled it away from them both, depositing it in his pocket. Not even little children are innocent.

When the congregants rose for communion, I took off.

Day 226

I had a fantastical revelation when I met with Thurman today.

The session began in the usual way, with her nagging questions on grief and guilt and my non-responses.

In the middle of making one of her more pointed remarks, though, she reached back unconsciously to scratch the back of her neck, but then jerked her hand back in a fast motion that drew my attention. She then smoothed her hair back into place.

But her hair-smoothing was too late—I'd seen on her neck what her hair had been hiding. How had I not recognized her before? Yes, she'd looked familiar, but after meeting with her a few times I'd begun to think it was a new familiarity, not an old one.

Now, though, I was certain, completely certain. I knew this woman. I knew her outside of this environment and outside of this hospital. I knew her from long ago.

I managed to maintain a neutral expression. To avoid suspicion, I re-directed my attention to the arm of the sofa, where I studiously picked at the cracked leather.

I needed no further confirmation. All the same, as soon as she looked at her laptop, I took a quick peek at her framed credentials, now hanging on the wall. There it was. *Matilda B. Thurman.* She'd gone by Meg in med school. Maybe she still did, to her friends. Her maiden name was something Polish, beginning with a B. Something like Bialaski. She'd immigrated as a teen with her parents, and by now had almost eliminated her accent. All that remained were those few idioms and that occasional *ch* as in *chutzpah* when she said my name.

She doesn't know that I know. This new knowledge is precious, golden. I need to preserve and guard it, save it for the right moment.

I can use it to save myself.

Day 227

I went straight to Ji-young's office this morning. She agreed to see me without an appointment.

I needed to explain that Thurman was holding a vendetta against me for something that had happened in the past, that she was punishing me by refusing to clear me to return to surgery. I'd demand that Ji-young clear me herself, or at the very least, allow me to see some other psychiatrist.

Yes, that was my plan going in.

Once I faced Ji-young, however, who stood there squeezing and loosening the tiny balls of her fists, I had second thoughts. Did I really want to divulge to this woman that I'd had a one-nighter with Thurman decades ago? She'd ask why I hadn't said something sooner. The last thing I wanted to admit was that I hadn't even recognized Thurman until I caught a glimpse of the port-wine stain on her neck.

Not only that, but Ji-young might say that any past relationship didn't matter, especially if I didn't even realize its existence until this week. She'd ask if I'd discussed this revelation with Thurman, and then insist I do so. Or maybe Thurman had already told her. Nothing would come of it then.

One fact I was convinced of: Thurman knew who I was. She'd known it all along. Why else had she so carefully shielded that birthmark from me, continually smoothing her hair over it that way?

So I changed my mind about telling Ji-young. It'd be better to hold on to my nugget until I found the right circumstance to capitalize on it. When revealing it to Thurman at the crucial moment, I'd say I had known from the start and had been acting the gentleman, not wanting to embarrass her. That would give me the upper hand.

Another consideration came to mind too. Something I wouldn't want to admit to Ji-young, and hardly wanted to admit to myself. It was this: I've gotten used to Thurman. The thought of starting anew with another psychiatrist suddenly seemed unthinkable.

In the end, I simply voiced my frustration to Ji-young about the length of the process to get the documentation needed to return to surgery. She stared at me in evident bemusement, then bobble-nodded as she recommended patience.

Day 230

I can't stop thinking about the brief tryst I enjoyed with Thurman so many years ago. Although we were fellow students, she was a year ahead of me—I barely knew her. We did attend one lecture class together, and at the close of the semester, we ended up at the same party one night.

I can't recall many details of the encounter. After a few drinks, we'd landed on a sofa together, pleasantly exploring each other's torsos. When she invited me to her apartment, how could I say no? Once in bed with her I discovered the birthmark. Nearly as large as a pancake, it spread deliciously around the back of her neck, ending in sort of a tail beneath her left ear. I kissed every portion of it tenderly, amorously. The blood-red of it was erogenous beyond all telling. Aside from that, I recall only my delight in her muscular peasant body and her old-world style of sex.

I left as soon as she'd fallen asleep.

I wouldn't have minded a few repeat sessions, but I didn't have her number. Nor did I see her on campus again—the class we'd attended together was over, and it was summer. I tried her apartment, but she'd moved away.

Had the realization of our past physical acquaintance dawned on Thurman over time? Clearly she's known for a while. What would possess her, though, to hide her knowledge? Maybe she's desperate for patients, or maybe she just enjoys tormenting me.

Day 233

It's increasingly useless to go to my office. Families are drifting away, even ones I've served for years.

I needed a respite, a getaway. When I asked Rosie if we could take a short trip, she nodded a bit sadly but made no objection. As we packed our bags, I belatedly fretted about the prospect of too much time with her, but by then it was too late to go alone.

I made a quick call to the kennel to book a spot for Patton, and after dropping him off, we headed north on the interstate, with no definite destination. We conversed along the way, not about anything serious—first the weather, then the sights and sounds and smells of the countryside. When those topics were exhausted, I began telling her stories about nurses, patients, and parents. I mixed light-hearted tales with more somber narratives until I could get a handle on her mood.

In our early years together, she used to laugh so naturally, so generously at my small attempts at humor. I'd use a documentary-style voice to describe familiar people's faces in the most obscure medical terms. Okay, so that wasn't exactly highbrow, but wasn't it, in its way, even better? And it was only with Rosie I could let my goofy side come to the fore. The Mac side.

It took so little to make her happy, yet over the years I came to begrudge her even that. How many times had I denied her the simple pleasure of pleasant company, only because it was in my power to do so? My pride was my pleasure, my bitter pleasure.

Now, though, away from everything, I experienced a reprieve from myself. I tried to please. Rosie's low-amp laugh acknowledged my efforts.

With each passing mile, I breathed a little more deeply, as if I'd been unable to take in sufficient oxygen for months.

Even the breaks from conversation held some peace—a companionable peace. I didn't know what she was thinking. Probably dark thoughts, like my own.

Once Michaelina was in my life, I thought I could forget my son. Often I did. But the times I spent so blissfully with Michaelina sometimes made me miss the Jackass more. I didn't want to miss him, but I couldn't seem to scrape his existence off the surface of my brain. During the silent spells on the drive today, I recalled again my long-ago unfulfilled expectations of my son's speedy return, and my inability to admit my concerns to Rosie. I had wondered at first whose sofa he might be sleeping on, whether other parents knew what was going on, and what they were saying about it.

When no news trickled back to me, I figured he must've left town. I'd heard of teens becoming vagabonds, riding the rails, bonding with each other. In a pique, I'd cut off his cellphone service, thereby throwing away the opportunity to contact him even if I wanted to. Why had he been so impatient? If he'd only stuck it out, we'd have gotten past the angst of his adolescence.

As Rosie and I drove across a bridge with the wide Ohio River beneath us, I shoved these ruminations aside. My stomach growled. We went through a drive-through and ate lunch as we forged ahead. After a double cheeseburger, however, I was sleepy. It'd been a draining week, a draining month. At least my surgeries had gone well.

I corrected my thinking. I wasn't conducting surgeries. And I did have a problem, the girl Zoe who was permanently blinded.

I asked Rosie to take the wheel for a spell. As I rule, she doesn't drive when we're both in the car. I have a justified phobia of riding in any vehicle she controls. But what did it matter now?

We pulled off at the exit to switch seats.

Consulting my phone, I located a bed & breakfast a few hours' drive away in Cincinnati and made a reservation, then entered the address into the GPS. The road was straight and smooth, and I dozed, waking only when we exited the highway.

The B&B was one of those big Victorians, close to downtown. I was glad to observe a little bustle there, a hubbub of complete strangers unaware of me or my affairs. We checked in and deposited our bags. Our room contained only one bed, a queen. The less time spent in the actual room, the better.

We headed out for a walk and discussed dinner. Rosie is easy to please in restaurant choices, a virtue I always attributed to her lack of culinary sophistication. Today, I decided to have no opinion either. There was freedom in that.

On our stroll, we stopped at each restaurant we came across, perusing and discussing the menu. Not because it mattered, but because it was something to do while waiting for a civilized time to dine.

In the end, we tacked back to the B&B. Their restaurant seemed as good as any. Facing each other across the candlelit table after the congenial drive, our conversation facilitated by a bottle of wine, we seemed to connect on a level we hadn't in years. By the time we ordered dessert, Rosie was almost giddy.

It was still early. Upstairs again, I showered, shaved, and took my time in the bathroom, admitting to myself I was almost nervous. Rosie has never denied me, not once. And really, hadn't we had some good times in those early years?

But those times were in the ancient past. Initiating anything in this place seemed impossible, after everything that's passed between us.

And beyond that, the old fears still haunted me. If I lose myself—inevitably—how can I face her afterward? The persistent tangled feelings—her veiled disappointment, my own desperate clinging, the aftermath of shame—retained their unsettling familiarity.

When I finally exited the bathroom, Rosie was sound asleep. I climbed into bed gingerly and stayed well to my own side. After my long nap in the car, though, I was wide awake. I didn't want to disturb her by switching on the lamp to read, and I couldn't tolerate my own thoughts lying in the dark.

I donned my robe and went downstairs.

In the living room a fire smoldered in the grate. A young couple, chatting on the sofa, glanced at me briefly. A little diverting conversation would've been welcome just then, but they returned to their tête-a-tête and ignored me.

I settled myself into a side chair—not as comfortable as the sofa would've been—and opened a nearby magazine as if to read. The couple lowered their voices. I listened while pretending not to.

The woman's face was anemic-looking, accentuated by light-colored eyebrows plucked to a fare-thee-well. Her hair, short and gelled into points, gave her a porcupine look. She did most of the talking. Her tone was authoritative, yet coaxing, as if expressing expectations to a wayward child. She clearly had the upper hand in the exchange.

I felt sorry for her husband or whatever he was. His puppy-dog eyes never strayed from her face. He leaned in towards her, nodding slowly as she spoke, acknowledging her words. At the same time, his tightened lips and crossed arms belied his seeming acquiescence.

Their conversation centered on a new job the woman had been offered in LA. The thought of having such a conversation with one's wife made me cringe. The woman stated her terms, and, based on the man's body language, I expected him to cut her off. Every time she made a statement, however, he'd circle in his reply, never giving her a direct response. Like a boxer in a ring, he avoided his opponent's punches, sometimes by ducking or dancing away, but often by clenching and hugging.

When he didn't fully accede to her wishes, she didn't push him away. Instead, she'd slightly amend her stated expectations or soften her demands. Eventually, though, she'd go back to her original proposition. Then the man would draw in a long breath, shift in his seat, and they'd go at it again.

The couple seemed able to talk endlessly. What struck me was not so much the length of these negotiations, but that neither one of them was ever visibly irritated. They didn't raise their voices. Neither stalked off in frustration or anger.

I concluded they must not be very much in love.

Day 234

Today began propitiously. It ended disastrously.

Despite getting to bed late, I was up before Rosie. I went down to the dining room, picked up a newspaper, and returned with a mug of tea for her. She sipped it in bed, while I read the paper lazily in a bedside chair, occasionally glancing over at her in a sort of conflicted satisfaction.

After a continental breakfast, we took a walk along an old, graveled causeway beside the river. The weather was clear and a little too cold to be pleasant, with the wind whipping in our faces. Conversation was strained again. I thought of the couple I'd observed the night before. Even though they had a clear disagreement, they managed to keep going. I'd left while they were still negotiating, leaving me wondering whether they ever reached a resolution.

In the afternoon, we attended a matinée at an artsy theater, then had an intelligent discussion about it. At dinner we again shared a bottle of wine, though Rosie drank less than the night before. We talked about funny movies we'd seen over the years, and I made her laugh with a few silly impersonations. Her face lit up in the candlelight, offering a glimmer of the carefree and trusting person I'd once known.

Maybe this evening would end differently from the last. I found myself thinking about protection, but had nothing with me. Surely there was no way she'd get pregnant again—she was over 40 now. And it would make her happy, my going without.

I had a further thought, one that was so unfamiliar that I nearly laughed out loud. What if she did get pregnant? Admittedly, a new baby would be no replacement for Michaelina, yet wouldn't there be a sort of salve in it? I'd been a better father to Michaelina than to my son. Until the end, anyway. Maybe third time would be the charm.

By the time we were drinking our after-dinner coffee, an alien anticipation enveloped me. Rosie herself emanated not just a glow from the wine and candlelight, but a sort of tentative attitude in her speech and movements that I interpreted as her having thoughts similar to mine.

I couldn't have been more mistaken. Out of nowhere, she brought up the subject of John.

John!

I was so aghast that I said nothing at first, allowing her to jabber on about how much he'd changed, how much I'd like him now, how much it meant to her that we all be together as a family, especially in these difficult times. Once she started talking, it was as if a dam had burst.

I barely listened. This wasn't how I'd planned it. It was *my* prerogative to broach the subject of the Jackass when I was ready, not hers. All I could think was, how could she do this to me? There we were, having an enjoyable time together, building up some emotional capital. And then, in a three-minute outburst, she fritters it all away.

The worst was that she was oblivious to her blunder. When she finally paused to take a breath, I shut her up instantly. I won't repeat the words I used. I'll only say they were effective. Her response was silence, utter silence.

I had wanted—intended—to discuss our son, but not this evening. Tonight was supposed to be about us. The Jackass would come later in the equation, after Rosie and I fell into a more substantial sort of reconciliation. And the timing should've been mine to determine. It galled me to think that even after all these years, that boy still had the ability to come between us.

I'm now lying on the couch downstairs in the communal room, and this is where I'll spend the night.

Why did I do it? Why reject her overtures about John when that's what I want too? Rosie's words activated some part of me, a part that felt I was being manipulated. Her words implied I needed to be cajoled into doing the right thing.

My response, though, went overboard. I should've listened to her, and at least compromised. Even if I'm not ready to see the Jackass myself, what harm could there be now in allowing Rosie to talk with him or for them to have lunch together, with my blessing? I should've suggested that.

I'm the one who's been trying to control Rosie, not the other way around. I have to stop. When someone assumes control of a situation that should be mine to control, it's humbling. Haven't I learned that lesson yet, that the shortest road to humility is by accepting humiliation? I failed today. And when I fail, I have to quit justifying myself.

Day 235

A dispiriting day. A day when, in a bolt of awareness, the hideous visage of evil flashes before you, and in that flash of horror your true enemy is laid bare.

One might have expected that after last night's pious ruminations, I'd have gone to Rosie first thing in the morning and thrown myself at her feet, begging forgiveness. Pride, however, is not so easily dispensed with—it rose again with the sun, full-chested and bedazzling. My rationalizations returned to me in force.

I started off by entertaining a doubt that even a full-blown apology from me would do any good. Then I convinced myself that it would embarrass Rosie for me to tell her I was sorry. Finally, I decided it'd be better to make it up to her a little at a time, to ease into it, that actions were better than words.

In the end, I did nothing at all.

I hate myself for it. But even if I'd apologized and she'd forgiven me, the magic was gone. We cut off the rest of our trip. This fresh split between us was raw, torn from a scar that hadn't yet healed.

The silence on the drive home afforded an abundance of time for my uneasy thoughts. With my gaze fixed on the road mile after mile, I forced myself to review progress on my bargain with God. At times I feel I've made real strides. Usually, though, the moment I have that thought, things fall apart again. And when that happens, my temptation is to give up, to go back to the patterns that provide a measure of comfort even in the midst of pain.

Yet I have to admit that despite my failures, when I'm actively working on humility, it does make a difference in my relationship with Rosie. Now is when I need to look at the big picture, the long term, and not give way to discouragement at setbacks. My failures, if I could learn to embrace them, would serve as another source of humility. And with this blasted psychiatrist beating me down at every turn, I need Rosie's support.

If only she didn't make it so difficult.

The entire drive, I felt her wilted presence beside me. Before I blew up at her in the restaurant, we'd scraped together a modicum of emotional unity. I'd forgotten how enjoyable, how satisfying that could be. Even if our connection was weak at times, I was thankful for it.

In the car, though, I couldn't talk to her. I couldn't formulate any thoughts that seemed within my power to articulate. If only Rosie would break the silence, I told myself, I'd respond with good cheer. Yet even now I wonder if I was lying to myself.

Owen popped back into my head. When I'd scuttled his promotion, he, to all appearances, had forgiven me. He, a virtual stranger. Yet with my own wife, I was back to the silent treatment. If I'm honest, that strategy hasn't taught her anything and doesn't make me feel any better. Well, maybe it does, in a perverse sort of way, like a drug providing a momentary high. *The silent treatment* shouldn't be called a treatment, as if it's some sort of medicine or therapy. It should be called the silent torment.

The weather was inclement on the way home, a depressing drizzle that froze in stipples against the windshield. I was determined to drive through it. I'm certain Rosie was as anxious as I was to get home, where we could retreat to our separate rooms.

We were nearly there—only about an hour away. A few icy patches developed on the highway and traffic slowed.

That's when it happened. Some idiot, not paying attention to conditions, rear-ended us. Not badly—our airbags didn't even deploy. I pulled over and hopped out of the car to give the driver a piece of my mind. But the man who exited the pickup truck was even angrier than I was. He launched a verbal attack, blaming me for the accident, claiming I was driving too slowly and had braked unexpectedly. His heavy brow clenched over his deep-set eyes, and his hairy hands twitched at his sides as if he could barely restrain himself from striking me. He wasn't a tall man but he was beefy in the shoulders. I'm not one for physical altercations, so I scaled back my own reaction, hoping to settle the Neanderthal down.

I glanced back towards Rosie. I couldn't see her expression because she was facing forward in her seat. I wanted to check on her but had to deal with this moron first.

In his rage, the man wasn't just unpleasant—he was ugly. Literally, physically ugly. He berated me at length. When he paused for breath, I insisted we exchange insurance information. He took numerous photos of the scene before hoisting himself back into his truck and speeding away.

I went to Rosie's side of the car and opened her door. The glassiness of her eyes made me blanch. I tried to converse with her, but her speech was slightly muddled and her voice distant and wavering, in a way that clearly had nothing to do with the snarl in our relationship.

Then she said, "Is Michaelina okay?"

I examined her expression for some sign she was teasing me. But she'd never joke about that.

I jumped back into the driver's seat and zoomed into traffic, searching mentally for the nearest hospital. I tried to ascertain from Rosie whether she might've hit her head on the dashboard. Maybe she'd drifted off to sleep with her neck at an odd angle when we were hit. When I received no satisfactory response, I focused instead on soothing her and explaining that we'd get her checked out right away. I glanced over at her every few seconds.

I careened off the next exit ramp and headed to the nearby regional hospital.

Our wait in the ER was interminable. If only there were blood, we'd get some service. I took her hand and stroked it as we sat there. With each passing minute, she seemed better, more coherent. By the time she finally received medical attention, she really did seem back to normal. Even so, the doctor wanted her to stay overnight for observation. I concurred.

I settled her into the hospital bed. Once she was back to her senses, the rupture between us reasserted itself and conversation ceased. I stretched out on a chair beside her. After sitting so long in the car, though, I was restless. Not only that, but after we'd given our names to the staff, I felt sure they were casting surreptitious looks at us. Maybe they knew I was the doctor whose daughter had been hit in our driveway. Maybe they knew about my suspension from surgery. Maybe they were all talking about how I'd blinded a little girl.

Maybe they even knew that I'd killed Michaelina.

I mentally shook myself, but couldn't let it go, not while I was in that hospital environment. After nearly two hours of silent misery, pacing back and forth in Rosie's room, I asked her if she needed me to stay. She said no, that she was just going to sleep anyway. I promised to return first thing in the morning. I pecked her on the forehead, the first kiss I'd given her in a long time.

I came home to an empty house. Patton wasn't even there to greet me—he was still at the kennel, which was closed for the night. The kitchen, bereft of Rosie's usual bustle, was cold and uninviting. I wasn't hungry anyway. I wonder now if Rosie really did go to sleep or if she needed to eat first. I'm hoping they haven't forgotten to order her a meal.

So I sit here writing, second-guessing my decision to come home alone. What was I thinking? I know better than anyone the kinds of neglect, mistakes, and infections that can happen in a hospital. I was thinking only of saving myself from gossip, discomfort, and paranoid thoughts. The self-centered, impatient me—Butt-cheeks—had made that choice. Now I see it as a missed opportunity for humility through humiliation.

However, if I were to make the long trek back to the hospital this evening, I'd surely find Rosie fast asleep. I can serve her better tomorrow if I get a good night's sleep here.

Rosie's not the only one on my mind tonight. The whole way home I thought about the Jackass. I wasn't able to absorb Rosie's information about him when she'd provided it, not when I was so infuriated by her introducing the topic at all.

But that's not my son's fault. It's time to recognize that the old animosity I've felt toward him isn't surging up the way it used to. Maybe it's been dissipating for a while without my noticing. I'm having trouble pinpointing why I've been angry with him all these years. It now seems like some ancient myth that no one ever got around to debunking.

I know what to do. I'll forgive him. I'll forgive him for his teenage rebellion, for abandoning us as he did, and for not coming back. Forgive him even if he doesn't ask for forgiveness.

Yes, I need to finish this year of humility strong, and to include my actions toward my son in the deal. If I want to salvage my relationship with Rosie (and I do, I do—despite last night's debacle), I have to accept John. John, not the Jackass. It won't be easy, not after more than five years' separation.

My efforts with Rosie are bearing fruit. Not perfectly, but who could've imagined our ever enjoying each other's company again like we did at the start of our trip? And if John is changed as much as Rosie claims, maybe it'll all work out, after some initial awkwardness.

Yes, once we're home, and after Rosie and I make just a little more progress, I'll propose a reconciliation with John. That way it won't seem as if I'm merely acceding to Rosie's desires, but that I made the decision myself.

Rosie will be overjoyed. I can picture it, the tears of gratitude welling up and dancing down her cheeks. It'll be like the day she gave birth to him.

Disasters can have positive consequences. Today is a case in point. By any objective measure, this was an unpleasant day. Yet now, at the end of it, I'm experiencing a kind of epiphany, a watershed moment in which the route to take is obvious and the path unimpeded.

Day 236

I was blindsided this morning. Completely and utterly blindsided.

Information was fed to me, or more accurately, spouted off to me. What was communicated was beyond any of my previous attempts to understand or interpret events. No way could I have anticipated this. No way in hell.

I slept little last night. Up at five, I skipped my run, since Patton wasn't there anyway, and headed to the hospital. I wanted to be with Rosie the moment she woke up. My thoughts on the drive were cheerful and anticipatory. I'd give her a solid kiss this time, smack on the lips. That would show her our argument about John was over, and I was going to make amends.

Once there, I took the staircase to the fourth floor. Rosie's room was the last one down the hall, on the right. As I passed the nurses' station, though, something caught my eye. A man was just exiting Rosie's room. He didn't look like a patient, or a doctor or staff member either. He sauntered down the hall in my direction.

The notion that Rosie could be having an affair entered my mind. That'd explain why she acceded so easily to my suggestion that I leave her at the hospital and head home. And maybe her cheating on me is the reason she'd abandoned her church. If she left me, people would say I deserved it.

Anyway, those were my thoughts as the man came down the hall. He was tall, with a good build, but had a slightly scruffy appearance—untrimmed beard and longish hair. I've noticed over the years that people wearing beards, unless they're Amish, have something to hide. Even wearing glasses instead of contacts, as this man did, is telling. They're either trying to mask a facial defect or bad skin or don't want people to see their inner selves. That's one bit of pop psychology I agree with.

The man neared me. I kept my eyes on him. Just as we passed each other he looked up, directly into my eyes. He startled, and so did I.

It was John.

He pulled up short and blinked at me. Blinked, as if trying to bring into focus a perplexing image.

I was confused, too, still busy shaking off my thoughts about Rosie having a lover. I blurted out, "What're you doing here?" I didn't intend to say it accusingly, but it might've come off that way.

John was instantly defensive. "I stayed overnight. *Someone* needed to be here with Mom."

Yes, that's the tone he used. I wasn't about to be usurped, though. "Why are you going behind my back?"

He looked at me incredulously. "Why? For starters, how about because you're a cruel, judgmental son-of-a-bitch?"

I glanced around but no one seemed to be in hearing distance, aside from a bed-ridden old man whose room we were standing outside of.

"You have no call to accuse me of that," I retorted. "*You*, of all people."

"*Me*, of all people? What, because I'm your son? That gives me more right than anyone."

Wanting to end this conversation quickly, I didn't argue. "All right, you've made your opinion known. Now out of my way." I pushed his arm, but he flung my hand away.

"Not so fast," he said, revving himself up. "I don't like what you've done to Mom."

I kept my voice low, trying to de-escalate. "I've done nothing to Mom."

"You call that nothing—letting her take responsibility for Michaelina's death?"

"I never blamed her, not once."

"You're a coward, not defending your own wife."

"She claimed it. I couldn't stop her. Evidently, she felt some need to take the blame."

"Are you kidding me?"

"Then why would she do it?"

His eyes narrowed and he paused, seemingly relishing my discomfiture. "You don't know, do you?"

I had no idea what he was talking about, but I didn't reveal my ignorance.

He emitted a short, mirthless laugh. "Unbelievable," he said, shaking his head slowly.

I suspected he had no real information, so with a surprise move and greater force I pushed past him and headed toward Rosie's room.

He followed me. "Mom blames herself, at least partly."

That much I already knew.

"You had to spite her, just because she wanted to spend time with me."

"I never spited her."

"You're the most spiteful person I've ever known. You're dripping with spite."

The last thing I wanted was for Rosie to hear this vitriol, so I turned right at the next hallway, and took another right soon after, then a left. Hospitals can be mazes—I began to feel like a rat running from aversive stimuli.

John followed so closely behind me that he tripped on my heel. "Mom was afraid to tell you why she felt guilty."

So they'd discussed the accident together. She'd never even discussed it with me.

I said, "I never asked her to lie for me."

"You let her take the fall though. You let everyone believe she was the one to kill Michaelina."

We passed a staff member who said, "Can I help you find something?"

I shook my head and hurried on.

"Do you know why she did it?" said John. "Why she confessed to running over Michaelina?"

The far-fetched, impossible reasons circulated through my head again, but I wasn't about to play some guessing game. We reached a bank of elevators and I pushed a button.

"You're an asshole," he said.

I said, "If that's all you have are epithets, I've heard enough." The elevator opened, but fearing that I'd be trapped inside with him, I turned abruptly away and started down the hall.

He said, "You're totally callous to Mom's sufferings, you know that?"

Coming to a staircase door, I opened it and went through. He followed. The disharmonious clacking of our feet as we scrambled down the stairway rattled me. I focused on my steps to avoid stumbling.

"You're the reason she can't eat or sleep," John said.

At the bottom of the stairs I came to an emergency door with a warning sign that an alarm would sound if anyone tried to exit.

I turned and tried to get around John, but he blocked me. He held his arm out against the wall so I couldn't get past. "I'll tell you why she took the blame," he said.

I looked at him, thinking I might stare him down.

He said, "You forced her to choose between Michaelina and me."

"I did no such thing."

"That's how it seemed to her."

"I can't do anything about her misconceptions."

"You made her miserable. She had to go behind your back just to spend time with me. When you saw her cellphone that day and discovered we'd been texting, you got all pissed off and then ran out to the car to take off in your usual spineless way. That's when the thought came to her that Michaelina might be in the driveway."

"So?"

"So... the thought of revenge entered her mind."

I looked at him blankly.

Then he said the words, the ones he'd followed me all this way to say. He hissed them: "She hesitated."

The words shot out at me as if a flame from a blowtorch, licking my eardrums, scorching my brain. It took only a moment for comprehension to flash through my entire body.

"It was only for a second. She regretted it right away and ran outside yelling for you to stop. But it was too late."

So that was it. John's words changed everything. Every belief I had about what'd happened and why. Every notion, every preconception, every rationalization. Everything I'd supposed about my wife. I desperately wanted to be alone with this new information. To be away from prying eyes, where I could nurse the implications in private.

But John wouldn't let me be. "She wanted to admit it all to you, to tell you about her part in it. But she was afraid you'd never forgive her. So she took the blame for you instead. It was her way of saying she was sorry. She didn't think it through, though. She never dreamed you wouldn't admit to what you'd done, that you were the one to run over your own daughter."

I looked up to the top of the staircase, but it remained deserted.

"Don't worry," said John, "Your dirty secret's safe with me. I promised Mom."

I'm not a violent man, but I nearly punched him in the jaw. Before I could make a move, though, he turned and bounded up the first flight of stairs. Just before he exited the door, he shouted down at me, "You weren't the only one to love Michaelina. Mom loved her, and so did I."

Those last words echoed into the empty stairwell.

I retrieved my wits and decided I couldn't let these accusations go unanswered. I dashed up the stairs and out the stairwell door, only to find John standing in the main lobby, phone in hand, probably texting Rosie. It was my turn now. I approached and told him he couldn't possibly have loved Michaelina when he never saw her.

He smiled at me then. A big fat *haha-the-joke's-on-you* smile.

"I saw her all the time," he said. "I held her in the hospital the day she was born. *You* had to rush back to work. *Someone* needed to stay with Mom."

I pointed out that some of us had jobs, important jobs.

He ignored that and repeated, "I saw Michaelina all the time. I took her to the park to give Mom a break. We went to story hour at the library, the children's museum, the zoo. We played together at the house."

"Michaelina would've told me."

"I went by my middle name—Chris."

"I still don't believe you."

"No? Well, I've taken hundreds, probably thousands of pictures and videos of Michaelina over the years."

So it wasn't Rosie developing into a decent photographer after all. It had been John.

Having made his point, he cast a final, summary glare at me and strutted away down the hall. I stayed put. I didn't want him coming back to Rosie's room. She didn't deserve to witness this kind of confrontation.

John stopped to talk with a young woman just emerging from the ladies' room—a petite woman. Petite, that is, in all places save one—her protruding belly. I observed with mounting disgust as he kissed the woman and slipped his arm around her. With their backs to me, they went out the hospital front door.

I returned to Rosie's room, smiling as if nothing had happened. She slid her phone under the sheet as I walked in, and I pretended not to see it. John must've texted her that I was back, and she didn't know if she should act surprised to see me. A trace of chagrin, or maybe annoyance, played across her features. I took her hand but received no feedback. I set it back down and moved away.

"Thanks for coming back so early," she said, but her words had no heart.

"Can I get you breakfast?"

"No thanks, I'd like to rest."

"Have you seen a physician?"

"No, but a nurse came in and said the doctor looked at my scan and blood work and everything's fine. I can go home as soon as the paperwork's ready."

Despite her protests about breakfast, I went to the hospital cafeteria and brought back a muffin. She picked at it, set it aside, then stole under the blanket and closed her eyes.

I slouched in the room's uncomfortable chair and read a newspaper until the nurse finally arrived to start the discharge process. We made it home without incident, and Rosie went directly to bed, claiming a headache.

So here I sit, and it's not even noon yet.

One thought occupies my mind: Rosie knew Michaelina was outside and didn't warn me. Not immediately, anyway. Not when she heard the mudroom door that led to the garage slam. Not when she heard the bang of the car door either, or the engine rev. Not when Patton began his furious barking.

Okay, she did come out of the house shouting—but at what point? Had she envisioned me backing up out of the driveway? Had she hoped to give me a scare? Or had she, for just those few seconds, seen an opportunity for payback? Maybe she thought it'd serve me right if the child I loved was taken from me, the way I'd tried to take John from her.

She'd hesitated. An evil wish, maybe even a prayer, had flitted through her mind that something bad would happen, that I'd be hurt the way I'd hurt her.

And God jumped right on it. He gave her what she wanted, even if she took back her wish a few seconds later.

The great Saint Eurosia, fallen at last! So you're capable of spitefulness after all. Capable of wishing for revenge, even to the point of endangering your own child. All your prayers, Masses, and confessions have been for naught, because in the end, you're no better than I am. No better than anyone.

So that's why you took the blame, not just publicly, but in your own conscience. Not because you were trying to excuse me, be kind to me, save my reputation, make up for past faults, or win me over. You took the blame because you hesitated.

And for how long? Those moments in time are compressed. Or maybe they're expanded, elongated. Warped, anyway. If for even a fraction of a second, that fraction makes all the difference in the world, the difference between pity and vengeance, innocence and guilt, life and death.

Don't get me wrong—I'm not claiming your delay cost Michaelina her life. No one can know. What matters is you wavered, and you did it willfully.

All these years, I've prided myself on being your teacher, but this was the one lesson you always resisted—the lesson of retribution. The lesson that loved ones should be punished when they disappoint us.

You finally learned it.

Day 237

I remember, so long ago, holding hands with Rosie. It's hard to believe that now, but whenever we walked more than half a block to the car or a store or anywhere, my hand naturally sought hers. When I took it, there was always a responsiveness—not a squeeze, exactly, just an answering hold that indicated her satisfaction in it.

However, that began to change soon after John was born. Once she was fondling her new baby boy, my taking her hand wasn't always welcome. She'd pull it away to carry the baby or the baby's things, to push the stroller, or to otherwise tend to him. I persisted for a while, and when we were out alone, we'd return to that hand-holding bliss.

But the frequent rejections got to me after a while, and eventually this token of affection was lost. And when tokens of affection are gone, affection itself isn't far behind.

Today, though, I experienced an unaccountable urge to take her hand. I've become weak, I suppose, dealing with this tragedy and the continual headache of Thurman. Anyway, this evening Rosie and I went to the store to pick up some dog food. It was dark out and unseasonably balmy. After depositing the dog food in the trunk of my Mercedes (I've gotten rid of the Porsche), I told Rosie I wanted to walk down the block to grab a coffee and would be back in five minutes. She elected to go with me. As we walked, I glanced down at her soft hand and began to reach for it.

I gained control of myself just in time. Embarrassed, I broke into a trot and reached the Starbucks well ahead of her. By the time she arrived, I was already coming out the door, black coffee in one hand and fruit tea for her in the other.

Rosie sensed something. As I handed her the fruit tea, our eyes met. There again was that look on her face, the expression I've come to know well. It's that special kind of consternation reserved for someone you can't stand, but can't manage without.

Day 239

I don't blame you, Rosie, truly I don't. Not for hesitating. You've suffered enough.

The fact is, I've endured relatively few negative consequences for my actions in this life, including my myriad infidelities. As punishment for my misdeeds, a just God might've meted out much worse.

But Rosie, you've never done anything deserving of more than a slap on the wrist. Yet the one time you do something objectively wrong—your one brief moment of hesitation—God slams down his hammer on you.

Day 241

It's a funny trick of the mind.

How is it possible to experience such a dramatic shift in perspective? The bombshell—Rosie's hesitation—has shattered my worldview. All my anger towards her, my resentment, my desire to blame her for the accident has dissipated.

Everything has changed. I can't look at her the same way. When I view the circumstances dispassionately, the logical response to this new information should be increased bitterness toward her. Yet my mind insists on the opposite. I can't comprehend the mechanism. This reversal in my attitude has nothing to do with my own will. It's happened automatically, as if some exterior being gained access to my mind's circuitry and flipped a switch.

It's not Rosie's hesitation *per se* that's caused this change. It's not the knowledge that Rosie, too, bears direct culpability for the accident. It has more to do with the realization that she must feel guilt too, guilt resulting from her own choices.

She, like me, was pulled by mysterious forces, evil forces, ones she couldn't stand up against. And she succumbed to them. We're the same, Rosie and me. We're on the same side now. Yes, it's Rosie and me, two sinners, against this God of hers.

Rosie's weakness draws from me a wish to protect her. Or maybe that's not strong enough. It draws from me a *yearning* to protect her. I feel an imperative to do everything in my power to lift the burden from her shoulders, to assuage her guilt.

I can't have her getting sucked down into that cesspool the way I have.

Day 242

The problem, though, is that my yearnings are of no concern to Rosie. The scenes with John at the hospital that have caused this change of heart in me have produced a countervailing effect on her.

Our situation is like apes switching positions, so that now I'm the one who wants to groom her, to pick those ugly lice off her, and perform other animalistic functions to demonstrate my obeisance. I'm already expressing, via my softened voice, tone, and attitude, that I desire for us to tackle this mess together in a new, united way.

But therein lies the rub. I may view her as the dominant one now, but she rejects that position. Instead of allowing me to tend to her, she takes little notice of me. She finds my subservience of no value.

Day 245

Today, I went to Sunday Mass again. I'm not entirely sure what I'm doing there—I have little desire to engage with the service. Rosie can't find out I'm going. She'd ascribe too much meaning to it, or else the wrong meaning. She'd think I was doing this to please her. But that's not it.

I've discovered a pew in the back corner, behind a pillar, where I feel comfortable. I arrived early enough today to find it unoccupied. A Bible had been left behind there in the missal rack.

During the service I paged through it. I prefer the Old Testament. The stories there are rife with dastardly deeds, with punishment and retribution—including God's. The stories don't seem congruent with the New Testament, which overflows with Jesus and his saccharine mercy. How is this the same God? And which God was it who effectuated Michaelina's death?

When the service wrapped up, I tucked the Bible under my arm and brought it home with me.

Day 248

After the hell I've been through these past two weeks, I still have to make emotional room to deal with that damn psychiatrist. I don't want to see her, and yet I need to. I've begun to see my visits to her as a just punishment. God's retribution, you might say.

Or maybe that's not the right way to put it. These visits somehow help to re-balance the universe, to bring about some invisible but unavoidable reckoning. They're a link between the past and the future. The unchangeable past, with its one-nighters and nurse-sex and Heather and a dead Michaelina, and an uncertain future, with an unmanageable John and bruised Rosie. And in between, a here-and-now with Rosie's incomprehensible God presiding over it all.

I'm drawn to these therapy appointments as a watchful deer to the stream. I approach cautiously, desperate to drink, but alert to the surrounding dangers. My eyes shift, my ears perk up and listen. But always, always, needing to bend and drink.

I tried to frame today's visit in a positive light before heading over. At least it was something to get me out of the house, to engage with someone other than Rosie, who was resisting my efforts. It would provide some distraction.

Not only that. I had my nugget of knowledge too, tucked into my pocket, away from view—knowledge of that birthmark and that body. I was ready to pull it out when I saw the chance to buy my release with it.

Dr. Thurman was a bit more pleasant when she greeted me this time. Not exactly smiling—she never smiled—but a bit more open-seeming. My hopes rose accordingly.

She began with, "So. How did things go this week?"

Not that great, I told her. I wanted to spend my time operating on patients who needed me.

"How'd you spend your time instead?"

How indeed? An aborted vacation with my wife, during which any chance of intimacy between us was ruined. An accident caused by an idiot in an ice storm that sent us to the hospital. An ill-fated confrontation with my son, during which any hope of our reconciling was catapulted to the netherworld.

And let's not forget the discovery that my wife had facilitated the death of our daughter.

These were not topics I had any intention of discussing. I told Thurman instead that my wife and I had gone on a brief trip to enjoy each other's company, that I'd had a visit from my son, and that I'd pruned my roses. Only one of those was an outright lie—it obviously wasn't rose-pruning time. I waited to see if she'd confront me about that, but she probably knew nothing about roses.

"Any thoughts about the topics we've been talking about?"

"Which ones?" I parried.

"Grief and guilt."

Oh, those. "Not very rewarding matters to contemplate, are they?"

"You might be surprised," she said. "Maybe not so rewarding right away, but maybe you've heard of delayed gratification."

I didn't dignify that with an answer.

"How will we get anywhere," she continued, "if you don't reflect on these things?"

I said I didn't want to get anywhere.

"You want that clearance, don't you?"

"Yes, just tell me what I need to say, and I'll say it."

"Things don't work that way."

I asked her whether she couldn't just write me another prescription if she was so all-fired concerned about my grief. (Not Xanax—the bottle of that was still sitting in the desk drawer of my office, unopened.)

"Pills aren't going to fix your problems," she said. "Maybe they can help for a bit. But no surgery until you can be all right without them."

"Forget the prescription, then," I said. I suggested she verify the stability of my mental state with a Rorschach test or some free association. I remembered those tools—vaguely—from my psychiatry rotation during medical training.

She clucked, which I interpreted as amusement. I went with that, pretending I'd been joking all along. If I could convince her I was feeling carefree and at ease, surely that would speak to my healed mental state.

She'd have none of it, however. Once again, she asked me to state what happened the day of the incident.

I noticed she didn't use the word *accident*. I said I failed to see how re-living it would help.

She said, "I see you're not ready. Take your time. We have plenty of time. All the time in the world."

Day 252

It's been several days since my last entry because there's nothing to report. I've been trying hard with Rosie. I've continued with our morning ritual, waiting for the double-flush and the footsteps so I can deliver tea to her in person. She thanks me in a low voice.

Outside of that, my efforts have been ineffectual. She won't let me do anything for her—every attempt is gently rebuffed. There's nothing I can make for her, move for her, fix for her, buy for her.

She's not angry, or even demonstrably sad. She's just listless. I can't engage her in conversation or get her to muster energy for any activity. I didn't realize I was capable of so thoroughly suppressing her spirits. I'm the boy who's peeled the light off a firefly, sticking it on his finger like a gem, parading about with his treasure, who then notices the dying insect on the ground. That's what I've done to Rosie.

With so little to do at the hospital, I've extended my morning run farther each day. It's getting to be too great a distance for Patton. On the way back today, a mile from home, he flopped down and refused to go on. I had to call Rosie to pick us up.

She reminded me about Patton's advancing age, and mildly remonstrated with me not to push him so hard. At last, even if unintentionally, I got her to speak up about something, to care about something.

Day 254

The only tasks that bring me satisfaction are ones that please Rosie. I do the dishes for her and take out the trash. Any time she speaks, I respond with enthusiasm, but the words never lead anywhere.

She doesn't ask for help with her crossword puzzles any more. They stack up on the coffee table half-finished, or often, not even started. And she's begun to sleep in a lot, or least to spend a lot of time in bed. I wait as long as possible for her to get up so I can deliver her tea.

I wait until Patton is running around in circles and ready to wet the floor.

Day 257

Yesterday I purchased a little hotplate for Rosie's tea mug, because of her sleeping in. This morning I left her tea on it so I could get Patton out. When I returned home, however, Rosie was gone from the house. The hotplate was unplugged, and the tea untouched.

Why is it that when I'm ready and willing to please my wife, nothing I do matters to her? Before, if I'd asked her out to dinner, she'd have perked up like Patton before our run. If I so much as sat near her on the sofa, she'd beam and edge closer. Now she has no interest in dinner out and seems not to notice if I sit beside her.

I can't force her. No, what I need to do is discipline Butt-cheeks. He's ruined everything. He's the one who caused the estrangement from my son, and now my wife. He's responsible for Michaelina's death. It's past time he was taught some hard lessons.

Day 261

Thanksgiving Day. What have I to be thankful for? And who's there to thank?

Thanks for nothing, I say to whoever is listening. Thanks for taking my daughter from me. Thanks for taking my surgery from me, my son from me. Thanks for making my wife hate me. Thanks for destroying my life.

Rosie and I were invited to Maude's house for the holiday. Their brother from Illinois and his caustic teenage kids would be there too. Rosie, for once, was up before me. She was charged with making a pumpkin pie for the occasion—I woke to the smell of it. She can make a tolerable pie, and her pumpkin version is quite good. Still, the spicy odor did nothing to improve my mood. A pumpkin pie is not worth eating, not able to be enjoyed, without Michaelina.

After my run, I gave Patton a chew bone in celebration of the day. At least he'd have something to be thankful for. Then I sat and read the remains of yesterday's paper. Rosie had mangled the section containing her crossword puzzle more than usual. But did I say anything? I did not.

That was to be my last effort on her behalf for the day. The part of me that desires to please her had mysteriously deserted. A nasty, resentful part ascended, determined to block memories and emotions and concern for others. I let him have his way.

Around eleven, Rosie asked if I was ready to go.

I told her I'd decided to stay home.

Her face paled. She said it would be good for me to get out of the house.

Good for whom? I said I wasn't feeling well.

Her brow furrowed momentarily but smoothed out quickly. "Should I stay home with you?" She voiced the question in a neutral tone, the kind she was incapable of pulling off without a major effort. Of course, that very effort gave her away. She was anything but neutral about this.

I called her bluff. "That would be nice," I said.

The muscles of her face began working beneath the surface in a monumental struggle to hide her emotions.

When she opened her mouth to speak, I interrupted her. "On second thought, never mind. You go. I'm going to lie down."

She drew in a long breath and exhaled it quietly. She began protesting the arrangement.

I waved away her objections. "You go ahead. Have fun."

Nothing I could've done would've made her happy anyway. If I went with her, she'd have no chance of enjoying her family, not with the mood I was in. And if I stayed behind, she'd feel guilty about leaving me alone. The worst scenario would be if we stayed home together.

She turned to go, then glanced back over her shoulder.

"I'll leave you some pie," she said.

"No thanks—my stomach's acting up."

After hovering around another 15 minutes, she finally slid out the door.

I spent the day binge-watching old episodes of *Breaking Bad* as I worked my way through a carton of ice cream.

So I hurt her again. But there was no way around it, not today. Holidays are a concentrated version of the day-to-day misery of existence. They're made for pain.

Day 265

It's as if a thick blanket of invisible particulate matter now covers everything, and I can't avoid breathing it in. It constricts my throat and lungs; it steals my appetite for food and work and any sort of pleasure. The mass of particles imparts a sort of electricity, dispersing a negative charge in the surrounding air, ready to explode at the tiniest spark.

Yet it never does. It just hangs there, blurring everything, spoiling everything about life that could otherwise be good, or at least tolerable and comfortable. I've suffered, but the small sacrificial acts I've inflicted on myself during this year of humiliation don't seem to be ones that Rosie cares about. Oh, she never indicates by word or gesture that she doesn't want me near her. It's that her whole being emanates an aura of resignation and indifference. I don't think she's trying to punish me, or even attempting to make some sort of statement. It's more like she's just given up. I've concluded she cares about one thing only: bringing John back into our lives.

I dread that. A reconciliation would be difficult after our recent encounter. I shouldn't have spoken to him as I did, but I was unprepared, thrown off-guard. He didn't help matters by lashing out at me.

Furthermore, he's not the John of my imagination. I don't know him—he was no more than a boy when he left, and now he's 24. His shoulders have filled out, his jaw is wider, and he's even a bit taller. He has his own motivations, opinions, and points of pride. These are a mystery to me.

Christmas will be here soon. I can't stand another dismal holiday like Thanksgiving.

Day 268

At dinner tonight, I told Rosie my plan.

A light kindled in her eyes. For a moment she was that firefly again, the one whose glow could dazzle my world.

But I feared a misunderstanding, so I clarified. "Just John. I'm not ready for that pregnant woman too, not on Christmas."

The spark in Rosie's eyes extinguished.

"This first time might be awkward," I explained.

I didn't say it, but how could John apologize for his desertion, for how he spoke to me in the hospital, and for his part in Michaelina's death, with that woman listening in? Adding her to the mix would complicate a sensitive situation. John has his pride too.

Rosie looked down at her plate and gave her head that determined little shake I've come to know so well. The one I hate.

"Let's leave things the way they are," she said.

What was that supposed to mean? Things couldn't be much worse than the way they were. Did she have so little faith in me, that having our son over would actually be worse than the nightmare we were living now? The two of us drift about this empty house, occasionally entering each other's orbit, but unable to muster any real engagement.

I've never admitted to her what a deep wound John had cut into me by his departure, how painful these years without him have been, how Michaelina was the only liniment I had. With her gone, the injury has flared up again, and aches more acutely than ever.

Nor can I admit it to her now.

Day 269

I blame the Xanax for what happened today.

I hadn't planned to take it. But it was something to do. Something different, something that could possibly break the cycle of these endless days filled with endless ruminations.

When I opened my desk drawer at the office, the little bottle rolled forward, jostling the pills inside. The clatter was like the warning of a rattlesnake whose nest has been invaded.

It was the danger that attracted me. Or maybe not the danger, but the opportunity not to care, the abandonment of principle. Even as I swallowed the pill, I reminded myself that I didn't need to. I wasn't taking it out of weakness or craving, but out of defiance. I was defying myself. I was denying myself the satisfaction of not needing it. Afterward, I deposited the bottle in my pocket.

The pill did its work in relaxing me. That made me angry, yet even my anger seemed strangely blissful.

So yes, I was relaxed in Thurman's office today—too relaxed. I sank into that ectosymbiotic sofa and spread my jellied being across its surface. I had the sensation it was feeding on me, on my angst.

Thurman asked me to tell her about a surgery that didn't go well—but not the one that caused my suspension.

When I asked why, she said it was to explore a circumstance when I'd felt a small amount of guilt. It could even be a circumstance in which my actions were fully excusable. According to her, most people, except psychopaths, feel guilty when something goes wrong in a situation where they have decision-making power, even if they're not at fault.

Examples popped into my head. After all, I've been a surgeon for a long time. Surgery is a risky business, no matter how proficient the surgeon. I had an inkling, though, of where she was going with this line of questioning, and

I wanted to thwart her. So I told a story that wouldn't fit her narrative, one that I thought she couldn't deconstruct:

About six months ago, a mother brought her daughter to see me. The girl was around ten years old and presented with a rare case of facial infused lipomatosis, a condition caused by a genetic mutation that results in an overgrowth of fat affecting just one side of the face. The result was that she had one grotesquely large cheek.

In this case, the excess fat had infiltrated surrounding tissues, including the muscles, dermis, and submucosa, but I could detect no abnormal vascularity or malignancy. In the end, removing the adipose mass was relatively straightforward.

At her follow-up exam, I was pleased with the surgical result, and said as much to the girl. To my surprise, she shot me a tearful, almost angry look. When I asked why she was dissatisfied, she said it was because she was still ugly.

I looked with raised brows at the mother, who requested that I step outside with her into the hall. Tears welled in her eyes. God how I hate crying women. She told me that ever since the initial consultation, her daughter had been weepy in the mornings, not wanting to go to school. There'd been no improvement in her emotional state post-surgery, even after the swelling had gone down.

The mother asked if I remembered saying, in front of her daughter, "*She would've been a pretty girl.*"

Thurman clucked. "You would say such a thing?"

I told her my off-hand remark was true—it even seemed to me a compliment of sorts, at the time. And after the surgery, the girl looked much improved, more or less normal-looking to the typical observer. The scar was well hidden, and she had pleasant features. I'm an expert, though, who could see the reality. I knew her face would never be perfect again.

"*Hoo.* So. You still think this was a compliment?"

"I wouldn't use the word compliment, no."

"When you were a child, maybe adults talked to you that way?"

"An adult? No." As soon I said that, I wished I hadn't.

"A child then. A playmate."

I hesitated. Thurman was a raptor, a falcon, circling far above me, peering down with her scope-eye. Spotting movement on the ground, she zeroed in on it—on me, her prey, in a manner that was becoming familiar.

"Why tell that story and not a messed-up operation?"

I looked at her.

My story was supposed to be a way to talk about something removed from myself and Michaelina. I thought it would distract Thurman, send her into a therapeutic cul-de-sac. But it hadn't worked out that way. Instead, I became a cowering animal, holding my breath as her wheeling shadow passed over me. She was forcing me think, to plan, to anticipate her next move so I could circumvent it.

The problem was, telling the story revealed something to me that I hadn't realized before. My interaction with the little girl had caused me to feel more guilt than any unsuccessful surgery ever had.

Thurman somehow sensed my realization. She sniffed guilt in the air and drew near my thoughts.

But she was off base. She wasn't understanding what my guilt over the little fat-cheeked girl was all about. It had nothing to do with Michaelina.

Here's where the Xanax effects came in. That drawing near of our minds morphed into a kind of physical attraction. Thurman's peasant face and muscular body allured me. I called to mind the satisfying encounter we'd had so many years ago.

I felt a sudden need for her to understand me, for her to not think badly of me. I had to make her see that my treatment of that girl reflected my own past, my own childhood.

So I told her another story, one that required no thought. A story that had repeated itself in my head so often over the years that I didn't see how it could possibly arouse any new emotion in me.

I told her about Butt-cheeks. The real story.

As a child I was good-looking. However, I was slightly heavy, and for some reason the extra weight gravitated to my face. My Aunt Shirley used to pull me close and poke her forefingers into my cheeks, saying, "This boy has so much brains they're spilling out into his cheeks." I was smart, so I experienced her comment as praise.

At the start of seventh grade, my mother bought me a pair of new gym shorts and some underwear. They were too large for me—I hadn't hit my growth spurt yet. I was bothered not only that they didn't fit, but because they suggested that my mother perceived me to be that size (the shorts were wide, not tall). I complained.

As usual, she brought the matter to my father. He told me to get over it—that I'd grow into the shorts (I didn't want to grow into them) and that my mother couldn't be running to the store every time I didn't like new clothes. Besides, they'd been on sale.

So I was forced to wear them. We played basketball in gym class the first week of school. I was a superior student, but, as an only child without much in the way of friends, and a father uninterested in sports, I was an inexperienced ball player. I'm competitive by nature, though, and worked hard to improve. Even so, my efforts on the court were belittled by the other boys, as if I shouldn't be allowed to be of any consequence on their turf.

I don't know how it happened. To this day, I don't. The gym teacher was immersed in a conversation with another teacher. The basketball rolled in my direction. I lunged for it, sliding across the floor and burning my knee, yet still missing the ball. Lying there, I pulled my knee to my chest—all my focus was on that pain. I heard a laugh-snort from a tall boy named Joel. His guffaw was followed by a rippling of suppressed chuckles that grew into a tsunami of laughter. I wanted to join in, but my knee stung and I couldn't see the joke. I figured they were laughing because I'd fallen.

When I finally stood up, though, I felt a coolness move across my backside that could mean only one thing. A hotness followed, shooting up my neck and into my face. I pulled up my underwear and gym shorts in a single motion, but it was too late.

Joel, still laughing, called me Butt-crack. After that, whenever the gym teacher was out of range, he ran up to me and hissed the name into my ear. The next day the name morphed to Crack-face. Eventually Joel settled on Butt-cheeks, because of my large cheeks.

The name spread. Boys started calling me that in the lunchroom, hallway, bathroom. There was no escaping it except by not going to school, and that wasn't going to happen.

The name wasn't the only torment either. Anytime we were unsupervised in the locker room and my back was turned, one of the boys would sneak up behind me and pull a pair of underwear over my head. And not clean underwear either.

I remember examining myself in the mirror at home, mentally comparing my face to that of my classmates. Even though the name had emerged from the basketball incident, I had to admit that there was a kernel of truth to it—hadn't my Aunt Shirley noted it numerous times? Yes, the size of my cheeks was outside the norm. I'd never given it a thought before, but it began to weigh on me. Not only did my cheeks have nothing to do with the size of my brains—as my aunt had claimed—they were an embarrassing facial aberration.

The recognition of this fact, the taunting of my classmates, and my powerlessness to change the dynamic made my school life nearly unbearable. I was obsessed with correcting the problem, but there seemed no avenue open to me. I tried to eat less—of course that didn't work. I said something about my face to my mother, without revealing the teasing, but she merely shook her head and said I was being silly. There was no way to broach the topic with my father, who probably would've called me Butt-cheeks himself if he'd only had more imagination. The next time Aunt Shirley pulled me close, I pushed her away. Forcing my hurt onto someone else provided some consolation.

Other kids acquired unpleasant nicknames too—Mole, Pizza Face, Gollum, and the like—but they either didn't care, or were able to hide the hurt better than I. They laughed and ribbed each other. I couldn't make light of it the way they could.

When even the girls at school started addressing me by that name, I began to have visions of going into the hospital for an operation, a doctor cutting my cheeks open and pulling out the excess fat, and then my returning to school in triumph.

In the summer before high school I shot up in height. I was still no taller than average, but it was enough to thin me out. Objectively, my cheeks were no longer fatter than anyone else's. The name, however, persisted.

Eventually, I went on to college. The name was gone, but not the after-effects. The years of teasing had caused me to maintain a social aloofness. I devoted the spare time that should've been spent hanging out with friends to studying. I had dreams of becoming a doctor, and the previously nebulous idea of fixing my own face grew into a concrete vocation to fix those of truly disfigured children. I needed to prove myself to be superior to those who'd treated me so heartlessly.

How many times have I gone over that basketball incident in my mind—did my shorts really fall down on their own, or had a classmate pulled them down? Was it my mother's fault for buying the too-large shorts? Or my father's, that when I complained, he wouldn't act? Or was it my own fault for not insisting on other shorts, or just wearing my old ones?

As I write this, I'm unsure if I voiced all these thoughts to Dr. Thurman. When I finished the story, I looked into her eyes. Was she seeing me? Was she attracted to me? Maybe she was thinking about sex.

But no—what had I been thinking? How could a story that made me appear so foolish result in her being attracted to me? I broke off eye contact and tried to shake off my confused thoughts.

She clucked and said, "Such a business."

Then she asked if my having been bullied myself made me feel guilty about saying the little girl "would've been pretty."

No doubt I've said plenty of hurtful things in my life. Who hasn't? But I don't expend a lot of effort choosing my words so as not to offend. I was bullied, and I (Butt-cheeks, that is) learned to bully too.

The girl with lipomatosis reminded me of my Butt-cheeks past. My comment to this girl's mother wasn't an off-hand remark—I'd said the words on purpose. Saying them was like scraping dog crap off the bottom of my shoe onto the sidewalk, ripe for someone else. Like shifting a sticky bit of crap to the other side of the scale of justice. It seemed a perfectly fair thing to do at the time.

What value is there, though, in avenging petty insults from the past? I've accomplished everything I've set out to do in my life—become a successful craniofacial surgeon, built considerable wealth, garnered prestige and honors far beyond those idiots who called me names in middle school. Hell, I even operated successfully on a child who had one butt-cheek.

Thurman asked me if I was trying to get rid of my guilt about Michaelina by dumping on this other girl.

"No," I said.

She ignored my response and said there were better ways to manage my guilt. We'd talk about them next time.

Next time, though, I won't be doped up.

Day 272

I invited Rosie to dinner and a movie tonight. She tried to beg off, claiming fatigue, but I had to divert my mind in some way.

I pressed her and she agreed. The movie was a melodrama I found unconvincing and silly. Rosie, though, appeared fully absorbed. During a particularly maudlin scene, she began sniffling. A sideways glance revealed tears shining in her eyes.

Rosie, you're the same sweet, sensitive person you've always been. I need some of that sensitivity to be directed toward me. Do you see how I'm humbling myself for you? I need my attempts at kindness to find some receptivity in you.

Day 273

Today I bought a Christmas tree. I thought it might cheer Rosie up, but when I opened the door to bring it in, she took one look and fled upstairs. I hoped she was running to get the decorations, but the abrupt closing of her bedroom door squelched that notion.

I set it up anyway. She's always taken charge of decorating—early on with John and in recent years with Michaelina. This time I did the whole damn thing myself.

I brought the boxes down from the storage closet, untangled the lights (I'd never have left them in such a state) and wound them around the tree. The ornaments were also in a jumble. I picked out the colorful balls and dispersed them throughout the tree in a pleasing pattern. Then came the season-themed ornaments, the Santa Clauses and sleds and fake candles and such, and then the more personal ones we'd accumulated over the years, including several from patients' families—a teddy bear, a smiling baby face, and even a stethoscope ornament.

Next, I forced myself to confront several ornaments Michaelina had chosen at the mall: a tiara ornament, a princess sitting on a sparkling globe, and a Cinderella-like carriage. I hung them all. Lastly, I came to a construction-paper snowflake that Michaelina had made. A photo of her was pasted on one side, and on the other, a drawing she'd made of herself. It looked remarkably like the one on Rosie's mug, just slightly more sophisticated in style. I placed it in the most prominent place on the tree.

I was about to put the box away but noticed one last bit tucked under a loose flap. I pulled at it and out came another homemade ornament, this one constructed from various pasta shapes spray-painted gold and glued to a piece of cardboard in the shape of a frame. In the center, attached to some green construction paper, was a childhood photo of John. On the other side was his own drawing.

Unlike Michaelina's simplistic sketch, his was a meticulous colored pencil illustration of our family at the time. Rosie wore a red dress, me a white lab coat, and John a T-shirt and jeans. Our hairstyles and fingers and shoes were all well-articulated. The way he drew our eyes, with irises and sclera and even eyelashes for Rosie, surely demonstrated advanced ability for one so young. At the bottom were the words 'age 5,' written in Rosie's hand.

In his rendering, we all held hands and smiled. I ran my finger over the figures, tracing the outlines. Was this the reality back then? Or only John's dream picture of us? Maybe it's my own memories that are faulty.

That ornament hadn't graced our tree in years. I placed it next to the snowflake, so that the pictures drawn by our two children hung side by side.

Day 274

I opened my pilfered Bible today for something to do and came upon the story of Abraham and Sarah. In their old age, God promised them a child. But after waiting eons for the fulfillment of that promise, Sarah became impatient and skeptical. She told Abraham to sleep with her maid Hagar to produce an heir.

Anyone could anticipate that this plan, like the plot of a bad TV sitcom, would end in disaster. But Sarah urged Abraham on, and Abraham obliged. He probably couldn't believe his luck—told to have sex with his wife's maid, with his wife's blessing! I'll bet he made the most of it.

Hagar bore Abraham a son—Ishmael. Her love for Ishmael was proprietary; she allowed Sarah no role in the relationship, and instead continually mocked Sarah for her inability to conceive. Sarah, as expected, was pissed off. Once God's promise was belatedly fulfilled and Sarah bore her own son—Isaac—she forced Abraham to expel Hagar and Ishmael. From then on, two distinct generative lines formed—from Isaac, the Jews, and from Ishmael, the Arabs. There's been no end to grief in the world ever since.

Hadn't Rosie practically pushed me into my own infidelities? And wasn't she the one, with her proprietary love for John, who essentially forced me into my own unavailing way of relating to him?

There's been no end to grief for us either.

Day 276

Today I was back on my guard against Thurman. She began today's session by saying she wanted to discuss my relationship with my son. How did she intuit he was on my mind?

Consulting her laptop notes, she repeated to me what I'd said months ago about my anger with John for being in covert communication with Rosie.

"Before, you told me you were cut off from your son," she said, "then, a few weeks ago, you told me you had a wonderful weekend trip that included a visit with him."

"I never said my conversation with him was pleasant."

She frowned. "Too bad."

I'd blown it again. I thought of changing my story, telling her I was just kidding, that things were going swimmingly with John. She'd find a way, though, to snarl those words too. I side-stepped the issue, saying my relationship with my son was irrelevant to the question at hand.

"I'll judge that," she said, adding that maybe I was feeling guilt about my son too, and we could approach the problem from that angle.

"You're caging me in," I said.

"You made your own cage. I'm trying to help you out."

I snorted at her implication.

She sensed she'd caught me off-guard. In her impatience to take advantage, she began throwing questions at me, hardly pausing to see if I'd answer one before lobbing the next. They were all of this nature:

"When did you start getting resentful of your boy?" "You were jealous of him because he took all your wife's attention, isn't that right?" "Did it make you feel guilty, not talking to him, cutting him out like that?"

Each question lit a new fuse in my brain, until it was primed to explode.

I could divert this conversation by revealing my golden nugget. I could shatter her cool front by saying I knew who she was and had known it all along. I could share my memory of her muscular body—hot, tensed, working beneath me. I could ask if she wanted me again as I wanted her. We could lock the door…

But I sensed the timing wasn't right. I needed to wait.

In the meantime, her questions were mental torture. Like a military prisoner, I'd hold out as long as possible. Even if I suspected I'd cave eventually, I'd never do it willingly.

These distracting thoughts prevented me from providing any response at all.

Thurman tapped her pen on the desk and sighed. "You're not paying attention. We'll try something easier. How about this—tell me a story, any story, about your son when he was a boy. Some kind of strong memory."

I didn't even need to think. I told her this:

When John was in seventh or eighth grade, he got in trouble for a situation at school involving two classmates. One of them had been taunting the other about his stupidity. The second student was in fact pretty stupid, if I recall correctly. Neither of these boys was a friend of John's, but after John had witnessed weeks of bullying, he made a plan. In English class, he surreptitiously removed both boys' typed essays from the homework bin. He whited out their names, forged their signatures on each other's papers, made photocopies to make them appear as originals, and returned them to the bin. Sure enough, the dim-witted boy got an excellent grade and the smart student, a poor one. As you might expect, the smart boy discovered the ruse in short order and complained. John's role was quickly detected, and for his trouble he himself received a failing grade on the assignment. I'd rebuked him for pulling the stunt, but he merely smiled and said, "So what?"

So what.

Thurman asked me why this incident made such an impression on me.

"Because of the failing grade. It was obvious he'd be caught," I said.

Thurman spread her hands flat on the desk. "Hmm... Maybe it made such an impression because you were bullied yourself."

I couldn't see what that had to do with it.

"Three boys are in the story," she said. "Which one do you identify with?"

"None of them," I said. "It's a story about my son."

She ignored me. "You're not like your son—we can agree on that." Her scope-eye narrowed. "Are you like the bully?"

"Why would I need to belittle someone else to build myself up? I was always the best student in the class."

She repositioned her feet under the desk, grinding her toes into the carpet, moving herself into heavy-lifting mode. "So. Only one boy is left."

I didn't see the point of this exercise. "Why do I need to identify with any of them?"

"Let's try this, then," she said. "What was your son trying to do? Was he really trying to get a better grade for the poor boy who was the victim?"

"I suppose so."

"But it was obvious he'd be caught, you said. Maybe John was smart enough to know that, too?"

I said nothing.

"What if there was a boy who stood up for you when they called you Butt-cheeks? What if everyone laughed at him for taking your side but he defended you anyway? How would that make you feel?"

We both knew the answer to that.

Thurman continued. "Suffering for someone else—that's what your son did. That's how we show compassion, right? Your boy was the antidote to bullying, the anti-bully. You should be proud."

I didn't like where she was heading.

"Why does this story strangle you?" She leaned forward, sensing riches ahead. "Maybe you're resentful no one stuck up for you in middle school. Maybe you resent your son because your own Butt-cheeks story makes you the victim, but your son's story makes him the hero."

I disputed her analysis, which only caused her to cling to it more tightly.

"After that incident, is that when your relationship with your son started going bad?"

"*No.*"

But my too-quick, too-emphatic response emboldened her. Her leg danced beneath the desk. She sprang forward with her line of questioning. She was under the rainbow now and closing in on the pot of gold at the end of it.

"Your son being so kind made you angry. Every time you saw him, it reminded you that he was a savior and you were a victim."

I rejected this interpretation. When she asked for mine, I told her I was sick of this psychoanalysis. Why was it necessary to interpret every minutia of human behavior in this convoluted and perverted fashion? Why couldn't the explanation simply be that I was being the best father I knew how to be?

I regretted saying that.

She waved her hand and continued her rant.

"You tried to bring your son down to size—your size. You couldn't look at him. You didn't want him in the house. You made him go, didn't you?"

I tried to shift my position on the sofa—unsuccessfully. It had swallowed and digested me.

"You bullied him. You forced him to leave," she said. "That's how you tried to make him a victim like you. And when he didn't come back begging for your help, when he didn't give *you* a chance to play savior, you were humiliated."

"I survived without my own father's help, and with a wife and baby besides."

"Yes, but you had a degree and a bright future. Your son, on the other hand, had only just turned 18. He wasn't going to medical school or even college, right? But he was above you in goodness. That bothered you."

I gripped the armrest of the sofa, wanting to tear it off. I was the unwilling bystander to Thurman's joy and good fortune. The reflection from the pot of gold lit up her entire countenance.

I finally found my voice. I stood and said, "I'm no victim. And he's no savior."

There was a knock on the door and a nurse appeared, asking Thurman if she needed anything. Thurman told me to sit down and I did. She sent the nurse out with a head gesture.

I thought we were done but she continued, in a softer tone. "You didn't like looking at your own son. His face was always reminding you of what he was and you weren't. Sure, you're intelligent and successful, but you're not so kind like he is. Compassion is worth more. Even you (yes, she said *even you*) know that. You should be admiring your son, but you didn't want anyone throwing a shadow on you."

"He's not as wonderful as you make him out to be," I said. "Since he was a teenager, he's only treated me with contempt."

"*Hoo.* Maybe you baited him? Maybe you found ways to bring out the worst in him so he'd have nothing over you. You treated him badly to make him have contempt for you."

I wouldn't dignify her assertions with a response.

"You were his father so he acted the way you wanted." She clucked then and shook her head. "Such a business," she said. "Just a child, he was. Your child."

Day 277

This morning, I took Rosie her tea. There wasn't a trace of put-on humility about it. Genuine self-loathing filled the gap.

Yesterday's encounter with Thurman wouldn't leave me. I'm reflecting on it now, as I write. Fine, I'll admit it—it's not true that John only treated me with contempt. It's just that the times he did are the memories I've enshrined.

He wasn't—he isn't—such a terrible person. For one thing, he's been good to Rosie. I haven't had the opportunity to witness that these past five years. And he does possess filaments of innate kindness that I'm lacking, as well as fibers of mettle knit densely into his character. His ability to build a life for himself with so little support took courage and determination. He's had cause for resentment too. I see that now.

As I've said, a saint doesn't let you wallow in your sin. I'm thinking now that John could've ignored me in the hospital, but he didn't. He chased me down to confront me with my fault. And he was there at Rosie's bedside the night before, when I'd gone home.

As long as I had Michaelina in my life, I could keep thoughts of John at bay. Now that she's dead, John has resumed an outsize role in my consciousness. Most times I turn aside the painful ruminations, but other times I fantasize about being together again. The old pipedream begins with his approaching me, downcast and ashamed in a prodigal-son way, begging for forgiveness and anxious to make amends. Me, the magnanimous father, the wise elder statesman, waving away his apologies, looking upon him benevolently, assuring him that everything's all right now. My son nearly bursts with gratitude.

Yet the fantasy never goes beyond that. The fact is, I have trouble envisioning how our relationship as father and son could work going forward. If, in reality, he approached me in the deferential manner I envision, would I really forgive him? Forgive his worst sins—the sins of not deferring to me, of not needing me?

Day 278

Nothing is happening. I'm having difficulty writing anything. The world is becoming a blank between my visits to Thurman. Seeing her is the only outlet for my misery.

I received an unexpected phone call today—from Owen, of all people. He invited Rosie and me to celebrate New Year's Eve at his house. You can probably guess my immediate reaction—what could possibly be worth celebrating? And hadn't he received the hospital memo that I'm *persona non grata*? But before disparaging the inappropriateness, not to mention the futility, of issuing me such an invitation, he added, "Not a large party. No one from the hospital. Just an intimate dinner party among friends. You and Rosie, and my wife Aimee and me."

I resisted noting that Owen and I were more colleagues than friends, and that I'd never even met his wife. Such a get-together held little prospect of pleasure. On the other hand, Rosie would agree to it, I was pretty sure. We'd be going out again as a couple, something we hadn't done in so long. She'd have to talk to me then.

I accepted the invitation.

Day 279

Here's an appalling father-son story from the Bible. King David had a son—Absalom—whom he loved dearly, even after Absalom murdered his own half-brother, who had raped Absalom's sister. Fearing his father's response, Absalom lived in exile for three years. David was furious with Absalom, yet he still mourned every day of his exile. Eventually, he sent a messenger to invite Absalom back to their city as an initial rapprochement, but declined to see him in person. The story doesn't say why, but I know. It's treacherous territory, this space occupied by fathers and sons. Love and hate live side by side.

Eventually, Absalom planned a betrayal. He began a campaign to win the hearts of the people while he built up an army. David was forced to defend himself, but he gave explicit instructions to his officers that Absalom was not to be harmed. David had become wise in his later years. He understood that nothing on earth, not even power, was worth the destruction of his son.

The commander of David's army, however, saw only the danger of the rebellion. He killed Absalom himself, then buried the body deep in the earth. David famously grieved the death of this traitor-son in deep agony.

That's the mystery of the father-son relationship. How is it John can exercise this power over me? I can't forget his treatment of me, yet he's still my son, the fruit of my loins.

Day 280

The Christmas tree's been up for weeks now. I'd hoped that hanging John's ornament on it would serve as a signal. Rosie, though, resolutely stays out of the den.

Nor has she relented in her decision not to invite him for Christmas. I haven't asked her again, but the way she spurned my original suggestion makes me avoid questioning her. At the same time, her declining to have John over has only increased the desirability of it. So has the fiasco of my running into him at the hospital. There, I saw him in the flesh. I spoke to him. He exists. All I think about now is seeing him again.

I never used to fear death. Death was for other people. If ever the notion crossed my mind that I myself would die someday, I felt utterly taken aback. The idea was absurd, like a bad practical joke being played on me. Even knowing the reality on a scientific level didn't make it ring true for me emotionally.

But Michaelina's death changed everything. Now, I fear my own death as well as my son's, like David did. David was on familiar terms with death—he'd tried to preserve the life of his newborn son (from his illicit affair with Bathsheba) by fasting and praying, but the baby died anyway. He tried to save his son Absalom's life, but Absalom was assassinated anyway. Why should I have more power than King David, the apple of God's eye, to save my own son? I couldn't save my daughter. I can save no one. I can't even save a child's life with my surgical skills anymore. I've lost any ability to save.

Including any ability to save myself.

Day 281

With nothing happening in my life, all I can write about are Bible stories and nightmares. Last night, I dreamed that John was blind. Stone blind, yet he walked confidently, talking and laughing, without stumbling. I kept wondering how he could be so happy when blind, but he only smiled at me.

Then we were at a state park, hiking a trail on the cliffs. Overgrown brush blocked our path. John, though he couldn't see, made his way through with ease and got ahead of me. When I emerged from the brush I entered a clearing, one with a large expanse of grass. John was far into the distance by then.

Up ahead I spotted a cliff, one with no guardrails. I tried to call out a warning, but my voice wouldn't work. Patton appeared from nowhere and raced toward the cliff, barking. But John wouldn't stop. When he disappeared over the brink, I woke up with my heart racing.

Day 282

Dreaming of Michaelina is a rarity, something precious. In my dream last night, I'd built her a house. But when I presented it to her, she wasn't as delighted as I'd hoped—something about it disappointed her. We stood in the kitchen. Black ink covered her hands and her pink outfit, from playing with my Camlin pen. I lifted her up to the sink and she turned on the faucet and put her hands under it, but the ink wouldn't rinse off. She wiped her hands on my shirt, blackening it. The water in the sink continued to run. I couldn't turn it off—the faucet handles just rotated endlessly—nor could I locate the shut-off valves underneath the sink. The neighbor boy Trevor looked in at the window. I rapped on the glass to make him leave, and he promptly disappeared. When I turned around, though, he was in the kitchen with Michaelina and me. He held a kitchen knife. But no—it wasn't Trevor holding the knife; it was in my own hand. I was the one holding the knife. It wasn't a kitchen knife at all, but a surgical scalpel. Michaelina sat on a throne at the table, pointing at me with a scepter. The scalpel in my hand dripped with something white. Was it paint? Milk? I shied away from comprehension. An ominous feeling made me sense that if I knew what I'd cut open, I'd die of shame and grief.

When I awoke, my shirt was soaked in sweat.

It wasn't a dream I could share with Rosie, but I needed to tell someone to ground it in my memory. It felt more like an experience than a dream, as if I'd had a new encounter with my daughter.

Day 283

Usually I'm able to sneak out for my therapy appointments without Rosie noticing. Or at least I believed she didn't notice. This afternoon, though, she caught me just as I was leaving. I tried to divert any questioning by saying I was just heading out for some fresh air. It was sleeting at the time, however, which didn't lend credence to my story. Her eyes flashed and she asked me pointblank where I was going.

It would've been easy to lie, or to say it was none of her business. I was thrown off, though, by her uncharacteristic confrontation. Maybe I'd underestimated her. So I told her I had an appointment with a psychiatrist.

Her countenance morphed into one of her signature multi-expressions—apprehension, curiosity, and relief commingled. Maybe she'd thought I was seeing another woman.

I hustled off.

The admission offered me a little release, despite the humiliation. And at least it spurred some sort of reaction from Rosie—a flicker in the ashes of her emotional hearth.

On the way to Thurman's office, I worried that if I told her my dream about Michaelina, she'd dissect it, pick at its innards like a freshman biology student with a frog corpse.

But when I described it, she only said, "*Hoo*. What an awful dream." The words were said with sympathy, as a friend might say them, as if she intuited my reason for telling her. As if she understood it was worth dreaming of my girl, even if the dream was a nightmare.

Then she said, "Something new for you to consider. Maybe Butt-cheeks isn't a bully at all. Maybe instead he's a vulnerable child inside of you. Your blustery parts—pride, impatience, anger, judgment—maybe are trying to protect Butt-cheeks from getting hurt even more."

A wildly implausible theory.

She continued. "Let's look at one of these parts. How about your impatience, this part of you that needs to be so intolerant and annoyed with everyone around you. We need to get in touch with this part, to understand who this part is and its motives."

I scoffed. "So now I have some sort of multiple personality disorder?"

"Not a disorder, no. We all of us have many parts that make us who we are. All are good parts, all trying to help us function and protect us from harms. But some parts, by trying to be helpful, just make things worse."

"I'm not buying it. You're trying to trick me into admitting I'm some kind of psychopath."

She waved my protest aside with fluttery fingers. "Beneath all these turbulent parts, you have a good self. I see it. These other parts of you, that arrogance and even anger, are good too, but they go overboard trying to keep you safe."

"Safe from what?"

"That's what we need to find out."

"How's that supposed to happen, by magic?"

"No. Just slowly. I can help. You can get to know these parts. We'll start with an easy one like that impatient part. Tell me, what does that part look like? Maybe even it has a name."

"This is insane. I want no part of it."

"Haha, a joke?" She tapped her pen on the desk, then checked her watch. "Okay, we won't go more in this direction today, but you give it some thinking this week."

"I have no interest in 'giving it some thinking.'"

A trace of some emotion—amusement?—flickered across her face. "So," she said, "I challenge you then to *not* think about it. That won't be easy, because something inside you is crying to get noticed and helped."

Day 284

Christmas Day. Even today, Rosie didn't go to church. She hasn't for months now. The Rosie I've known is slipping away.

Her faith was her sustenance. It sustained her, and she sustained me. Her not believing anymore, not praying, is killing hope for us. That was our last line of defense, the one place she'd held her ground against me all these years. That and her attachment to John.

I went to Christmas Mass without her. I don't care if she knew where I was going or not.

My usual spot was taken. The whole damn church was taken, packed to the rafters. Who were these people, coming to Mass only on Christmas? What was the value? It'd be like taking a bath once a year. Yet their presence must count for something. *My* presence must count for something.

The Christmas carols only blackened my mood. Somehow, they blacken me. I feel a smudge on my face. I need to bathe but can only watch others dip into the now giant baptismal font when the water's stirred up. I stand in the back with other latecomers, unable to move into the stream. I, the one most in need of ablution.

The running gear I wear is inappropriate. People stare. Or no, it seems I'm not dressed at all. I'm naked and filthy. A line forms for communion and I'm pushed into it. I walk, keeping pace with the crush of white-robed people moving to the front. I'm forced to present myself to the priest, who offers me the host and says *Body of Christ* and I open my mouth. But what he holds in his hand isn't a host. It's a bloody bit of flesh with a splinter of bone protruding from it. I see what the bone is. I know whose blood it is.

I turn and try to run but the crowd presses against me. They glare and goad and accuse. Someone grabs my arm, then the others take hold too. The priest has stopped communion and stands to the side, nodding approvingly. The congregants push me up the steps of the sanctuary and past the altar. They raise me up, handing me overhead from person to person until I reach the crucifix. Underneath it, a nurse with naked, gargantuan breasts sits on a man's shoulders. She holds my legs and pushes me up so that I stand on those breasts while clutching the upright beam of the cross so as not to fall. I want to get back to the ground, but when I wrench one leg free, the nurse grabs my foot and slices off a nickel-sized piece of flesh. She pops it into her mouth and chews in an exaggerated way. I reel in pain. The crowd waves their knives. To get away, I pull myself up the cross until I reach the block that holds up Christ's feet. I cling to those feet, wishing only for something to cover my own nakedness.

Day 285

The ground continues to shift beneath me. I don't know what to say to Rosie. She drifts about the house, performing her functions like a hired wraith. Our every interaction is fraught with a vaporous meaning I can't grasp or bear. I've stopped bringing her tea because she's stopped drinking it.

There's something she wants from me. I thought it was allowing John back into our lives, but she rejected my overtures on that. I can't ask her what's wrong outright—everything about her demeanor toward me precludes that possibility.

Day 287

This evening I entered Michaelina's room for the first time since her death. I used to go in there every night when she was alive. After a long day at the hospital focusing on the disfigured faces of children, gazing at my little sleeping beauty's smooth face was a tonic. Her features would be at rest, her breathing slow and relaxed, not like the stertorous breathing of some of my compromised patients. Witnessing the peace there helped me to fall asleep more easily afterward.

This time, though, the bed was empty. I picked up a stuffed animal and smelled it, searching for that fresh, little girl scent, but it had dissipated, replaced by a slightly musty polyester odor. Michaelina's princess dolls were all lined up with their fixed smiles. Nothing could perturb them. Is that what I'd wanted in my own life?

Michaelina owned one of those dolls that was custom-made to look like her, with porcelain skin-tone, round blue eyes, and brown hair. I held the doll close and lay down on her bed, under the canopy. I stroked the hair of this faux-Michaelina and separated out one tress to rest in front of her shoulder. Then I held her above me, as I used to do sometimes, giving my girl again her moment of supremacy. She was the sovereign, looking down on me from heaven. I begged for her mercy. She had to listen to me, to have pity on me.

Michaelina, though, wasn't just a little girl anymore. She was a nine-year old, then a teenager, a young woman with a career, a wife and mother, a graying grandmother. For each stage of her missed existence, I apologized to her—out loud, for real. She won't live those years, have those experiences, because of me. My needs, my petulant attitudes took precedence over her very life. That's the way it was. The unfortunate, appalling, rottenness of the way it was.

"Michael."

Rosie stood in the doorway.

I dropped the doll and leapt from the bed, dinging my forehead on the sharp edge of the canopy.

She said in a soft voice, "You all right?"

I rubbed the spot on my forehead for effect, and said, "It's nothing."

She remained in the doorway, just looking at me. I had no way to get past her. I wanted to say something more—I really did. But what good would saying it do? One of these days, though, we'll need to have it out. Just not today.

I moved to the door and she stepped aside.

Day 290

Thurman was right that I'd have trouble not thinking about these different parts of my subconscious. The idea still seems like bullshit, but I'm ready to try anything.

Immediately I feel impatient, so I go with that.

"Who are you, impatient part? Show yourself to me." I visualize a test proctor looking at his stopwatch. "What makes you so impatient?"

He glances at me, then taps his watch, as if that explains everything.

I persist. "What is it you want?"

"For you to hurry along," he says.

"Where to?"

He shakes his head. "Doesn't matter. Just move your mind along somewhere else. Nothing to see here."

I get the distinct impression, however, that there *is* something to see here. I confront him. "Would you mind moving to the side so I can see what's behind you?"

"No, that wouldn't be wise."

I expect he's right.

Day 293

Owen called today to ask my permission for his sister Darla and her husband Steve to join us on New Year's Eve.

Hell no, was what I wanted to say, but it was *his* party, not mine. So I said sure, of course. Now I can only hope that these superfluous guests don't detract from the occasion. I do find myself looking forward to seeing Owen. I can relax around him, trust him not to judge or mock or speak indiscreetly. He's a human white noise machine, softening and occluding the sharp racket in my brain.

What I haven't figured out is why he wants to be around *me*. Me, a disgraced physician. He can't be that hard up for friends. People adore the Owens of the world. The Owens listen to your complaints and boasting without attempting to outdo you. On the flip side, maybe some people dislike that trait. When people like Owen are that humble, it takes away the joy of outshining them.

I still wonder, though, if his humility could be an act. Or worse, a setup of some kind. I need to be careful.

Day 295

Nightmares come frequently now. Last night I dreamed of Owen entering my office at the hospital and asking if he could call me Butt-cheeks. I tried to escape him, running down the stairs, then taking an elevator, which took me deep into the earth. Wherever the elevator door opened, hospital nurses blocked my exit. Owen appeared. He said, "Let's be kind. Let Butt-cheeks through." Eventually I got around the nurses but got lost in the parking garage. I couldn't recall which vehicle was mine. I landed inside a Ford Fusion and managed to head toward home, but I lost control near the driveway and veered toward the fence. Michaelina was riding her bike behind it. I couldn't see her, but I knew she was there. I tried to slam on the brakes, but they stopped responding, no matter how hard I pressed. Crashing into the fence woke me.

I told Thurman the dream, leaving out the part about Michaelina.

Thurman clucked and asked me about the fence I'd constructed between myself and my wife. She wanted to know whether we were having sexual intimacy. As usual, she'd misinterpreted.

It was interesting, though, that I'd gotten her thinking about sex. Was she wondering whether, if I wasn't having sex with Rosie, I might be free to have sex with her?

Then a new thought emerged. Maybe this was a trap. Thurman would trick me into sex, then accuse me of sexual assault and refuse me the clearance to operate again. I said, "Did Rosie put you up to this?" Rosie would have evidence of adultery and receive a large financial award in divorce proceedings.

But when I suggested Rosie's involvement, Thurman said I looked disturbed.

"Wouldn't *you* be?" I said.

I must've raised my voice, because she tensed in her chair. That only increased my agitation and I blurted out something more, something I won't repeat here. Catching myself, I reined in my volume as I reiterated my suspicion that she was in cahoots with Rosie. I wouldn't be surprised if she'd been talking with the nurses on my staff, too, and maybe even Heather.

"Who's Heather?" she asked.

She turned to her laptop and tapped something in. She said, "How long have you been bothered by this paranoia?"

But she didn't know about Rosie's betrayal, that my suspicions in this case were justified. I said, "Rosie's behind everything. She went behind my back to communicate with John. She couldn't get her own daughter to obey, couldn't keep track of where her daughter was. Even when she figured it out, even when she knew Michaelina had gone outside, she didn't stop me. Did Rosie tell you that, about her hesitating? I wouldn't be in this damn predicament—"

I cut myself off.

Thurman's head popped up from the laptop. "What are you saying?" Her eyes were bulging, not scoping, and the pitch of her voice was a half-octave higher than usual.

I backtracked. "Nothing," I said. "I'm not saying anything."

"You were talking about the day of the incident, when your daughter was in the driveway."

"Absolutely not." I was going to ask her what she was inferring, but didn't want her even to state it. So I made up some other story about a time when I wanted to take Michaelina with me on an errand, and Rosie didn't know where she was.

Thurman turned away from her laptop to look me in the eye. As she opened her mouth for a pointed remark, my pager beeped. I was being called in for a quick consult on a patient with a complication after surgery—a surgery someone else had performed. I was still needed for something. I rose to leave.

But before I could escape her gaze, she said, "You're not irredeemable, you know."

Day 296

After yesterday's session with Thurman, I was ready for New Year's Eve—not so much an evening of celebration as an evening of losing myself in drink.

I did latch on to a madcap hope that Owen's party would inveigle Rosie into opening up. My plan was to steer copious amounts of wine and champagne into her glass. She'd talk then. We'd talk things through, laugh, be ourselves again.

Maybe we'd even have sex.

In the event, none of my fantasies came to fruition. First, it turns out Owen is a teetotaler. That figures—it's consistent with his Ned Flanders-style character. Still, it's false advertising to invite someone to a New Year's Eve party without announcing upfront the absence of booze. Upon arrival, we were offered some kind of mildly bitter mocktail that gave the illusion of an adult beverage with none of the salutary benefits.

The food, at least, was delectable. Owen's wife Aimee—a French-born schoolteacher with wispy hair styled high on her head, a wafer figure, and a propensity to lean in while conversing—did the cooking: grilled scallop hors d'oeuvres with a fusion sauce, filet mignon, braised artichokes, potatoes Dauphinois. Still, I couldn't help remarking on the absurdity of a Frenchwoman serving such a dinner sans wine.

Owen and Aimee exchanged a glance, one that communicated shared amusement, as if this question had been asked of them countless times. Aimee said, "Owen believes wine dulls the taste of the food and makes dinner conversation turn uncivilized."

"You believe that too?"

"I respect my husband's preferences, and his long experience."

Owen's sister Darla piped up. "Men are like wine—some turn to vinegar, but the best improve with age.'"

Was she talking about Owen, or implying something about me? I replied, "Sounds like something a woman would say."

"Actually, it's a quote from one of the popes."

Darla's husband Steve chuckled from across the table. Steve was a glad-handed knee-slapper type, the kind of man who shaves his head when he first starts balding, then wears his new look like a prince. His eyelids were slightly lowered in perpetual amusement. His occupation—wealth management—explained everything.

Darla's face sported a female version of Owen's neotony. Unfortunately, the baby-faced look was no more appealing on her. She reminded me of a ventriloquist's doll, with her small round face, too-rosy cheeks, and pixie-style hair with its almost polyurethane sheen. Rather than leaning in like Aimee, Darla was in a constant state of brisk head-pivoting on her stick-like neck, snapping her attention to whoever was speaking.

Meeting other men's wives always made me grateful for Rosie. Sure, I'd appreciate a wife with Aimee's culinary skills. And while Darla clearly had the sharpest brains of the three, Rosie's more languorous style of interaction was so much easier on the nerves.

The women congregated during appetizers and sat next to each other during dinner. I paid little attention to their conversation, which revolved around cooking and what it was like growing up in France. I bent my ear occasionally in their direction to ensure the topic did not involve children. Aimee and Darla must've been briefed in advance.

The men, too. For their part, they steered clear of surgical or hospital topics. Steve's presence was helpful in that regard. We talked of the stock market and upcoming public offerings and an idea he'd had recently about short selling.

Although the meal was nearly perfect, the apple galette was slightly overbaked, which I remarked on.

Darla said, "'Cookery is an unselfish art. Cooks, like artists, are inspired by a worthy audience.'"

At the lift of my left eyebrow, she quickly claimed to be quoting a famous chef, saying, "I meant only that sometimes it's harder to be a good guest than a good cook."

Was she including herself in that assessment? I turned to Rosie, who was smiling. Was it okay to be amused by this woman?

After dinner, Aimee excused herself to put their kids to bed—they'd finished their movie—while the rest of us repaired to the large living room. Darla and Rosie seated themselves in closely arranged chairs in front of the fireplace. We men had settled, whether by accident or by Owen's design, in a sofa arrangement at the opposite end of the room. I couldn't make out the conversation of the women. Rosie's laugh surprised me. I wasn't sure how I felt about the fact that Darla, this total stranger, could prod Rosie to enjoy herself, without any wine even.

Soon after, they began speaking in hushed tones. I strained to hear the topic, but without success.

Meanwhile, Steve—bless his soul—magicked a flask of bourbon from his jacket and poured us both a glass, with no objection from Owen. In fact, the après-dinner appearance of liquor seemed a ritual both men had come to expect.

When Aimee returned, the women rejoined us. Darla watched me drain my glass. "Ahh," she said, "'Courage is a vitamin best swallowed with whiskey.'"

This time I refused to be goaded. Instead I said, "What are you, some kind of walking Bartlett's?"

She grinned at me, as if I'd caught her with a hand in the cookie jar.

As we pulled on our coats, Darla and Rosie exchanged the kind of farewell that suggested a bosom friendship had blossomed. Darla announced to all how much she'd enjoyed herself, but was just as glad she hadn't imbibed, as she had work to get done the next day.

"On New Year's Day?" I said.

"O-oo-oh yeah," she crooned, as if boasting of the colossal task awaiting her. I'd assumed she was a housewife like Rosie.

Now, until that point, our gathering had felt reasonably normal. *I* had felt reasonably normal. Only at the end, only at the moment we prepared to leave, did it dawn on me: *the whole purpose of this shitty little party.* Why hadn't I recognized Owen's machinations from the start? I should've paid more attention to this sister of his. Backtracking in my recollections, I realized she'd been surreptitiously observing me all evening. And not just observing—hadn't she provoked me multiple times with those quotations of hers? Tried to throw me off, then gage my reaction?

I understood then what this final baiting at the door was about. I was expected to ask her what she did for a living. That's what a typical person would do. Rosie didn't ask—she must've already learned it. I wouldn't do it, though. I wouldn't play into their hands. I refused to bend to destiny.

Fate would have to wait.

Day 299

I've just recounted the money, and it's all there—$20,000 in hundred dollar bills.

For days now, I've been reflecting on Owen's party. The guests were all informed of its purpose beforehand. They had to have been. And that Bartlett's woman—Darla—had connived further with Rosie during the party. I just know it.

My plan to get Rosie drunk hadn't worked. She'd enjoyed herself anyway, but none of that enjoyment redounded to my subsequent benefit. On the ride home, she'd been pensive, expectant, though not in any sexual sense. We chatted a bit about the evening and the guests, with Rosie hesitating between sentences, offering me multiple opportunities to ask questions about Darla, to exercise my curiosity about her.

I wouldn't do it.

And the moment we were home, Rosie reverted to her silent, walled-off self.

I wrote the other day of fate. Fate is scheming against me, I can feel it in my depths. Fate is teeing up future events without my imprimatur. These events are forming a pattern, a grid, a web that's surrounding me. Fate has its legions of co-conspirators—Owen and Darla and Thurman, and even Rosie. Each of them is gripping a corner of this sticky web, lifting the edges and moving to enclose and entrap me.

This morning, I must've felt an instinct to fight fate. That's the only explanation I have for what I did.

I went to the bank to make a withdrawal. What I encountered there was atypical. Instead of the cheery greeting from the staff I expected, the teller at the window spoke in a low voice, glancing furtively at the guard.

Then she excused herself—to get the money from the vault, she said. But moments later I was summoned to a back office and questioned by a bank officer. Evidently, all cash transactions over a certain amount have to be reported to some governmental entity, to track potential money laundering from criminal activity. So now I can't even access my own hard-earned money without suspicion. The officer wanted to know the reason for the withdrawal, but when I refused to provide one and threatened to take my not inconsiderable business elsewhere, she relented.

As the teller counted out the money, my hands fidgeted on the counter in anxious anticipation. It was then I noticed how filthy my fingernails were. It must've been from working in the garden, I thought. But then I recalled that I hadn't touched my roses all day. It had to have been yesterday. Or maybe the day before. But had I not showered since then? And it was January—I had no reason to be working in my garden at all.

From my fingernails, from my body odor, from some strange transmission in the air, I realized the teller must know the truth. And if the teller knew, everyone knew. They knew I killed my own daughter, and that I did it out of spite. But it couldn't have been out of spite, because it was an accident. Did they know that—that it was an accident? I almost asked the teller, but her narrowed eyes—which were knowing, yet indifferent, like a cat's—alarmed me.

It's evening now and I'm not sure how I spent the rest of my day. I haven't done anything with the money. The fact is, I can't recall what I withdrew it for. Was it to fix the Porsche? No real damage had been done, but you know how expensive Porsches can be to repair, especially old classics like mine. The dent must be small, a mere scratch, but I can't bring a picture of it to mind, and I don't want to go look at it. I'll call the garage tomorrow and have it towed. It can be made as good as new.

Day 300

This morning I woke early after a mostly sleepless night, during which I ruminated on how the teller had found out. Maybe there was a story on the news that I'd missed.

It didn't matter, though, how people were finding out. I only knew they were, and because of it, I had to get away. That's what the money was for.

I gave Patton a quick run around the block—he was disappointed with the brevity of it—then hopped into my Mercedes.

Yes, I own a Mercedes now, a new one. I sold the Porsche right after the accident. I'd somehow forgotten that yesterday. All this gaslighting is affecting my mind.

I took off in an easterly direction, doing 90.

After a few hours on the road, the hilly landscape turned mountainous—steep and winding. I could easily make a turn too fast, I figured. Accidents do happen—I know that better than anybody. Or I could be pulled over for speeding. My hang-dog expression might make the police suspect something more. They'd search my car, ask about the telltale dent on the back bumper.

But then I remembered—it's a different car now.

I had to get a better mental handle on things. My memory hasn't been as lucid of late. I've made some mistakes, some miscalculations. As I drove, I tried to clear my head of the tangles that've wound around the neurons in my hippocampus.

I drove fast, hoping that a bit of adrenaline might prove useful in one way or another. My Mercedes faithfully hugged every curve, like a drunk with a cheap prostitute. The state troopers must've been on holiday—none were there to shine a purifying flashlight in my face.

At a rest stop I thought to call Rosie. Even if she was in on it, I didn't want to cause her additional anxiety. I couldn't find my cell phone though. I looked between the seats, under the seats, in the glove box. I couldn't have left it at home. I never forget my cell phone. That's something Rosie would do.

I hadn't thought to bring a coat, but I sat outside on a bench anyway. I considered my future. What if Thurman never cleared me? Even if she did, my practice was already essentially ruined. Finding a position elsewhere seemed doubtful. And anything less than a surgeon would be a humiliation.

Yes, yes—acceptance of humiliation is the best form of humility. But who ever believes that in the moment?

Noticing my fingers had turned numb, I returned to the car. After a few more hours of driving and listening to *La Boheme*, I felt a bit better. I'd gained a fresh perspective. It was this: I was going to die regardless. Even without suicide, death was inevitable—this nightmare would end at some point. I latched onto this new outlook, which was surprisingly consoling.

The next time I got gas I found a pay phone—service stations deep in rural areas still have them. I dialed Rosie's cell, and after six rings she finally picked up with a *hello* that was faint and unenthusiastic. I paused without identifying myself. Had she been waiting for my call? Or dreading it? Maybe she'd been hoping never to hear from me again.

Suddenly, I could think of nothing to say to this woman. What did she want from me anyway? What was done was done. Yes, it was my fault.

Everything that's screwed up now is my fault. What else could I do to satisfy her—announce a news conference? Post it on social media?

Maybe I'm expected to vomit up an actual apology. Then here it is in writing: *I'M SORRY, ROSIE*. Is that good enough? I've spent nearly a year in this purgatory, and I've got nothing to show for it but your feeble hello in my ear. And at home, your turned head, your wilted movements, your muffled sighs. You can talk, you can laugh—I saw that at Owen's party. You're trying to cheat me, to trick me somehow.

I don't know what you want from me. But when I heard your anemic *hello*, I knew what *I* wanted. I wanted to reach through the phone, take hold of you, and wake you up to the doom we're heading for. Then I'd carry you to the bed, the way I used to in the distant past. Not playfully like in the early times, not with candles and crosswords. No—I'd have you definitively, in the way that would cloak my need, my fears.

I can't have you though. I can't take you because I've taken too much already, and have nothing to offer in return. You don't need me, not the way I need you. That gives you all the power.

The theorists have it backwards. The key isn't the woman's submission, it's the man's. The woman accepts you or not—the power is hers. When she agrees, it's the man who yields, who's overwhelmed by his need. In the end, he has no choice but to surrender. He relinquishes not just his body, like the woman, but his control, his very essence.

But we men don't want to admit it. Our egos can't handle it. So we move through the world in our cocky fashion, pretending for all we're worth that we rule not only our own bodies, but those of our women. Meanwhile, the women snicker behind their hands.

I admit to it, all of it. I admit it, and I acquiesce to it. Who am I to refute the meaning of the universe?

Yet now, when I need Rosie more than ever, when I'm willing to surrender all the miserable crumbs I have left into her possession, she offers me only that anemic hello. But I didn't express any of that on the phone. How could

I? At that moment I didn't care about her or her lousy power over me. I hung up on her without a single word. I got back in the car and drove another hundred miles.

Only one thing pecked at me. Even if I didn't care about Rosie and her weak hellos and the saving power she refused to wield, I did care about Patton. He still needs to get out for a run, even if he's getting old. And what I've done or haven't done makes no difference to him. He harbors no reservations, bestows no anemic hellos.

I'd purchased him as a puppy for John's 14th birthday, hoping the novelty of a dog would displace his burgeoning interest in chasing a different kind of tail. John named him *Yellowcard* after some punk band, popular at the time. All he wanted to do with the dog was run around the yard with him, pet him, and snuggle with him. Sure, he'd walk him and feed him (overfeed him, really), but he didn't clean up after him. And he wanted no part in the tedium of training. Obedience, though, had to be enforced from the start or the dog would be worse than useless. So I took on the training. And the more I involved myself, the more John allowed me to. Or maybe I should put it this way—the closer I got to the dog, the less John was inclined to spend time with him. Eventually he lost interest entirely. If I was going to care for the dog, however, I wanted a more dignified name, so I changed it to *Patton*. Under my tutelage, he became a disciplined and loyal canine, the envy of the neighborhood.

At the time, I felt I'd saved our family from the humiliation of a spoiled dog, the type that leads its owner on a walk rather than vice versa. Looking back, though, I wonder if my taking over was wise. Rosie had expressed concerns. I see now that John's better qualities, namely his persistence and his easy-going nature, were brought to the fore when he engaged with the dog. Maybe his nurturing a fondness for it was of greater value than my fostering its obedience.

Why does my every thought lead back to that boy?

I returned to the interstate but headed in the opposite direction—toward home. When I arrived late in the evening, there was a strange car in the driveway—an older Volvo. I was fairly certain it didn't belong to any of Rosie's friends. I parked on the street, with my vehicle shielded by some shrubbery. It was no use, though, because the moment I got out of the car, Patton barked—with enthusiasm—from inside the house.

I walked near the front porch but stayed to the side to scope things out. The last thing I wanted was to confront some lover. If a man were there, I'd leave and never return.

Sure enough, a man did open the door. He poked his head out to look around. It was no lover, though—it was John. Patton skirted past him, bolted out, and practically leapt into my arms. I leaned over and rubbed the top of his bristly head.

When I looked up again, John was no longer in the doorway.

As I entered the house, I glanced around but didn't see him. Rosie fluttered about me, telling me how concerned she'd been, especially when she'd come across my phone, and then when she got a hang-up after answering a call.

I didn't care about any of that.

"Where's John?" I said, shoving Rosie aside and marching through the living room, dining room, and into the kitchen. Scouring the place, I looked behind curtains and into closets.

"John and Shayze—that's his wife—were concerned too," Rosie said, shadowing me, catching at my sleeve as if to restrain me. "We wanted to be together to decide what to do."

I completed my circuit. Arriving back in the foyer, I flung open the front door just in time to see John starting up the Volvo, and the woman—Shayze—levering her highly pregnant body into the passenger seat.

Something occurred to me then, something quaked in me and shook loose, like a hard nut from a tree: John's apology was immaterial. He'd been a mere boy when he left us. A headstrong one maybe, but I was the adult. I'd allowed him to go, and had made his return virtually impossible. And I'd done nothing to help him financially or emotionally all those years—they must've been hellish at times. My pardoning John shouldn't even have been part of the equation. I'm the stumbling block, not John.

I could've, I should've rushed out, forced upon John my own festering apology. But I was a pillar of salt, unable to move.

"What a coward," I muttered to myself, as John pulled the car out of the driveway and sailed down the street.

Rosie, standing behind me, said, "You can hardly blame him, can you?"

I swung around to face her, and she startled.

But I said nothing to correct her misconception.

Day 301

Yesterday turned out to be just the appetizer for today's confrontational feast. I'm still digesting it.

I'd gone in to the hospital in the morning, but was back before noon. Upon my early return, I detected a note of chagrin on Rosie's face. That should've served as a warning. The minute I was occupied with the newspaper in my study, she disappeared from the house. In the past weeks, I've become acutely conscious of her whereabouts from one moment to the next, and I'll wager she's just as cognizant of mine. She used that knowledge today to slip past me.

I stationed myself near a window with a view of the driveway to await her return. She was gone over two hours. Around 2:00 pm a car pulled up out front and dropped her off. I was unable to see the driver. I met Rosie at the door. Suspicions formed as she removed her gloves and coat in a controlled hurry.

"Where've you been off to?" I asked, in a studiously casual tone.

As she stowed her gear, she practically hid behind the open closet door. I could see why—the outfit underneath her coat was too stylish for her to have been grocery shopping, or out with her sister Maude. Her cheeks sported a fresh blush, the fiery type generated not from make-up, exercise, or brisk weather, but from alcohol.

She said, defensively, "Out to lunch."

I bit back a snarky comment.

She attempted to beeline out of the room, but I blocked her. "With whom, if I may be so bold as to inquire?"

"If you must know…," she said.

"*Must* I know?" I retorted. "Will it be of interest or value for me to know?"

The air went out of her. "Okay, then. I had lunch with Darla."

"Lunch with Darla," I repeated. A common police interrogation tactic—repeating a speaker's words to get them to continue talking.

"Yes, lunch with Darla. She invited me and so I went. I hope there's nothing wrong with that." Her voice embodied a slight slur.

"No, no, nothing at all. You appear to have enjoyed yourself."

"As a matter of fact I did. Darla's interesting."

"Oh yes. All those quotations."

"Huh?"

"Never mind."

"And she's a good lis—" Recognizing her near-blunder, she self-corrected. "—a good conversationalist."

"What have you told her?" I demanded, surprising myself with my own forthrightness. A determination was rising within me.

Rosie's cheeks turned rosier, or perhaps more accurately, they burned with heightened fire. Her jaw tightened and her breath quickened, puffing out margarita fumes. "You know what, Michael? Sometimes I need someone to listen to me."

So this was how to get a rise out of her. This was good. "How about talking to your husband? What's wrong with me?"

"*What's wrong with me?*" she mocked, using the same police tactic on me. I wouldn't bite though. Besides, I couldn't begin to explain what's wrong with me.

"We haven't been communicating at all, in case you haven't noticed," she continued.

"And whose fault is that? I try to get a word out of you, and you recoil like a discharged pistol."

"That's because you get angry."

"What? I never get angry."

"You're angry right now. You're seething with anger."

"How can you say that? I'm standing here talking to you in a totally calm and reasonable manner."

"If you could see yourself, you'd see how angry you look."

"So now *you're* the expert in facial expression?"

"I only know my husband. And I don't know why you're so mad at me."

"I'm not mad at you." Yes, I was frustrated by her accusation, but I withheld any outward show of anger to prove my point. "Furthermore," I said, "I resent your insinuation that I can't control my emotions."

"That's not what I said."

"You implied it. You won't talk to me, because you think I can't control my anger. Can't you see how disrespectful that is? You're trying to manage me."

"You're putting words in my mouth."

"You're treating me like a child."

That did it. The tightly stretched drum of her temperament split wide open. Sparks flew at me from her flashing eyes, her sputtering mouth.

"If you don't want to be treated like a child, then don't act like one!"

How many margaritas had she had? "Look who's angry now," I said.

"Of course I'm angry! I'm furious. And I have every right to be. Let's talk about the way you treat *me*. How do you think *I* feel when I say something totally innocuous that somehow offends your *delicate sensibilities* and then you stop talking to me for weeks on end? I try to be good, to say the right things. I don't want to make you angry, I do everything to avoid it. If you want to call it managing, then fine. And guess what? I'm not the first wife ever to do that! And if I notice you're getting mad, yeah, I try to soothe you. You're like a baby needing a nipple."

I ignored the insult, focusing instead on the present. "So that's why you've been moping around the house, barely speaking to me for months now?"

"It's all about you, isn't it? Always about you. Where's the room for my own grief? My daughter was killed, almost right before my eyes, by my own husband, who was too angry with me to spare two seconds to look behind him!"

Then the big one.

I said, "Is that why you lied about the accident and covered up for me? Because you think I'm a child who's incapable of taking responsibility for my own actions?"

With that pointed question, her anger dissipated with a sort of dying hiss, as if I'd doused the fire with a bucket of ice water. Thin water filled her eyes. She shivered.

"It wasn't that," she said flatly.

"Then what? John claims you knew Michaelina had gone outside, but you hesitated because you were angry, you were fed up with me. Is that it? That because I wouldn't sanction your liaisons with John, you entertained the evil thought, for a couple of seconds, that you'd get revenge on me if Michaelina was hurt? But when it happened, you blamed yourself. You took the blame because you hesitated."

Rosie sniffed up her nose and swiped at her eye with a bare hand, smearing her mascara in a diagonal line down the malar bone of her left cheek.

"I did hesitate, but that wasn't the reason."

"Then why, why?"

"She looked at me with exasperation. I hesitated for the same reason I always hesitate. Any time I try to stop you, correct you, suggest the smallest modification in your behavior, you get mad and I have to take the brunt of it. And I was just so tired of it. You were already furious after discovering I'd been seeing John. What if you found a way to prevent me from ever seeing him again? That was all I could think about. I was thinking only about what your anger would mean for me. That's why I hesitated. I wasn't thinking of Michaelina at all—she was safe in her room. Then it hit me—Michaelina *might* have gone outside. In fact, she probably *had* gone outside—that would be just like her. The whole thing played out in my mind then, like a movie preview. Michaelina going outside, getting on her bike in the driveway, behind the car. And you, so angry you don't even look before backing up. That's when I ran outside, screaming for you to stop. But my yelling only made you gun the car out faster."

"If that's true, then why did John say—"

"Maybe John's angry too. He has his own perspective. He can't figure out why you hate him."

"I don't hate him." That was true. I had ceased hating.

Rosie sighed forcefully and rolled her eyes away from me.

I let that go. I'm capable of letting things go.

"Fine, you don't hate him," she said. "Whatever you say."

Again, treating me like a child.

"But just so you're aware," she said, "the way you've acted toward him, whatever you want to call it, gives him a certain viewpoint."

I didn't want to hear about John's viewpoint, especially not as it concerned me. Soon enough, I'd work things out with John. At the moment, though, there were more pressing issues to attend to.

"What did you tell Darla?"

An expression of almost smugness stole into Rosie's face. "If you must know—all of it."

I restrained myself from grabbing Rosie's shoulders and shaking her. I merely said, "How could you? She's a complete stranger."

Rosie's brief emission of tears congealed, leaving a patchwork of glossy streaks coursing through her makeup and down her cheeks. "Actually, I hardly needed to say anything," she said. "Darla already knew."

"What? How?" This was worse than I'd imagined.

"Okay, maybe she didn't *know*, but she strongly suspected. Things didn't add up, she said, not from what she'd seen online and heard from Owen. And how you acted at the New Year's Eve party, your reaction to some comments she made—that helped her connect the dots."

Even now, wracking my brain, I can't think of anything I said to give myself away. That scares me.

"At lunch, Darla laid it all out for me. I didn't tell her, she told me. And I couldn't deny it. That would be lying."

Lies. They can be powerful enough to destroy you, yet never show up when they're really needed.

"Isn't lying what you've been doing up til now?" I said.

Rosie's smugness vanished. "Yes. And I'm ashamed of it." She was quick to add, "But Darla's discreet. She won't say anything, not even to her own husband. Not Owen either. She promised."

"I don't believe that. Women talk. That's what women do."

"I haven't talked, have I? At least not before today. I haven't even said any of this to a priest, or to Maude."

I was tempted to point out that she'd discussed everything with John but didn't want to bring him up again. So I only replied, "Thank God for small favors." Then, "Still, I don't see why Darla stuck her nose in, why she confronted you about any of this."

"I wouldn't call it confronting."

"What would you call it?"

"Helping. She wants to help."

"We don't need her help. We don't need anyone's help."

"We don't?"

At that point my curiosity got the best of me. "What help is she proposing to provide?"

Despite the reasonable question, Rosie tilted her head and gazed into the distance. "She didn't say."

"What? Didn't you ask?"

"No. And she didn't say that explicitly—that she could help. It's just a strong sense I got."

Something more was going on here. I've seen how Rosie can lie, and do it convincingly. Despite the watershed conversation, I'm no closer to knowing what's really going on inside her head. Was she lying now? All this could be a plot to ensnare me, to wring a public confession from me and get me out of her hair. She doesn't respect me anymore—this conversation proved it. She doesn't want me, doesn't need me. She has John and Shayze and Darla. Probably a lover, too. That would explain so much. I can't stop Rosie from seeing people, from talking, from plotting against me. And if Darla can figure it out, anyone can.

An idea struck me. "Are you paying her?"

Rosie seemed taken aback. "All we did—"

"—was have lunch, I know. But you gave me away, betrayed my confidence. There had to be a price. Or do I have it backwards, and she paid you? Is she a tabloid writer or something?"

Rosie blanched.

I shifted course. "No matter. My life isn't worth crap now anyway. I'm decaying before your eyes."

She said, "What're you talking about?" She was stalling, avoiding the inevitable.

I said, "I won't let it end that way—with me, rotting away as you watch."

She looked at me, aghast, as if leprous flakes of flesh were already detaching from my body and floating to the floor. Something in her eyes convinced me we were heading for disaster.

Then she took my tainted hand and stroked it. She soothed me. Maybe I *am* no more than a baby needing a nipple. But is she offering me a nourishing breast, or only a rubber pacifier?

Day 303

Last night, as I lay in troubled sleep, Rosie crept into my room. It wasn't her footsteps per se that registered in my brain. It was her trying to tread lightly that agitated my subconscious and woke me.

I had no idea what she'd come in for, but even if she were about to shoot me, it was better to give the impression of sound slumber. She must've been there to check on me, afraid I'd take off again. I expected her to leave once she saw me sleeping.

So when she crawled into bed beside me, I suppressed a gasp. She settled herself gently on top of the covers, seemingly intent on not disturbing me. I lay on my back, my face turned slightly away. She inched closer. Then she laid one arm over my chest.

The sensation of that bare arm had an effect on me that's difficult to describe. Its heft, its coolness, its very placement pinned me in some way to the bed. Physical intimacy with Rosie, especially after that post-lunch conversation, was the last thing I wanted. Rather than responding, lifting my hand

and touching that arm, caressing it, my only desire was to fling it off, to push her away in one decisive thrust. But I dreaded the thought of the discussion that would ensue, alone with her in the dark bedroom.

I remained immobile while considering my options. I could strangle her. I could turn over with my back to her, scare her off with faux snoring. Or, I could lie there and do nothing.

In the end, that's what I did—nothing. At first, my discomfiture was extreme. So substantial did that arm feel on my chest that I could barely breathe. The heavy floral scent of her deodorant wafted up from her exposed underarm, adding to the sense of encumbrance.

After a time, though, I adjusted to the sensations. As I lay motionless, some of my irritation dissipated. I began letting go of the tension that had revved up my nerves and I allowed my defenses to drop. Being pinned had its advantages. My shallow breathing gradually grew deeper, until I drifted off into a cavernous sleep.

When I woke, daylight pierced the curtains, and she was gone.

I felt immensely better on my morning run with Patton. My mind was clearer. I came up with an idea that would get me that release from Thurman. It was this: I could demonstrate grief if I wanted to. I could even parlay my mistake from last session—when I'd accidentally revealed too much—into a claim that assigning blame was my way of dealing with grief and guilt. That'd give Thurman a bone to chew on.

What a mistake that turned out to be.

When I arrived, Thurman greeted me in her customary manner, but I detected a sub-current of tension not palpable in past meetings. For one thing, she sat a little more upright in her chair. And her scope-eye was exceptionally active.

As I plopped down onto the sad sofa, it heaved a heavy sigh beneath me.

Thurman's first words were, "You need to go into the hospital for a full evaluation."

What? That wasn't the direction I wanted things to go.

"No," I said.

We debated, but I was adamant that I felt fine. If I went to the hospital, they'd just release me anyway.

Thurman could see that. She could see I was doing well, that I'd improved. So she relented, but with a compromise. "Come see me every week then. No more every two weeks."

I didn't object. The frequency of visits would be immaterial once I executed my plan.

I was impatient to begin. So before she said anything further, I launched into my rehearsed *mea culpa*, explaining how devastated and contrite I was about the accident. I reproached myself. I should've been watching my daughter, should've checked on her as soon as Rosie had headed out to the car. Mustering the requisite facial expressions, I told her how horrific it's been, how difficult to face my part in it, how intensely I've been grieving all these months.

I managed to draw out my performance for several minutes. Thurman's nodding expression indicated acceptance of my confession and her approval of it.

The problem was that I hadn't adequately prepared for her follow-ups.

First, she wanted to understand the 'context' for my grief—when and where I experienced it.

I thought for a minute to come up with something credible. I told her I felt sad when I peeked into Michaelina's bedroom and saw her princess dolls, when I saw a photo of her, and when I arrived home from work and she wasn't there to greet me.

Such bullcrap.

Then she asked what I do when I experience those feelings.

I wanted to say that I do nothing, that I set the feelings aside and move on with my life. But that answer wouldn't satisfy her. So I went further. I told her, "I say to myself, *I miss Michaelina.*"

Except I didn't say that. That's what I *meant* to say. But what came out of my mouth instead was, "*I miss you, Michaelina.*"

A terrific knot formed in my gullet. The fact is I've never said those words before, because what good is it talking to the dead? What benefit is there in pulling Michaelina from her grave, dredging up the cold dirt in search of the warm, pulsing little body, when all I'd discover is defeat and decay?

I was beside myself. This doctor, this woman, had no right to witness my grief. She'd tricked me into thinking about my response to Michaelina's death. She made me think about it, because to cover up the truth I first had to figure out what the truth was so I could tell her something different.

So now my truth was uncovered, fully exposed to her. Worse, it was exposed to me in my own consciousness. The truth lay there, exposed, like that damn breast again, just waiting to be sucked. Only with tremendous effort was I able to restrain myself from taking advantage of the obscene comfort it presented.

Because the truth was this: I grieved not just when I saw Michaelina's dolls, but every time I walked past her bedroom door. Not just when I arrived home and she wasn't there, but at every meal I had to eat at our empty table. Not just when I saw a photo of her, but every time I saw a little girl. I was sick with grief every time I got in a car, saw a bike, heard a siren. Every time I stepped into the operating room.

And every time I recognized Michaelina's likeness in my wife's stricken face.

I didn't tell Thurman any of this.

But my eyes burned and my facial musculature twisted with the effort as I held back, held back, held back…

Day 304

I'm writing in the morning, because I need to record my thoughts before they're forgotten.

Last night I lay in bed unable to sleep. I pondered the occurrence of Rosie's visit to my room the previous night. Why had she offered her silent, one-armed comfort? I half wished her to come back again, but the other half shrank from the thought.

In the midst of my ruminations, she did return. Again, she laid her heavy arm across my chest. Again, I feigned sleep. This time, however, I didn't doze off. I just rested under that arm, more or less contentedly. I'm not a new-age believer, but as a doctor, I'm aware of nerves in the epidermis, the underlying electrical impulses, and the impact of skin-on-skin contact. I received and absorbed everything that came through that contact, without moving a single muscle.

I've never seen Rosie as a strong person. Too often I've taken advantage of her weakness. Yet she's the one who's initiated this physical contact. Her lying next to me isn't a gesture of need, but of support. Maybe she's strong after all. It's her strength I need right now.

Pride is the root sin, or so I've heard. I'm proud—I've been upfront about that—but I've spent nearly a year trying to course-correct. Pride, I've learned, amounts to loving yourself too much. After all that's happened, though, I'm unsure whether my problem now is too much self-love, or too much self-hate. I suppose in the end the two dispositions are equivalent—they're both based on too much consideration of self.

After an hour she eased herself off the bed and left the room.

Day 305

I've begun looking forward to Rosie settling herself in bed with me. I don't acknowledge her presence, but I believe she's figured out I'm awake. Thankfully, she doesn't press me, for how could I ever confide what's going on in my head? I'm all nerves now. I have no control over events.

That heavy arm of hers is a bulwark. These night visits might not be resolving anything, but they're softening things. It's not that we have more daytime conversation than before, but the tone of what we do say has become milder. The eggshells we've been walking on are still there, but it's as if we've both put thick fuzzy slippers on.

Day 308

I continue the motions of going in to work—most days, only for a few hours. I putter about to look busy. My new ritual is to scour the scientific literature for any new developments in the field. After a short time, though, it's as if a liquid oozes from my brain, coating my eyeballs and preventing absorption of anything I read. I then pace the halls, working through imaginary surgeries in my head, difficult cases in which novel or sophisticated techniques are required. But I have trouble focusing.

Instead, I find myself conceptualizing new schemes to thwart Thurman and obtain my release. Or, I try to colorize my faded images of Michaelina. Increasingly, when I attempt to bring her back, I find only a big blank. At night, she haunts my dreams, lurking behind corners or walls, always just out of sight, just out of reach.

And John regularly inserts himself into my thoughts. I wonder what he's thinking, how he perceives me. I can't get into his brain. Or Rosie's, for that matter. Or Thurman's or Owen's or Darla's. My sense of being shut out grows daily. I can't decipher the motivations of those around me, while they seem able to peer right through me. My substance is receding, wasting away, rendering me transparent. At the same time, I'm not sure anyone cares enough to look at me.

Day 309

Grief, guilt, sex. All of them begin with or end in death of some sort.

Today's session started out well. Thurman reminded me that we have made progress recently on my feelings of grief.

Progress—yes, our sessions are working. *We* have made progress. A tiny surge of dopamine welled up and pooled in my head when she said '*we.*'

Thurman and I are growing closer. I want more of this *we*. I'll cooperate more, I decided.

"Today we'll start tackling guilt," she said. "How are you managing your guilt?"

It was time to be more open. I explained I was managing my guilt with a bargain I'd made with God.

Her eyebrows shot up.

I said I'd been reluctant to talk about it because it was meant to be a private pact, but that by describing it now, I was evidencing my full cooperation. Furthermore, my ability to set this goal and work methodically toward it demonstrated the soundness of my mind, that I could work through my guilt in a productive manner.

She needed details. I described the first deal I'd tried to make, the one that would spare Michaelina's life. When the Almighty hadn't come through, I decided to humiliate him by keeping up my end of the bargain anyway. Humiliation was the worst of life's sufferings—being called Butt-cheeks as a child had taught me that. I reasoned that if I actively pursued humility, I'd outsmart God. He'd be the one who'd feel the guilt then.

Thurman tapped the point of her pen a few times on the desk. "I'm not getting it," she said. "You're trying to be more humble, fine. But you're going to transfer your guilt to God? You're going to manipulate God into taking the blame for you?"

When she phrased it that way, it sounded ridiculous.

Maybe it was. I can't even explain it to myself now in a way that makes sense. Maybe it was just a story I told myself to make my guilt bearable, to make it possible for me to make reparation to my wife for what I'd done. A way to justify letting go of my pride, letting go of being right, and punishing myself by serving the woman I wanted to blame—the very woman I'd allowed to take the blame. I could only undertake the plan, however, by telling myself my actions weren't for Rosie's sake, but for a larger, more cosmic purpose.

I couldn't say that to Thurman—she'd never understand something so psychologically and spiritually complex. I needed to move the conversation in a different direction, so I asked for *her* ideas on managing guilt.

I expected her to train her scope-eye on me, but instead her eyes softened.

She said, "A good start would be to work on forgiving yourself."

Ah. She had no idea what she was asking, the extent of what I'd have to forgive myself for.

I tried instead to clarify the situation by telling her the story of Abraham and Isaac. "God told Abraham to kill his son Isaac. Abraham was willing to do it, too—to prove his obedience. He tied up his son and drew his knife, raised it high to prepare for the plunge. But God stopped him at the last second."

"So?"

"So—Abraham was willing to give up his son, but I wasn't willing to give up Michaelina—not even if God had asked me to."

The scope-eye returned. "And you're saying what? That if you were okay with Michaelina dying, then God would've saved her?"

I didn't reply.

"*Hoo*. You're not thinking straight. Are you reading the Bible a lot?"

"I wouldn't say a lot. Some of the stories I hear at Mass."

She rearranged her feet under the desk. "Going to church a lot?"

"Why's that important?"

"I didn't say important. Just that sometimes, becoming all of a sudden religious, becoming *over*-religious, can be a sign of something serious."

"I'm not religious at all. I don't even believe in God."

She leaned back in her chair and crossed her arms. "You just told me you made some agreement with God."

I explained. "It's Rosie's God, not mine. Rosie's God is behind everything, controlling everything."

"Are you hearing a voice, this voice of Rosie's God?"

What does it mean to hear a voice? Is it to become aware of something you feel compelled to do? What was the nature of the voice telling Abraham to sacrifice Isaac, then telling him to stay his hand?

I asked her whether she knew the story of David and Bathsheba.

She gave me a blank look.

"David, the king, witnessed the beautiful Bathsheba bathing on a nearby roof. He commanded his servants to bring her to him and he had intercourse with her. She conceived his child. David needed to cover up his sin, so he had Bathsheba's husband killed on the battlefield. That way no one would know he'd fathered her child."

Thurman tapped her fingers on the desk. "So you're saying…you're saying you killed someone to cover up something?"

"No! That's not it. Don't you see? David stole another man's wife. He was unfaithful and then compounded his infidelity with murder."

"And?"

I was annoyed she wasn't seeing any connections here, connections that to me were obvious. Was she being purposely obtuse?

"God said he'd make David pay for his sin by killing Bathsheba's baby—their baby. And he did it, too."

"*Hoo.* So you think God killed your daughter because you had an affair?"

"Not exactly. Or I wouldn't put it that way."

"You've been unfaithful to your wife?"

There it was. The question I'd waited for, the one that gave me the opportunity to reveal my golden nugget of knowledge—to trap Thurman and force her to give me the release I needed.

So I smiled and said, "You should know."

"Pardon?"

"You should know." I added, "Don't think I haven't seen it."

She played dumb. "Seen what?"

"Your birthmark. The port-wine stain on your neck. One time you accidentally revealed it to me when you scratched the back of your neck."

She looked at me with wide eyes.

I was forced to be more explicit.

"You've known all along, haven't you? The way you've talked to me. Every time you said the words '*your wife*' with that little emphasis. You brought up my wedding ring months ago and asked why I didn't wear it, implying I'd been dishonest with you about being married. You remembered I didn't wear it back in med school, that you wouldn't have invited me to your apartment if you'd known it."

She interrupted. "*What?* What're you saying?"

"Then, when I became your patient and I didn't recognize you right away, you acted as if we were strangers. You wanted to keep the truth from me. You're the one who's been dishonest, not me. You wanted to torment me. You've kept that clearance from me all this time, just to get revenge, haven't you? And smoothing your hair down all the time, covering up that birthmark."

I paused to take a breath. Thurman's fingers moved to the keyboard of her laptop, trembling as they floated above it, as if she wanted to type something but didn't know where to start.

"But I figured out who *you* were a long time ago. Now you'll have to give me that clearance so I can get back to surgery. Give it to me or I'll report you."

Then, instead of typing, she moved her hands to her neck and lifted up her hair. She turned her head to both sides.

Where was that birthmark!? I'd seen it. It had been there, hadn't it? "You've had it removed," I said.

She looked at me in what I felt was fake incredulity.

"In med school," I said. "That's when we did it. You remember that, don't you?"

"What are you talking about? We didn't go to the same med school."

"You can't deny it. Your maiden name was Bialaski or something like that."

She stood, went over to the wall, removed her framed diploma, and came over to hand it to me. I wouldn't take it though, or even look at it. She set it on my lap. I let it slide off and rattle to the floor.

"You've had it altered," I said.

She returned to her desk and stood behind it, hands on her hips.

"We'd taken that class together," I said, "and there was a party afterward. You invited me to your apartment." I began describing our being in bed together. How I'd begun by kissing that wine-red birthmark, then moved down her neck—

She stopped me. "*Hoo, hoo, hoo!* You think we had sex? You think if we had sex I'd take you for my patient? So unprofessional!"

I accused her of angling to get into bed with me again. I detailed how she'd been aloof initially, but had recently started being nice to me, manipulating my emotions, making me become emotionally dependent on her. She wanted me to want her. Once I gave in, when we were together having that old-world sex again, and I was kissing that birthmark lovingly, that's when she'd finally say, "Now you've proven you're alive and capable and loving. Yes, you're ready to go back, ready for surgery again."

I stated all this, although it hardly needed stating.

She didn't see it that way though.

In a slow, exaggerated fashion, she shook her head. "You need a different doctor. This isn't working out so great."

I stood, prepared for a confrontation. "No! You haven't cleared me yet. If you don't clear me, I'll report you to Ji-young."

She stood as well. "Go ahead," she said. "Report me to Ji-young. She'll give you another doctor."

"I don't want another doctor. I want you."

"No. This is a problem."

"How is it a problem?"

"Some angry part of you has been activated. I'm getting afraid of you."

"Afraid of what?" I nearly shouted it. She was ceding power to me, but I didn't want that power. I needed *her* to be in charge, to control what was happening, to see things through. I would submit.

She asked me to settle down, to ask my angry part to step aside so we could see what it was protecting.

I couldn't. Why wasn't she understanding and acting? I had to change course, say something to hold on to her. It had to be something big.

So I said it. "I didn't do it on purpose."

"What?" she said. Her scope-eye went bonkers, adjusting and readjusting the zoom. "What didn't you do on purpose?"

I didn't know Michaelina had gone outside. I didn't know she was behind me in the driveway. I didn't hit her on purpose.

Did I say that to Thurman, or just think it?

She said she'd walk me to the ER. That they'd help me get a handle on things.

I asked, "Will they be able to clear me?"

She asked my permission to call Rosie.

That request woke me up from what seemed like a bad dream.

I said no. Then I walked out, with a hand gesture that made it clear I was going alone.

The remainder of the day I spent walking around campus, watching the harried doctors rush by in their infernal hurry. Twice I passed by the entrance to the ER.

Day 310

It's 3:30 am. Rosie's come and gone.

I've figured out why she doesn't stay. It's because she has a lover waiting for her in Michaelina's room. Some nights, I hear them making love on Michaelina's bed, under the canopy. When the sound of their thrills reaches my ears, my heart races and I have trouble breathing. My mouth fills with saliva and I try not to vomit. Where is Patton, I wonder, and why doesn't he bark?

Tonight, after hearing the noises, I got up to check Michaelina's room, but the lover was gone.

I need to pull myself together, but my thoughts won't coalesce around any oasis of comfort. I feel nearly as bad as the day of the accident.

Accident. What really is an accident? I read recently that the term 'car accident' is out of fashion. Calling something an accident implies it couldn't be helped—like a lightning strike. Car accidents, however, can largely be avoided. Instead, it's now called a 'crash' or a 'wreck.'

Thurman mercifully calls it "the incident." She's guessed the truth, though. That's why she's afraid.

She doesn't understand though. She's concluded that I killed Michaelina out of spite, to get revenge on Rosie. That's why she told me to go to the hospital. She thinks I'm dangerous. She thinks I killed Michaelina on purpose.

Did I?

I need her to help me understand what I did.

Day 311

I never did get back to sleep last night. But no matter—I don't need much sleep anymore. Once I had my coffee, I was hyper-alert, ready to accomplish something important: I needed to see Thurman again.

Having no appointment, the receptionist tried to turn me away. I said I'd wait. After she made two or three calls, a security guard appeared and spoke to a nurse outside Thurman's office.

I picked up a magazine and paged through it, pretending a patience I didn't feel. I tried to control my fidgeting, to self-calm. Even so, I caught myself—mid-sentence—vocalizing my thoughts. Even my breathing was loud.

After an interminable 40 minutes, I was ushered into Thurman's office.

I sat down and adjusted myself on the sofa, grinding my rear-end into its familiar crater. I was here for the long haul, the finale.

Thurman sensed it. She leaned back in her chair and looked at me expectantly. There was no scope-eye this time. Her indolent manner was one you might expect of someone nearing the end of a movie as the credits begin to roll.

"Tell me what happened," she said. Her voice was soft, like a mother soothing a frustrated child on the playground with a bloody nose.

Her tone did soothe me. My mind cleared. I felt myself situated in the eye of a hurricane, enjoying the momentary preternatural calm, while knowing the storm on the other side was gathering force.

I told her what happened—everything.

I told her about the text conversation between Rosie and John, the one I'd discovered on Rosie's phone. I related the argument we'd had, my absolute fury. I described leaving the house, slamming the door from the mudroom to the garage, climbing into my Porsche and slamming that door too. The garage door was already up. I started the engine and shifted into reverse.

Patton barked from inside the house. I ignored him. Rosie came outside, shouting for me to stop. Without looking at her, I instinctively calculated from the increasing pitch of her voice that she was running across the porch, onto the sidewalk, and out toward the driveway—all the while yelling for me to stop.

I wouldn't stop, though—not for her. I wouldn't listen to her, not after what she'd done. I wouldn't give her a chance to explain or allow her the opportunity to ask forgiveness.

It was in my power not to stop, not to do what she wanted. I could prevent her from reaching me, from explaining and apologizing. I only had to hurry.

There was no time to look over my shoulder. No time to look in the rear-view mirror. Not if I wanted to get away from her.

I gunned the car out of the garage.

I hit something. The strike made a loud thump.

It was okay though—I knew right away what I'd hit. It was Michaelina's little two-wheeler with the training wheels. That's what it was. She'd left it out in the driveway. Michaelina herself was in the house. Yes, she was in the house, safe in her room. Rosie had sent her to her room.

All the same, with the sound of that thump, all the hurry drained out of me. I shifted into drive and moved the car back into the garage. A scraping sound came from beneath the chassis. I parked, got out, and looked behind the car. Yes, I'd hit her bike. There it lay, mangled, one handlebar caught on the fender and one wheel jammed beneath the vehicle.

Rosie reached me. She wasn't shouting any more, but whispering, the kind of choked whispering that comes from your mouth when the breath has been knocked out of you. She whispered, "Michaelina." But she wasn't saying it to me. Nor did she look at me.

She offered no explanation or apology about her betrayal. That wasn't why she'd come out of the house. That wasn't why she'd shouted for me to stop. I'd been mistaken.

"Michaelina's in the house," I said. I believed it to be true. I willed it to be true.

But even as I said it, my eye caught a lump of pink off the side of the driveway. A lump of pink on the lawn. The pink lump was a sweater—Michaelina's pink sweater. It was pink, except for the streaks of red. Streaks of bright red that turned to blotches as I approached. Streaks that were turning to blotches, and blotches turning to puddles.

Michaelina lay on the grass, on her side. She'd remembered to wear her helmet, the darling girl. A helmet is made for protection, for protecting the head. Under the helmet, Michaelina's hair was spread veil-like across her face, covering her eyes. I didn't want to move that hair, to look into those eyes, didn't want to see those eyes that might not look back at me.

I mustered my courage and moved the veil of hair anyway. I moved it aside for the sake of the seconds that might matter. Her eyes were closed in unconsciousness. Gently, I removed her helmet. The helmet that had protected her head. I flung it across the lawn.

I knelt down. I supported Michaelina's neck while turning her on her back. I pressed my fingers into her neck, against her carotid. I couldn't detect a heartbeat. I began chest compressions, calculating how hard to press to get the heart moving without exacerbating any internal injuries.

Rosie's presence surrounded me. She seemed to be standing in front of me, next to me, and behind me all at once. Her voice had returned. The sounds coming from her mouth were like groans, except more high-pitched.

I got Michaelina's heart going. I pulled out my phone and dialed 911.

While waiting for the EMT, I examined her more closely. She'd been hit on her right side. The blood soaking her pink sweater was flowing from her right forearm. Her fractured ulna had pierced the skin near her wrist, just below the cuff of the sweater. The bone protruded nearly an inch. An inch of white-pink bone, edged with red at the break. That broken bone was good news, I told myself. A broken bone isn't life-threatening. And if her arm had absorbed some of the blunt force impact, it may have lessened other damage.

When I examined her midsection, though, I felt two displaced ribs as well as some crepitus—a crunchiness beneath the skin. Crunchiness from crushed bones. I kept an eye on her lips. If blood seeped out between them, it could mean a flail segment of a rib had punctured her lung or other organ. A fractured rib can slice through your innards with no resistance—smoothly, slickly, like a warm knife through butter.

The bleeding from her wrist worsened. I shimmied the bone back into place as best I could. Then I pulled off my necktie for a makeshift tourniquet, twisting it onto her arm and tightening it with a pen from my pocket.

All the while my wife filled the air with her keening. I didn't look at her. I asked her to keep clear so I'd be able to restart CPR if needed. The full assessment of Michaelina's condition would have to wait for imaging at the hospital.

I recounted these events to Thurman in sequential order as if I had them well-ordered in my memory, but I didn't. In reality, once I started the car, succeeding events all seemed to happen simultaneously—Patton barking, Rosie shouting to stop, my gunning the car, and the sound of the thump.

Dr. Thurman, elbow on desk and palm propping up jaw, listened in silence.

I then confessed to every action I'd committed afterward—how I'd allowed Rosie to claim fault, how I'd rationalized that to myself, how I hadn't admitted to anyone that I'd been the one to hit my daughter.

I told her what we learned at the hospital. That Michaelina's ribs, fractured on impact, had cut through her intestines and colon, probably as she'd made contact with the ground. The openings had instantly flooded her abdomen with her own waste. The surgeons had cleaned her out, but bacteria had hidden somewhere, probably in multiple places. The surgeons resected the damaged gut, but the germs had taken hold. That's what ultimately killed her—infection. The immune cells in her tiny body, fortified though they were with armies of antibiotics, weren't strong enough to fight it off.

When I finished my story, Thurman made no immediate comment on it, but instead said, "What about that girl blinded from surgery? Was that your fault too?"

Blame and guilt all over again! I'd just confessed to killing my own child. Now I'd have to admit this too?

But I wouldn't, or maybe I just didn't know how. I wasn't sure if I was guilty of that or not. Something was distorted in my recollection. All I knew was that I needed this nightmare to end.

Thurman would help me. She'd wrangled one confession from me; why not go for it all?

I raised my eyes to hers, to her soft eyes. Encompassed by her gaze, I was awash in mingled pain and pleasure. Strangely, euphoria took over. I'd agree to anything she wanted, do anything to please her.

And I knew just what that was. I hung my head and said, "I need to go to the police."

She nodded solemnly and let me go.

I made my way to the parking garage and my car, where I slumped into the driver's seat, crossing my arms over the steering wheel and leaning my head against them like a pillow.

I don't know how much time passed. At some point a lot attendant came up, looked in the car window, and asked if I was okay. Without reply, I started up the car and drove off.

I wasn't done thinking though. I needed more time to steel myself, more time for figuring out how to make my confessions—as Thurman was expecting of me. Lovely Thurman.

I took a circuitous route in the general direction of the precinct. After passing St. Bartholomew's, I turned around and entered the empty church lot. I parked and dragged myself up the steps. Someplace quiet was what I needed, someplace to think. I envisioned myself encountering a priest with nothing better to do than spend the afternoon kneeling before the altar, like they do in movies. I'd approach him and he'd ask me in a kindly voice how he could be of service. Maybe he'd even invite me into that confessional box.

But the church was locked. The door had a high window in it and I looked through. I could see straight down the center aisle to the altar. Above and beyond it was the crucifix.

On that crucifix, though, Jesus wasn't the one hanging—*I* was. I was the one being crucified, or about to be. I saw myself on that cross—exposed to the world. Humiliated. Left alone to twist and die.

Okay, not alone. Rosie would be there. Rosie's always there. She's Mary Magdalene—the sinner, the one who's been forgiven much because she loves much. The one who, even in the presence of such horror and despair, clings to the crucified one with her mysterious and incomprehensible and stultifying love.

I couldn't take that. No—if I had to go I'd just slink away somewhere. Anything but that public cross.

I sat down on the church steps. The bottle of Xanax bulged in my pants pocket. I removed it and took out a pill. I swallowed it dry and it stuck in my throat, melting slowly against my esophagus.

A small girl rode by on her bike, accompanied by a man who was likely her father. I got up and followed them. The girl zigzagged along the sidewalk, unsteadily, yet at the same time instructing her father to move faster, not to fall behind. The father made a pretense of speeding up, although if he went any faster, he'd get ahead of her in no time. I moved at their pace, keeping them in my line of sight.

As I watched them, I felt another hard nut shaking loose in my head and falling. To my surprise, I discovered that watching the father and daughter didn't hurt. Not so much, anyway.

I felt better, lighter. The weight that had pressed so unrelentingly on my psyche had lifted. Telling Thurman the whole story had eased my mind.

Yes—I'm better. I'm good, I thought. The wound was cleaned out and stitched up.

I went back to the car, reconsidering my decision to turn myself in to the police. I'd committed no crime. A police investigation would only stir up trouble, only prolong Rosie's agony. After all, going to the police had been my idea, not Thurman's. I no longer needed to justify myself to her.

I drove to the nearest park and left my car in the lot. Instead of walking on the trail, however, I picked my way through a thicket and then ambled into the woods beyond. By accident, I disturbed a couple of sleeping does. They leapt up and ran off, white tails flying, then stopped and stood like statues, glaring at me.

The dank smell of the woods conjured in me a remembrance of childhood. To be a child again! To have no worries beyond a stupid name a classmate might call me. As I walked, each tree I passed served as a handhold to steady me. I hadn't touched a tree in years and was astounded by the strength of their trunks. Even those only six inches in diameter were rigid, unable to be budged with my strongest push. I encountered a massive oak and ran my hand across its rough surface and stuck my fingers into the deep furrows. A piece of loose bark chipped off.

Within the trunk of that oak lay the long history of its existence. The first years of its bloom and pliancy were concealed deep within the concentric circles. Each passing year left its dark edge. I sat down against the trunk. Hairy acorns littered the ground.

I drew my knees up. I needed time. So much time has been misplaced, so many pieces have gone missing.

The police would have to wait.

It was dusk when I arrived home. Rosie was sitting on the edge of the sofa, hunched forward, elbows on her knees. I sat and clutched her hand. I told her I was done with surgery for good, that I couldn't manage it anymore.

She didn't ask for an explanation. Instead, she released her hand from my grip, patted my arm, and went to the kitchen to heat up my dinner.

I'll redouble my efforts, finish out my year of humility. It's not that I have something to prove anymore. It's that I need practice. I need to trust like a child again.

Day 312

I considered staying home from the hospital today. Thurman would've told Ji-young that I'm a danger. I've ceded my therapist-patient confidentiality on that point.

But I went in anyway. And sure enough, mere moments after my arrival, the department admin showed up to escort me to Ji-young's office. I asked him to wait for a moment outside my door. I thought to gather my personal items. After some dithering, I concluded that nothing really mattered. All I took, besides my medical bag, was the photo of Michaelina—the one with the tress of hair in front of her shoulder. I wrapped the frame carefully in some tissues and tucked it into my bag.

Winding our way down the long halls, I endured a gauntlet of barely concealed stares and whisperings.

In Ji-young's office, there was no head-bobbing this time, only headshaking as she informed me that I was on indefinite leave, effective immediately, that I was not to speak to the media, and that I'd be hearing from the hospital's legal department.

No handshake was offered—her small tight fists never loosened.

I didn't bother returning to my office. On my way out, I was intercepted by Owen, inviting me to a cup of coffee at Starbucks. I agreed to the coffee, but insisted we find a place off-campus.

After walking a half mile or so, we reached one. We had only just gotten our coffees and found a seat, when who showed up but his sister Darla.

"Fancy running into you two here!" she said.

"Oh, it's Bartlett. What a surprise," I said dryly.

"Nice to see you too, Michael."

"What, no quotation?"

"How about, 'Better late than never'?"

"I believe that's an adage, not a quotation."

Owen, ever the expert at repairing rifts in conversation, said, "You want a quote? Here's one from Einstein about running into someone unexpectedly: 'Coincidence is God's way of remaining anonymous.'"

I responded with a James Bond line that I thought more appropriate: "'Once is happenstance, twice is coincidence. Three times is enemy action.'"

"Ha! But I've only met you twice," said Darla.

"So far."

She laughed, although I was serious. Even if I don't believe in coincidence, I do believe in fate. Or at least in the inexorable. Whatever you want to call it, I was tired of fighting it. The fiend had me in a headlock, coercing me to play my part, to submit. "So, Bartlett, what brings you to this part of town?"

She and Owen—the two babyfaces—swapped a glance of deep sibling understanding.

"A case," Darla said.

"So you're a law—"

"An attorney," she said, pre-empting me. Lawyers don't like to be called lawyers.

I toyed with the fiend. "I suppose you take malpractice cases, to help that brother of yours when the scalpel slips?" I cringed at my own joke, especially since it had been my own surgery that'd gone wrong, not Owen's.

"No, I mostly stay out of the civil courts. Too dull for my tastes."

I already knew the answer to my next question but asked it anyway. To seal the deal.

"What flavor then?"

She smiled. "Criminal defense."

Day 313

I was sitting in my study this afternoon, reading the Bible, when Patton barked vociferously. I didn't pay much attention, figuring the commotion only signaled the arrival of a package.

Unfortunately, it wasn't UPS, it was the police. Rosie ushered them in.

I wondered if Thurman was responsible for alerting them. But we'd built up trust, hadn't we? And she'd gotten what she wanted—I'd quit surgery, I'd been expelled from the hospital. I wasn't a threat to anyone anymore.

When it happened, though, I realized I'd been waiting for it. Waiting for nearly a year, and in some way expecting it, for nearly a year. Maybe even wanting it.

It was Detective Wolanski again, escorted by the same uniformed cop who'd visited us after the accident. The same faces. The same sick feeling welling up in me.

A third plain-clothes officer accompanied them this time, a Detective Shorr.

I glared at Rosie for opening our home to them, but she only said, "Search warrant."

Politely, Wolanski offered to show it to me. I declined, with less graciousness.

First, the detectives wanted our cell phones. I handed mine over without concern—they'd never be able to get in. Not to mention that if they did, I had nothing incriminating on offer. Rosie's phone, with her *1234* password, would be an open book. Heaven knows what they'd find there.

The detectives wanted my car keys, too, even after I told them I'd replaced the Porsche.

Rosie and I were 'invited' to sit on the sofa. The uniformed cop kept us company, while the detectives explored the house's main and lower levels. Judging by the time invested, the search seemed somewhat cursory, as if they had something particular in mind and weren't expecting to find it in those parts of the house.

My worries began when they went upstairs. I'd taken precautions against my journal being found—not with the police in mind, but rather Rosie. I've concealed it in a loose-leaf binder labeled *Protocols for antibiotic prophylaxis in orthognathic surgery*, a title not likely to arouse curiosity. The first several pages are filled with jargony surgical notes, for good measure. I keep this binder in a bookcase in my room wedged between several similarly named binders.

Still, I was on edge. The detectives rummaged around for quite some time. Meanwhile, Patton, who had been relegated to the back yard, whined at the door. My eye was trained on the staircase.

When the detectives finally came down the steps, they carried no binder.

What Wolanski did have, however, was a zippered plastic pouch, opaque blue, which I happened to know was filled with 200 hundred-dollar bills. I'd failed to hide that as cunningly. The detective set it down on a chair near the uniformed cop, presumably so I'd take note of its discovery.

Both detectives then exited the side door of the house. Patton immediately barked at them, but they didn't let him back in the house.

Wolanski must have separated from Detective Shorr, because she began shouting his name from the porch, as if he were some distance away. As if she'd found something important to the case, something so spectacular that she couldn't bear to leave it for even a moment to walk over and get him.

Nothing was out there though. Nothing on the porch, in the yard, or in the garage, either.

When the detectives returned to the house, they wore no giveaway expressions. Wolanski held only a notebook. Schorr returned my car keys.

The detectives requested to speak to me in private. I invited them into my study and closed the door.

Detective Shorr started asking questions, but not ones I was anticipating. He asked nothing about the cash they'd found, but instead said, "How well are you acquainted with your neighbor, Herman Miller?"

I wanted to say, "Better acquainted than I'd like to be," but thought better of it. Instead I said, "Not particularly well." I said Herman was a decent enough neighbor, and all the better one for keeping out of my business.

Shorr grunted softly. Then, in a way he evidently intended to sound offhand, he said, "Let's go back to the day of your daughter's accident." He asked me to recount the events of that day.

My mouth opened but no words came out. He then clarified by asking me to start from the minute I got up in the morning and include details about where I was physically located at each moment, and what was happening around me. In particular, he wanted to know what had occurred immediately before I went outside and discovered Michaelina on the ground.

I asked if Matilda Thurman had called him.

"Thurman? Is that another neighbor?" He scribbled on his pad.

An unpleasant tingling attacked my underarms and groin. Blood seeped into the vessels of my face. I tried to demur, claiming it was all a blur, that it was nearly a year ago and hard to recall. But that wasn't true. Every detail was scratched into my mind like fingernail impressions in curing concrete.

Detective Wolanski butted in, repeating the request in an apologetic rather than suspicious tone. Consulting her notebook, she read back to me the statement I'd made way back then.

"You said, 'I didn't realize Michaelina had gone outside. When I came out, I saw she'd been hit. I started CPR and once her heart was going I called 911.'"

She looked at me with eyebrows raised.

Here was my chance to rectify the great omission, to take it all back, to let go of it all. Why did I still resist? I'd just made a full confession to Thurman, demolishing any remaining connection with her in the process, and losing my position at the hospital in the bargain. Maybe I resisted because there was finally a crack of light seeping into my life, brightening my relationship with Rosie.

"Why are you bringing this up now?" I asked.

The detectives swapped a look. Detective Schorr said, "New evidence has come to light."

"Which is…?"

The detective's face vivified with the keen pleasure of possessing valuable information he had no intention of sharing. "All in good time," he said.

"For now," said good cop Wolanski, "we just want to make sure we have your side of the story written down."

I attempted to proceed, despite the feeling that I was now trapped for good. More or less ignoring her specific question, I began to describe a fairly typical day, starting with my run, while trying to plan what I'd say at the critical part.

The longer I spoke, though, the more trouble I had. The lies weren't coming with such fluidity. I stumbled and stuttered. My confession to Thurman—that outlet she'd succeeded in opening—couldn't simply be closed and sealed. The healing wasn't finished. My world was still off-kilter and couldn't continue that way without toppling.

All the same, I couldn't come right out and say, "I killed Michaelina." Even writing it now is like stabbing myself.

If I set the record straight, there'd be a scandal, or worse. Everyone would believe I'd purposely pinned my daughter's death on my wife, pressuring her into falsely admitting guilt. People would think I threatened her, even. My reputation—or the tattered remains thereof—would be fully ruined.

It wasn't totally ruined now, not yet. People knew my daughter had died horrifically in her own driveway. They knew I'd performed an unsuccessful operation, blinding a little girl. The masses would recognize that as an unfortunate mistake, adding to my bad luck. Right now, no one thought me a monster. They would, though, if they heard the real story. It wasn't as if I'd come forward with the truth on my own. The whole fishy affair would reek.

For some reason Owen popped into my head. How would Owen respond in such a predicament? He desires approbation as much as I do—just a different kind. This situation, however, would never have happened to him. But then, who'd ever have imagined it happening to me?

I've never cared about people's opinions. Plenty of people don't like me, and I don't give a rat's ass. In a way I revel in it. It's a way of being superior—the lord cares not what his vassals think. This was different though. Being perceived as abrasive because of my superior status is not the same as being thought a killer, and a lying, conniving, cowardly one at that.

I'm recording these thoughts as if I'd had time for them, with Detective Wolanski standing there, pencil poised. Maybe I did think them, or maybe I'm just fleshing them out now.

We humans have evolved to be hypersensitive to the subtle meanings behind micro-expressions. One type of eyebrow twitch might mean a man is joking with you, while a slightly different kind might suggest he's about to kill you. I attempted to garner additional information from Wolanski's face, just as I'm certain she was doing with mine. My eye was drawn obsessively to her protruding chin, but it offered no clue to her thoughts, beliefs, or plans.

In a fraught situation such as this, it's impossible to prevent those micro-expressions from surfacing. Moreover, I had to imagine this detective had received extensive training in how to detect dissembling. So when she gave her partner a pointed glance, I figured my charade was over.

I asked Wolanski's permission to remove something from my pocket. I pulled out Darla's business card, the one she'd so presciently pressed into my palm yesterday at the café.

All along I've known what the end game would be. I've known there'd be hell to pay. And I've barely begun to shell out. My self-imposed plan for humility counted for not more than a feather on the scale of justice.

Oh Jesus, Jesus.

Day 314

Last night I was sleeping soundly when Rosie arrived. This time, instead of laying her arm across my chest, she wriggled one arm underneath my back and wrapped both arms around me, then laid her head on my shoulder.

That not only woke me, but destroyed any pretense of sleep.

I lay still, trying to ascertain her intentions. What did she want from me? I had nothing to give. No thoughts to share, no words, and certainly no actions. Her body was pressed against mine. I could barely breathe, so overwhelming was this presence, this closeness. I shuddered. She held me more tightly.

A painful knot formed in the lower part of my throat that almost choked me. I had trouble getting air in, then had to force it out in spasms. Dry spasms that I struggled in vain to control. Rosie whispered to me, but her soft words were lost in the hair of my chest. She caressed my hand.

Why had I forced her into such a corner? She'd hesitated—she'd become capable of hesitating—with her daughter in harm's way, because of me. I'd trained and conditioned her. I was guilty, and because of me, she was also implicated.

Now, she waits for me. She understands the apology needs to originate with me, that it's not something you can ask another person to do.

She whispered into my chest again. I could hear the words this time, gentle words of encouragement and gratitude. Then she began recounting her regrets, but I stopped her. I reached for her chin, turned her face up toward mine, and put a finger to my lips. She'd interpret my gesture as saying, *Never mind, let's be quiet and not talk, especially about that.*

What I was really doing, though, was apologizing to her.

Day 315

This morning, Rosie and I attended Mass together.

When I first made the offer, she wavered. I assured her I had no hidden objective. It'd be something to do together, I said.

We went downtown to St. Bartholomew's, where Michaelina's funeral had been. The newer parish near our home, where I had been going in Rosie's stead, is one of those brightly lit, church-in-the-round structures with cushioned seats and no ornamentation. I prefer the old style—the vaulted ceilings, hard varnished pews, darkened stained glass, and mawkish statues—a style that's both penitential and celebratory.

I knelt with Rosie. No prayers came to mind. That didn't matter—I hadn't come for that.

What had I come for, really? What was I to say to God, there on his turf? In my original plan, I was to bring God to heel. Kneeling there in that pew, though, I wondered how such an outcome could possibly manifest itself. I recalled how much more favorably I viewed Owen after he responded to me with humility. Was I now expecting God to look more favorably on me, to treat me more tenderly?

As the liturgy began, I imbibed it all—the priest's embroidered robes, the somber rituals, the chanted responses. I drank it all in, not in gulps like a convert, nor in distracted sips like a cradle Catholic. Not even as a skeptic, gargling mouthfuls and spitting it out. Instead, I was like an ailing man taking his tonic. I didn't care whether it was to my taste. I suspected it might be snake oil, yet at the same time I hoped for some mysterious salutary effect.

When the line for communion formed, Rosie stayed with me in the pew. Two old sinners, that's what we were, not fit to put ourselves forward to the feast.

No—that's not precisely true. Rosie hasn't sinned in the way I have. Her level of reverence, though, is such that she doesn't approach the altar without preparation. She needed confession first. I see the appeal of that—unburdening yourself in that small dark space to someone who can't reveal your secrets later.

I watched the communicants process to the front. They knelt in long rows at the altar rail, some receiving in their hands, others tilting up their chins to receive the host on their tongues, like baby birds fed by their mother.

When communion had finished and the priest and servers were busy cleaning up the remnants, my eyes wandered beyond them and settled on the cross hanging high on the wall behind the altar. It was an old-style crucifix, not like those anodized resurrected Christs with arms outstretched, floating in front of a cross. This one, carved of wood and painted, portrayed the crucifixion more graphically. The artist captured with some realism the torturous effects mere gravity can inflict on a body pinned to wood. Everything was pulled downward. The entire figure slumped. The punctures in the hands where the nails entered weren't just holes, but more like long rips. Blood dripped downward in streaks and runlets from the torn hands and feet, the wounds on his head, and the sliced flesh in his side.

I'd never looked at a crucifix so closely before, never examined it in this clinical fashion. The ubiquity of the symbol in our culture has rendered it a virtual cliché. This one, though, with its theme of physical gravity, inspired in me an emotional gravity. The corpse wore a clean and neatly tied loincloth over its genitalia, an adornment incongruous with the rest of the depiction. Would the Romans really have allowed him to be covered, or was the cloth a fig leaf, an aesthetically and historically mandated embellishment to spare the viewer? A crucifixion, the most ignominious death the most depraved minds of the time could devise, surely wouldn't have sanctioned the mercy of a loincloth.

The ultimate humiliation, that's what it was. If Jesus were God, why had he agreed to it? He'd prayed beforehand in the Garden of Gethsemane that it not be so. No one, not even the Messiah, actively desired humiliation or to be put to death.

The last time I'd spoken to God was in the hospital when Michaelina had been near death. That's when I'd made my bargain. Had Jesus, before his death, made a bargain of sorts too? During his crucifixion, Jesus had asked his Father why he'd abandoned him. The question implied that his Father had reneged on some sort of implicit pledge. Yet Jesus then bore the rest of the punishment without complaint.

And he'd endured the contempt of the crowd. Had he also viewed himself with contempt? Was he humiliated not just in others' estimation, but in his own? That's the kind of humiliation I could comprehend, the kind of Christ I could relate to. Maybe that was how he brought his own Father to heel. By accepting, by embracing the total abnegation of self, he proved he was as good as God. He proved that he was one with God.

In contrast, my own humiliation wasn't thrust upon me—I'd courted it myself.

Day 317

Despite the recent police search, I felt better this morning than in a long time. I'd called Darla right after the search to let her know she'd be hearing from the detective. My plan was to go for a run, shower, then get a haircut from Harris. I hadn't shaved in days, not since the hospital had let me go. Afterward, I'd meet Darla at her office.

But first, tea—Rosie's drinking it again. I steeped the Earl Grey in the Michaelina mug, heaped the contents with the proper amount of sugar, and waited for the toilet's double-flush above me. That idiosyncrasy doesn't bother me anymore. In fact, the sound consoles me. It's a sign of the Presence of the Other. The Other who awaits, who's prepared, who's favorably disposed and ready for communion.

I carried the tea upstairs, along with coffee for myself. I leaned against the wall, and Rosie sat in her chair by the window. The sun splayed its revealing rays across her face—her care-worn, time-beatified face. We talked of nothing in particular.

As I came downstairs, Patton raced in circles, then stopped and shook his floppy ears in rebuke for the delay. I sat on the bottom step, set the empty mugs aside, and gave him a thorough rubdown. Then we headed to the park.

The trouble started at the end of my run. I stopped at a port-a-potty near the trailhead. On exiting, I believe my photo was taken. A woman in casual business attire—not hiking gear—pretended to take a selfie, but she had me in her sights. Then, on returning home, I found a media van parked out front. Someone must've leaked information about the search warrant. With my cellphone confiscated, though, I couldn't check the news or call Rosie on our landline.

Rather than give myself away, I sailed past the house and headed back into town to locate a payphone. After a half hour of fruitless searching, I needed to hustle to make my regular appointment time with Harris. He'd be unlikely to comment on my sweatiness and running gear.

At the barbershop, Patton whined about being left in the car, but it was cold out and I cracked the windows for some air. Just as I was about to open the front door of the shop, the sight through the glass stopped me short. Another customer was in my chair, and Harris, with his rough old face and protruding ears, was talking animatedly with him. They shared a big laugh. I'd never heard Harris laugh before—not once. As I walked in, the little bell above the door tinkled. Harris glanced up and our eyes locked. He registered no surprise, but the grin disappeared from his face. With his head, he motioned me over to the waiting area.

I asked to use the phone. I called Rosie and in a low voice told her not to answer the door under any circumstances. "What if it's the police?" she wanted to know. "It won't be," I said, with more confidence than I felt. "The media want your reaction—do you want to give it to them?" Impatience rose within me, but I beat it back. I'll be forever beating it back.

Harris had stopped conversing with his customer halfway through the haircut. I suspected his sudden silence was caused by my presence. I watched him as he worked methodically around the man's head, scissors flashing. Despite my waiting, he didn't rush through his task.

The laugh I'd heard from him moments before echoed in my ears; the image of him chatting amiably with his customer filled my mind. Harris had been enjoying himself. Which was the real Harris? I thought we had an understanding, that even if we were on different planes socioeconomically, we were alike in our no-nonsense natures. We both eschewed the fake, glad-handed spirit of the commercial world.

But I was wrong. He'd only been adjusting his response, catering to his patron's preferences. His current customer wanted jolly conversation and Harris was eager to provide it.

What did that say about me? All these years, as he stood ready to serve me, he must've made his little calculations. Each time I sat in his chair, he must've reminded himself, "Here's the guy who wants no conversation. I'll just grunt a few times until I get my tip and he's out the door." Maybe then he laughed at me.

Harris, it turns out, was more sophisticated than the adulating bank tellers and grocery store clerks, but no less obsequious after all. My money just purchased the illusion of sympathy.

He finished up with his customer and received his fee with a smiling thanks that he never gave to me. I waited as he swept up the hair and indicated he was ready. His chair's red leather arms, darkened with age and oil from the fingers of countless customers, received me, but I found no comfort in them. How many times, sitting in this chair, had I experienced a surge of camaraderie with this man? Yet he wasn't like me at all. Even here was a lie about love.

As usual, he said nothing as he cut my hair. But instead of launching into the shave directly afterward, he hesitated, then held the mirror out to me and said, "I thought maybe you was wanting a beard. You look good."

So even Harris knew. I snatched the mirror from him and looked at myself. *I should change my appearance?*

I insisted on the shave. He seemed extra slow about it. Was he savoring the chance to remove the facial bristles of an infamous doctor, a possible criminal? As he worked his straight razor, he cleared his throat a few times. When he finished and spread the hot towel over my face, he said, "I had a neighbor once. They was hunting, him and his son. He shot his son by accident. It was all over the news." He paused. "He couldn't take it. Offed himself the next day."

I hardly knew how to reply. Was he suggesting a similar course of action for me? My face was obscured under the towel, which suddenly felt like the hood a man wears at the gallows. *Quickly, draw the razor across my throat*, I nearly told him.

Then he added, "No sense in that. Everybody makes mistakes. Some's worse than others, but that's just the luck of it."

In my case luck wasn't much involved, but I wasn't about to engage in conversation about it. I fingered the Xanax bottle in my pocket. Isn't that what I'd been keeping it there for—in case I couldn't take it anymore? I visualized myself swallowing the remaining pills and falling into a deep and eternal sleep. If only I could assure myself such a sleep would bring me peace.

No—I'm only kidding myself. I'm a coward in that as in so many things. The day I took off speeding in my car had taught me that. I'd never kill myself because I still have pride left after all. Or in any event I still place some kind of value on my life.

Afterward, I met with Darla, who cautioned me that an arrest could be imminent. I needed to arrange my affairs.

When I returned home, the news van was gone.

Day 318

Late last night, instead of Rosie coming to me, I went to her.

I stepped softly into her room. She must've sensed my presence, because she turned in bed to face me. In the darkness, I could see only the shine of her eyes, but not her expression. Her lying there in the dark, turned to me, distressed me almost as much as when I first brought tea to her that morning nearly a year ago.

I thought of an excuse for my intrusion—that I'd forgotten to ask her something, but that it could wait until morning.

I didn't, though. That part of me has learned to step aside.

As I approached the bed, she opened the covers for me. Clearly she'd been expecting me. I wondered—for how many nights? I slid in beside her. Without a word, she laid her soft arm across my chest, making this encounter like the others, easing the way.

To be sure, I wasn't there to claim any rights, to control, or to force a re-establishment of anything. I was there because it was the right place to be. Because I needed her. We needed each other.

Maybe now, after everything, I did have something of value to offer. At least I could place myself in her presence. The rest would have to take care of itself.

And it did. Her ear was near my lips so I kissed it gently. She turned her face to me and kissed me on the tip of my nose. I smiled. We gathered our bodies together. I took up her hair and smothered myself in it, breathing in the vanilla scent of her shampoo.

This might seem like old territory. Yes, but the terrain had become unfamiliar, like going back to your old neighborhood and finding a hurricane had blown through, shifting landmarks and sweeping away the old paths. This is no metaphor for Rosie's body—no, every welcoming part was just where it belonged. But here was a new landscape, a breathtaking one. I was the boy returning to the neighborhood after the storm. Wreckage lay all about me, filling me with awe at the devastation and feeling a party to it, while at the same time reveling in the possibilities for discovery and rebuilding.

I ran my fingers over the flesh on either side of her mid-section. And I laughed. Laughed because the situation was so incongruous, so inviting, so real. I laughed because of the absurdity and the seriousness. My recognizing it, and giving in to it instead of fighting it, sent me soaring. Rosie laughed too and poked me in the ribs, tears streaming down her face.

In the midst of it all she called me Mac and I laughed harder. Maybe this whole year of humility was leading to this one thing, that I could let go of my pride in this one place.

And the letting go did come about. Her hips tilted in the old way and swung open like a door. Like a gate, a heavenly gate, swinging wide to greet me. To welcome me home.

I finally have an inkling of what Rosie's about. She's understood the paradox from the start. How sex isn't to be taken lightly, yet is best undertaken light-heartedly. How desire can be as much metaphysical as physical. How so much of it was giving up and giving in. How it could fill you with a terrible sense of loss, or of becoming lost. Then, being found again, re-created as someone new.

Day 319

Thurman's office called first thing, saying she wanted to see me today.

I'm weak, conquered. All my opposition to her machinations, her manipulation of my psyche, has vanished.

When I arrived, her first words were, "You went to the police. Good."

I didn't correct her misapprehension, but instead asked why she wanted to see me, now that the truth was out and the whole thing over.

"*Hoo!* All over? We only just got ourselves to the beginning."

I sunk into her old accomplice, the sofa, and awaited instruction.

"I've been thinking," she said, "I see it better now that it's not so much guilt you feel. Guilt is how you feel after doing something wrong. You can recognize that and make amends and live with that. If you were only just going about your business when you backed into your little girl, that would be one thing—just a very awful mistake. But I see more behind it, more that's harder to let go of. I think you wrestle with shame. That's what's killing you."

I sighed. "I see no difference between guilt and shame. No effective difference, anyway."

"The difference is very big. Shame isn't just doing something wrong, it's making you believe *you,* your very person, is wrong."

How could I dispute that?

She sat forward in her chair, pleased with her new interpretation. "By counting on your pride and self-importance to keep your childhood shame hidden, your behaviors only got worse and caused disaster. So you try this scheme of humility to make amends. But even your humility is trying to prove something. Showing up other people, showing up God. That's not real humility."

"No matter. It's all turned to humiliation anyway."

She clucked. "Humiliation is no good either. When someone humiliates you, they cut you down to size, but you realize they're wrong, that you're not at that low level they cut you down to."

I listened in cowed silence.

"No, it's not humility or humiliation. It's shame you're hiding."

"There's generally good reason for hiding shame."

She shook her head. "You think you're set apart, that no other father has done something so terrible as you. But other children die too when their parents make a big mistake. And don't forget all the near misses—it's just luck that saves other parents from the same fate. What about the time they left the balcony door open and their toddler was halfway through the railing before they noticed and grabbed her collar just in time? Or the close call when they jaywalked and didn't have hold of their little boy's hand and he darted out into traffic, but the truck squealed to a stop just in time? Or when they were in a rush and left the baby in a hot car for several minutes, or the time they left the pool gate open and they hear a faint splash just after they turn off the vacuum cleaner…"

"Enough! Even if you argued negligence in their cases, they didn't do those things out of anger."

"Okay, maybe not anger, but maybe self-absorption or carelessness. That was you, too. You didn't back into your girl because you were angry with her. It was anger with others, pride that your authority wasn't respected, impatience to get away from your wife. These emotions have been working so hard to protect you, to hide your shame. You've been hiding from shame your whole life, ever since Butt-cheeks."

I exhaled a long sigh. "That information is of no value. If I harbor shame, it's hidden even from myself. I see no way to release myself from it."

She leaned back in her chair. Her tone turned soft. "You forget about empathy. Being honest with people—people who care about you—can help. Does no one show you compassion?"

I thought of Owen. When I talk to him, I feel almost normal. Rosie's shown empathy, too.

"Even more important than compassion from others, you need to show it to yourself."

"Right."

"Seriously. You need to talk to these parts of you that keep your shame hidden. Be grateful to them for their hard work protecting you from pain. But then you need to ask them to step aside so you can find that part of you that's aching, the part you've pushed away for so long. You need to be a friend to that part, to show him your empathy. The goodness in your real self can heal that part of you that's so weighted down with shame."

Day 320

Despite my skepticism, I later closed my eyes, as instructed by Thurman, and tried to loosen up my mind. In doing so, I seemed to find myself in a dense forest, experiencing a sense of danger. A musk-like odor, as from a wild animal, filled my nostrils, but I couldn't see clearly. Something was happening in that forest, something of importance, but I could get no further.

Nevertheless, I felt a bit better. Not that I believe in these multifarious parts of my psyche existing in any concrete way, but I'll admit that by viewing my own consciousness from a different angle, from a more detached viewpoint, I experienced a measure of emotional relief.

Day 321

The police came today with a Miranda warning and arrest warrant. I was handcuffed and muscled to the squad car. I hung my head as the news cameras clicked and rolled.

Rosie wasn't home. I was glad of that. She'll learn soon enough of my whereabouts.

Upon arrival at the station a sergeant made me empty my pockets. He opened the bottle of Xanax and sniffed it, then insisted I remove my belt and shoelaces, even though I told him there was no call for that—I wouldn't make any trouble that way.

He examined the oddly shaped stone among my possessions. I made him promise to keep it for me.

I used my phone call to speak with Darla, who said we could probably avoid a sensational trial if the case were handled carefully.

"Sure," I said, "but what I want right now is a pen and a sheaf of looseleaf."

Darla demonstrated competency in this small matter, as this evening, the guard handed me a short, dull pencil and several sheets of scrap paper.

Day 323

The thin mattress in my bunk is covered in plastic. Its antiseptic smell suggests it's been wiped down, but when I lay my face against it to sleep, I can't avoid its stickiness and the sense that it's been embalmed with human secretions of every kind.

A square of security window allows me to look into a sort of courtyard, but the pane is grimy, turning the outside world to dust and ashes.

The overhead lights burn my eyes. They're dimmed at night but never turned off. I cocoon myself in the rip-resistant blanket to shield my eyes and minimize the amount of my skin that fuses with the mattress. The downside of this method is waking up every few hours in a sweaty panic, feeling as if I've been buried alive.

There's a toilet behind a four-foot wall in the corner of the cell, and a doll-size sink. The toilet stinks, as there's not enough water dispensed to it to fully flush the contents. It appears not to have been cleaned in half a century.

Lawyers have been in and out all day. First my regular tax attorney, to have me sign some power-of-attorney papers, then lawyers from the malpractice insurance company and another one hired by the hospital. They all look alike, with their shadowy blazers, bespectacled distance, and tsk-tsk airs.

Then Darla arrived. She was in lawyer mode—abrupt, all business. No quotations. "Arraignment's tomorrow," she said, "so if you can hold on another day here we'll get you out on bail."

She wanted to know what the police might've discovered in the garage during the search, and what evidence I could've left behind in the car. I told her the Porsche was long gone, and the garage had been cleaned since then.

"Then all we can do is wait for the preliminary hearing to find out what they have."

She mentioned the potential for a plea deal, raising no questions about why I had covered up my role in the accident. I suppose she didn't need to, after her discussions with Rosie.

Day 324

Around three in the morning, the guards put a drunk in the cell with me. He fell into an immediate deep sleep and snored like a jackhammer. After an hour, just when I was ready to get up and shake him, someone came to bail him out.

My arraignment today was brief, but informative. The female judge, unsettlingly young, spoke with an imperious intonation, the weight of sovereignty behind it. She pressed her lips together frequently, as if every aspect of the case displeased or disgusted her.

The prosecuting district attorney, a man with narrow, flinty eyes that darted frequently in my direction but never seemed to take me in, was competent and well-spoken. Just my luck.

I'm being charged with depraved heart murder—a form of second-degree murder in which someone knowingly engages in excessively reckless behavior that results in another person's death. I'm also charged with two counts of making false statements to the police.

Darla petitioned for bail but was denied. Evidently, my lying about my role in the accident, coupled with the $20K in cash they found when searching my bedroom, constituted sufficient evidence to deem me a flight risk.

Day 325

Rosie was allowed to visit me today. I downplayed the seriousness of my situation, made jokes, did silly impersonations of the jailers, lawyers, and the succession of petty lawbreakers who've stayed briefly in the cell with me, just to get a smile from her. That's all I wanted, just a smile. I'd asked her to bring in any crossword puzzles she hadn't completed, so I could finish them with her.

Instead, she brought me my Bible (the one I pilfered from the church), which I'm allowed to keep.

I touched her hand through the small slot at the bottom of the plexiglass barrier, but I wanted more contact. All those times I'd cut her off from my affection haunted me now.

On her new cellphone, across the table, Rosie showed me a video news clip of my arrest. It featured a photo of me in my running shorts with a stupid expression on my face, a port-a-potty in the background. The report has proliferated.

We didn't speak of the charges or the impending trial. I asked if she was staying with Maude, which I'd suggested, to have some company as well as to stay clear of the media. She hesitated before answering, seemingly weighing how her reply might affect me. Now, more than ever, she manages me.

"Actually, I'm staying with John and Shayze," she said. "They invited me, and with the new baby coming and everything, I thought it made the most sense."

I didn't ask what the "everything" part meant. That things had regressed to the point that she was now living with our banned son seemed incongruous, even funny. What mattered before no longer matters, for me or for her. We're living in an alternate universe.

I also met with Darla, who said, "I didn't want to push you the other day, but I need to know every detail of what happened. Be as objective as you can. I won't judge—that's not my role." Every bit of information, she said, would serve as a tiny piece in an intricate puzzle. Those pieces would help her see a picture she could turn into a story to persuade the jurors. Right now, she was only developing the framework. At the preliminary hearing, we'd learn what evidence the prosecution had. From there, she'd explore potential responses and complete a narrative we'd follow during the trial.

Telling her about the accident was easier than expected. She kept her nose to her writing pad and took copious notes.

Upon concluding, I remarked that my confessing seemed anticlimactic.

"That's because your admission of guilt is immaterial now," she said. "They must have evidence you did it. It's better not to dispute that, unless you want to keep implicating Rosie."

I did not.

"Good. What matters now is the motivation."

Day 326

This place isn't so bad—no news media here. No cell phones, no internet. No obligations or decisions to make. No maximizing food choices and no criticizing the chef. It's oatmeal or toast and coffee for breakfast, bologna and cheese sandwiches with lukewarm tea for lunch, and soup or a plate of rubbery meat and overcooked vegetables for dinner. I haven't much of an appetite anyway.

There's peace in a place where one's depraved heart, the very organ that's supposed to love, is powerless to do additional damage. Depraved heart murder is just a step below premeditated murder. It seems I was only a step away from killing Michaelina on purpose.

Yet, I'd convinced myself that Rosie was ultimately to blame. What is blame, really? Blame is holding someone else responsible because it's impossible to believe that you yourself could've done something so stupid, so evil, so humiliating. You couldn't have done it because you're better than that. The action has to be outside of you.

I never truly blamed Rosie. I just couldn't admit to an atrocity that I believed my true self wasn't capable of committing.

Day 327

Today, they brought in a man who must've done something pretty bad—no one's come to bail him out. I avoided conversation as much as I could, but he seemed to need to declare his innocence, insisting that his girlfriend had done it (whatever "it" was) and was now trying to pin the crime on him to get rid of him. Her bed was already occupied by a new dude, he claimed.

Something about a jail cell disables the mind's gatekeeper, the one who concerns himself with the consequences of spoken words and revealed emotions. Here, thinking is painful; talking is relieving. Maybe that's why so many criminals confess once they're in here.

Or maybe it's the lack of distractions. Outside the cell, one need never think—something always fills the void. In here, though, you can't get away from thinking. At the same time, your thoughts are not fully you. They're like another person—a silent judge standing over you, aware of the minutiae and motives of your every action. Maybe that's also why prisoners kill themselves—not from fear of punishment, but from the inescapable horror of self-reflection.

The cellmate asked what I was in for, and when I said depraved heart murder, he grunted and didn't question me further. At last, someone who doesn't keep up with local news.

Day 328

When Rosie visited today, I questioned her about Shayze, this putative wife of John's. She's first generation Jamaican American. She and John had married in Las Vegas, not wanting to deal with our family situation. That was nearly two years ago, and they'd known each other for a year before that. That means Shayze knew Michaelina too. Rosie informed me that they were both at the funeral. Shayze apparently had approached me and shaken my hand. John, camouflaged by beard and glasses, had stayed in the background.

The revelation of this deception sent the blood rushing up my neck. They'd conspired behind my back even more so than I'd imagined. No doubt they'd discussed me, analyzed me, probably mocked me. At the very least they must've been amused at my cluelessness. And all the while I believed they were docilely carrying out my wishes.

But instead of lashing out at Rosie's revelation, I merely nodded.

The truth is laid bare now. The layers of lies that had afforded comfort or protection have been peeled away. The existence beneath is stark and raw. Still, I won't turn away.

Day 329

I've been thinking about my rose bushes. It's pruning season. How I'd love to be outside in the brisk air, caring for them. No matter how dead they appear on the outside, when I slice through the canes, the pale green interiors are moist and filled with the promise of spring.

Michaelina, that one time, pricked herself on a thorn and hated the roses forever after. She'd rejected them wholesale—the vivid colors and velvety petals and beguiling fragrance—because of the sting of the thorn.

I choose a thorn now, the largest I can find. I bend it where it joins the stem, and gently tear it from the cane. I probe the sharp tip with my thumb. Gripping the torn part between my thumb and forefinger, I place the thorn just behind my left ear and press the point firmly into my flesh, working it in until it hits bone. I leave it there, resisting the urge to pull it out, ignoring the silent scream my brain produces. The pain flowing through me allows me to think more clearly.

Here's the substance of my thoughts. Why is it I'm a worse person now than before this year of humility began? Why am I so incapable of change?

I try to understand this powerlessness by opening my mind to the foreign parts of my psyche. Again I come upon a forest, thick with evergreens. I intuit danger there, feeling once more the presence of a wild animal lurking nearby. I move quickly through the trees and into a clearing that leads to the rocky shore of a lake. A small, faint island is situated in the distance. As I step onto the strand, a bear appears in front of me. Her coat, black and glossy, reflects the sun as she lumbers back and forth between me and the lake, obstructing my view.

"I want to see that island in the lake," I say.

She growls.

Just then, the piece of torn toenail loosens from its position behind my ear and falls to the floor. The pain peters out, and with it, the mental clarity.

In an instant, I'm flooded with irritation at this whole scenario, at losing my daughter and my practice and being charged with crimes and forced into this jail cell and being expected on top of it all to figure out my own mental complexities. Most of all, I'm annoyed at the very notion that some hidden part of me, some embodiment of shame, is waiting for release.

This will never work. I am above this. I am strong. The great black she-bear is me.

Day 330

Fathers and sons have been messed up forever.

With little else to do, I find myself reading and rereading their stories in the Bible. Abraham nearly sacrifices his son Isaac; he also abandons his son Ishmael. Noah curses his son Ham's descendants. Isaac favors his son Esau over Jacob, and Jacob steals his father's blessing. David's son Absalom tries to usurp his father's throne and is assassinated because of it. Even Christ's relationship with his heavenly Father is fraught. The Father expects obedience from him in everything, "even unto death."

The prodigal son wastes his father's inheritance. He repents, and his father forgives him. But that story was a parable and not true to life. Besides, in this jail I cannot scan the horizon, watching and waiting for John's return. I have no robes or rings, no access to a fatted calf.

No matter—I don't want to see him now anyway. Not until I've learned self-effacement.

Day 331

"A faithful friend is a life-saving remedy, such as he who fears God finds" (Sirach 6:16). Owen, who visited me today, is my faithful friend. Or he would be, if my faith were of such caliber as the Bible suggests is required. All I know is there's not another person on earth—besides Rosie—I was as happy to see as Owen. The man has a sixth sense about what topics are welcome and which are not—even in an extraordinary situation such as this.

What did we talk about? *Michaelina.* Owen recalled how she'd come with me to the hospital one day. He'd seen her in my waiting room area as he passed in the hall, recognizing her from the photo in my office. He paused and watched her. Sitting by herself and holding a doll, Michaelina scanned the craniofacial patients around her. Quietly, she got up and wandered over to a girl about her age whose mother was holding a tiny infant with a cleft lip. Michaelina patted the girl's arm and said, "Don't worry, my daddy can fix her face. She'll be as pretty as a princess." The other girl said, "He's a boy, silly." In response, Michaelina screwed up her face and planted a sharp kiss on the baby's forehead. "At least he won't be a frog."

Owen burst out laughing at his own story, and I joined him.

That story opened a valve. I talked to him of Michaelina and what I missed most—the quizzical looks, springy step, precocious posturing, and flashes of willfulness. Owen listened closely, then responded in his typical (yet how atypical) manner, convincing me somehow that all was as it should be, or at least that events were now heading in a salutary direction. He didn't steer me, yet his easy responses aided me in steering myself. Yes, that's how I'd put it—every revelation that came to me when speaking with him seemed to originate within me, even though I doubt I'd have had those revelations without his aid.

He helped me to think less about Michaelina's death, and instead to reflect more expansively on her life. At bottom, it was the same as everyone else's— she was conceived, born, lived, suffered, and died. I won't call her flawless, and who knows what faults she'd have developed as an adult, especially under my tutelage. As a young child, though, she was pure, and blessed with my intelligence, Rosie's imagination, and John's determination. Curious and joyful, she lived in the moment. Any minor pains and sorrows were fleeting.

Until the day I backed into her.

The arc of her life was truncated, but it wasn't pointless. What was the point then? First, she was loved. I adored her, and so did Rosie, John, and even Shayze. She was loved by her preschool teachers, classmates, and friends, especially Trevor from next door. And she loved all of us. What more is there to a successful life than to love and to be loved?

Her death was a tragedy, but her life, a glory.

Day 332

A new cellmate has joined me. I don't know his name or the charges against him. He doesn't speak much, which is good, as what he does say is not exactly edifying.

His head has been recently shaved, and he's missing his left eye. A thick pink scar, evidently from a deep cut that was badly sewn up, curves from the corner of his empty socket around his zygomatic bone, then tapers off and dissolves into his nostril. With his left middle finger, he traces the path of this scar along his cheek, starting at his eye socket and looping down to his nostril, then up again, repeatedly. He seems to derive great comfort from this compulsion.

His remaining eye is yellowed and bulging, as if he has a thyroid condition. When he thinks I'm not paying attention, that bulging eye observes me.

Later, meeting with Darla, I asked if I could be transferred to another cell.

"What do you think this is, a college dorm?" she said.

The irritation in her response reminded me of myself, or of the late me. I couldn't fault her for it. Someday she'll have her own opportunities.

This evening, wanting to establish good terms with my new cellmate, I graciously moved to the bottom bunk.

Day 333

Court is a mixed blessing. Away from the jail, my senses come alive again. I can't get enough of the sight of other people—their colorful clothing, lively murmurs, and varied faces. I take in the long clean lines of the courtroom, the chance to see objects at a distance. I run my palm along the wooden rail in front of me and am astonished at its smoothness. You wouldn't think a courtroom could have odors, but it does—a mixture of furniture polish, cloistered breath, and anxious sweat.

I'm learning more about the court system than I ever wanted to know. At today's preliminary hearing, a grand jury was convened to hear the evidence against me, to decide if there was 'probable cause' to hold the trial. The only good news was that the charges of lying to police were dropped for lack of evidence. New charges were added, however, related to the surgery that blinded Zoe: first, aggravated assault with a deadly weapon (for intentional use of force), and second, reckless endangerment, stemming from the fact that I knew my vision and judgment were impaired—but that I hid this situation from the surgical team, hospital administrator, and psychiatrist, and blithely continued performing surgeries.

The sworn testimony from my hospital colleagues was unpleasant. (Owen, thankfully, was not involved in Zoe's surgery and thus was not asked to provide a statement against me.) It's purported that I used medical procedures that weren't warranted, resulting in her blindness. This information had come out when detectives discovered my surgery privileges had been revoked.

Most damaging for the depraved heart charge, though, was the discovery of a witness—the neighbor boy Trevor, whose statement was presented as evidence. Looking over the fence that day, he saw Rosie come out on the side porch and scream for me to stop, just before I backed up from the garage and struck Michaelina. Moreover, during the house search, the detectives had examined the distance from the porch to the garage door. Detective Shorr had sat in the car in the garage, engine running, while Detective Wolanski shouted from the porch. They determined I would've heard Rosie yelling, even with the car windows closed, radio on, and Patton barking. They'd made a recording and it was played for the grand jury. The key element of the case is that Rosie had yelled for me to stop, and I didn't. They were correct about that—I did hear her shout. I heard Patton barking, too, and I ignored them both. Having assigned the blame to my wife sets the seal on my guilt.

Beyond the criminal charges, Zoe's family is filing a civil suit against the hospital and me. I'm also facing a medical malpractice suit. Even more lawyers, supplied by the insurance companies, are in my future.

After the hearing, I asked Darla whether my conviction could really rest on the testimony of a child with a developmental disability.

"Not exactly," she said. "It's true that none of this would've come to trial without his belatedly telling his father what he saw. But his value to the prosecution is only in establishing you as the driver of the car. Once that's a settled point, which we're not disputing, then Trevor has no further use to their case. It then boils down to your thinking. That's why the tape is so damaging. If they can prove you heard Rosie shout for you to stop and you didn't, they've won."

"But the recording's just a simulation, not evidence."

"Yes, and I can cast doubt on it in all kinds of ways. Nevertheless, a jury may decide that the recording itself is unimportant. They may think, not unreasonably, that by not looking behind you before backing up, you disregarded an obvious risk, and are just as guilty."

Day 334

In this jail cell, I'm the dregs, the ashes, the detritus—lower than the lawyers, the guards, the other prisoners, and my cellmate. They wield power and control. I am unprotected.

Perhaps this hopeless physical and mental state is what I need to help me find the shamed child, the one saddled with the name Butt-cheeks. He's well hidden, though. I can't see him or feel him. To locate him, I first need to get past the bear.

I wish Thurman were here to help me.

Day 335

My cellmate's name, I've finally learned, is Blake.

This evening, Blake found my Bible, hidden under my mattress. (Not much of a hiding place, but options are few.) He opened it, and the loose pages of my journal fluttered to the floor. He picked them up and read several passages out loud. How strange to hear my words read back to me! They no longer seem to belong to me. It's as if putting the thoughts on paper has deleted them from my internal hard drive.

As for Blake, it's the first time I've seen him smile. Yet the smile was less one of amusement than of portent. When he finished reading, he tucked the pages back into the Bible. His finger explored his scar, back and forth, up and down, as he contemplated something he didn't care to share.

He wants me to continue writing.

Day 336

Michaelina's absence still presses on me, from above and behind but never in front of me. I generate fewer concrete thoughts about her. To be clear, I don't mean that days go by without my thinking of her, only hours. When she's present in my thoughts, it feels like the edge of a migraine softening, making you want to press your finger into your supraorbital notch to make sure the pain is still there, almost wanting it to be, because the sensation of it dissipating is so cathartic.

With the easing of the pain comes a sense of betrayal that I'm allowing her to slip away from me. To lose the constant ache of loss—is that disloyal? Because of my responsibility for that loss, the question seems unanswerable. I feel a moral urgency to make amends by keeping her memory alive, and my guilt as well.

Rosie has revealed the existence of a trove of photos and videos from John, chronicling Michaelina's short life. Are these photo-relics a comfort, or a colossal chastisement? I'm absent from them; they were recorded without my knowledge. Rosie and John and Shayze took turns with the camera. I'm the one left out. It seems the obliteration of my life began years ago. And who is to blame for that?

When Rosie visits, she shows me samples of these photos and videos on her phone. Through the marred visitor plexiglass, I can never see them quite clearly. And anyway, it's eerie to view my little girl performing in front of the camera, living an entire life I had no part in.

Today Rosie played a video of Michaelina and Shayze cavorting outside in the rare snow. They belted out a song from a wintery Disney princess movie and danced around each other, picking up handfuls of snowflakes and flinging them at each other. I recognized the song as a favorite of Michaelina's, one she'd sung incessantly around the house. At the time, the lyrics came across as sappy, new-age, girl empowerment crap. I remember hoping that Michaelina would tire of the song quickly.

This time, though, the words pierced me. As Michaelina sang, she turned to face the camera. *Let it go*, she sang, as if speaking words from the grave: *The past is in the past! Let it go!*

Day 337

All those rubdowns I've given Patton over the years—who knew they were more for my benefit than his?

That unfortunate time I backed out of the garage and hit Michaelina, he'd barked long and loud, but I paid him no heed. He's owed an apology. I picture him now, hovering about, alternately flapping his ears and nosing me on the arm. I pull him close. I drape my arm over his back and lay my head on top of his neck. As my emotions drip onto his fur, I rub them away.

Day 338

Blake hasn't had any visitors except the public defender. Today, however, he was gone most of the day. I expect it was for his own arraignment, although he doesn't discuss his case.

I had the cell to myself. I can hardly communicate my jouissance.

Day 339

When asked, I explained to Blake that jouissance is something like a combination of sadness and loneliness.

Day 340

Blake has voiced his displeasure at how little I've been writing. I explained how awkward it feels to write something that a stranger will read. The other day, when he read aloud that passage I wrote about Michaelina, I could hardly bear it.

In his opinion, I lack incentive, motivation. He's found a way to help me with that. I promised to write daily.

Day 341

Craniofacial surgery can require harvesting skin, flesh, or bone from a distant part of the body to build up or otherwise improve the face. One part of the body loses, and another part, judged to be of greater importance, gains. Both parts have to sustain injury before the healing process can begin.

I've never chosen suffering. What sane person would? And yet that which no sane person would choose, has been chosen for me. That's the struggle. If God exists, is almighty, why would he deem the death of an innocent child necessary to change me? That's a stumbling block, a mystery I can't comprehend or accept.

I wonder what would've happened if God had kept his side of the pact—the side I'd assigned him—and Michaelina had survived. Could I have lived with that gift, with God accomplishing what I was unable to do? Would I have humbled myself in eternal gratitude? Or would I, the man of science, have reverted to form? After Michaelina's death, evil received its answer. To wish Michaelina alive, I'd have to wish there were no evil to begin with.

That'd be wishing myself out of existence.

Day 342

My time here must be made to be of some value. I need to think and write, to write without caring about my words being read aloud. I must put my thoughts into written words, or they'll escape and I'll never recover them again. They're all I have now, all that grounds me—my written words.

Day 343

At a pre-trial conference today, Darla pushed for a plea deal, but was unsuccessful. Apparently, not only does the DA see this case as an easy win, but it'll generate fawning press coverage prior to the election and bring out the votes, especially among women.

"It's the cover-up," Darla explained, "your laying blame on your wife. That's destroying us here."

"I never lied."

"That's even worse. It paints you as conniving, as someone so calculating and detestable that he manages to cast blame on his own wife while not explicitly lying. The prosecution expects the jury to find this behavior so repugnant they'll readily convict you on the second-degree murder charge." She opened her mouth to say something more, then closed it.

I urged her on.

"It's all so lurid," she said. "A media sensation, especially with you blinding that girl in surgery. That additional charge will make the jury more eager to go against you."

"Can't I just plead guilty and be done?"

"Sure, if you don't mind 20 or 30 years in the state pen."

No comment from me.

"I strongly advise going through with the trial. We'll get some compassion from the jury when they hear your side."

"I have a side?"

"Sure, everyone has a side."

"So I'll testify then?"

"No! That's what you've hired me for, to present your side of the story effectively. When I explain what you've been through, they may empathize and view your actions as a sort of temporary insanity."

In a previous life, I would've questioned the competence of this lawyer. But that was then. Now I'm dependent on others, Darla foremost.

Day 344

Rosie told me that when she went back to the house to collect some things, Trevor had stopped by to visit.

I wish to God I'd been there. I imagined the scene: Patton barked wildly, running back and forth in a paroxysm of joy. I opened the door and there stood Trevor. He didn't look at me or speak. Instead, he put his hand out to Patton, who licked it rapturously.

The reason Trevor was there didn't matter. I didn't care that he'd witnessed the accident or told his parents. I didn't care about his disability. I cared only that he'd been Michaelina's friend.

In that moment, I loved the boy.

I asked him in. I yelled upstairs to Rosie, "Trevor's here!" She came running down and smiled at him. I wondered aloud whether we had any refreshments and she hustled into the kitchen. I asked Trevor if he'd like to see Michaelina's room and he nodded. We climbed the stairs together and entered her room.

This was why we hadn't touched it. We'd kept it intact for this visit from Trevor. I told him to choose something of Michaelina's to remember her by, anything he wanted. He nodded. First, he ran his fingers over the coverlet on her bed. Then he went to her child-size velveteen sofa and picked up her teddy bear and smelled it. He moved to her dresser and looked at each doll, stroking the hair on several of them. I opened Michaelina's closet door and he touched her dresses. He pulled out a ruby-colored cape, one I'd seen him wear when assigned the role of prince in one of Michaelina's make-believes. He took it off the hanger and draped it over his shoulders.

I crouched down to his level, my face inches from his. He didn't look me in the eye, but he was listening. I took his hand and said, "I made a mistake that day. A very bad mistake. I'm so sorry." I didn't call it an accident. How could I, when he knew better? His eyes turned liquidy. Then he hugged me, in that brief but fierce way children have.

In the kitchen, he ate chocolate cake and drank lemonade while I sat beside him. I wrote a brief note to his parents, explaining about the cape and letting them know Trevor was welcome over anytime.

Day 345

Life in jail is boiled down to a slow-moving syrup.

Time here is both precious and expendable. Vast swaths of it fill the day. But when a visitor arrives, the clock starts ticking. I hear the sound of it in my brain. I can't tell myself I'll say the important words some other time. I'm on my deathbed each time someone comes to call.

I'm a love-needy child. I say what's on my mind and hope it will please. I'm a child with no control over my life, who has no choice but to trust those who do have the power.

I try to please you, too, Blake. You can see I'm trying. I thank you for taking such an interest in me, for helping me overcome my faults.

Day 346

Yes, Blake is helping me. I'm learning not to be selfish, for example. I consider Blake's needs first. I give him the space he needs. When he performs his morning push-ups, I stay in my bunk. When he moves to the bunkbed to do some modified pull-ups, I slip over near the door. I proceed slowly now in all I do, as quick shifts in position seem to disturb his peace.

I'm not to look at his scar. That means not making eye contact with him, although he's welcome to look at me as much as he likes.

When I hear the soft chugging of Blake's snores at night, I sleep soundly, delighting in his contentment.

By the way, he's confided to me that he was framed. He's innocent of all charges.

Day 347

Darla now says that an insanity defense is our best option.

"I'm not insane," I told her.

"I've talked to Dr. Thurman and Rosie," she said.

When I gave her a blank look in return, she said, "There are incidents, behaviors, and examples of self-talk that could be construed that way, enough to promote that theory."

"That's their interpretation," I said. "Sure, a couple times I felt near the edge, but not anymore. Besides, confinement in a mental institution would itself drive me insane."

"I get it, but your stay there would probably be a lot shorter, and more pleasant, than in state prison."

"Pleading insanity would be the end of surgery for good. I'd lose my medical license."

"That's likely to happen regardless."

That shut me up.

"I'd be a poor attorney if I wasn't honest with you," she continued. "We have a promising mental illness case here. If we don't go that route, I'm less sure—"

"No way."

"At least think about it."

But I didn't need to. Insanity could maybe mitigate my culpability for Zoe's injury. For Michaelina's death, however, I was fully responsible. No punishment could make up for that, certainly not a stay in a mental ward. And this much I've learned from my Bible readings: justice and mercy are two sides of the same coin—and it's the only currency that can purchase my mental freedom.

"Forget it," I said.

Day 347 (again)

I wrote in my journal earlier today, but now I have something else, something crucial to add. Not about anything I've done—that's all in the open now.

It's about Blake. And no, he hasn't confessed any crime to me.

It's that he 'owns' my journal now. I expect he plans to give the pages to his lawyer, hoping to parlay my (forced) favorable representations of him into a character reference, to help him get off lightly or go free.

I must do something to prevent that.

Not because of the pain he's inflicted—strangely enough, the sharpness of it somehow helps me to recognize myself. It's that I need to prevent him from hurting anyone else.

He's threatened that if I report the abuse, he'll come after Rosie or John or Shayze, or the baby they're soon to have, when he gets out. He's confident of his ultimate acquittal, and I have no way to assess the veracity of his claim. Even if unlikely, he reportedly has associates who would do his bidding. My case is all over the news—it wouldn't be difficult to locate my family. And who will protect them while I'm in here, or put away for good?

If I tell anyone outright, I'll be transferred to another cell. Blake would know I was behind it and my family would be endangered.

All I can think to do is write my testimony on this page, hide it as best I can, and have it ready to slip to someone trustworthy at a moment's notice. Blake is cunning, but not so bright—if he sees I already wrote an entry for Day 347, surely he won't look for another from the same day.

Blake: if you do discover this piece of paper, know that I'm no better than you. I only reveal this situation to help save you from yourself, as you've likewise helped me.

For any of your actions toward me, past or future, you have my forgiveness.

Day 348

The hope of holding on to my medical license, which I mentioned yesterday to Darla, was only a smoke screen. Truth is, I no longer miss being a surgeon. Somehow, I've dropped the desire for it like a used tissue.

A surgeon is something I was in a dream long ago.

Blake and I have been studying the Bible together. He's found the passages I've marked about fathers and sons. He reads them aloud, and we pick them apart for their meaning. Today's was Hebrews 12:5-11:

> My son, do not regard lightly the discipline of the Lord,
> Nor faint when you are reproved by Him;

> For those whom the Lord loves He disciplines,
> And He scourges every son whom He receives.

He asks for my interpretation and I provide it. Then he gives me his.

Blake is a good man, one who studies the Bible daily and desires to help others.

Day 349

We prisoners take our daily exercise in a courtyard. It's not what the word 'courtyard' might suggest to you, although perhaps the 'court' part is close. There's no resemblance to a real yard—no grass to speak of, no shrubbery or trees. No scent of roses except in my imagination.

At first, when circumnavigating the seamed concrete sidewalk that loops around the compound, I observed only bleakness. Here and there a stray weed, a reject of the plant world, would rear its head in defiance of the seeming law against greenery.

On my own lawn, I'm strict about eliminating weeds. But here, meanings and values are reversed. How I now love the sight of a weed! Especially the lovely dandelion, with its multitudinous yellow petals bursting in shameless brilliance. I soak in the color. Then a day or two later, I find the flower transformed into an ashen puffball. It's funny how despite my vigilance, I never see a dandelion amid its magical transformation. It's one thing, then, magically, it's a totally different thing. The dandelion's life culminates in disintegration of its own head, its very death seeding new life. Sometimes I collect the dandelion seeds and surreptitiously plant them in cracks in the pavement around the yard.

Even more felicitous than a dandelion is the open sky above me. The guards haven't figured out how to take that away. It's the same glorious sky a saved man beholds. Sometimes I walk with my eyes trained on the vision above me. I've become adept at pace and cadence, no longer bumping into the prisoner ahead of me. I'm in rapture when the sky fills with fast-moving, multi-layered clouds that seem to tell some mysterious story. As I walk in the midst of these mists, I become part of that narrative. To others I appear static, substantial, while in reality I am a vaporous thing—supple, roving, seeking the entry point to be subsumed into the heavens.

Day 350

Blake and I are becoming closer. I think it's okay to write that.

Day 351

It wasn't okay to write that, I discovered.

Still, he insists that I keep writing, and that I show him each day what I've come up with. I oblige.

Day 352

Thoughts of my impending trial fill me with dread, yet I yearn for its completion. It must be like this for my patients, the teenage ones, when awaiting their reconstructive surgery.

My patients. I have no patients.

When Rosie visits, I experience a modicum of release. But even then, her revelations bind me to the past. I no longer object to anything she says or does (that'd be like the drowning swimmer disputing with the lifeguard), so she's become bold. Or somehow firmer.

She spoon-feeds me information about John and Shayze, testing my tolerance with small bites. She confirmed that John often babysat during the day, but Michaelina was never told that John was her brother. In Michaelina's presence, she addressed John by his middle name—Chris, short for Christopher. That way, if Michaelina ever mentioned him to me, she'd refer to him as her babysitter Chris. I do, in fact, recall Michaelina talking about a sitter named Chris. I'd also assumed Chris was a girl, an impression reinforced by our having an occasional evening sitter by the same name.

Michaelina probably mentioned Shayze in her chattering to me as well. That must be why her name sounded familiar to me. I probably assumed that Michaelina was just mispronouncing something. As was often the case, I wasn't paying attention.

John and Shayze also visited Michaelina in the hospital in her dying days. They stayed in a different waiting room, summoned by Rosie during those few times I'd slept.

Where is the Michael who's infuriated by such disclosures?

He is becoming the ashen dandelion.

Day 353

Blake is slumbering peacefully. I take out a fresh sheet of paper.

I breathe slowly, deeply. A childhood memory surfaces. A boy plays in the front yard on a cloudless day. He spots something red near the curb. Investigating, he finds a red rubber ball, like those used in gym class. When he shows his father and asks him to play catch outside, his father just shakes his newspaper open and begins reading. The boy is persistent, practically begging, to no avail. His mother comes to shoo him out of the room. He's near the front door when he overhears his father say to her in a low voice, "You're the one who wanted him. You play with him."

I can't help the spillage of tears at this recollection. I wonder that the boy doesn't feel anger, but when I probe, I sense what he feels is shame. Shame at not being worthy of his father's love, that to his father, his existence means nothing. Or worse than nothing—his existence brings an unwanted burden into his father's life.

I say to the boy, "I see your pain."

He looks at me with trust-filled eyes. I open my arms and he jumps into them. I hold him tight against my chest. His heavy head, with hair smelling of freshly cut grass, rests on my shoulder. I sway back and forth, the motion calming us, melding us.

After a few minutes, I set him down. "What should I call you?"

"I'm little Mac."

"Let's get out of here, little Mac," I say.

His face breaks into a grin. He climbs on my back, and we fly to the island in the lake. For a moment, we observe the black bear pacing on the shore in the distance, separated from us by an expanse of water.

I set the boy down. Holding hands, we walk further inland, until we emerge into a glade of magnolia trees. The sweet odor of the big white blooms is carried to us on a gentle breeze streaming across our faces. Behind a tree we find a red gym ball and we toss it back and forth, laughing at bad throws or when an easy catch is missed.

I'm euphoric at finding and comforting the child. My body is awash in sensations of lightness and a tingling joy. We agree to meet again.

Before we part, he makes a request. I promise to carry it out at the earliest opportunity.

Day 354

I slept long and deep last night. Strange, but I haven't had a single nightmare since landing in jail. What is it about this place that blanks out areas of the brain?

Sometimes, to pass the time, I pull up words from my old profession, to be sure I still can. Today, I constructed this sentence: *the localized collection of extravasated hemoglobin is generally inconsequential, although an epidural hematoma that occurs between the dura matter and cranium can be serious.*

I try to perform little services to make Blake more comfortable, like a shoulder massage after his workout. I allot him a portion of my meals. I don't need the food, but I'll admit giving up my pillow was a sacrifice.

Day 355

Darla delivers periodic updates on preparations for the trial.

Blake continues to read my journal pages aloud each day, and we discuss. He furthers my quest for humility. With his assistance, I can admit on these pages that I, Michael, am an asshole and dipshit.

He asked me to explain yesterday's sentence about hematomas in plain English, so here it is: Don't worry when a person talks about their personal memories, but when they try to hide their thoughts, that's when you should pay attention.

Blake's become determined to have an impact on my life. I recognize him now as the mediator sent to help me abandon the last dregs of my selfishness and pride. He's an agent—an angel—sent for my sanctification.

Sanctification has several definitions, Blake. One is 'to set apart for special use or purpose.'

Day 356

The face—its amalgamation of bones, sinew, cartilage, muscle, and skin—is the outward manifestation of one's identity. When we're humiliated, it's not called losing pride or losing control, but *losing face*.

I've lost face. When I view myself in my mental mirror—

No. That's what I've given up.

The anniversary of Michaelina's death approaches. The anniversary, too, of my pledge of a year of humility—an artificial timeline, as if I could control how long the process would last.

I wish to be done with grief, while still retaining the sensation of Michaelina's existence. But how? The impact of my daughter's life affords me a vague conception of eternity. Not in quite the way I described earlier, like the permanent disruption of molecules from the ripples in a pond. Eternity isn't the same as infinity. If Michaelina lives on in eternity, it's not that she's living for all time. It's that she's outside of time, and therefore in some mysterious sense must always have existed, and always will.

Day 357

As Michaelina lay near death in the hospital bed, she opened her eyes for a fleeting moment. I've guarded that memory as a little flame, afraid that sharing it would reduce whatever warmth and illumination I've gained from it. Or worse, that someone would find a way to blow it out. To convince me it didn't happen.

But it did. Michaelina opened her eyes and looked directly at me. When I put my finger to my bottom lip, her oxygen mask shifted slightly. The movement was barely discernible, but she was clearly nodding in acknowledgment.

I leaned over to kiss her cheek. When I straightened up, her gaze was no longer on me, but past me. Somehow, underneath that mask, her face radiated a smile. Not that her zygomatic muscles engaged. Rather, she was smiling in a face-glowing way, the way people sometimes have of lighting up at a sight or memory that so fills them with delight that a physical smile is both insufficient and unnecessary.

Then her eyes unfocused and the alarm sounded. Rosie woke and leapt from the cot. Emergency staff rushed in and resuscitation efforts began. I stood aside, knowing she was gone. I'd witnessed similar scenarios before, with other people's children. Those times I felt helpless and frustrated, to be sure. But at Michaelina's deathbed I was the parent. I was the one experiencing the evisceration of hope, the black hole that forms when the medical team steps back and removes their masks. When the doctor looks at his feet instead of you, and says, as if it requires saying, "It's over."

Such a clinical way of saying it, too, with less emotion than remarking that the clock has run out at a football game, and your team has lost.

My anger at losing Michaelina wasn't directed at the doctors. It was focused on Rosie. Because of that anger, I didn't tell her that Michaelina had woken up for those few seconds. That final interaction was the tiny pearl in my gritty oyster shell, all I had left of my daughter, all I could still claim as my own. To pry that shell open and part with it… I couldn't do it, at least not then. So I never told Rosie that Michaelina had forgiven me.

That she'd forgiven us both.

Day 358

When Rosie visited today, she was bursting with news of our new grandson.

Photos of the tiny thing showed Shayze's coloring, but with features all John's. The baby's facial landscape exuded complete normalcy, which is to say, unadulterated beauty.

The cycle continued—an innocent babe with its smooth flesh, unmarked by scar or bruise, undespoiled by scalpel. Parents filled with happy expectation, never dreaming their relationship with the child could take a devastating turn.

I'm glad I wasn't there for the birth, or the joyous aftermath. They'd have expected me to coo and adore. But a fear lingers in me, a fear of ruining anything I draw near to.

Day 359

I was provided with a suit and tie today, chosen by Rosie from my closet. How odd to dress myself in such foreign clothes, as if for a costume party.

The trial began after jury selection. Nine women, three men were chosen. They'd all heard of my case in the news, so some pre-judgment would be inevitable. I was heartened by one juror who when questioned said, "Killing my own kid would be my worst nightmare." Another admitted to briefly losing his son at the park one day while busy scrolling on his phone. One was a dermatologist. I can't decide whether a fellow physician would be more empathetic or more critical.

Voir dire was followed by motions *in limine*. Darla moved to exclude the recording taken by detectives in my garage but was shot down.

The trial began. Rosie sat just behind the rail. Thankfully wives aren't required to testify against their husbands. John wasn't present, which disappointed me until Darla told me he was to be called as a witness so wasn't allowed in.

In his opening statement, the DA paced languidly in front of the jury box, as if successful trial proceedings required little energy on his part. He told the jury how I'd lied about backing out and hitting Michaelina and how I'd let my own wife be blamed. He claimed that I'd purposely blinded Zoe in surgery, and that I had a track record of being impulsive and intolerant and a bad father. To hear him tell it, I was an evil and callous man, an ongoing danger to society who needed to be locked up for eternity.

Darla's opening statement was brief. She made no attempt to cover up my role in Michaelina's death, but rather played to the jury's sympathy, focusing on how I'd suffered immeasurably since the accident, not only in grief for the loss of my daughter but for my guilt.

Trevor was called to the stand first.

"How old are you, Trevor?" asked the prosecutor.

Trevor gave his birth date.

"Let the records show that Trevor is eleven years old. Trevor, do you see any persons in this room who live next door to you?"

Trevor's eyes flew to Rosie. As Trevor had difficulty with gestures, the judge allowed him to leave the witness box. He went and stood in front of Rosie. Then, when asked if there was another neighbor in the room, he came and stood in front of me.

After he returned to the witness box, the DA asked, "Trevor, please think back to the afternoon of about a year ago, when you were ten years old. Tell us about the last time you saw your friend Michaelina."

Most kids would look to their parents when asked such a question, but Trevor looked straight ahead. He said, "Michaelina rode a Schwinn."

"Yes, that's a brand of bike. Did you see a car back up from the garage at your neighbor's house?"

Trevor said, "Cruella De Vil drives crazy." Murmurs arose from around the court, probably wondering whether Trevor was going to accuse Rosie.

The DA, though, appeared unconcerned. His nostrils flared as he drew a huge breath. "Did you see a person get out of the driver's seat of that car, just after the car hit Michaelina?"

"'After them, after them!'" said Trevor, quoting Cruella from the Disney Dalmatians movie. "'You idiots. You imbeciles.'"

"Objection," said Darla. "Prejudicial."

"Sustained," said the judge. "Please strike Trevor's last words from the record."

The DA continued. "Trevor, please show us the person who was driving crazy like Cruella De Vil, the person who was driving the car that hit Michaelina. Please go stand in front of that person."

Trevor came over and stood in front of me. Uncharacteristically, he looked directly at me. In his eyes I saw Michaelina. Michaelina reproving me, but with gentleness.

"No further questions, Your Honor," said the prosecutor.

"Nothing from the defense," said Darla.

Once my role in killing Michaelina was established, the prosecutor called Detective Shorr to the stand, who described how he'd sat in my car with the engine running, radio on, and garage door up. He testified he could easily hear Detective Wolanski shouting from the side porch for him to stop.

They played the recording made from inside the car. On it was heard a cacophony of sounds—loud classical music, Patton barking, and a woman's voice yelling, "Detective Shorr! Detective Shorr!"

The playback had a strange effect on me. It was a caricature of events, akin to a Saturday Night Live send-up. The absurdity of it made me want to laugh. Maybe I did laugh.

In her cross-examination of the detective, Darla tried to elicit skepticism about the validity of the recording. She asked the detective whether the Mercedes in which he conducted the simulation was the same car that hit Michaelina (it wasn't), and whether different vehicles could have different acoustics. She asked him how old he was, and whether it was possible his hearing was more acute than mine. Also, wasn't it possible that someone specifically listening for a voice would be more likely to hear it than someone who had no expectation of hearing it and whose mind was on other matters? Couldn't the dog's bark have meant any number of things, such as excitement that a squirrel was running by? Couldn't Detective Wolanski's voice have traveled farther than Rosie's? And even if I'd heard Rosie yelling to stop, wasn't it likely that I'd interpret it to mean that she had something to tell me, such as that she was sorry for making me angry, that she wanted me to pick up something at the grocery store, rather than that Michaelina was in the driveway?

Next up was the 911 operator, who confirmed she'd taken the call from me on the day of the accident. The recording was played for the jury: "My daughter was just struck by a car and is seriously injured. She's unconscious, bleeding profusely, and appears to have internal injuries. Send an ambulance immediately." Even though Darla had shown me a transcript from discovery, hearing my unemotional voice made it seem far more damning. The prosecutor asked whether I admitted on the call that I'd been the one to strike Michaelina. Darla objected, pointing out that the contents of the entire call had just been played back to the jury.

In cross-examination, Darla got the operator to agree that occasionally callers are unemotional, that they could be in shock or trying to calm someone else on the scene.

The first responders were brought in next. They'd made assumptions, based on Rosie's words and hysterics, that she'd been at fault, but it wasn't their role to question, just to save the child.

Things got more uncomfortable when the social worker from the hospital was brought forward. She read from her hospital notes, which said that Rosie had confessed to backing up the car and hitting Michaelina. She was asked if the accused had made any effort to contradict his wife. Answer: he had not.

Darla's only cross-examination question, on whether the social worker was aware that Rosie had received a strong dose of tranquilizer, was objected to by the prosecutor and sustained by the judge.

The trial recessed for the day. Darla felt it had gone as well as could be expected, although I needed to work harder to maintain an expression that appeared contrite, or at least neutral. Tomorrow would likely be more difficult.

My Bible study with Blake has been paused. Instead, he insists on a blow-by-blow of the trial. Then he wants me to write down every detail I can recall.

Day 360

First to witness today was Ji-young, the hospital administrator. She claimed she suspended me from surgery not because I was a danger, but out of compassion—I was evidently suffering from the loss of my daughter and needed a rest.

To be clear, Ji-young didn't give a rat's ass about my suffering. Anticipating the hospital will be sued, she was forced to downplay any known problem. When Darla cross-examined her, she sweetly praised my talent as a surgeon, value to the team, fantastic track record, etc., vertically bobbling her head and keeping her unclenched hands flat on the ledge of the jury box, as if to keep an eye on them. She'd been heartbroken when the accident happened, she said, and had been monitoring me closely ever since. To make sure I was all right, she'd even offered me a counselor.

The DA said, "Please tell us this counselor's name."

"Matilda Thurman."

"Is that *Doctor* Matilda Thurman?"

"Yes."

"Is she a psychiatrist?"

"Yes."

"Did you *offer* Michael the chance to see a psychiatrist, or did you *require* that he see her?"

"I required it, for his own benefit." She maintained that she'd had no qualms about my return to surgery. "After all," she said, "we believed it was Michael's wife who'd caused their daughter's death. We had no reason to think he was suffering from anything but normal grief."

Dr Prezic, the resident who'd operated alongside me in Zoe's surgery, was next on the stand. She had challenged my methods during the operation. Under the prosecutor's questioning, Prezic hedged as much as possible (the hospital lawyers must've coached her too), but in the end was forced to agree that in her opinion, traction force wasn't needed to correct the ocular adhesion. But when asked by Darla if traction force in those circumstances was within the limits of reasonable surgical protocol, she said yes.

Thurman was called. Darla immediately objected to her being questioned, for reasons of therapist-patient privilege, but was overruled.

"When did you start seeing Michael?"

"About a month after the accident that killed his daughter," said Thurman.

"Have you seen him regularly since then?"

"Not exactly. At first, we had only three sessions together."

"And why did you stop?"

She looked over at me and made eye contact, but the scoping eye didn't engage. "I couldn't prove he was having a problem, and he didn't want to keep seeing me."

"It was your professional opinion, then, that Michael had no mental illness at that time?"

"I'm not saying that. He was suffering, yes, from mental distress, but I couldn't diagnose him with anything specific."

"Did you prescribe him medication?"

"Xanax—twenty tablets—just to see him through his first times of grief."

"To your knowledge, had he been continuing to successfully operate without problems?"

"To the best I knew, yes."

"You started treating Michael again several months later, though, is that correct?"

"Yes, after what happened with the little girl Zoe. The hospital took away his surgery privileges and made him see me again."

"Did Michael admit to you that he was the driver of the car that hit Michaelina?"

"Yes, but only about six weeks ago."

"Did he also confess to injuring Zoe on purpose?"

"No."

"Did he admit to having difficulties operating?"

"I wouldn't say that. He did have some problems with his vision, but he saw an ophthalmologist and the problem cleared up."

While pausing to form his next questions, the prosecutor breathed deeply through his flaring nostrils, as if picking up the scent of something putrid in Thurman's answers.

"In your opinion," he said, "was Michael having mental health issues already, when you first started seeing him, before he operated on Zoe?"

Thurman looked in my direction, but her focus was on something above me, beyond me. "Yes, something was not so right, but he covered it up enough that I couldn't—"

"Thank you. You say he was covering up his mental problems. For someone to cover up a problem suggests they know they have a problem, doesn't it? Do you believe Michael knew he was having problems but that he purposely forged ahead anyway, resulting in the blinding of Zoe?"

Thurman gave a long answer, too long for me to recall in detail. She talked about my lack of self-awareness, unwillingness to communicate openly, and the vagaries of motivations. When the attorney insisted on a yes or no, Thurman said she honestly didn't know.

He left it at that. Darla declined cross-examination but reserved the right to call her back to the stand later.

Media stories about my case have attracted revenge-seekers. A succession of nurses I'd fooled around with were brought in, and either acknowledged an affair with me, or worse, accused me of sexual harassment. Darla objected vociferously to their testimony, on grounds of irrelevancy. Her objections were overruled when the prosecutor argued this information spoke to my bad character and lack of commitment to my family. But when the questioning veered too far into details about sex, the objections were sustained. In cross-examination, Darla emphasized how long ago these incidents had occurred and suggested they were immaterial to the current charges. She questioned the memories of these nurses, and asked whether it was possible I'd changed since then.

Heather showed up as well. Although I'd been forewarned of her appearance, it did nothing to mitigate my unease at having our lengthy affair and aborted marriage plans made public. She'd aged well, as I would've expected. Her vindictiveness and poorly concealed pleasure in witnessing my humiliation, however, detracted significantly from her looks. During her testimony about our former relationship, I felt Rosie's eyes on me. At least Darla was able to force Heather to concede that I'd broken off the engagement upon discovering that Rosie was pregnant with Michaelina.

Next, the prosecution called John. I couldn't help staring at him; my eyes feasted on his face. I wished he would've shaved off the beard and removed his glasses before taking the stand. Even so, beneath the veneer I recognized the boy I had known, the boy I had loved.

John was asked to confirm the text conversation with Rosie, the one that had precipitated my backing up the car from the garage in anger. The texts had been lifted from Rosie's phone and were now entered into evidence.

"How would you characterize your relationship with your father?"

"Problematic."

"How so?"

"Aside from one accidental encounter a few months back when my mother was in the hospital, we haven't spoken to each other in almost seven years."

"And why is that?"

"Honestly, I'm not entirely sure. He seemed to hold some grudge against me from not always following his rules. At some point in my teen years he just stopped interacting with me."

"Stopped interacting with you at all?"

"Pretty much. If he ever spoke to me, it was to berate me. So I moved out when I turned 18."

"Where did you go?"

"My friends' parents took me in here and there—I slept on a lot of couches. When the weather was warm, I just camped out."

"Your father never tried to contact you?"

"No."

"But you kept in touch with your mother."

"Yes, to the extent I could."

"How did you feed yourself?"

"At first, besides mooching off friends and their parents, I did a fair amount of dumpster-diving. But when my mother learned of that, she began to skim off money at home and get it to me. It wasn't easy because my father had an eagle eye for expenditures. But she stretched her food budget and bought her clothes at thrift stores. She helped me even after I started working."

"What is your profession?"

"Freelance videographer. I do pretty well now, but it's taken years to build up a steady clientele."

"How did your father feel about your maintaining a relationship with your mother?"

"He didn't know about it. He'd given orders that she wasn't to speak to me."

"So would it be safe to say that your father would've felt betrayed by you, and by his own wife, when he discovered you were keeping in touch?"

Objection—leading the witness. Sustained.

"What happened when your father discovered the texts on your mother's phone?"

"I wasn't there, but my mother said—"

Objection—hearsay. Sustained.

"Did you know your sister Michaelina?"

"Yes."

"How often did you see her?"

John rubbed the inside corner of one eye. This was hard on him. I hoped he was okay.

He said, "Several times a week. I held her in my arms in the hospital when she was born, and held her hand in the hospital after the accident."

"All without your father's knowledge?"

"Yes."

The prosecutor paused for John to use a tissue. Or maybe the pause was to build anticipation for his next question:

"Your father hated you, didn't he?"

Objection—irrelevant.

"Your honor, this goes to the long history of antipathy Michael has evidenced for his own children."

"I'll allow."

"I repeat. Your father hated you, didn't he?"

John flashed his eyes for a millisecond in my direction, long enough to notice that I was watching him intently.

He gave his head a little shake. "I don't know."

"He wouldn't speak to you for almost seven years, and you 'don't know' if he hated you?"

Objection—badgering the witness. Sustained.

"No further questions."

Darla didn't cross-examine but reserved the right to question him for the defense.

The prosecution rested.

Day 361

Since yesterday, I can think only of John. That's what the trial has been reduced to. Nothing else matters—only what John thinks, what John says.

That mindset is what got me into trouble today.

Darla met with me early. She said the case wasn't looking good, not after John's testimony. I tried to explain how meaningful and significant his statements were, that he seemed to understand I didn't hate him. That maybe he even realized I love him.

Darla, however, brushed my notions aside. She insisted we use our remaining case to arouse sympathy among the jurors.

I begged to testify myself. "The jurors need to witness how sorry I am. I can show that." What I really wanted, though, was to show John how sorry I was.

"That's a big risk," she said.

We batted the question back and forth. While not making any promises, Darla agreed to walk me through some possible questions, ones she might ask and ones that might come from the prosecutor. She seemed satisfied with my responses, only occasionally adding, "You may want to give more detail there," or "Maybe best not to mention that." I had to be mindful, she insisted, to limit my answers only to the questions asked, and not give the prosecution openings to undermine our case. I could talk about my failings and my remorse—why I hadn't spoken with John, why I didn't look behind me when backing up, why I let Rosie take the blame, and how I'd been wracked with guilt ever since.

When we arrived in the courtroom, I searched for John to no avail. I whispered to Darla, "Where's John?" She reminded me he was a witness—a very unsatisfactory answer. How was I supposed to show him my remorse without his presence, without his needing to sit quietly and receptively when I spoke?

Darla questioned Thurman first. "Did Michael ever speak to you about his childhood?"

"Yes."

"What was it like? What was his father like?"

Objection—irrelevant.

"Your honor," said Darla, "Michael's background puts his actions into context."

Overruled.

Thurman related what I'd told her of my father's strictness and lack of affection.

Then Darla asked her about Butt-cheeks. *How did Darla know about Butt-Cheeks?* I was suddenly glad John wasn't in the room.

Thurman had plenty of information there. She described at length my childhood as an outcast, how I was victimized by bullies.

Then Darla asked, "Did Michael enjoy his sessions with you?"

"No," said Thurman.

"But he kept coming, didn't he? Why?"

"He showed up because he was forced to, in the beginning. We met for just a few weeks. But then—"Thurman stopped and looked about the witness box, as if for a pen she could tap. Finding none, she drummed her forefinger lightly on the ledge of the box. "Then he was suspended from surgery. He couldn't wait to see me then, for a chance to get back to the operating table."

"You didn't clear him, though, did you?"

"No."

"Why not?"

"All this grief and guilt, they were eating him up from the inside out."

"You mention guilt. What was he guilty of?"

"Of backing up into his daughter and killing her, and blaming his wife. But he didn't tell me about any of that until after many sessions."

"Why do you think that was?"

Objection—speculation. Overruled.

"For one thing, he was afraid of giving me information that might stop him from getting back to surgery."

"For one thing? What was the other thing? Is there another reason he wouldn't talk about Michaelina's death?"

"I think he blocked out his guilt. He didn't want to admit it even to himself."

"But eventually he did, correct?"

"Yes."

"How did he act during his confession? Was he contrite?"

"Yes, he was a big mess with all the crying."

"Nothing further," said Darla. The prosecuting attorney declined cross-examination.

Darla next called John to the stand. I watched him enter the courtroom and followed his every step.

"Would you characterize your father as an angry man?" Darla asked.

If John felt my gaze, he didn't show it. "I wouldn't call him that. He can be proud and resentful and unfeeling, but he hardly ever expressed anger outright. He was more of the type to stew in silence."

"He must've been terribly angry when he found out you and your mother were continuing to communicate against his wishes?"

Objection—the witness wasn't present. Sustained.

"You encountered your father several months ago, after your parents' fender-bender, when your mother was in the hospital. Had your father changed? I mean, his personality, was it different from the last time you'd seen him?"

"I couldn't say. My memories of how he was before are kind of faded. I was only a teenager."

"I understand. You said he rarely expressed anger outright, but when you spoke with him in the hospital, was he angry then?"

John grunted grimly. "Yes, more livid than I'd ever seen him before."

"Livid with you personally?"

"Yes."

Darla continued. "John, on the day your father backed up and hit Michaelina, could your father have been angry enough to kill your sister Michaelina on purpose?"

Objection—speculation. Sustained.

"Was it your impression that your father would sometimes get angry with Michaelina?"

"No, that's not my impression at all—the opposite, in fact. He adored her. I believe he'd figured out how to be a loving father, at least to her."

"So he reserved his fatherly anger for you."

"That's how it seemed."

"If you weren't on speaking terms, if you played no part in his life, why do you think he'd be so angry with you when you met in the hospital, angrier than you'd ever seen him before?"

Objection—speculation.

"Your honor, this speaks to the issue of what kind of a father Michael was."

"I'll allow."

"John, why would your father continue to harbor so much anger toward you after all these years?"

This was the exciting part. John looked over at me, kind of quizzically, his head tilted, as if he'd never thought to ask himself this question. As if he wanted to understand, to understand *me*.

The courtroom was still. The usual ambient noises—whispers, throat-clearing, creaking benches, the slight whoosh the door makes when closing—were magically silenced.

John said, "On some level, I suppose my father still cares about what I think. He still cares about me."

See?

In cross-examination, the prosecutor asked John about his new baby. "A boy, isn't it?"

"Yes."

"Congratulations," said the prosecutor. He fiddled for a moment with his necktie. "Tell me," he said. "If your father were released today, would you feel comfortable allowing him to hold your newborn son?"

Darla leapt to her feet. "Objection—speculation and irrelevant!"

Overruled.

John did all he could to avoid a clear answer. He said, "That's unlikely to happen, since we're not on speaking terms."

When pressed further, he said I probably wouldn't be interested in holding his baby, then averred that his wife would have to make that decision. In the end, he was forced to reply.

"No, probably not."

That response didn't bother me. John was right, absolutely right to keep me away. After all, I'd blinded Zoe in surgery. John's a very sensible father.

I suppose in desperation, Darla called me to the stand. She began by questioning me about my childhood. Because revelations about Butt-cheeks had already been brought up in Thurman's testimony, the topic was easier for me to discuss. And although it was unsettling to paint a picture of myself as pitiable, I could tell that my story was having a favorable impact on the jury.

"Were you upset that Michaelina died?" she asked.

"Yes," I said, nearly swooning, "I loved her so much."

"Did you feel guilty about letting your wife take the blame?"

"Yes, yes!" I almost shouted. It felt so good to admit it publicly at last. Then, addressing Rosie across the room, I blurted out, "I didn't mean it. I was angry, but I never meant for you to take the blame."

The DA objected, and the judge intervened. "Michael, please direct your answers to the attorney and jury." But Darla tossed me a private smile, encouraging me.

"So you're sorry, then, for getting angry, for backing up into Michaelina without looking, and for letting your wife take the blame?"

Objection—asked and answered. Sustained.

I hung my head. I'd intended to generate some tears, but for some reason I felt closer to laughing than crying. The absurdity of the whole proceeding—which focused on all the wrong things—tickled my brain.

Darla must've noticed. Her smile disappeared. As she paused to find a way to redirect, I tried to save the situation, to cover up my amusement by confessing to even more. "I'm sorry too about Zoe's blindness. In her case, I was only angry that—" I was just about to explain to the jury when Darla interrupted me with, "No further questions."

The DA, meanwhile, was scribbling notes so furiously that he only stood when the judge prompted him to proceed.

"You just said you were angry during surgery," the prosecutor said, his nostrils going haywire, the scent of the hunt in the air. "Was that during the operation that blinded Zoe?"

Here was my opportunity to explain, to make it up to Darla, who was looking deflated. But she'd understand, and so would the jury once they heard it all. "Mainly I was angry beforehand."

The DA harrumphed in annoyance. "Please clarify. Were you angry or not when you used force in the procedure that resulted in Zoe becoming blind?"

"Yes, but I'd never hurt her on purpose," I said.

"She *was* hurt, though, because of your anger, correct?"

I shook my head. "My anger didn't cause anything."

"But her blindness was the result of a decision you made during the procedure, wasn't it?"

"No, it wasn't my decision."

Murmuring arose throughout the court room. Jurors shifted in their seats. I had everyone's attention. Before the prosecutor could pivot, I continued. "The reason Zoe needed the procedure in the first place," I said, "was because of a car accident. Her father had been the driver. I remember being a little disturbed that this man was getting his daughter back, good as new, even though he'd been at the wheel. The irony and the injustice struck me as monumental—*I* was the one who could fix faces. I could heal this stranger's daughter and not my own. Zoe would live and have a happy life."

"And that's when you performed traction, when you were feeling angry about this injustice?"

Objection. Overruled.

"No. By then, the Xanax had kicked in."

"You took Xanax before the operation? Why?"

"I already told you. I was angry with this girl's father. I didn't want to be angry, because I cared about my patient."

"What dose of Xanax did you take?"

"Three tablets. 6 milligrams."

"Would you say that's a standard dose?"

"It was a little high but justified under the circumstances."

"What circumstances were those?"

"Needing to correct an adhesion that—" I stumbled.

"What were your thoughts when trying to fix the adhesion?"

The recollection flooded back. "I remember now. I was recalling my bargain with God." The prosecutor raised his brows, and I realized he hadn't been informed about that. "It was a pact I'd made to save Michaelina's life. It didn't work, though. I kept my end of it, but God didn't keep his."

"What does this have to do with the operation?"

I took a long, cleansing breath. "When confronted with tragedy, people say, 'God has a plan,' or "God has his reasons.' I've thought a lot about that and it's just not true. God doesn't make plans—that's a ridiculous notion when you think about it. A plan is a human construct, an attempt to exert control over events. And reasons are what human beings come up with to justify their plans, or to make sense of why their plans don't work. God doesn't need to make sense of things. He doesn't need reasons."

"Again, how does this relate to the botched operation?"

"Have you ever heard this: 'The heart has its reasons that reason doesn't know'?" I looked at Darla, hoping to invigorate her with my quotation from St. Augustine, but her expression was indecipherable.

"Please explain," said the DA.

"In my heart I was taking the correct action. I can't come up with reasons after the fact."

"Didn't that action entail serious risk?"

"All surgery has risks. Living has risks. Only dying has no risks."

"But why take that particular risk in surgery when there were alternatives?"

There I was stuck. I couldn't recall. I'm not sure how I answered the question, but this time I couldn't prevent a tiny chuckle from escaping when I contemplated this prosecutor's relentless inquiries into reasons and intentions and motivations, when God didn't need any of those. There was something funny as hell about that.

He didn't pursue that line of questioning further, but merely asked, "On the day of the accident, did you gun your car out of your garage without checking to see if your daughter Michaelina was behind you?"

"Yes."

"Was it possible she was on her bike in the driveway?"

"I wasn't thinking about her then."

"Just answer the question. Did you know it was possible that your daughter was on her bike in the driveway?"

"I don't know. I mean yes, she could've been. Yes, she was."

Then Darla stood back up. Her temporalis muscle drooped. Being a defense attorney isn't a good occupation for her. She asked me to explain my bargain with God in more detail, which I was happy to do. She let me talk as long as I wanted. Then she asked, "How did you know it was Zoe's father driving the car when her eyes were injured?"

I didn't know how I'd become aware of that, although she pressed me to search my memory. Then she referred to some notes and said, "Would it surprise you to learn that Zoe's injury was not the result of a car accident, but from being thrown over the handlebars of her bike when she hit a pothole in the road?"

That information did surprise me. I thought perhaps Darla was making it up, but Darla's not exactly an inventive person. I'm thinking she should be an English teacher. She loves quotations, and evidently there's no place for them in a courtroom.

She followed up by asking, "Do you love your son John?"

I was so busy thinking about Darla's new occupation that it took me a moment to comprehend the question. When I did, my eyes instinctively searched for John in the courtroom. But no—he was a witness and not there.

"Yes," I said, "Of course I love John." I looked at Rosie, whose face displayed her signature multi-expression of pleasure, pain, and a kind of semi-relief.

"If you love him, why didn't you speak to him for almost seven years?"

I said, "It was a mistake, that's all. A misunderstanding. We're fine now."

"Why did you forbid your wife from speaking to him?"

I wasn't sure what she meant. "Rosie and John talked all the time." I was elated to point this out. "There are hundreds of photos and videos of them together."

I wrote earlier about how justice and mercy are two sides of the same coin, but that's not quite right either. That analogy assumes that the two forces are equal and opposing, and that their application is as arbitrary as the flip of that coin. I see now that justice and mercy are one and the same. You can flip the coin all you want, but justice and mercy will always land together—heads up—because they're not distinct entities. God dispenses both in a single feat.

I'm reminded of Blake and the way he fingers his facial scar as he observes me and contemplates his own experience of justice and mercy. Watching him, it's as if I can feel the scar myself, as if I too can caress the gruesome ridge in the otherwise smooth skin and derive my own significance and satisfaction and even delight from it. Yes—delight. That's what's left to me now, only the duty to delight. How easy it is, too. Each object reveals its beauty, and each event its awe-filled anticipation of becoming.

The closing arguments didn't come off as I expected. True, the prosecutor touched on all the damning evidence: "Michael wanted to punish his wife. Why? For continuing to be a mother to the son he'd rejected. In his anger, he guns the car out of the garage without looking behind him, despite his dog barking in warning and his wife screaming for him to stop. And when he sees his daughter Michaelina badly injured on the ground, he harms his wife further by laying the blame on her. Then, wracked with guilt, the accused begins performing erratically in surgery. He knew he was unstable—that's why he took a megadose of sedative prior to operating on Zoe in surgery. In his anger and bitterness, he wielded his sharp and deadly medical instruments on her, blinding her for life. Members of the jury, you see before you a man who abandoned his own son and forbade his wife from maintaining a relationship with him. A man whose wife is so afraid of him that she confesses to his crime, just to avoid his anger. A man who, even as his daughter lies on the ground unconscious and dying, provides an unemotional catalog of injuries to the 911 operator. A man who cheats repeatedly on his wife and sexually harasses the nurses who work with him. You see before you a man with a long pattern of contempt and profound disregard for the wellbeing of others—a menace, a danger to his own family, his patients, and to society. I ask you to find him guilty on all counts."

The strange thing was, he didn't deliver this speech in the kind of fiery, impassioned tone one sees in television dramas. He said it all rather softly. Almost, well, apologetically.

I didn't know what to anticipate from Darla. She rose and stated that although I was a flawed person, as we all are, I was also a gifted and respected surgeon who'd saved the lives of many children and helped countless others to live more normal lives. I'd been devastated by the death of my daughter at my own hands and had already suffered enormously. I'd experienced horrific mental trauma that had affected my surgery without my full understanding. However, she said, in the year since these events took place, my character had changed markedly for the better. I'd acknowledged my guilt. It wouldn't serve society's best interests to lock away such a talented surgeon who would suffer for his actions for the rest of his life.

By then it was mid-afternoon, and my stomach growled. I was seized with fear that I wouldn't get back to my cell in time for my dinner tray. On Thursdays we're typically fed a beef stew that isn't half bad, with its starchy potatoes and soft carrots that dissolve against the roof of your mouth.

I needn't have worried, though. The jury deliberated less than an hour before delivering their verdict. They were probably starving too.

Day 362

When I woke this morning, my first thought was that I was late making Rosie's tea. I threw off my blanket and went straight to the kitchen, where I put the kettle on to boil. Patton nudged me impatiently. I rubbed his back and asked him to hold on. The double-flush and creaking footsteps sounded above me. I made tea in the special Michaelina mug, brought it to Rosie, and we chatted amicably. I next entered John's bedroom and sat on his bed, tousling his hair until he woke and stretched and smiled at me. Next I crept into Michaelina's room and watched her sleep. I examined every detail of her face—the soft lashes, the upturned nose, the rosebud lips. She, too, awoke, and leapt from her bed to hug me.

I was pulled from my reverie for an early confab with Darla. "A pre-sentencing investigation is being conducted today." She stared at me meaningfully. "In light of events yesterday, I'm pushing for an alternative sentence, a 'specialized treatment departure.'" She began to explain but I cut her off. What need have I for explanations or reasons? Everything has connected and converged into goodness, even if no one else is seeing it, seeing the line of unbroken glory that swerves and ascends and renders explanations and reasons immaterial.

My other visitor today was Thurman. Yes—Matilda Thurman came to see me in jail. She told me she's not named in the civil suit against the hospital, having covered herself well. I smiled.

We leaned toward each other across the wide table.

"*Hoo*," she said, "Such a business." But her scope-eye didn't scope. It was round and relaxed. There was even a sparkle to it.

I asked about the weather.

She talked of diagnoses—PTSD-induced psychosis and paranoia. This was important for me to know, she said, because it would be coming up at the sentencing hearing. Did I want her to explain it in more detail?

I shook my head. "I'm better."

She looked at me a little clinically, I thought, or maybe just with curiosity, but she only said, "I'm glad."

"Do you like roses?" I said.

Through the plexiglass slot, she pushed toward me some brochures about Belize, where even a doctor with a felony conviction could find work. Or, as she put it, "a place where someone as talented as you could make yourself useful someday."

This was supposed to be my hope now. Like the others, Thurman didn't understand that plans were of no use.

I said, "I've been meaning to tell you something."

"Yes?"

"Your office needs a new sofa."

She grinned. I'd never seen her smile that way, never seen her teeth up close before—they were white, regular. Things must be all right then.

"A new sofa?" she said. "The one I have is perfect already."

Day 363

Is it God forgiving me, or me forgiving God? Either way, I no longer need to justify or defend myself. How is it you can work and work against a fault with seemingly no progress, then one day it disappears, or at least ceases to disturb you?

At the sentencing hearing this afternoon, Darla pushed for the sentence diversion. Her reasons were heartfelt, persuasive. I was dazzled. Even if rationales mean nothing to me now, I was swayed by her eloquence. (No, Blake, I can't remember her exact words. Would you rather I make something up?)

Next, Thurman was invited to provide a professional opinion. I will paraphrase her: "My sessions with Michael went on for almost a year. He did make some progress, but I see now from his testimony during the trial that some regression is going on. At the beginning of seeing him, I think his mind was sound. But afterward, the way he held back his grief made me have reservations about his mental state. But I couldn't give a diagnosis to prevent his doing surgery. And then later, he got more and more paranoid and filled with delusions. By killing his daughter and letting his wife be blamed, he ended up with psychosis."

Owen showed up and provided a carefully worded statement that he was my close friend (bless you, Owen!), and that he'd witnessed my extraordinary mental distress after Michaelina's death. It had affected my judgment, he said, but I was a highly resilient person, an exceptional surgeon, and a top mind who would undoubtedly bounce back quickly if given the treatment I needed.

Ji-young added to the chorus of those believing a mental ward was the best option. While she was giving her lawyer-prepared statement, I took the opportunity to observe my son John, seated next to Rosie. He must've felt my gaze upon him because he turned in my direction.

Eye contact is a curious thing. Maintaining it consumes a surprising amount of brain power—we often need to look away to concentrate on our thoughts. That's normal. If you don't look away, people think you're a psychopath.

So when John glanced in my direction, we locked eyes, but for only a few seconds. No matter, though—a world of understanding and compassion can be communicated in that timespan. I was inundated with emotions impossible to relate here now.

Rosie spoke next, saying she takes responsibility for implicating herself as the one who hit Michaelina and not correcting the record. If she had, I wouldn't have been so tormented and maybe that poor girl Zoe would still have her sight.

After speaking, Rosie turned to John and they embraced. Woman, behold your son. In the Bible, mothers fare far better with sons than fathers do.

The prosecution produced their own psychiatrist, who'd been present at the trial but hadn't testified. Darla told me later he'd been prepped before the trial to counter any plea of 'not guilty by reason of insanity.' Now that I'd been found guilty, however, he weighed in by agreeing I was seriously mentally ill, and in his opinion I should be put away for good.

It was mid-afternoon by then. The judge wanted time to consider the statements and findings. She'll give her decision in two days.

Day 364

During outdoor exercise, a few raindrops spattered my shirtsleeve.

The boy, Mac, pulled at my arm, reminding me of my promise.

Before the guards could shoo us inside, I made a break for the center of the courtyard to greet what looked like an imminent downpour. Sure enough, the purple heavens broke open and torrents of rain plastered my upturned face. Water—holy water—streamed through my hair, down my forehead, and coursed into my open mouth. The taste was newness and purity itself. The guards shouted obscenities from under the eaves, but were unwilling to confront the deluge to force me back in. I stood there for several magnificent minutes, soaking in the celestial immersion.

Just as quickly as the clouds had rolled in, they parted, revealing the bluest of skies and the whitest of sunlight.

I'm clean now. Nothing will defile me again, nothing external ever can. Inside, I'm healed. The boy and I are free.

Blake took exception to my waterlogged body, but no matter.

Rosie arrived in the afternoon. She chided me gently about my appearance. I said nothing in reply, I swear.

I did plan to tell her where in my erstwhile bedroom she could find my journal. If she moved out of the house permanently—and who could blame her?—I wouldn't want it inadvertently landing in a stranger's hands. Somehow, though, the words didn't get said—in her presence, the information lost all urgency. I spoke only enough to reassure her, to save her from worry. I didn't feel like talking. I wanted only to gaze at her beautiful face and project my love to her.

Blake took more than his usual enjoyment in my company this evening. Also, because I won't be returning after tomorrow's sentencing, he allowed me to select our final Bible reading. I chose Philippians 2:1-18. A few words I've memorized:

> Do all things without grumbling or questioning, that you may be blameless and innocent, children of God without blemish…
>
> Even if I am to be poured out as a libation… I am glad and rejoice…
> Likewise you also should be glad and rejoice with me.

Day 365

It's not Day 365, as written by my father (Michael), but ten days later. I, John, am writing this final entry in his stead.

My father's journey is at an end. I'm not talking about the sentencing—the judge had intended to impose a year of supervised treatment, with the first three months in a facility. That sounded about right.

But just before the hearing, Darla approached my mother and me to break the news.

I insisted on seeing him. A profusion of bruises, some of them days or even weeks old, covered his torso. His hair concealed a large contusion on the back of his head. And just below, decorating his neck, lay the fresh stains of strangulation.

His journal was the devil to locate. I've read it twice now, including the loose pages recovered from his jail cell. After reading and rereading, absorbing and digesting the contents, I still have trouble understanding him—the man beneath the chipped armor.

The most revealing entry of the entire journal is probably the one I didn't get to read. The detectives inspecting his cell had collected a few torn bits of paper from around the toilet—the bulk of fragments having evidently been flushed away. Darla was allowed to examine the tiny scraps remaining, but she could make out nothing of value, only a few partial words: *'you discov,'* '*orgivene*' and '*Day 347—agai,*' in my father's handwriting. I'm thinking this was a second journal entry from that day. It's uncertain whether it was my father or his cellmate who was so intent on obliterating the page, but the words on it must've been significant, and likely included information pertaining to what led to my father's murder.

Also not clear is why my father told no one about the abuse. This seems senseless—we could've gotten him transferred to another cell, safely separated from that criminal. So why the silence? Maybe he was so mentally weak by then, so thoroughly under the cellmate's domination, that he felt powerless to act for his own benefit. Or maybe he'd developed a taste for suffering, relishing it as a kind of cleansing or reparation.

But neither of those explanations sound like my father. Despite his faults, he always maintained a stubborn strength of purpose. Most likely the cause for his reticence was simple pride—the pride he could never quite free himself from, the pride that ruined our relationship.

According to his writing, he was wracked with remorse, and pursued a year's worth of humble acts to compensate. Yet through all his self-reflection, he seemed unable to come to terms with himself, or to recognize that pride was woven so tightly into his being that there was no rooting it out without self-annihilation.

At the pre-sentencing, when we made eye contact, I sensed there a bid for connection, a yearning. Not of a hungry or desperate type though. Instead, his eyes held a curious kind of contentment, as if reconciliation itself didn't matter—only his desire for it, his communication of it, his consent to it.

His journal, I see now, boils down to a love letter of sorts. Was this his final accomplishment—allowing himself to be destroyed for love of me? Odd, how in the end he could become a paradigm.

In the woods he'd visited before his arrest, I found the oak tree he referenced, or close enough. Hairy acorns littered the ground. A dislodged chunk of bark rested against the trunk.

I took a photo, then sat as he had, my back against the tree. Around me, emerald grass grew in haphazard clumps. I intertwined my fingers with the damp blades, palms down, and inhaled the honeyed air. My restlessness was curbed by a resolution to remain, to wait for a sign or some kind of insight.

As I lingered, the muted light filtering through the branches nudged me with soft colors—first blue, then rose, then blue again, an indigo blue that stretched and deepened and insinuated itself across the broad swath of sky. Stars with pointing beams glinted at me. A high-branched owl cried out in jarring, echoing petition.

I drew up my knees in anticipation.

Amid the night's embrace, a gust of chill air brushed against me. I shuddered. The weight I'd carried for so long seemed to shift and groan within me, shaking loose, and slowly unraveling into dry, useless fragments—mere relics of my discontent. The rising wind swept them up and away to some foreign place.

With the pull of the milky moon, deliverance at last found an outlet. The runlets that coursed down my face became as if streams—torrents flowing over my chest and shoulders, down my arms to my hands, still pressed flat against the ground. I watched as creation's deluge slipped through my fingers, sank into the soil, and disappeared into the dark and fertile depths.

ACKNOWLEDGMENTS

This book would not have been possible without the support and feedback of family, friends, and other writers.

First, I am deeply grateful to John Rees, Sr., who read this manuscript multiple times. His invaluable insights on structure and the addition of new characters helped shaped this novel into its current form and truly brought the story to life.

My heartfelt thanks go also to my early and late readers, including Linda Rees, Sarah Scherrer, Greta Carswell, Ellen Green, Carmel Slattery, Nancy Tunick, Ian McKeown, and my daughter Maggie Kennedy. Your perceptive feedback and encouragement kept me motivated throughout the writing process. Special thanks to the St. Mary's Bookstore writing group for their camaraderie and kind words.

Lastly, but most importantly, many thanks to my dear husband, Martin de Porres Kennedy. I could not have produced this novel without his constant support, patience, and early feedback. It was while editing his novels that I was first inspired to try writing my own.

Thank You for Reading!

We hope you enjoyed *The Year of My Humiliation*. If so, please consider leaving a review on Amazon and Goodreads. Reviews support and encourage independent authors and help other readers like you to find great reads.

For more novels, visit **lilyfieldpress.com**. Sign up for our mailing list to learn early about our new releases.

Thank you for your support and happy reading!

The Editors, Lilyfield Press

More novels from Lilyfield Press:

Falling As She Sings, by C.J. Sursum

Torpedo 8, by Martin de Porres Kennedy

Manayunk, by Martin de Porres Kennedy

A Philadelphia Catholic in King James's Court, by Martin de Porres Kennedy

Made in the USA
Columbia, SC
26 June 2025